Christobel Kent was born in London and educated at Cambridge. She has lived variously in Essex, London and Italy. Her childhood included several years spent on a Thames sailing barge in Maldon, Essex with her father, stepmother, three siblings and four step-siblings. She now lives in both Cambridge and Florence with her husband and five children.

A
SECRET
LIFE

Christobel Kent

sphere

SPHERE

First published in Great Britain in 2019 by Sphere

1 3 5 7 9 10 8 6 4 2

Copyright © Christobel Kent 2019

The moral right of the author has been asserted.

A CIP catalogue record for this book is available from the British Library.

Hardback ISBN 978-0-7515-6882-0
Trade Paperback ISBN 978-0-7515-6883-7

Typeset in Bembo by Palimpsest Book Production Ltd, Falkirk, Stirlingshire

Printed and bound in Great Britain by Clays Ltd, Elcograf S.p.A.

Papers used by Sphere are from well-managed forests
and other responsible sources.

MIX
Paper from
responsible sources
FSC® C104740

Sphere
An imprint of
Little, Brown Book Group
Carmelite House
50 Victoria Embankment
London
EC4Y 0DZ
An Hachette UK Company

www.hachette.co.uk

www.littlebrown.co.uk

For my dad
Christopher Kent 1923–1992

It had turned cold at last, after the long mild spell: overnight the temperature had dropped. The sky outside was a bright empty blue and where the sun hadn't yet reached the glass an edge of frost still misted the window at one corner. The early light dazzled in the small, bright white space. She hadn't bothered to pull the curtains but the sun didn't wake her.

The room was warm, overheated even and just as well because she was naked, or close enough. There was a half empty bottle of red wine on the side, the glitter of a party shoe on its side on the rug and a little overnight bag had been flung open and was spilling underwear. Sooner or later they'd come and root through it all with gloved hands, a finger through the underwear, lifting it, looking at each other then down into the little bag for what treasures she might have brought with her, what equipment. Looking for a sign, what kind of woman is this? It was all evidence, now.

Her eyes were open, staring up at the Anaglypta of the ceiling that had been painted over ten, twenty times like everything in these old streets. Front doors, window frames, railings, the bell pushes at the doorways with one name overlaid by another, little strips of sticky tape, calling cards. They said it was all change with the new rail link but then when hadn't it been all change? Change had always been life, in London. Forge ahead, push on. Except in Soho one name might have got stuck down over another but the same bargains always seemed to be being struck on the grimy yellow-lit stairways; it had used to be change in the way a termite mound is always changing but always stays the same. Now the upheaval looked set to turn the whole anthill inside out, and steel and glass were pushing up through the old uneven pavements, opening cellars, shining light into basements.

She was past considering that, now, just like she was past sunshine and blue skies. She lay on her back on the floor on a deep-pile synthetic sheepskin half under a coffee table. Her head was back, chin up, her hair spread out around her head all gleaming and her lips parted, just a fraction, dry lips in the unforgiving light, and purpled, swollen. The tongue was visible.

One bare leg – the left – lay straight out in front of her, she would have been recognisably a woman just from the gleaming curve of her calf, even if the rest of her hadn't been on display. The right knee was up and had fallen outwards to rest against the coffee table; she had on a silk slip feathered with lace, a pale pink like the inside of a shell, that had been pushed up so high it exposed her all up to the underside of her breasts. Their

2

skin gleamed bluish-white like skimmed milk in the sharp pale light, pale up into the tender armpits where her arms had been flung wide open.

The darkening place was from below her upturned chin down to her collar bones. Something terrible had been done there, it was mottled, a hatching of dark red turning purplish-green with the beginnings of bruising. They'd decide very quickly she'd been strangled, the men with their evidence bags. If you looked close you could see her open eyes had a reddish, bloodshot look, where the pressure had burst the tiny vessels. There was some blood, too, smeared on the synthetic sheepskin, so there could be other injuries, when they turned her carefully with their gloved hands. They weren't here yet, though; for the moment she was alone.

She was cold enough to have been dead eight hours or so, dead long before the streets turned quiet down below the little room, in fact they probably would have been around their noisiest, with last orders being called and punters heading to find more drink and a bit of a dance, the smokers on the street jeering and sloshing their pints and the taxis cruising with their lights on. She wouldn't have seen the light change beyond the window, she wouldn't have seen the inky sky, the pinprick stars fading in the bright blue morning. Never no more. She was gone.

Chapter One

Her bag was packed and standing by the front door, Tabs' dinner was out on the side cooling, and Tim was waiting. He'd texted her from the office, first thing. Call in on your way to the station? Georgie stood in the hall, looking at herself nervously in the big chrome-edged mirror and wished for the mirror of her childhood, Mum's one with its soft kind speckled glass. It had never looked at home here, though.

She smiled at her reflection uncertainly. Not quite ready. Not quite sure. Hesitated. Was her coat too warm? It was almost November but it felt like late summer, sultry. Crazy weather. She ran back up the stairs.

Tim would have none of it, *this global warming business*, but Georgie disagreed. Silently, of course, well mostly. But the glaciers *are* melting, she'd said, stubborn last Sunday evening, as on the big TV shoals of fish raced and wheeled across a blue screen, Tabs looking up at her.

As for the evening in town, she'd expected Tim to say no, if she was honest. A girls' night out, a rowdy gang of them on the town getting back together properly after all this time, a dodgy room near King's Cross afterwards where they could giggle and haul out a chocolate stash and raid the mini-bar. She hadn't gone into all that, of course. Even Tabs would have been shocked, wouldn't she, her well-behaved mum, pillar of the school office, pining for an evening getting a bit pissed and going dancing. But Tim had just nodded absently: he had a big client giving him grief and timidly Georgie had made use of that, because she found she wanted to go. Really wanted to go. And by the time he'd inquired into the details more closely, it wasn't ten of them any more but whittled down to four, then three.

Back upstairs in the bedroom Georgie stripped off her coat in a sudden sweat of anxiety and flung it on the bed. She told herself she had plenty of time. She'd be ridiculously early for the train then early to London for a night out, turning up with her little stuffed bag at six in the afternoon; they'd be able to see her a mile off, the mum from the suburbs.

Looking around Georgie grabbed her old raincoat instead: she'd already spent long enough working out what to put in her bag, flicking through the party dresses that had got squeezed up in the corner to give Tim's suits room. It had been like looking through old pictures, another life. The red sequins. The navy shift with the low back; she hadn't even dared try that one on, for fear of it getting stuck over her bottom pulling it up. The fringed one, that you could dance in and all the silk tiers would shimmy.

6

The longer she'd looked, the more she'd had to fend off despair, but she'd forced herself. She needed a safe dress, and a spare. Not so safe.

She hadn't danced in how long? Fran's wedding, six years ago. Fran had been one of those supposed to be coming tonight, on the train from the South Coast where she ran a fancy B and B these days but one of the kids had chickenpox, or something.

The thought of having a dance had been what clinched it, what had made Georgie cling on, determined, to the thought of this night out, that had made her plot and strategise, as meticulous as she once had been at work over the submissions that had come to her for scrutiny. Cook meals ahead of time, arrange a playdate for the next morning, a sleepover maybe, sweet-talk Tabs until she was actively looking forward to her mum being away for the night. And today, ticking everything off: she'd hung out the washing, emptied the dishwasher, made the dinner.

A moment of panic. Shoes? Were the shoes right – no. In the bright neat room, she stopped herself, there's no room for anything else.

'So whose idea was this, exactly?' His tone had been amused. 'Cat's idea,' Georgie had said, hardly looking up from the vegetables she'd been chopping, how long ago, a month and more, not daring to catch his eye, casual.

'Oh yes. Well, you're hardly likely to get into trouble with her, I suppose.' Turning a page of the newspaper at the Saturday breakfast table. 'How many kids's she got now? Three? Four?'

Cat was back in their lives – well, Georgie's – after

five years living off in deep country, she was practically up the road, her husband in a new job. Eight miles away, and they'd already managed to meet four, no, five times.

'Three.' Finding herself defensive, on Cat's behalf. Three boys, they'd run her ragged but she was still the same Cat. Since she moved back they'd met up for coffee two Saturdays in a row when Tim was playing tennis. A sneaky drink in a wine bar near Cat's after school while Tabs was at drama club. Cat had come over for tea twice, once with the boys, once without, when they'd moved from tea to prosecco: that was when they decided. A proper girls' night out was what they needed. Cat's idea, but one glass down and Georgie had practically bitten her hand off.

We all used to work together, at the big tax office. People would glaze over when she said what she used to do, before Tabs. But they'd be surprised, what lurked behind those starchy shirt fronts. It was probably different now, it was probably all out in the open, it was dress-down Friday and LGBTQ liaison officers but it had been fun then, guessing what people got up to at the weekends. Portly Simon who covered Lincoln's Inn, with his nipple ring just visible through his shirt.

It was where she'd met Tim. Kind, responsible straight-as-a-die Tim.

And now Georgie reached into her wardrobe, grabbed a pair of high-heeled sparkly sandals and stuffed them in the top of the bag.

'Right,' she said to the empty air. 'We're off.'

★

A stopping train, but Georgie didn't mind. She floated, smiling, looking out of the window. The sun was getting low over the trees and the world looked like a happy place, lines of washing, a red-brick crescent of houses with garages, striped lawns and hedges. Across the aisle four women occupying a table seat had turned to look at her briefly then huddled back over their table, looking at a map.

The track had skirted the forest first, where it was still deep green, a few leaves just turning to rust only now in the unseasonable warm, and that hazy undergrowth. Epping Forest, Tim insisted that meant they lived in the countryside but the map said different, Google Earth said different. At night the lights of the city cast their glow this far, over the woodland; it felt like a smoke-haze more than a barrier. Tabs would stare into the trees, fascinated, on the rare occasions they drove into town. It should have been tamed, somehow, Georgie always thought on those drives, with Tim grumbling about the traffic, by the cars that wound through it but it was still a strange place. Some of the trees were very old, bent by age, twisted into odd shapes and the ground underneath them soft and grassy. The train rattled faster and they were crossing the undulations of a golf course, a game going on in the late afternoon light and beyond it the glint of skyscrapers in the setting sun.

They'd been happy for her. Everyone in Tim's building seemed to know she was off on a night out.

Georgie had been anxious, parking the car carefully next to Lydia's little yellow one on the forecourt, so Tim could drive it home. Anxious that something would have come up that would stop her going which was irrational, silly: he would have told her on the phone if there'd been anything. And then Lydia looking up from her desk outside his office had smiled, kindly. Lydia couldn't be more than twenty-five but she had always looked at Georgie like that: it did rub Georgie up the wrong way sometimes, she had to admit, but on this occasion she was only grateful. Lydia had buzzed Georgie straight through. And then Tim was coming round his desk towards her, and smiling, and the panic had subsided.

There'd been that moment, a couple of weeks earlier over breakfast when he'd looked up and asked mildly what exactly the plan was, this evening on the town and she'd confessed a few details, the hotel room, the bar they would start out in and he'd raised an eyebrow. 'Already booked?' but then he nodded, seeming to accept it, with a frown as if he'd been outfoxed. A smile next: kind Tim, thoughtful Tim. He loved her, she could see that. He wanted her to be happy.

He'd stepped towards her in his office an hour ago and taken her gently by the elbows. 'You look lovely,' he said softly, his smile broadening. Georgie had reached reflexively for her earlobes, the little diamond studs he'd given her when Tabs had been born. 'Lovely,' he repeated, and leaning in he kissed her there, on her neck, just below the ear. Over his head she had seen Lydia smile, indulgent.

The train was in the city now, rolling slower, level with the upstairs windows of a terrace, bathrooms and extensions. They came past an old Victorian school, the playground milling with children letting off steam before heading home. A little boy running like an arrow for his

10

mother in a parka, who had bent to receive him with her arms out.

Tabs. Georgie felt it like a pain suddenly, blinked her eyes closed. Tabs would spend a couple of hours with her new best friend Millie then Tim would collect her, he'd be on time, she'd told him twice when he had to be there, while he rolled his eyes at the thought of having to interact with *mums*. The shepherd's pie cooling on the kitchen counter: it was Tabs' favourite, she'd be fine as long as she didn't get told off for dropping her bag on the floor or playing on the iPad. As long as Tim warmed her pyjamas on the radiator and left the light on in the hall when he said goodnight. At the thought of Tabs' head on the pillow Georgie felt a tight knot in her stomach, she felt the evening slipping away from her.

Across the aisle there was a burst of laughter and Georgie opened her eyes. She made herself think of Cat. Cat got out, Cat had fun. Cat who had three sons she loved angrily – *little sods* – and Georgie's memory of them, as small boys very close in age, scrapping and gap-toothed, was roughly only sweet, only loving, too. Cat who had been taken aback – horrified, even, to hear Georgie'd never left Tabs overnight before.

'Come on,' she'd said, when they'd been talking on the phone and Georgie had introduced it into the first tentative plans for an evening out, plus hotel, 'come *on*.' And then, briskly and without pausing for breath, 'We'll have to do something about that. It's not—' and at last a hesitation. 'It's not *good* for you, George. Out there in Stepford or wherever it is, stuck in that school office all day.' Georgie silent. 'Come *on*.'

11

And Georgie had taken a deep breath and said, 'Well, I'm sure nothing would – I'm sure I can – I'll talk to Tim.' Of course she'd laid a bit of groundwork before she'd got around to it, but she did talk to him. Eventually.

The train chuntered on through grey brick, slate roof-tops, the old tenements that bordered the City and its towers as the light faded. The group of girls around a table in the seats across the aisle seemed to be on the same sort of mission as Georgie, though no doubt they wouldn't have guessed it of her, with her unmade-up face and her flat shoes for the journey and her raincoat prop-erly buttoned. Friday night and they already had the high heels on, fishnets, leaning over the table to get closer to each other. One of them had got out a bottle of wine and plastic glasses.

Georgie looked down into the streets, the street lights blinking on as they went over a bridge and a chain of red buses stationary in rush hour traffic and quite suddenly the old days didn't seem that long ago, although they were.

Long, long ago before she met Tim, she calculated. Tabs was five, so Georgie was thirty-seven now, she'd met him when she was twenty-three. Those old days came back to her as a kind of glow: Fridays looking forward to the weekend, Saturdays buying something nice to go out in. The feeling of Saturday morning, the sun always seemed to be shining as you headed out to Topshop. And dancing on a Saturday night.

One of the girls over the aisle glanced across at Georgie and she smiled, feeling herself flush: the girl raised a glass as the train swung against a bend and they all jostled, laughing, against each other.

Georgie leaned her head back and looked out of the window.

The tracks were multiplying to either side of them and other trains came into view going in both directions, faces turning behind glass, a shuttling exchange and sudden darkness as they entered one of the wide old brick tunnels that meant they were there. Almost. *You'd think*, thought Georgie, standing for her bag and feeling anxiety mix with excitement as the train eased to a halt, *that I'd never been out on my own before.* The girls were clattering for the door ahead of her and she let them go, pushing their way into the commuters waiting patiently on the platform. Tired blank faces looking forward to a very different sort of Friday night but in that instant Georgie would even have gone for that life, the bustle of an office, the slog of the commute.

Under the high curved girder roof the station was packed with people heading home, echoing with their noise. Pushing out at last Georgie was at the wrong end of the platform. Hurrying, bumping, apologising, she searched and searched the heads bobbing ahead of her because Cat had said she'd be there, she'd be at the barrier. A departure was announced, loud but inaudible and there was a surge of bodies, people carrying brief-cases and takeaway cups, then it cleared and she did see Cat, beyond the barrier, in profile staring up at the arrivals board.

For a second she wondered if something was wrong. Georgie stopped abruptly and a man ran into the back of her, muttering. Cat had had her hair done, she looked different and maybe it was the light or seeing her in profile

13

but she looked older, and tired and – *Is this all an awful mistake, aren't we all too old for this, for anything?* – Georgie felt a stab of panic. Then Cat turned her head, and smiled, and waved. And it was OK.

Chapter Two

The family room was at the top of the old building: low ceilings, dormer windows with a view of rusty-looking treetops and it had three single beds and one double. Georgie looked around, trying to stop her spirits dipping too much. The décor was standard: tired thirty-year-old furniture, limp curtains, floral carpet: on the outside the hotel had looked nice enough, a Georgian end of terrace but inside, from the minuscule veneer – unmanned – reception desk to the fraying stair carpet it was not much more than a fleapit. There had been a smell of stale food and bathroom cleaner on the stairs.

Cat dropped her holdall on one of the singles with a sigh and looked around.

'Well,' she said, 'it was cheap.' And shrugged. 'We're going to rattle around in here, aren't we? Unless Holly does turn up. But hey.' Patting the bed beside her and twisting to grab her bag. 'All the more room for us, right?'

Georgie peered into the bathroom: it looked clean enough, anyway. And felt her spirits begin mysteriously to rise again. She could hear the traffic from the Euston Road and around her, London. The red double deckers inching along and the garden squares and the railings and the tall old brick and stucco buildings and it was the neat little close they'd lived in ten years that evaporated, unreal. And when she turned there was Cat, struggling with the foil on a bottle of champagne. Looking up at Georgie and grinning, 'It's not cold, but—' and the cork popped and Georgie had to run for the bathroom and grab the plastic-wrapped plastic cups.

And it wasn't cold but in a way, thought Georgie with the first sip, that made it even better. A taste of the old days, before fancy hotels and Tim making sure everything was perfect down to the number of cubes in the ice bucket. 'Cheers,' she said. Cat grinned, her glass already empty.

Cat was thinner, since two weeks ago, was that it? She'd been talking about diets for as long as Georgie could remember, but they didn't usually work.

'You all right?' said Georgie cautiously, and Cat frowned, comical.

'Why wouldn't I be?' she said. 'How *long* have we been looking forward to this?' And sloshed some more pink into her glass, getting to her feet, stalking the room, peering out of the flaking dormer window.

It suited her, whatever it was. It made her look older but mysterious, with shadowed cheekbones. Her dark eyes looked very dark. Georgie looked down at her own stubborn soft belly and sighed theatrically, but – maybe

16

it was the warm pink fizz effect – her heart wasn't in it, finding fault. She lay back and patted it, and the sigh was happy.

'Sorry it's just us,' said Cat, turning back. Georgie opened her eyes and struggled upright.

'Sorry? No! I'm happy as Larry,' she said. 'It was our plan, wasn't it? We always said, if no one else comes we'll still have fun.' Which was true: she could hardly remember the others Cat had tried to recruit, mournful Katy, bossy Suzanne, giddy Lindsay. What she could remember was their old selves anyway and who knew what they'd have turned into, fifteen years later? 'I might have got stuck talking to the one who bred dogs in Cornwall and never got to talk to you and then what?' she said and Cat began to laugh, laughed till she sat down.

'Well, Holly's still a possibility,' she said. 'She's here at least, in London, it's down to whether she can get away.'

'Get away from what?' said Georgie and Cat shrugged.

'God knows,' she said. 'The clutches of her many admirers? Or maybe just work. She's in advertising now and it's long hours.' Rolling her eyes.

'Ah,' said Georgie, trying to stop herself deflating but as if Cat sensed it she was on the bed straight away and nudging her out of it.

'So,' she said. 'What we wearing?'

'Well,' said Georgie putting her glass down carefully, 'I wasn't sure so—' opening her case, but Cat was there at her elbow peering in. Pulling out the safe navy jersey dress, neat and modest, grimacing.

'You're kidding me?' Turning to frown into Georgie's face, smelling of wine and perfume. Laughing, but not

17

unkind, Cat was never that. Dropping the dark fabric disdainfully on the bed. 'So what else you got?'

Spying the heels and dangling them from a finger. 'Now you're talking.'

Leaned lower, and saw it, pulled it out, a flash of gold. Expensive, a surreptitious purchase passed off across two credit cards and never worn, because of the expression she could picture on Tim's face. Gold silk, light as tissue. Georgie couldn't remember what had possessed her to buy it – except— 'I think it might be too tight,' she said faintly, and Cat threw back her head and laughed.

'As if,' she said, collapsing on to the bed and leaning to pour them each another glass, sitting up, holding Georgie's out to her. 'We're not talking parents' evening, baby,' she said, 'This is ladies' night.'

Chapter Three

The two of them, Georgie and Cat, had started work within weeks of each other, fourteen years ago. The big old office building on the roaring Euston Road, two girls – and they hadn't been so far off being girls then, either, Georgie had been twenty-three, barely out of nappies it seemed to her now, soft, fair Georgie, dewy-faced, wide-eyed. Going to work for the man – the tax man, as it happened. Two girls among the men in their suits and ties, they'd had to stick together.

The office offered excellent benefits, too, equal opportunities, prospects: good maternity benefits. Georgie had noticed that clause in the recruitment drive at her university: it turned out that Cat had too, though she didn't learn that for a good couple of years, during which they had been determined to show the men and each other how good they were at statistical analysis and how unsentimental they were about sex. Cat had been the one, shouting it on the dance floor one Friday night under the influence of God knew what. Skinny as a bean back then. *I'd love it*, she said, half closing her eyes, arms out, spinning under the lights. *A baby.* And shrugging, unabashed in the ladies' later, deftly wiping the smudge of mascara out from under her eyes. 'I don't know what's wrong with that. Wanting a baby.'

Cat with her straight chopped black fringe and red lips and her tiny waist.

It hadn't turned out quite like they'd planned. Did it ever? Twelve years older, not much the wiser.

So: drinks. Maybe dinner – but then maybe not. Dancing, a room in a fleapit for the night and they could pretend they were twenty-five again.

And now, tottering down a warm dark street in Soho that smelled of beer and street food and pavement smokers and hanging on to Cat for dear life, Georgie wasn't sure she wanted to be twenty-five again.

They'd been in one bar already – they'd left the hotel in a taxi, both of them in the heels too high for walking and giggling about it – that Cat had directed the driver to. A big place off Leicester Square that was part of a chain: big and rowdy – and full of twenty-five-year-olds. Their laughter had subsided pretty much the moment they'd walked in but there'd been a corner booth miraculously empty and Georgie, too self-conscious still to remove her mac, had gone to buy drinks. She'd waited patiently to catch the barman's eye then not so patiently as she was elbowed out of the way by a succession of blokes in suits smelling of aftershave, who didn't seem to even see her.

She didn't want to be twenty-five and thoughtless. She

wanted to rewind just a little bit, that was all. Past the train ride, past Lydia's little yellow car on the forecourt and Tim standing up behind his desk to give her his blessing, further back than that, past these last four, five years of pacing out the rooms she lived in, bedroom, kitchen, school office, go into reverse. Not too far, don't go back too far. Maybe as far as holding out her arms for Tabs to be put into them, all strange and new. That might work.

Turning from the bar at last in the overheated noisy barn of a room, with two stupidly overpriced drinks in her hand, to look across at their table, she'd seen Cat – still bundled up in her coat too and that wasn't like Cat, not when there was a nice off-the-shoulder dress under-neath, tight and black – frowning down at her mobile. Gingerly, hands full and bag swinging from her shoulder Georgie negotiated a cluster of office girls still in their work shirts and finally collapsed on the banquette beside her. Cat looked up, absent, blank.

'All right?' said Georgie.

'Ah, oh – oh—' Cat blinked.

'You were on the phone?' Georgie said, setting down the drinks. It was deafening in the room and she had to point at the mobile, face down on the table.

Cat's face cleared, 'Oh,' she said, beginning to shrug off her coat finally – big and fluffy, leopard-printed – then changing her mind. She pushed the phone away a little across the table, and took the glass. 'Holly. She's just extri-cating herself from a situation, she says.' Rolling her eyes, though without much conviction. Georgie could have sworn her mind was elsewhere.

'*Extricating*,' said Georgie. Holly coming back into focus

21

now, with her high-arching eyebrows, rolling words like that around. Checking her lipstick in the mirror, talking about getting out of tax and into something glamorous.

'Yep,' said Cat, and pulled the phone toward her and turned it face up again.

Georgie still couldn't see the screen and couldn't tell if that was deliberate. 'What?' she said.

Cat looked up from the phone, pursing her red lips. *Should have put lipstick on*, thought Georgie automatically, not sure if she'd even brought any. 'Holly doesn't fancy this place much,' she said, and looked around the room as if seeing it for the first time. A riot of wooden panelling and neon signs and barstools, something for everyone. 'Says it's for the bridge and tunnel crowd.'

'Bridge and tunnel?' Georgie had only a vague idea what she was talking about.

'Like in New York?' said Cat helpfully. 'Not that I've ever been. People that come in from the suburbs. But I think she means it's for provincials.' Grinning broadly now. 'Wannabes from out of town. People like us.'

'Aha,' said Georgie, taking a long drink from the glass, tasting mostly water now and setting it back down. Wanting something stronger, something that tasted of something. Something to take the edge off being ten years older than everyone else in the room, and the prospect of seeing Holly again. Grinning back, and then Cat was on her feet, reaching for her bag. Her glass empty.

'Anyway,' Cat said, reaching for her bag. 'She'll meet us some bar called Le Something. One of those streets off the square. Soho Square, we can just about manage that, can't we?' Wincing and reaching down to her

22

stockinged feet in heels. 'She says they know her there, you can dance. And if we get a move on we'll catch the cheap drinks.'

Ladies' night. Women – *ladies* – get in free, first drink half price. And up ahead the neon signed loomed, green and red, and underneath it a shaven-headed bouncer, big as an ox with hands clasped in front of his crotch, turned to give them the once-over.

He looked to left and right, his face in shadow under overhead light although there was no one else queuing for entry. Paused, stepped to the side and one arm was reluctantly spread to usher them through.

They stepped inside, into the dark.

Chapter Four

Frank had watched the tall guy working out how to break in on the women for half an hour now but they weren't interested. He had been watching them under the low lights, and it didn't look like they even knew he was there but every time he took that crucial step closer there was a shift and a back was turned on him. The tall guy was patient, though. Frank had observed that, too.

The first one through the door had smiled at him, uncertain, then switched it off. Standing awkwardly, soft and fair in a mac, something shining underneath it that she was a bit unsure about. She was holding a handbag tight against her front. And then her friend was bustling in behind her, shoving her on so she laughed, a big laugh, tripping over herself and then the pair of them hesitated, on the edge of the dark room.

Frank caught Lucy's head turning from behind her little mahogany counter: Lucy the queen of hat-check, married to the boss. She must have seen the new arrival smile at him. Not much got past Lucy.

The blonde nervous one still had her coat on and he liked that look, a shy Brigitte Bardot in a trench coat, but the other one was swinging her big fake fur number from a fingertip and looking around. She was the one in charge, turning her friend in towards the bar before they got to Frank.

Down at their end of the low-lit bar Dom was polishing a glass slower than you could think was possible when they approached, choosing him – Christ knew why, Dom from North Island, a fuzz of beard and a daft bow tie and no fucking clue how to make a reasonable Sidecar, what was he even doing in a place like this? – to take their order. Frank would have said the women were late thirties.

Dom was nodding slowly as the women leaned down over the cocktail menu and Frank's radar saw movement in the big dark room. No one was dancing yet, Dom was keeping the music on his early setting. The into-the-groove setting.

Frank had customers to serve. Vince and a couple of cronies were in, working out if they were going to wait it out till it got busy. There'd been a flurry at eight, a dozen suits coming in off some conference or other singing 'Hi Ho Silver Lining' until Dom looked up, affronted, from his laptop and his mood music. Then only one suit was left in the room: they'd gone without him, not a backward glance. Survival of the fittest, leaving the weakest one to fend for himself, was it? – only he didn't look like he needed looking after, come to think of it.

Had he even been with them in the first place? Giving off confidence, anyway, even if there was something not quite right about the suit, too short in the sleeve. Something not quite right about the set of his head, either, the angle of him, looking round. Eyes in the back of his head. Older than Frank? Maybe.

The guy was sitting on a stool around the corner – half out of sight in the window that was curtained for night-time in the same red velvet – when Frank saw the small movement that meant he had noticed the women. Shifting, one leg going down to meet the floor.

Then there had been something different about him that made Frank, still with his hands flat on the chrome bar top, lean forward. He didn't know if it was the way the lanky bloke shifted, the careful way he set his glass down – but then the moment was gone because then another woman had arrived. Tall, leggy, model-girl stride and to his surprise she was with the two at the bar because she swooped from behind them and the fair one jumped. Frank could smell her scent from where he stood and he wondered if he knew her from somewhere. Big smile sweeping the room as she leaned between the two early arrivals, her hand cupped round her ear, making introductions.

She had a little wheelie suitcase with her and was straight off to the Ladies' Cloaks, swish, swish, head up, pausing only to order a drink, an Old-Fashioned, waving it at Dom with her hand in passing. Leaning across the counter to exchange a word with Lucy.

Dom had blinked awake to stare at her, then scrabbling for the right bourbon while Frank restrained a sigh. On the dance floor a few girls had started dancing. In the corner directly opposite to where the tall, quiet guy had paused halfway down from his stool. Quiet guys – everyone thought they were harmless. Not always, they weren't.

The blonde was standing, uncertain, closer to Frank than to Dom and she half turned and there it was, they were looking at each other. 'All right?' he said, first thing that came into his head but also, she didn't *look* quite all right. Waiting for her drink. There was a hint of panic in her eyes. 'Dancing gets going around ten,' Frank said and it seemed to have been the right thing because she smiled, a beautiful smile.

'I like a dance,' she said and he heard it in her voice, unmistakable.

'You're not from out of town after all then,' he said, leaning in. Tilting his head, pretending to consider, but not too long. 'Crystal Palace?' he said, musing. 'No.' Lifting a finger. 'I know.'

She was staring. Her friend with the fake fur was talking to Dom but that wouldn't last much longer: Frank had a knack for this, though. South London, and her accents. 'Brockley Rise.'

She put her hand to her mouth, delighted. 'What?' she said, breathless. 'How did you know?'

He shrugged, modest. 'Made it my life's work,' he said. Offering a hand across the bar. 'Frank,' he said. 'Soho via Lewisham.'

She moved her hand toward his, hesitating, 'I'm Georgie,' she said, 'Born in Brockley Rise but now—' and the hand waved off to the north somewhere, 'it's the suburbs.' He nodded, seeing the wedding ring. Diamonds in her ears. Thinking, *She's spoken for.* 'It's not the same, is it?' she said and her hand hovered there between them but then her friend had sensed something, turned sharply and she brought her hand back to her side of the counter and the friend was sliding her drink over to her, one of Dom's terrible martinis, giving him a frown.

And Lucy was leaning out from between her velvet curtains and gesturing to him, violently. Men's toilets, again: *shit*, thought Frank. Sometimes he wished he wasn't considered the alpha male in this place when Eddie wasn't about to catch Lucy asking him to unblock anything. He felt the impulse to apologise to Georgie from Brockley Rise, he felt an odd reluctance to leave her that wasn't just down to whatever was waiting for him to deal with in the gents'. But her back was to him now, all he could see was the vulnerable back of her neck above her coat collar, flushed, downy. He slipped out.

Frank took his time washing his hands, after. If customers only knew. Knew what there was behind it all, what it looked like Monday morning with the lights all on and the floor yet to be swept.

And when he came back in, the tall man had broken them up: he was talking to the one who'd come in last, with her wheelie suitcase.

She was looking the other way when he came back in, *Georgie* a flush on her cheek and her glass empty, and then she turned and slid her coat off, careless. The gold dress caught the light and her soft shoulders rising out of it were suddenly very bare. As Frank watched she held the glass out to the tall guy, across the other woman's shoulder, and he took it.

★

Holly, Holly, Holly.

The room swam briefly around Georgie, the sparkling downlighters and the rows of coloured bottles like stained glass, red and green and gold and the moving figures on the dance floor. The square-shouldered barman at the far end of the counter, the one who'd known where she was from who'd stood there with his hands flat on the counter smiling at her, had seemed for a while now like the only still point – and then suddenly he wasn't there.

I *do* remember you, Holly.

The minute she came through the door, then as she threaded her way on high heels through the crowd. Pretty Holly. Her cheekbones were sharper, she was narrow-faced like a fox. Was that the right animal? If Holly was a fox, Cat was – a cat, and what was Georgie? Her own outlines were fuzzy, indistinct: she'd be one of those little ponies, stubbornly untidy, motionless in snow. She looked across the bar and caught a shard of herself, between bottles, blank.

Now Holly had her back to Georgie, talking to the tall man who'd come over to them: Georgie could see the sharp blades of her shoulders in a cut-out vest and she could see his elbow, in dark cloth, resting on the bar. The other side of Georgie Cat was leaning across the bar top in her tight black dress chatting up the barman in his bow tie while he nodded, disengaged.

'What's with the suitcase, Holl?' Cat had said, amused when she wheeled it, bump, toward them at the bar, bringing the street air in with her, exhaust fumes and the squeal of brakes. 'I thought we were the out-of-towners.' She'd already told Georgie, Holly lived in some mansion flat somewhere, paid for by a man.

'I'm between lovers, darling,' said Holly, airily.

'Kicked you out, has he?' said Cat, 'About time too.' And Holly had given her a quick sharp look before laughing, loudly, head back and hair rippling. And leaning down and exclaiming, *Well, it's little Georgie, look at you.*

And Georgie, remembering her vividly all of a sudden, had started to say something about her perfume, about remembering her perfume and an outfit she had used to wear all that time ago but Holly had shaken her head impatiently, miming that she couldn't hear, leaning down with her hand cupped around her ear. So Georgie had just mumbled, *Nice to see you again, Holly* like the polite little out-of-towner she was.

She'd looked for the square-shouldered barman then, who had known she wasn't an out-of-towner. Who'd known where she was from, down to the square half-mile, who probably knew Dad's street and the cherry tree outside it, but he wasn't there. And then she'd caught the man's eye, from down the bar to where he sat in the dark. Had she been aware of him all along? He'd been further off, before, had he? And now he smiled at her, kindly, as if he'd seen what had happened quite clearly, and bringing one long leg down from his barstool. She'd had to look away. A tall man.

But when he'd got to the bar Holly had turned to him and he'd stopped, easy, his eyes sliding over Georgie and settling on Holly and they'd begun to talk, the tall man and Holly. Because he was taller than Holly even in her high heels he leaned down. Georgie must have moved because he looked past Holly to her, coolly, while he was talking, then his eyes were on Holly again.

Was it the booze? Georgie didn't feel drunk, exactly, but then it was a long time since she'd had more than a single glass of wine, ten years at least, they didn't go to parties. Not real parties, anyway, just the odd work do where there was no dancing, just standing and talking and being polite till your face hurt. She felt a little numb, immune – that *little Georgie*, in Holly's voice, what had that been, maybe just her manner, maybe just being sweet – as if she had been lifted a little way off the ground, to where everything was softer, easier: she could just stand here, smiling at that little piece of herself reflected behind the bar.

Cat was leaning across the bar and was re-tying the other barman's bow tie for him. Georgie felt she couldn't be drunk because she could see the man's vague expression exactly and every detail of Cat's long fingers, broken skin at the knuckle from washing up, a roughness at the pad of her thumb, a chip in the varnish.

She wasn't happy. Cat wasn't. The revelation had come halfway from the last bar to this one, hanging on to each other at a set of traffic lights, jammed between a gang of tourists behind them buying Union Jack mugs from a stall and taxis touting for business. Cat had let out an explosive sigh.

'What is it?' Georgie had said and for a moment Cat had said nothing, just stared across at the little red man forbidding them to walk. Then a longer sigh.

'Just tired,' she said. And rattled it off quickly. Settling in to a new place, the boys, her husband Harry never home, money was tight. With a quick glance sideways at Georgie, who knew straight away there was something else, something she wasn't saying.

'Is it—' but then the little man turned green and Cat had jerked her arm and that was that.

Now in the glow from behind the bar Cat smiled into the barman's face, and obediently he smiled back.

They had opted for dirty martinis, Cat pouting as she said it which was the whole point, after all, and now Georgie's glass sat on the bar, almost empty, just an olive and a little oily trace left and she drained it. With the burn and the taste Georgie felt the stir of something, she saw a whole other life unroll like a carpet, a red carpet, the gangway to a big glittering ocean liner. If she'd been brave enough. From behind the bottles Georgie saw her own downturned mouth. She'd let Tim look after her, after – after that first time and God knows, women all over the world deal with that, don't they? And much worse. It was only a bloody miscarriage. Bloody. Georgie pulled herself up straight. She turned to say it to Cat, her revelation, but Cat wasn't there.

There she was. Further down the bar and Georgie could see that the boy – he was a boy, he might have a beard and a bow tie but he couldn't be more than twenty-five – had a laptop he was showing Cat at the end of the counter and it must have had music on it, because he traced a finger over the screen and it came on loud, and then Cat had raised her arms over her head and was moving. Georgie could see a shadow of stubble under her arms and her radiant smile then some guy was there on the dance floor in front of her, obscuring Georgie's view, his arms up to mirror Cat's. Georgie turned, feeling herself beginning to move too, and she was nodding, smiling because it was an old track everyone knew and it had worked.

The space was filling up, heads nodding in unison, ten bodies, twenty. But as she swayed Georgie became aware that something was wrong, she didn't know what and then she realised, she still had her coat on. She wriggled her shoulders out of it, bare skin to the warm air, felt for a hook under the bar and there was one. As if she'd been here before, in another life.

Did Tim dance? Had he ever? Georgie couldn't remember suddenly, and she almost laughed: she could only see his face, she felt him shake his head at her and then she turned and saw that the other barman was back from wherever he'd been, what had he said his name was? Frank, flushed but serious in his suit jacket and frowning. At her? He'd been so friendly. She wanted to say, *What?* To lean over the bar and ask him, *What exactly am I doing wrong?* but then Holly shifted and it was the tall man looking at her past Holly's sharp bare shoulder, looking at Georgie and Georgie alone, and he was smiling at her. He tilted his head and his smile was warmer. And careless, certain, Georgie leaned past Holly, and her glass was in her outstretched hand, and he took it from her.

Chapter Five

Something hurt, all down one side of her body.

Eyes closed Georgie tried to turn over, not even sure if she had been lying face down or up. Something was wrong, it took too long, it was too difficult, her body too heavy. The bed felt different, harder, narrower, she reached across for Tim and her hand flapped in empty air.

And then it came, a sudden quick eruption of panic: she couldn't feel her hand, her leg wouldn't move and even her face, her face felt numb. Georgie lay, feeling her heart pound, unable to move. *Other hand* – she willed it, and it did move. It moved. She eased herself over, off the dead hand and leg, stiff and sore, and the other side moved. Her body responded. Dead leg. Dead leg, that's all. She opened her eyes.

A low ceiling lightly furred with dust, a dormer window, the corner of a cheap wardrobe and a thin curtain letting in grey light. She looked sideways and saw Cat's face turned towards her, scrunched in sleep, panda-eyed with mascara, the cover pulled up. Beyond her, on the third bed along the wall she could see a clump of streaky hair and a naked arm drooping to the floor. Holly, lying face down. Her little wheeled suitcase, its handle still raised, stood at the foot of the bed, unopened, her clothes in a pile on the floor, the inner arch visible of a high-heeled shoe on its side. Georgie stared at it, she couldn't remember what, how – she lay very still, feeling life return to her left side, it tingled, then it hurt, that horrible feeling when a numb limb comes back to life. She must have slept very heavily, she must have—

From nowhere sweat beaded on Georgie's forehead, the back of her neck. Her head pounded, and the skin of her cheeks felt raw and hot. This wasn't her, hungover in a horrible hotel room.

Gingerly she sat up and winced, raising a hand to shield her eyes from the dull grey light that slanted through the little window. In their beds Cat and Holly hadn't moved, humped shapes in the dawn. *This isn't you*, she thought, wanting to be off the bed and gone, back to the station, get on the train, sort herself out, brush her teeth. She shifted in the bed but everything whirled suddenly, and she sat back on the thin pillow and put a hand to her forehead. Her hand felt hot and under it her head throbbed.

This isn't you. This isn't real. Saturday morning and she should be calling up from the kitchen to Tabs, out of bed. Tim with the newspaper, legs crossed in the living room, turning his head to smile as she laid the table, croissants and coffee.

There was a bottle of water on the side table: Georgie was sure she hadn't put it there. She unscrewed the lid and drank, a gulp then sipping, carefully. Still no movement from Holly; Cat was snoring slightly, one nostril squeezed shut, mouth open. Neither of them knew what her life was, not even Cat, not really. Cat had only been to the house when it was empty of Tabs, of Tim. Looking round Georgie's kitchen and laughing at how clean it was. At Georgie hopping off her stool to wipe a wine spill as if she was going to be arrested, that was what Cat had said, laughing and frowning at once. 'Chill, George. You want to see the tip my kitchen is, I'm surprised health and safety hasn't been round.'

The air in the room seemed to thicken, hot: she felt it on her cheeks, struggled upright. And then abruptly Georgie knew she was going to be sick. She stumbled out of bed, knocking painfully into a chair, keeping going.

The bathroom lurched at her: it was cramped, cheap, tiled in brown and orange. Toilet bowl and bidet side by side and she only just got there in time, and vomited: she didn't even have to heave, it poured out of her, hot and sour. Sweat beaded across her forehead, under her arms: the porcelain was cold under her hands, against her cheek, she felt poisoned, sick. She could see the crust inside the toilet bowl of ancient scale and it came again, and again, until her belly was sore with the effort and she leaned back, sweating, against the bathroom wall.

The cold tile against her back, hair plastered to her damp cheek, Georgie looked down at herself. She shivered; she was half naked. The slip she'd bought specially for the occasion (although she'd never have said that, she'd have

36

said, *It's nothing special* though it was silk), that she'd laid out carefully on the pillow last night, had rucked up. One knee up, the other leg stretched out, her round thigh, a nick on her shin where she'd caught herself shaving, painted toenails, white, white skin. There was something funny about her knee. It hurt. Georgie shivered again, looking down at it.

Something was embedded in it, a bit of gravel? She put her hands palm down on the tiled floor to push herself upright and they were sore too, grazed in the ball of the thumb, the palm. A bruise on her shin. Her body in that flash of a second seemed to belong to someone else, taken apart and reassembled, sore at the joints. Her head stuffed with cotton wool, or mould, a grey blur where last night should be. Outside she could hear a jackhammer going somewhere, shockingly loud.

Georgie closed her eyes and made herself keep still. It had been so long since she had a hangover she'd forgotten what it was like. That nasty feeling that you've done some-thing awful, said something stupid and everyone is talking about you now. It was chemical. That was all.

Last night. *Wait and you'll remember:* she waited. Taxis with their lights on, hissing past in the street. It had been raining. A hot night. Then swaying in the hotel's cramped hall as they let themselves in, the bulbs too bright in ugly wall sconces, the empty reception desk, the little bell. A flash of memory came then, she remembered leaning towards it, laughing, her hand hovering over the bell and someone had stopped her, shushed her.

The worn carpet on the narrow staircase coming up to meet her too fast. Now Georgie's eyes blinked back open – she'd tripped. Tripped on the stairs. Now she looked down at her knee. A wave of nausea came with the lurch of memory and she scrabbled back to the toilet bowl, hair hanging down either side of her face but there was nothing but a streak of yellow bile left. Georgie reached for the toilet flush, feeling the sweat of shame and sickness on the back of her neck and her upper lip as the water swirled in the bowl.

Behind her she heard the door open and weakly, her palms still sore, everything still wrong, wanting Cat, she turned.

Holly was leaning against the doorjamb, holding a bottle of cola. She was wrapped in pale silk, something short with deep sleeves. 'Well,' she said with a sigh and stepped inside, pulling the door closed behind her. 'One of those nights, hey.' Long legs, gleaming. A flash of no knickers as she crouched and then she was sitting beside Georgie against the wall, smelling of perfume, eyes smudged with last night's make-up, sharp knees raised. Georgie felt a kind of despair come over her, she didn't know at what, at Holly's scent, her smoothness, the pale expensive silk swathing her, at her not being Cat. She leaned away, pushing helplessly at the robe to protect it from her own sour smell, sweat and sickness.

'Oh, come on,' said Holly, jostling her. Impatient but not unkind, and Georgie felt tears just waiting, hot behind her eyes. Holly held out the bottle and Georgie took it. She sipped: waiting to see which way the sugar would go. It stayed down. Better. She offered the bottle back to Holly, who shook her head, one eyebrow raised.

Tabs when she was sick, wanting Fruit Shoot. Mum

bringing Ribena to Georgie, way back when. Something settled, gingerly, inside her.

Holly rested her head back against the tiled wall and Georgie stole a glance sideways. It had been so dark in the bar last night, just a blur of twinkling disco light and the different colours of bottles behind the bar, she'd hardly got a look at Holly. Just the impression, legs and hair and the flash of teeth when she smiled. The suitcase rattling carelessly across the dance floor when she arrived and her head turning from this side to that side, acknowledging the attention.

And after? Taxi, hotel, rain. It was a blur. There was something on the edge of the blur. Georgie turned her head as if that might send it away. Send it all away, back into the dark.

In the cold bathroom light Holly looked a bit rougher round the edges and Georgie felt mournful knowing that made her feel better. Rougher – but not worse. A bit more blurred, more relaxed. Her hair still looked good, expensive, making Georgie wish she got hers done more often. Tentatively Georgie prodded at the normal thought, letting it settle her. Like a nice hot bath, or cleaning her teeth. Hairdresser every two months instead of every six: Tim wouldn't mind. This was just a hangover, it would pass.

From beyond the door came a sudden snore, and a grunt, and Holly turned her head to Georgie, catching her looking. Smiling. 'You weren't the only one, see,' she said, and her shoulder pushed into Georgie's again. 'What's the betting she can't remember a thing when she wakes up?'

Georgie groaned involuntarily and Holly pushed herself off the wall, leaning forward over her sharp knees, examining Georgie.

'You OK?' she asked, narrowing her dark-smudged eyes.

Georgie swallowed, fragile. 'I can't—' she began, but revised. 'What happened?' she said. 'I can't – I can't really remember how I got—' looking down at the slip, pushing it down to try and cover her thighs. The silk was pale greyish, oyster they'd called it and she'd thought it was a sophisticated colour but against it her skin looked grey too. 'I mean – I remember coming up the stairs. I tripped over. I think I hurt my—'

She stopped. The room, though. That memory was confused. Coming into the room. Holly reaching into her handbag and pulling out a flat bottle of something amber-coloured, brandishing it. Georgie put her hand to her mouth a second, feeling her stomach wobble.

'You had – was it brandy?'

Holly shrugged, amused. 'My bad,' she said. 'Just a nightcap. I mean – we'd probably had enough already, yeah, but—' And shrugged again.

'But what actually happened? Did something – oh—'

Because she remembered something. She did. The hand reaching past her to cover hers, above the night bell on the reception desk, the wrist in a suit cuff. She blinked, and it was gone: she'd dreamed it, or imagined it.

Holly smiled, sympathetic, reaching an arm round her. The perfume again, enveloping Georgie: she stiffened reflexively, made herself relax.

'One of those nights,' said Holly, 'Wasn't it? Cat was spark out by the time you came up.'

'What happened?' Georgie could feel herself redden, stubborn, on the verge of tears again. Holly tilted her head, put a cool hand to Georgie's cheek a second, then she let the hand drop, patted her on the shoulder, once, twice.

'Chill,' said Holly. 'Nothing happened. Just − one of those nights.' And the ghost of a wink, a sideways smile.

'What did I—' Georgie had another question, but she thought better of it, the sickness in her belly told her, *just stay quiet.*

Holly's smile widened, as she held Georgie's gaze, knowing. 'Nothing happened,' she repeated. And then that look softened and was gone. Holly leaning back against the white tile, quite relaxed, reassuring, a hint of tiredness, a hint of concern but nothing more than that. Georgie had no reason not to believe her.

Nothing happened.

It didn't feel that way.

Chapter Six

Sunday

The room was hot, sweltering behind the heavy curtains. Even before she woke fully, Georgie could still feel the ache under her ribs, she could still feel her limbs sore and heavy: she lay motionless, trying to make the feeling go away.

Beside her Tim stirred: she didn't want him to wake and so when she turned her head to look at the clock she did it carefully.

The feeling was still there. Was it only yesterday? She'd come home on the train feeling hollowed out, the muscles of her abdomen sore from vomiting; she had sat on the train with her overnight bag, looking at the other people without really seeing them. Dread in the pit of her stomach.

Out through the brick tenements, the tower blocks, other railway lines and industrial units and then the green of the forest had started to appear. She had looked back a moment, and seen the whole city, the scale of it. Stretching back for miles all grey under the low warm sky, to the east the starburst of skyscrapers and she'd felt herself shiver, as if she was coming down with something.

When the taxi dropped her off she had already been able to see Tim pacing in the hall behind glass. She had approached diffidently, slowing down the closer she got because the dread somehow was all tied up with this moment, of her stepping back over the threshold.

She'd told herself, it would all be all right when she got home. All the way, leaving the hotel with her bag and turning to wave, walking to the bus, going through the barriers at the station, she'd waited for the feeling to pass, just chemical, just hangover, but it had stayed.

Then Tim had seen her and he was flinging the door open and on the doorstep Georgie saw his tennis bag straight away, and a flush went through her. How could she have forgotten? Saturday afternoon was tennis.

On the pillow now she turned her head slowly. He was facing away from her, his back rounded.

She'd been so scared in that moment on the doorstep, a panic out of nowhere, but then as if he knew, he had been pulling her against him, bestowing a kiss distractedly somewhere, above her ear, 'Tabs'll be back at five,' he said, speaking into her hair and she had held very still, squeezing her eyes tight ready to smile when he looked at her. But he didn't: he released her and in the same moment he was off down the path with his keys jingling. Just turning back as he let himself into the car and she raised a hand to wave and off he went, too fast round the corner as always.

So much for that. She could see Cat's face. Hear her voice. 'Come *on*. This is your husband we're talking about. Love of your life. Do you think he doesn't know what a girls' night out is all about? We all need to let our hair down now and again.'

43

The flush came on Georgie again now in the hot room and she pushed the covers away gingerly. Perhaps she *was* coming down with something, because yesterday, alone in the house despite the warm day all she had been able to do was shiver.

Yesterday. The day had seemed to go on for ever: the weekend stretching out ahead of her, before normality could return.

Putting down her bag in the hall, tiptoeing into the kitchen, filling the noisy kettle she had felt like – like someone who didn't belong there, like the cleaner, or a burglar. Without Tabs in it the house had felt cold and empty and alien. She had gone upstairs and looked in Tabs' room: neat as a pin, the duvet pulled completely straight, cushions and soft toys in a row, as if it was a bedroom in a hotel. A photocube on the bedside table with pictures of her: the one facing Georgie was of her with Tim, on a fairground ride, Tim's arms right round her holding her steady and his face pressed against hers, beaming.

She had thought then, *While I was out there, dancing, Tim was home alone*, and she had shivered again, at the memory of the dark dance floor. Her hair flying, catching on some man's button. His? Yes, his. Him smiling and disentangling it.

And then when they had been waking up in that horrible room in a hotel that could have been a brothel, thinking about it – who had booked it? Cat? Holly? – Tim had been making his own breakfast, filling the kettle, packing his own tennis bag.

Georgie had stood in the kitchen waiting for the kettle

to boil, pinning all her hopes on a cup of tea, trying not to shiver. Now, in bed, she put a hand to her forehead, tentative: it was clammy, yes. It would be too easy, wouldn't it? To lie in bed, pretending to be ill, so as not to talk. The sweat cooled: she lay still.

Maybe she was coming down with something, maybe it was not getting enough sleep, she wasn't used to that. In bed by ten, although she often woke at four. Often. Always. Woke certain she'd done something wrong and she just had to work out what it was. And then lay there, with things running round in her head, mostly about Tabs. Trying not to want another baby. Trying.

Standing in the kitchen yesterday where she hadn't even turned on the lights, the Saturday afternoon grey and dull beyond the window, Georgie had thought, maybe, a hot water bottle. They kept them in the garage, for some reason: and it was true, a hot water bottle was an untidy-looking thing, flopping, antique, their covers always grubby, they had a habit of springing out of drawers and landing like fish on the floor. But every cool night when she was a kid Mum had used to fill her one, and underfloor heating wasn't the same.

It had been properly chilly in the garage: it was a while since Georgie had been in there because it was Tim's domain. His neat tool shelves, his power drill, his fold-out work bench. She stood, trying to remember where she'd seen it.

It was Georgie's talent, finding, if she was allowed to stand and think, and Tabs loved it. It seemed like magic to her, she liked waiting while Georgie closed her eyes and held up a hand, she clapped and clapped when, opening her eyes, Georgie led her straight to it, the special pen or the science workbook or the merit badge. And now Georgie knelt, looking under the work bench and there it was, or rather *they* were, three hot water bottles in various states of disrepair. She reached for the most presentable one, red rubber with a floral cover, and stopped, awkwardly, half under the bench. There was a box against the wall that she hadn't seen before, a wooden box on its side, with a snap fastening, and a little brass padlock.

Crouched in the dim dusty space Georgie had looked at the box: in that moment it had seemed to her that Tim lived in another universe, the man who owned all this stuff. She took the hot water bottle and sat back on her heels. She'd never seen him use any of the tools he already had and here was another one. She shuffled back, up and out, the movement, or something, bringing her out in a sweat that cooled immediately. She went back into the house through the kitchen door, hurrying, hurrying: she filled the bottle, still hurrying, and she could hear Tim in her head, hear him clicking his tongue, exasperated, careful – and burned herself. Shit.

Stop. Stop. What's going on? Why are you in such a state?

Because Tabs wasn't there. Because she thought everything would settle down when she got home and it hasn't. Because Tim would come back from tennis and say something, she didn't know what, he would say something and Georgie wouldn't be able to look him in the eye.

Because she still couldn't remember how she got to bed on Friday night.

46

And then outside a car door had slammed and there had been footsteps on the path.

And Tabs on the doorstep, her own little pink wheeled suitcase parked beside her because she'd been on a sleepover and why hadn't Georgie known that, *Mummy, Mummy, Mummy.* And Georgie kneeling to receive her, 'Daddy fixed it with Millie's mummy,' Georgie was saying, while last night had retreated, back into the shadows.

The shepherd's pie on the side, not needed.

After that, things had settled, soft, Tabs bringing with her that little comforting tick of motherhood, her steps overhead, padding in and out of her bedroom, the bathroom.

Tim had come home late, from tennis and a few beers after the tennis, he said, they'd had something to eat too, only a passing frown at the hot water bottle, untidy on the kitchen counter and suddenly Georgie had been exhausted, so she had crept up to bed. Heard him watching TV, letting the cackle of voices lull her, the bursts of canned laughter. It would be all right in the morning. That was what she'd told herself.

And now the morning was here.

Out of bed, shower, clean your teeth, downstairs to make breakfast. It was early still, if she was quick – and then in that instant as she hesitated, readying herself for the quick quiet movement that would attract no attention Tim's hand came out and took hold of her.

It wasn't inevitable, sex on Sunday morning, sometimes it was Saturday, sometimes he was too tired, particularly after an evening with the tennis boys, which was normal, wasn't it? Once or twice she'd been tentatively on to

47

mums' chatrooms to see what other people did. All sorts of things seemed to be normal, which had unaccountably disturbed her. And now Tim tugged at her in the dark and she made herself soft, made herself relax. She moved into him, full body contact and he put his hands up under her ears, pulling her face towards him, looking at her in the dark, his fingers in her hair.

She swallowed, hoping he wouldn't hear. He didn't seem to. He turned her over and his hands were on her hips from behind and Georgie closed her eyes. She let the thoughts into her head, shapes moving in the dark, the feel of his hands but she didn't have time, he was quick. She waited, in darkness suppressing the old stiffening reflex, *no*, turning it into simple relief, until she was sure. Until his breathing slowed, regularised, and his hands slipped off her.

She closed the bathroom door behind her softly and seeing her face in the mirror – pale, pouchy with sleep, unmade-up and something else – and hurried past it. She heard the light click on in the bedroom.

Under the shower Georgie told herself, having sex was good. That was good, it meant things were getting back to normal, it meant – she put her hands up to lift her hair as she washed it, up under her ears and then she felt a lurch, back into panic. Her hands slippery with shampoo, she couldn't be sure – left ear, yes, there, relieved, how could she have forgotten she had them in, right ear – no. No. There was no earring in her right ear. No diamond earring, the ones Tim had given her at Tabs' birth, how could she – how could she—? The water ran on, drowning her, she grappled for the dial and pushed at it and the flow stopped. Blindly, eyes stinging with the shampoo she reached for a towel and in the same movement knelt, squatting in the shower tray.

It wasn't there. Could it have gone down the drain already? She sat back on her haunches a second, then set to work, quickly. There was a quick release on the drain cover and with clumsy fingers she prised it off. Water still beneath it, a swirl of hair half blocking the outflow – if it had come out in the shower it would still be there. She leaned back against the shower, and heard Tim clear his throat next door. He'd be reading in bed. Would he get up and make a cup of tea?

It could have come off in the bed. Couldn't it? Of course. That was where it was.

But she knew, the pattering of her heart told her. Deep down, she knew. She put a hand to the right ear: it was tender, but not much.

Blinked, and there she was on the dance floor, smiling as he disentangled her hair from his shirt button.

'Cup of tea?' Tim's voice from next door, on cue.

'Oh yes please, thank you.' It came out higher-pitched, more relieved than it should have but perhaps he wouldn't notice through the bathroom door.

She could hear Cat say, *Just tell him.* Exasperated. *Just tell him, you don't know where it came out. It's just an earring.*

She heard the bedroom door, and Tim on the stairs. The quilt was folded back neatly, exposing the sheet and she could see straight away there was nothing there but she looked anyway. Carefully, scrupulously, she felt across the sheet, shook out the duvet: she was on the floor and peering under the bed when he came back in. Georgie hadn't heard him coming back up, the first she heard was

49

him laughing and that was her chance, she knelt back and looked up at him.

'I—' her hand going up to her ear. But Tim got there first, his face already clouding.

'You haven't—' he said. Exasperated. Controlling it. Disappointed.

'I don't know – I thought it might have come out in the shower,' she said, desperate suddenly.

'But—' he was shaking his head, regretful. 'I'm sorry, sweetheart,' he said. He sat down next to her. A hand lightly on her shoulder. 'It wasn't there last night,' he said.

She stared. 'Why didn't you say anything?' she said, and could hear herself, querulous like a child. He looked at her. And sighed.

'Because you were asleep, sweetheart,' he said. 'You were lying on your side and I kissed you there, under your ear, that ear—' her hand went up to it reflexively, she hadn't remembered, she hadn't woken. His hand patted her shoulder now. 'I didn't think anything of it except that your ear looked a bit sore, I assumed you'd taken them both out and put them away.'

'So it must—' she shifted on the bed and he turned away from her to pick up her mug. 'It must have been while I—'

He turned back, and handed her the tea, shrugging. 'You know what,' he said. 'Don't worry about it.' Smiling, sad. 'It's only money.'

Staring down into her lap, the tea burning her hand, Georgie blinked back something, not tears, panic. Not, though. Not, though. Not only money.

And from across the landing she heard Tabs call.

★

It had taken five years of IVF to get Tabs. Donor eggs and donor sperm in the end, and thousands of pounds. Thousands, Tim's face grim and set as another round went for a burton, Georgie off work, and it turned into a full-time job, lying there having her ovaries manipulated. The hormones. The pregnancy tests, crouched on the loo not daring to look. *My little baby.*

Her world had blossomed that night, the night Tabs was born, everything Technicolor, a big beautiful cherry tree with pink pompoms on every branch, against a bright blue sky. Tim beaming, the next morning, so full of it she could hear him booming in the corridors outside, boasting, telling anyone who'd listen. And Georgie had lain there, floating on the narrow bed, her head turned sideways to gaze through the perspex of the cot.

She hadn't got pregnant from ordinary unprotected sex since that first time, when she'd been twenty-three.

They got through the day. Sundays always felt endless, didn't they?

Tim didn't really mention the earring again. Only to say, mildly, maybe she should call the hotel and see if it had been found, which made Georgie's heart sink because if only he knew what kind of hotel it had been he wouldn't have bothered.

Georgie did call: the receptionist listened, to give him credit (she remembered a young woman when she'd left yesterday morning, a narrow face although this was a foreign male voice), but there was an edge of amusement in his questions, *when, where, which bed* that gave Georgie no hope at all. If you worked on zero-hours cleaning contracts and you found a diamond earring, what would you do? Answering his questions, though, talking about that grubby low-ceilinged room, remembering the thin mattresses – the mildewed bathroom – while looking down from the bedroom window at Tim's velvety lawn, she felt that uneasy feeling that had never really gone away stir and grow, she felt the shiver.

'You friends check out two hour ago,' he said. She'd forgotten: Cat and Holly had made a weekend of it, hadn't they?

'Oh, I—' she began to apologise but he was still talking.

'Nothing has been give in with me,' he said, 'but if you leave you number.'

She did that, hastily, guiltily, and hung up. Cat and Holly wouldn't have been looking for any earring, would they? And if they'd found it they would have told her.

Later, when Georgie went looking for Tim with his coffee, calling up the stairs with Tabs trailing behind her, she found him in his study examining the insurance documents for the house. He looked up at her, preoccupied and murmured vaguely 'Just – you know, I thought we might be covered. They're named on the house policy. The earrings are.' And took the coffee. His eyes resting on her, mild, vague.

What if he asked, *Did you, could they?* What if he asked, half joking but not quite, 'What on earth did you get up to on Friday?'

He smiled. 'What about a barbecue this evening?' he said. 'Still warm enough, isn't it?'

Setting Tabs bouncing down the stairs, full of excitement; Georgie could follow, with a rush of relief that for the moment they didn't have to go there, talk about it any more. It would come up again, because they had been expensive, because Tim was a numbers man, a money man and a hole in the accounts would niggle at him, he wouldn't be able to help himself. But for now. Tabs skipping ahead of her, out through the kitchen, sticky hands on the glass to where her sandpit distracted her almost immediately.

The question was still there, though, in her head: sooner or later it would have to be answered. *What on earth?*

In the kitchen, resting her back against the counter, Georgie got out her mobile phone. Looking down at the little screen, looking up, around the room. Sleek matt cupboards without handles and matching toaster and blender and juicer. She'd chosen it all, in the big department store with Tim, so why didn't it look like hers? In a kind of daze she reached out and touched the kettle, forgetting it was hot, and let out a yelp. Stupid: it brought tears to her eyes, which was more stupid.

The kitchen Georgie had grown up with was nothing like this: there had been stained cookbooks on a shelf and toast crumbs and a table covered with stuff: papers and bags of bananas and Dad's fishing tackle. Brockley Rise: it seemed so far away but it was still there, wasn't it? Dad was, there were people, barmen in Soho, who knew it as well as she did.

The thought came into her head, comforting, a little lifeline, that Cat's kitchen was probably like that, boys barging in and out of it and with half an ear for where Tim was she got out her phone and dialled Cat's number.

Thinking, while it rang, *These things happen, don't they? On a girls' night out.*

★

53

Because there were things she *did* remember. Of course there were.

A girls' night out in some dodgy club, getting carried away to the music, you lose a button or an earring but you keep dancing, you have another drink. You talk too loudly, and then a slow dance with a man you don't know. A kiss — all right, but she hadn't asked for it and it hadn't been that kind of kiss.

At her ear Cat's phone rang and rang, and then Georgie heard Tim's feet on the stairs, and she hung up.

At seven, eight, it was still hot. There was something funny with the weather, whatever Tim said. Tim had pulled the barbecue — his pride and joy, a big, shining state-of-the-art contraption, with teak and steel and a hanging row of implements — out on to the paving. Tabs was standing beside him obediently, two feet away and if she came closer his hand would go up instantly. The fridge was full of meat, chicken marinading, a big steak, sweet-corn on skewers — and standing between the glass doors waiting to be told to bring it out Georgie could feel the heat, it made her queasy. She was still wearing a sweatshirt and jeans.

'I need to put something else on,' she said: Tim didn't hear but she went anyway, running on the stairs.

In the bedroom she'd stripped off the jeans, when she heard the buzz from the pocket, a text. Bending for it she saw the bruise she'd seen yesterday, darkening at her shin, and then another. Her inner thigh, high up, a patch of yellow-green. She touched it: it was tender, and in that moment her whole body felt tender, her neck felt sore, under her arms.

54

She took the phone from her pocket. It was from Cat. *You OK?*

Her heart was thumping, ridiculously. What did that mean? What did she mean? Why wouldn't she be OK? Although she wasn't, was she? Not OK. Before she could stop herself Georgie was texting back. *Lost a bloody earring.* Typed like that it didn't look so bad. Not so serious. *You didn't see anything did you? In the room? How bad was I Friday night?* Jokey, right? *What am I like?* Right?

She stared at the phone. No answer.

Cat hadn't been like that yesterday morning. When they'd been getting up. She hadn't been clipped or wary. She'd been sitting up when Georgie and Holly came back into the room, woken by the whispered conversation or – more likely – the repeated flushing. She had rolled out of bed with half her hair sticking up. Wrinkling her nose on the threshold of the bathroom and laughing back at them.

'We still making a weekend of it, then?' Holly had said, standing at the bar, before they even got going. She'd been talking to Cat: they'd tried to persuade Georgie to stay on too. The two of them, and the guy. The guy, leaning on the bar and watching her steadily. She remembered shaking her head, dreamy, tipsy, knowing he was looking. 'Got to get back to my husband,' she'd said.

Remembering that Georgie slid to the floor, bare-legged, leaning against the bed. Outside she could hear Tim, instructing Tabs.

She'd said that. So it wasn't as if she'd been acting young and free and single. She'd even felt proud, saying it, *I'm spoken for.* But there'd been other reasons for saying it:

I'm wanted, you see. Turning slightly then so she couldn't see him. The tall man. He'd told her his name, too. Frank had been the barman, but the other—? Leaning in to her, his mouth smiling, his eyes smiling.

At the bar Cat had been loudly proclaiming she was up for it. 'They can fend for themselves, Harry can do the football. Christ he can even stick their kit in the washing machine, he knows how it works.' Flinging her arms around, defiant and angry, that was Cat. But she gave herself away when she said Harry's name, her eyes just closed a fraction, her smile just softened. They couldn't get enough of each other, her and Harry.

Of course, she'd be on the way home, maybe she'd be home by now and no time to be on the phone, setting Georgie's mind at rest, maybe that message – of course. She'd called Cat, so the text just meant, *Why did you call?* Still, Georgie's heart was fluttering. She needed to get dressed, she needed to bring the plastic-wrapped barbecue food out to Tim.

But Georgie had been the one had gone home, and Cat had stayed on until the afternoon train on Sunday. For the first time, something about how Cat had behaved pricked at Georgie. She had enjoyed herself, hadn't she? Innocent fun. Bouncing between blokes on the dance floor, taking none of them seriously. One of them had leaned and whispered something in her ear, turning to laugh with his mates when he said it but Cat had just smiled, beatific, and said to him, *That sounds lovely but not just now. I don't think so.* 'Blokes,' she'd said in the toilets after, repairing the damage in the mirror. 'If you had sons you'd know, they can't help themselves.'

'George?' Tim was shouting for her. Hurriedly she reached into the wardrobe, tugging out an old sundress, blindly shoving the gold silk that emerged with it back inside.

'Coming,' she called back. Silence.

Inside the sundress, pulling it down in a sweat, remembering the hot dark of the dance floor. *They can't help themselves.* Cat knew men, with her sons and her Harry, but what did *she* know, Georgie, about them? Blokes. Her dad, pottering about his sheltered accommodation, worrying about the old bloke next door, down to the pub once a week for skiffle night, perpetually kind, perpetually anxious, the only woman for him had been Mum. Was that men? Tim, ordering the house around her, building it for her, putting his arms round her to welcome her home. At school there were no men to speak of, only the odd playground dad trying not to catch anyone's eye.

Downstairs, the phone still in her hand, into the kitchen. She set the phone down and brought out the meat in its bowls.

Are you OK? Cat's message sat on her screen. She wondered what they'd got up to, last night? Her and Holly. Had they talked about Georgie? Outside now, obediently, setting the bowls down on the table in the shade, peeling off the clingfilm. Tim barely looked up and she hurried back into the kitchen. Opened the fridge. Salad, sweetcorn. She hesitated.

Holly had been nice yesterday morning. Friendly. Reassuring. Friday night had been – a bit different. Friday night she'd been more aloof, but maybe night behaviour and morning behaviour are different, and maybe having

57

your whole life in a little suitcase in the Ladies' Cloaks made you more careful. Friday night swam in front of Georgie's eyes again. Leaning on that bar, Holly watching the square-shouldered barman move to and fro. *Nice man*, the thought popped into Georgie's head. Nice man who knew where she was from.

And then on the side, the phone vibrated again, quick. Georgie left the fridge door hanging open and picked it up. From Cat: Forget about it.

Which meant? Which *meant*?

'Geor*gie!*' Tim's voice, on the edge of angry, cutting through all of it. Georgie grabbed the salad and the sweetcorn and shoved the fridge door shut with her shoulder, catching her elbow on it and still feeling it as she came outside into the heat.

Tim in his apron, Tabs in hers, a cloud of smoke and the smell of meat cooking.

Which meant, *Forget it*. Don't give it a thought. *Pull yourself together, Georgie.*

She put the bowls down, Tim turning to look at her, and straightened with the smoke stinging her eyes. 'Isn't this lovely?' she said.

The weekend would end eventually, the traces of Friday night would be washed away, Tim would be back at work. Only a matter of hours and life would be back to normal.

Forget it.

Chapter Seven

Monday passed, and Tuesday, like normal days on the outside.

Lunchboxes, clean uniform, into school. Tim up and out, passing her in his suit as she stood at the kitchen counter in her dressing gown. The silk and lace slip had been exchanged for one of the T-shirts with cartoon characters she'd slept in more or less since Tabs had been born. Georgie had washed the slip carefully, by hand, after school on Monday and hung it out to dry. Under the dull glare of the October sky, still hot, it had dried in a moment and she had ironed it quickly and put it away at the bottom of her underwear drawer, kneeling in the bedroom and thinking a second, wistful, tentative.

The panic of the morning after had ebbed, leaving an uneasy curiosity, a guilty fascination whenever her thoughts settled on that night. The room under the eaves. A flash of memory now and again: had she raised her arms obediently to have the slip slither down over her, or had she invented that?

The diamond earring had not been mentioned again, and maybe it would be forgotten after all, until the next birthday came around and Tim would get her another pair, or something to replace them. The hotel didn't call, but Georgie went on thinking, thinking. In the school office at her desk, working in a kind of daze that Sue her co-worker tiptoed around, after one or two questions about the night out that Georgie mumbled something and nothing to in response, she found herself putting a hand up now and again, wonderingly, to her earlobe. Feeling for the tenderness.

She had put the remaining earring carefully in its little leather box, in her handbag, just in case.

The weather was going to change, maybe at the end of the week. She heard them say it on the radio as she made tea on Tuesday night, waiting for Tim to get home and remembering the rain in the Soho streets and then the germ of an idea started up, vague at first, dismissed at first. Could she go up to town? The thought of those streets on a cold morning was enticing, a bright autumn Saturday in London alone, like the old days – and not just for the freedom, for the shopping. She wanted to know, she had this vague daft idea that if she went back there, stood in front of the hotel, maybe, she would remember. It would fall into place: the steps, the railings.

But not two weekends in a row, there was Tim's squash, there was tennis, there was Tabs. He would roll his eyes.

Could she call the club? Le Cinq. Maybe she would get to talk to him, the nice barman, perhaps he would remember her? He had seemed to her like the kind of man, if he found someone's diamond earring, or if he saw a cleaner find one— and then the thought of the phone conversation alone – *Who? Sorry, love* – was enough for her to put the idea to the back of her mind.

Let it all settle. That was the thing to do. Trouble was, it wouldn't.

In the middle of the week, school was always quiet. The further it got from the weekend the more resigned the children were to their captivity. Usually Georgie felt the positive change: Wednesday you could relax, just a bit, things went more smoothly, there was more time.

This week wasn't like that, hadn't been from the start: however much she wanted things to settle back to the humdrum, they refused to. Even Tim had frowned at her, this morning and said, 'What is it?' when she raised her voice to Tabs. When she couldn't find her handbag and there was a muddy footprint in the kitchen and all of it conspiring to put her on edge, everything escaping her.

Growing up, Georgie hadn't imagined she'd be this person. Keeping everything neat, a place for everything: the house she'd grown up in hadn't been like this. Not a mess exactly – but the kitchen table had always had to be cleared for dinner, there had been a jumble of shoes in the hall. And she'd been the worst offender: Mum had always been in despair at the state of her room. It was one of the reasons Dad always used to take a while to sit down in the new house, walking round it like he wasn't sure if he was in the right place. 'How d'you find the teabags, George?' he'd asked her, gazing round the newly finished kitchen, the doors you just pressed for them to spring open. Half joking, half – half in despair.

She had always understood why Tim wanted it like this. The miscarriage had been as hard for him as for her, both of them so young, such a shock, just when they'd got their heads round it. And messy. The mess. She explained it to herself as nest-building: it touched her heart when she thought of it that way. She'd tried to tell Dad, when she had explained about the IVF and he had nodded as if he understood but he still looked around uncertainly every time he came to stay, not setting his overnight bag down till he was pleaded with.

And now the house, the big bright house with its wide windows and smooth lawn and empty surfaces, was saying something else to her. It was saying, You need to look after all this, it doesn't get done on its own, you can't let things slide. *One muddy footprint –*

Tim had stroked her cheek after he'd said it, *What is it?*, gently. 'You still haven't caught up on your sleep, is that it?' Shaking his head and smiling. 'I hope it was worth it.' And he'd kissed her on the top of her head and gone.

At her tiny desk in the window corner of the brightly lit school office Georgie was writing up an email about next year's activities week while two teachers stood behind her, bitching about a reception child they had identified as the source of the latest outbreak of nits. Janette Evans, close to retirement and sour, and Marie Webster, her acolyte, watching Janette's every move for how to be tough, how to be in control. They went on and on, round in circles, not quite coming out with it: *The mother's a lazy cow, single mother, there's an old fridge in their front garden, it's got to be her.* Georgie took a deep breath. School always smelled of reheated dinners and toilets, kids and their digestive tracts: how had she been here two years without even thinking about it? Perhaps she had a bug: she'd felt sick for days.

She became aware of Sue, at the door with her coat on, ready to ring the bell for the end of break, looking at her. She liked Sue, older, a single mother to teenage Tara, weary and understanding. Georgie smiled, uncertain, then looked quickly back at the computer screen.

She'd taken the job there a year before Tabs began school, everything in place to be a good mum, socialising with other mothers, acquiring colleagues. How old was Sue? Her clothes said sixty: patterned blouse, thick cardigan, but Georgie knew Tara was sixteen and she probably wasn't much more than fifty. She was kind, but not unconditionally. She'd been patient, this week, but Georgie was going to have to sort herself out, start smiling, start chatting, move faster.

Sometimes she could see Tabs, filing past the door for lunch or PE or outdoor play, and her heart lifted, jumped, out of the flatline. The work was easy, but she liked it all right. There was plenty to keep on top of. Sending email reminders, dishing out uniform forms, taking calls when kids are off sick. Chasing down truants and allergies and doctors' details. And outbreaks of nits.

'It's not brain surgery,' she had ventured to Sue once, like a traitor.

'That's what he says, isn't it?' Sue's eyebrows had been raised in outrage. 'Your husband.'

'Well—' Georgie hesitated, uneasy. 'I did tell him, it's a good job, and I like it.' Sue had shoved a hip on to the corner of her desk then and Georgie had thought she was going to go off on one. But all she said was, 'I'd like to see *him* do it.' And then gone out to buy milk for their tea, rather abruptly.

Georgie looked up again now but the doorway was empty and then from outside in the playground the bell began to jangle. You could tell when Sue was ringing, it travelled, loud and steady. Unhurriedly Janette and Marie departed, Janette's voice still droning.

The door closed behind them and it was just Georgie, for a second, for as long as it would take for Sue to see the last child in, and in that second she gave in, and lowered her face into her hands.

She'd thought work would help: jolt her back on track, it would all recede. Something and nothing, a night out, a break from the real world, just a few hours. A dream. It was just that – it kept coming back.

In glimpses. The way the club had looked inside, the coloured lights, the girl at the cloakroom. The sound of taxis hissing by in the rain, afterwards. And since she'd got back on the Saturday afternoon she'd felt like she was underwater. As if she couldn't quite hear things properly. As if everything was passing her in a blur.

'Georgina?'

Georgie raised her head sharply, face out of her hands. Nobody but her mother-in-law called her Georgina, or ever had, not even Mum.

'Are you feeling all right?' Sue in the doorway, half amused, half frowning. Sue didn't exactly do sympathy.

'Oh, sorry, yes, yes,' said Georgie, 'I was just – just – it's nothing.'

64

But it was something. Something soft and warm and dangerous, just out of reach, in the dark of her cupped hands.

'Giving your eyes a rest, yes, I know that feeling,' said Sue. And sighed. Around them the school had settled into quietness, the soporific fug that always followed the lunch-break. 'Well, tomorrow's Thursday. Think on that.'

Georgie smiled and nodded, looking back at her screen without focusing and eventually Sue moved off, to her own desk at the front of the office.

The three of them standing there, Cat on one side of Georgie, standing with her elbows behind her on the bar and looking out into the room, Holly on the other side turning to watch the barman walking back in from some-where behind the cloakroom, and him, *him*, looking past her at Georgie.

What *had* his name been?

The man who came back to the hotel with them. And that memory was sharp in focus, the memory that had come back to her the morning after and then evaporated again: his hand over hers at the reception desk's little bell, stopping her ringing it. Following her up the stairs.

And the shock of it prickled at her: in front of the computer screen she stopped, hands poised over the keyboard. That was new: that memory. He had been in the room with them. So when Holly said *nothing happened* – Georgie swallowed, lowered her fingers to the smooth warm keys. Dared not look right or left.

He'd told her his name, but she still couldn't remember it. And then her throat tightened: it had been her, Georgie, that had let him in. She had been the one had held the taxi door open for him and he had slid in beside her. His hand had been on hers. He had her hand in his and he had turned it over, soft, and raised it to his lips.

Mark.

She felt her lips open to say it, but had to stop herself.

He had been called Mark.

Frank stirred, heavy, in bed in the pale light. Something about waking up on your day off: everything felt different, before you even opened your eyes. Last night had been a late one and his head was banging in time with the scaffolders. He needed to change his life.

His mum had been saying it for years. She was a tough act to follow, bringing him up on a cleaner's wage single-handed, though she'd had Benjy five years now, her tame ex-copper and between them they kept up a barrage. The Cinq was beneath him.

Eddie was always talking about selling up but never did anything, it was more like a boast, the money he could have if he sold. Now and again Frank had found himself wishing he would, just to shake things up a bit. Eddie about the age to start playing golf, or playing house with Lucy, in his big mansion with the gravel drive out beyond the North Circular.

Something had changed, not overnight but not long back. A feeling, discontent, maybe you'd call it, with the world in general – all the shit in the streets, fast-food cartons and drunks sat with their legs out to trip you and the silver litter of laughing gas capsules and condoms and all of it – and with himself. Something had made him understand: you shouldn't mess about. Get pissed, shag people you shouldn't, drift into something you don't know how to get out of. Being at Eddie's beck and call, day and night: he'd started out pretending Frank was the son he'd never had, but if this was what being Eddie's kid was like it was a good job the old bastard hadn't had any.

Frank got out of bed. The flat wasn't picturesque, it was a white box on Dean Street in a small anonymous sixties block. Eddie owned the block: that and a couple of girly bars with flats over them and the Cinq, the property his nest egg. It had narrowly missed being compulsorily purchased for Crossrail: Eddie had been rubbing his hands ever since. It could be bulldozed, easy, and redeveloped. Eddie biding his time.

Frank opened a drawer, pulled a T-shirt on over his boxers and wandered back to the window.

She'd told him she lived in the suburbs, with a dreamy look in her eye. Shy Georgie from Brockley Rise. That was where she must be now, back out beyond the dirty edge of town in the green, where one forest blended into another. Where the old gangsters used to bury their victims, his mother had told him once but now it was where people like Eddie had their big houses.

She hadn't looked to him like your average mum on a night out looking for excitement, though. Frank had seen enough of them at the Cinq to know. And there it was again, the discontent, the sense that he'd taken a wrong turning somewhere, that twenty years ago, thirty, he should have been walking down her street in Brockley Rise. Waiting outside her door, being polite to her parents, planning for a mortgage. His ring on her finger, even if he'd never have been able to afford diamonds for her ears.

67

But while he'd been unblocking a sink in the gents' Dom had made her another of his dirty martinis and some other bloke had taken his chance, moving in.

Something wasn't right. She wouldn't have. Frank sighed: it wouldn't be the first time he'd got a woman wrong. He leaned his head against the window in the warm light, knocking it gently against the glass, over and over.

Back on the floor beside the bed, his phone buzzed and jiggled, the screen lighting up.

Frank took his time, the phone beginning to turn itself in a circle by the time he got there.

It was Eddie. Of course it was.

'Late one was it, son?' and Frank sat down on the bed, scratching his stubble. Got to get out of this place.

Chapter Eight

'Look,' Georgie said, trying to make it sound upbeat, not pleading. Not bloody desperate.

Because you had to know. When you couldn't remember something, you needed to find out.

'Cat. I just — there's something—'

The school playground was empty: the school had hummed with pre-lunch industry as Georgie carefully let herself out of the main entrance. She could see Sue through the office window, head down, minding her own business. She hadn't needed to say anything, just gestured with the phone and Sue had nodded.

Coming around the corner of a classroom with the blinds down against the midday light, she kept going until she got to where reception had planted a little garden, dusty-looking in October, in need of trimming back, but there was a bench under a big overarching buddleia. A bench where you wouldn't be seen or heard.

Because teachers were nosy: it was one of the first things Georgie had learned about them. Nosy and unhappy, and they liked nothing more than someone to judge. Parents and colleagues their favourite subject, and she was both.

If you sat on the bench you couldn't be seen from school: there was competition for it at break time, a lot of bum-shoving. Georgie sat on it gingerly. The school was on the edge of the village, and you could see where the trees began.

'Cat?' A sigh and she'd launched into it, *It's about Friday night, I just want to know* but then it had caught up with her, the sound of Cat's voice as she picked up. With the memory Georgie stood up, twitchy. She'd been like this since – since. Like her system was running twice as fast as usual. Food didn't stay in her: she could feel it now, her stomach loosening to water. 'Cat?'

She said it again, because Cat still hadn't spoken. They hadn't talked since Saturday morning, unless you counted the two texts. Five words in total.

And then it dawned on her. Something was wrong. Not with Georgie, with Cat. 'Is everything all right? Cat?'

There was a sigh, slow, something waterlogged about it. Tearful? Georgie paced, sat back down again abruptly and the buddleia showered her with tiny brown seeds. 'Look, forget me, never mind, it doesn't—'

But Cat answered, weary. 'Calm down,' she said. 'Nothing happened.' That again. Georgie found she was holding her breath.

'Nothing?' she said, looking away from the school.

The trees were dense quite close up to the road, she hadn't realised that. They didn't walk there, after the first few times: there were paths, but too many of them, they criss-crossed, and once you were out of the sight of the road — and anyway quite soon litter appeared, magazines with pages stuck together, cans and condoms. Waiting, Georgie looked back at the building, a light going on behind the long windows of the assembly hall. Cat cleared her throat.

'He was quite a gentleman, actually, as far as I could tell.'

'Really?' said Georgie, not quite relieved. Because she still wasn't sounding like Cat: she sounded jaundiced, cynical, where Georgie had wanted forgiveness. Or even to know what she needed forgiving for. Kindness would do, and Cat was always kind, wasn't she? Georgie felt slightly sick.

'Yes, really.'

'But he—' Georgie hesitated.

'He just got into the taxi with us,' said Cat. 'It wasn't really your fault.' Sighing. 'I mean, I wasn't in any fit state to argue, myself.'

'I remember that bit,' said Georgie. Him sliding warm against her and pulling the door shut, the taxi moving off before any of them could say anything, and then Georgie feeling laughter bubble up inside her. He'd been looking at her, that had been all it took.

Inside the taxi he had still been looking at her: he had taken her hand.

'But what happened after?'

The tiny seeds were scattered down her arm, clinging,

and she brushed at them, they clung. She remembered his hand coming round to stop hers, at the bell on the reception desk, his thumb soft in her palm, his back against her back.

How long since she'd had sex with Tim, before Saturday night? A month, at least. Two. Something about that felt odd. Absence made the heart grow fonder. She shifted, uneasy, at the thought that somehow another man being interested in her had left a trace. A trace she couldn't see or smell, but Tim could.

'I don't know why you let him into the hotel,' said Cat, stiffly. 'But no harm done, eh? He left again.'

'Right,' said Georgie, uncertain.

'You remember that bit, right?' Cat was still dry, withholding. Was it that there was someone else there? It was in the middle of the day, though. Harry would be at work, the boys at school.

'Sort of,' said Georgie. 'I remember—' Halting: she made an effort, actually to pin it down. Because, she realised, her efforts up until now, until Cat put her on the spot, had been not to remember. In case. 'I remember him coming up the stairs with us.' He'd been behind her. She remembered tripping on the worn carpet, falling upstairs. His hand on her hip from behind. Remembered not protesting.

Cat was still talking. 'Because you can't rely on me to remember past that, once Holly got that brandy out, I was pretty much gone,' said Cat. 'Until I heard the door close, when he went.'

'He came into the room with us,' said Georgie. She could see him standing there under the low ceilings, looking around, quite relaxed as if it was all normal, three in the morning, him and three women in a cheap room full of beds. Mark.

'His name was Mark,' she said.

There was a sigh, then Cat said, drily, 'If you say so.'

'I found the glasses,' said Georgie suddenly. That was new. She'd gone into the bathroom looking for plastic cups and come back out with nothing, and there they'd been on the bedside table where she and Cat had left them, after emptying the bottle of champagne. 'And then—'

She remembered Cat pushing hers away, the brandy slopping. She remembered Cat lying down, face down on the single bed. 'Should put her on her side,' he'd said. Mark had said. He'd leaned down to her, solicitous.

'Then I can't remember anything else.' It came out like a confession. Why couldn't she remember? Georgie got to her feet.

'You saw him off the premises,' said Cat. 'There. Job done.'

'I did?' Georgie stood very still. She didn't remember that. If Tim knew.

'I saw you go,' Cat said. 'I was spark out when you came back in – but you *did* come back, we both know that much. Because next morning, there you were, right?' That tired, rusty laugh. 'So like I say. No harm done.'

And Holly said, *Nothing happened.* Why did it feel like she meant the opposite?

Forget it.

'All right,' said Georgie. 'All right.' She needed to move, to get back to work, the permissions letters for activities week. The Christmas production timetable. From the school came the sound of a classroom full of chairs being scraped back, Janette's voice raised. And silence, from Cat.

'Cat,' she said. 'What is it? *You're* not all right. Please tell me what's wrong.'

'Oh, shit,' said Cat. 'George. Shit. I wasn't going to tell you.'

Inside the school hall, Janette's class began to sing.

They'd been so young when they'd started working together. They'd been kids. Her and Cat.

'Stage two, left boob, size of a Malteser.' Once Cat had reeled it off, her list. 'Harry found it actually, not me, he was—' she'd broken off there but not before Georgie had pictured it, Harry with his arms round Cat in bed, sweet grumpy Harry. 'Lumpectomy and a bit of chemo, so could be worse—' Cat had sounded immediately better, normal. 'Could be a lot worse.'

Georgie had been pacing, one hand cupped over her ear against the reedy little voices raised in the hall. They were singing 'The Lord's My Shepherd': it was a church school. She didn't know if Cat could hear, and hoped not. Like Georgie, Cat wasn't religious in any bone of her body.

Kids, and this was when you grew up. Stuff like this: hospitals. Biopsies.

'Stage two is—'

'Not as good as stage one but it's OK. It's good. It's not aggressive, blah, blah—' But Georgie could hear Cat's voice tightening up.

74

'Sorry I made you tell me,' Georgie said. 'I'm glad you did, though.' She couldn't stop thinking back down the years, and Cat's boobs, the running joke, Cat and her cleavage, out for every special occasion. Parties, weddings, funerals.

As it had been Friday night, squeezed up against the bar, Cat's eyes sparkling as she ordered dirty martinis. 'So – you already knew,' said Georgie. 'On Friday night.'

'I just wanted to forget about it,' said Cat. 'Still do, really. The boys don't know, OK? So—'

'I get it,' said Georgie. 'I understand. How's Harry?'

'Shitting himself,' said Cat. 'And lovely. Of course.'

'Well, if there's anything – what can I do? What?' *Stop asking stupid bloody questions about how badly you behaved last Friday night, for a start.* 'Cat, there must be something. Have the boys?' Tim would go nuts. 'Send casseroles?'

'Let's make a date for when it's all over,' said Cat. 'Another night out. That's all I want. Honest, it could be worse. *Honest.*'

Coming back into the office Georgie's face must have said it all, because Sue had taken one look at her and decided not to ask. Back in front of her keyboard, Friday night receded: because what was all that worth? It seemed like nothing, or even, something benign. A bit of reckless behaviour and everyone back to their own beds. Nothing. Life's too short.

On playground duty at lunch Georgie stood with her sandwich and the children whirling around her, the forest beyond them silent and green. One thing had stuck, stubborn, out of all of it, one thing, in Georgie's head: Cat and Harry. Harry, rolling over to take hold of Cat in bed,

75

had probably saved her life one way or another. They could work wonders these days, and stage two was better than stage three, and – Georgie didn't want to jinx it. She made herself stop.

As the children circled and ran, from the tarmac to the play area to the fence against the road, Georgie identified Tabs, running, running, on the grass, white socks, hair flying. It seemed so long ago that Georgie had felt like that. She wrapped the sandwich back up in its foil and guiltily thrust it in the bin: a bad example. Sometimes she wished she could go back and start again. Still have Tabs – but somehow start again.

Her phone buzzed. And as if on cue it was a text, from Cat: her heart jumped inside her at the name, on high alert, but it wasn't what she'd expected, it wasn't, *Don't tell Tim*, or *Do*.

Holls asked for your number, it read. Thought you might want hers.

She stared, again, remembering Holly's sharp knees, raised in the bathroom, the flash of smooth thigh, the narrowed eyes examining her and the hair went up, on the back of Georgie's neck. They were chalk and cheese, her and Holly. Why would she want to be in touch?

She knew why. Cat had been asleep – *No use asking me*, wasn't that what she'd said, deliberate? Spark out and snoring. But Holly hadn't. Out of nowhere, Georgie wanted a cigarette. Another message came through: Cat thinking again.

Watch yourself with that one, though, it read. No holds barred with Holly. Specially when she's on the rebound. A big heart emoji.

On the rebound: Holly roaming with her wheelie suit-case, Holly debris in outer space, looking for a home.

It could be Cat, kidding around, Cat pretending everything was normal, Cat teasing.

Miss, miss! Georgie looked around, stuffing the phone away hastily, because Jason Burke, a beefy boy from Tabs' class was tugging at her. Someone had got stuck in the hedge, a tiny girl from reception whose name Georgie hadn't learned yet, they'd only been back two months, crying because her hair was caught, there was a scratch on her leg and blood on her sock. It took Georgie a full five minutes to coax her out, disentangling the hair, hanky for the blood, talking to her the whole time to stop her wriggling, calming her when the bell began to ring.

When she looked at the phone again, stopping for a cup of tea with Sue halfway through the afternoon she saw she'd missed a call from Tim and opened her call list.

'What?' said Sue.

He'd phoned around two, had left a message. She replayed it, distracted. Something about a conference, this weekend, in Bournemouth. 'Talk about it tonight, OK?' She hardly listened. Hung up, swiped back to the call list. Stared.

'What?' said Sue again.

'Nothing,' Georgie said. 'Nothing – just—'

There was a number her phone didn't know, in the names on her call list.

She didn't make calls these days, not much, it was all texting. This was a call she had made to another mobile. At three a.m., last Saturday morning. The hours she had lost, a time she couldn't remember, a call she knew nothing about, made on her phone.

Friday night, Saturday morning. Whose number? Whose number was it? How had it got on her phone?

She stared at the number, her finger hovering over it, and for a moment she was thrown into absolute panic at the thought she had no memory of the phone call, at the sudden irrational certainty that it was Tim she called, even though that wasn't his number, there was his number at the top of the list. Just the thought of having called him by accident, just the idea, however impossible, of him hearing – whatever it was she had been doing, at three a.m. last Friday night, Saturday morning. She sweated, aware of Sue staring.

Georgie realised she had no idea what time they'd left the club, if it had been one or two or three. The three of them giggling drunkenly in the taxi? Four. Him too. On the stairs? And then it appeared, a memory so vivid it was almost physical, of her and the man, standing close in the hotel room with the phone between them.

She put the phone down, carefully, face down, as if it was a bomb that might go off.

'Nothing,' she said to Sue, brightly, but her heart was fluttering, fluttering, like a bird in her chest.

It came later, when Georgie had got up to do some photocopying. As if he knew, or she knew, she would be in the corner by the machine on her own, as if he knew, she knew that she needed to take her phone with her now, wherever she went.

That was how people behaved when they were having affairs: Georgie remembered overhearing that at a PTA meeting, a year five mum divorcing her husband. 'He never left his phone out, except that once,' she'd said in triumph. 'And I saw it on the lock screen.'

It rang. And she knew, somehow, even before she saw it, that the number, unknown number, would be ringing.

'Hey.' It was him. It was Mark.

Chapter Nine

It was getting late and Frank, standing at the window, open-necked shirt for his day off but still white, still cotton, had just opened a beer when he saw her coming across the road with a man in a suit whose face was turned away, looking back up the street.

Like Friday night coming back for him.

After Eddie going on about it, too, Friday night: could that really be why he phoned, on Frank's day off? Going on what Lucy had told him, Frank had been rude to her about sorting out the men's bogs on Friday night, when he hadn't. Eddie needling him about keeping the place running rather than flirting with the clientele until Frank saw what was behind it. Lucy liked to be alpha female all right.

And now. Dainty, she stepped up on to the kerb, in high-heeled sandals. Holly, he saw the muscle defined in her slim calf. He knew her all right if not her surname, the long-legged one with the wheelie suitcase from Friday night.

Holly who had been in and out of the club, not often but regular if you like, once every month or so maybe, at the edge of his vision, Holly with a gang from work or Holly kissing someone in the dark. Holly, friend of blonde Georgie. He leaned forward over the window sill, the can dangling from his hand. On the pavement Holly flicked back her hair with a practiced gesture, leaning against the man's shoulder and it puzzled Frank. How could those two ever have been friends, her and Georgie?

What did he know about female friendship anyway? A mystery to him. But something about it had bothered him from the off. If he'd seen that Georgie needed looking after, her mates should have helped, but she'd been cut loose. But there was Holly, right in front of him: he just needed to call down. *Hey, Holly.* That would put the cat among the pigeons, the man would look up, pissed off. And then what? Ask for her friend Georgie's number? He didn't need that.

What did Frank want to know, anyway? That they'd got home all right? Wherever home was. Holly had, after all, hadn't she? So no need to say anything. He didn't move though, rested on his elbows on the window sill, looking down.

He could see the tops of their heads now. Holly arm in arm with some bloke in a suit, he couldn't see the guy's face only the faintest thinning patch on top. Frank had an eagle eye for another man's bald spot: he put his hand up to his own head reflexively. Ruminatively he tipped the can back. He wouldn't mind being looked at the way Holly looked at her man in his suit, hair or no hair.

Could be him, couldn't it? And in that moment Frank decided it *was* him, the tall guy, the one moving in on them in the dark. So he'd ended up with Holly: that seemed better, to Frank. Two of a kind.

Now she had stopped, right there below him. Rummaging in her bag. She had got out her phone and looked at it, looked at it some more. Pressed a button on it. Then her attention went back to the bloke, snuggled up to him like he was Marlon Brando.

Women: Frank thought he'd got the measure of them then he realised he'd got it all wrong. Was he rich, this bloke? Was that why Holly was hanging on to him like that? If he didn't know better he'd have said it was love, the way she was looking at him.

Stepping away from the window, for the hundredth time Frank's thoughts turned back, to last Friday night, uneasy. He couldn't shake the idea that he should have asked that Georgie what school she'd gone to, where her old man went fishing or whatever. Something, anything: a dozen questions he could ask her if she was in front of him now, like, Did you get home all right? Like, Are you happy?

But she'd been taking a drink off the tall guy and then old Vince had moved in, in his pork pie hat and had got hold of her. He had been working his moves and Frank had watched her go: pink-cheeked Georgie had kept up, hand held out at waist level for him to take her and spin her, knowing how to turn. That always held his attention, too, a girl who knew how to move. Then the music had stopped and she'd instantly turned awkward and almost tripped over herself, hanging on to the bar, blushing, Vince tipping his hat to her. Old Vince. It hadn't been Vince who held his hand out to steady her, though.

That was when Lucy, slipping noiselessly up to the bar for service – she liked a cheeky negroni to sip, behind the velvet curtain – had caught Frank looking at her. Georgie.

Lucy'd known Holly, they'd had a word or two as she handed in her suitcase so she probably knew who the love interest was. She probably knew Georgie, maybe she even knew the lanky guy who'd managed to muscle in on their evening. Not a lot got past Lucy; if only you could talk to her like a normal human being without her reading everything into it. Without her pouting to Eddie about Frank chatting her up.

Frank stepped back to the window. They were gone, he didn't know where, Holly and her man. He didn't even know why he cared who Holly's man was, except it was the way she'd put a hand up to ruffle the man's hair. He'd pulled away slightly, hadn't he? Frank put his hand up to his own head again, feeling for the crown.

Lucy'd laugh, especially if he moved on to asking about the other two women, well, one in particular, the one with the golden dress and the beautiful shoulders and the shy look. *Frankie's in love. With a Friday night mum on the lash?* And that bloke sitting casual on his barstool, one long leg on the floor, ready to move in.

Ask Lucy if she'd seen him before because the more

he thought about the guy the less he liked it. The way he'd bided his time, watching the women, those three and no others, not shifting his attention to anyone else. They had bouncers for that, though, even the Cinq had a bouncer, Matteo from Sicily, built like a brick shithouse, shoulders bulging out of his jacket and only five words of English Frank had ever heard him speak.

Maybe he'd better ask Matteo. Maybe if Holly walked back round the corner he'd run down and ask *her*.

What happened, did you get home all right? and then she'd laugh at him because she was there, wasn't she? Safe and sound.

But something felt wrong to him. He leaned there at the window, till his back stiffened and the sky was almost velvety blue, and the crowd outside the pub had spilled on to the street, but they didn't reappear.

It was gone eight by the time Tim got home and Georgie had started to go over their conversation again, worrying. Had he heard something in her, some breathlessness?

'You didn't call me back.' She'd been in the village shop with Tabs after school when Tim got hold of her eventually.

What did she have to feel guilty about, anyway? A man she hardly knew had called her to make sure she got home safe. That she was OK.

Hey. The sound of his voice had been strange and familiar at the same time, she remembered it instantly, soft and intimate and she felt her limbs weak suddenly, she had had to put a hand to the photocopier.

'Hello,' she whispered. Then, 'I'm at work.' Hurried, panicking.

'Oh, God I'm so sorry, look, forget it. I just—' a laugh, 'I just found this number on my phone. It is you, isn't it?' A delighted sound to his voice.

Standing with her back to the wall beside the photocopier Georgie didn't have to say anything. Couldn't say anything.

'I just wanted to make sure you got back OK – look, I'm really sorry. You get back to work. I just wanted to say it was lovely – you were – it was lovely to meet you. I'll go now.'

What had Georgie managed to say? 'It's fine, look, 'bye. Thanks.' Something like that. Then it had been done and no one had heard and she had been standing in the corner by the photocopier staring at her phone and her whole body humming. Humming.

She'd forgotten to call Tim back. In the shop now, talking to him, she looked around, positioned herself so she felt unobserved, behind the newspaper rack.

There had been an edge to Tim's voice. He sounded not quite aggrieved, but curious. Tabs choosing what she wanted for her treat, humming to herself

'Oh, I was—' the excuse evaded her. The real reason hummed too loud in her head. Her head had been too full, was the truth, too full of other stuff but she wasn't going to say that. It didn't seem to matter, though: Tim quickly shifted to indulgence.

'Doesn't matter,' he said, kindly. 'Did you listen to the message?' He didn't wait for her to answer. 'Look – this is – it's my fault, I'd forgotten all about it but I've got to go off this weekend, leave Friday, day after tomorrow, that is.'

'Another conference?' Tabs looked sideways at her raised voice.

Georgie knew she should be used to it by now, there seemed to be one of these a month. Developments in legislation, stuff like that. Client confidentiality. Tim was careful about client confidentiality. Dinners and speeches and big hotels. But this weekend – she wished he was going to be here. She wanted things to be quiet and normal. She wanted the hum to go away and to sit next to him on the sofa and talk about their day and let it all settle down.

Tell him about Cat. Cat was what mattered.

'On the South Coast,' he said, terse and she knew why, because of that plaintive note in her voice.

'Sounds like fun,' she said, trying to correct it but that was wrong too.

'It's not going to be a holiday, you know.' He spoke sharply. He sounded stressed, Georgie realised and she turned in the little shop, this way then that way, not wanting Tabs' eye, Tabs pressed against the counter and looking up at her with the KitKat clasped in both hands tight as if someone might take it away from her.

'I'm sorry.' Georgie realised she was almost whispering and cleared her throat. 'I know, I know it's not, it's just—' searching for something to say, 'it's so long since we went anywhere together.' Her heart bottomed at the thought, out of the blue, but she couldn't stop now. 'I was thinking, maybe one time – maybe I could come too?' she tailed off into his sudden silence.

86

She'd hate it, wouldn't she? A hotel full of tax accountants. Tim had always been at the glamorous end of his profession, though she knew how Cat would laugh at that thought. He loved a smart hotel, his nice suits, a good car, wine. She could imagine him in his element down there, somewhere with chandeliers in the lobby. A picture was in her head, then of the family room in their King's Cross fleapit. If Tim could have seen it.

She swallowed, half wanting to giggle, half terrified. If he'd seen.

He sighed. 'No sweetheart, *I'm* sorry.' Softening. 'I'll make it up to you.' In a voice she hadn't heard for a while. The voice she used to hear after a good dinner, Tim coming into the kitchen and kissing her against the cabinets, his hands on her back. Maybe Sunday morning had been a new start. He *had* been stressed, and Georgie should have taken the initiative, shouldn't she? In bed.

Tabs was waiting by the till, Georgie scrabbled for coins, the phone wedged under her ear. They paid and left the shop.

'You *will* be all right?' There was something else in his voice. 'On your own, I mean?' He was uneasy: this was Tim, worried about leaving her alone. Poor Tim.

'Of course I'll be all right,' Georgie said, fishing in her pocket for the remains of her lunchtime sandwich, for Tabs to feed the ducks with. There was a silence, a hesitation, a diffidence: as if there was something he wanted to ask, but couldn't. She didn't know what it meant, and then a spark ignited, flared, a second of panic and the memory, of that call, at three a.m. was back. *Surely he didn't – he couldn't.*

'Why?' she said, before she could stop herself. 'I've been alone before, haven't I?'

Tabs was at the edge of the duck pond now, crouched, one hand held out. It wasn't enough to throw the bread, she wanted the duck to come to her. She could keep still for long minutes, a lifetime, watching intently. She wanted a dog, but Tim said no.

Nothing happened. Nothing. Georgie had thought she'd put all that away, Friday night behind her, but then he'd called. To say nothing, only checking up on her, only making sure she was safe. And suddenly it was all still there. Like the diamond earring: it was out there, somewhere, those soft dark hours were there, the hours of secret laughter in a hotel room, things she couldn't remember. Glittering in the dust, under a floorboard, in a dark corner.

But she knew why there was that tone in Tim's voice. He knew her too well and he was just worrying, because she was different, she was jumpy, she wasn't eating, of course he'd noticed. She felt sick. 'I'm fine,' she said, putting warmth into her voice. 'Honestly. See you later.'

She'd expected him at six, then seven, half past came and went and she felt sure, he knew something. What something? When she heard the car door slam she had readied herself – sorry, sorry – but he was smiling.

Raising her face to him for the kiss Georgie examined him, but there was nothing. No wariness, no suspicion. He was light on his feet, loosening his tie, cheerful. An arm round her waist, feeling for it, the familiar soft place. Then it slid down, resting on her hip.

Tabs ran up and flung her arms around his legs and Tim didn't even go straight to, *Have you done your homework?* It really was as if he was going on a holiday. As if he'd been worrying about something and it had gone away. Georgie shifted guiltily: she'd made him worried.

No harm in it. A bit of fun. A phone call. Just being polite, being caring. Forget about it.

And then he was on the stairs, taking them two at a time and Georgie watching him. She put a hand down, uncertain, to her waist, then her hip, trying to understand what it was he felt, when he put his hand on her.

'Mummy?' Tabs was looking up at her, anxious. 'What's wrong?'

She made herself smile. 'Nothing, sweetheart,' she said. Because how could you explain this, any of it, to a little girl, five years old? A little girl used to gazing proudly at her own soft smooth tummy, her chubby wrists, how could you explain that sometimes, you didn't recognise yourself? That one day her body might feel as if it belonged to someone else.

She tried Holly's mobile again, standing at the stove while Tabs' tea was cooking. Waiting, listening to the phone ring, knowing Tim was happy, upstairs, he knew nothing, she felt a bubble of something unexpected – guilty pleasure, excitement – as it rang. She wanted to confide. To Holly. *He called me.*

He was nice, wasn't he? His voice. His smiling eyes as he handed her the glass carefully. Mark. A gentleman – was it Cat said that? Saw them up to their room and she took him back downstairs. She would have thanked him, that was what she would have done. Stumbled back upstairs – or had that been before? He called to make sure she was OK.

A footstep overhead and the pleasure was mixed with something else, expecting Tim to walk in at any moment and she would have to hang up.

But he didn't. The call went to voicemail.

Chapter Ten

Thursday

Tim climbed off her, whistling, and bounded into the shower. On the bed Georgie lay very still. The old habit, when they'd been trying, wanting it to work this time and not daring to move. She remembered lying, with a flush on her cheeks, with her legs up one time, resting on the headboard. No need for that any more but she still lay quiet, not moving a muscle.

A new start. Maybe that was what was happening.

Way back when, she'd tried to talk to Cat about it. After the miscarriage, which had shocked Georgie much more than she could have imagined. She'd been young – but not too young to know what it was, surely? That it was a natural thing, how many times had she told herself that? Lying in an overheated hospital bed with her belly cramping and her head aching and watching the busy nurses and feeling completely alone, completely empty.

And Tim. *We can try again*, he'd been there saying that straight away, as she got out of the taxi, wobbly, that winter morning after they'd discharged her and she had looked at the stairs up to their flat as if they might have been

Everest. And although what he was saying, although the idea of having to feel that way again had horrified her to the roots of her hair, she'd just nodded dumbly. Floundering in the cold sea, you take what you're thrown.

It's a natural thing, it's just your body working properly. Cat had said that, too, well-meaning, not really understanding. Four and a half months – Georgie hadn't even been showing. She'd felt it though, sort of knot low down in her belly, in the soft extra flesh that had started to accumulate, the little cushioning that had not, in the end, been any use. It wasn't true. It had felt like the opposite, nothing natural about it, everything failing to work. It felt like an outrage.

There had been things she hadn't been able to tell Cat, things she couldn't even look straight at herself. Sitting on the bathroom floor with blood streaked down her calf, her back to the door, telling Tim he couldn't come in. And eventually he had and she'd sat on the loo with the lid closed under her, telling him not to look while he stared at her with that expression.

Tim had married her. That was what he'd done. Scooped her up, bought her a dress, booked a honeymoon, to stop her dwelling on it. The Maldives for two weeks, lying on a wooden jetty staring down into the bright blue sea at fish flickering in the shadows, feeling the sun burn her. She hadn't worn suncream and her shoulders had peeled and Tim had been there for that too, rubbing lotion into them, over and over and over. They'd snorkelled and gone for walks along the beach and eaten swordfish looking at the sunset and when she looked at the pictures Georgie could only stare at her empty belly, brown and smooth and round. The trace of a line down it, the brown line, linea nigra, that means a baby.

She should never have done it. That thought flashed into her head at odd times, at those four in the morning moments – including this morning, as a matter of fact – and then it flickered away, like one of those fish. This morning it had stayed longer, lurking in the shadows, a bigger fish. And then, sometime later, Tim had rolled over and put his hand on her.

Then there had been years, years and years, of trying and nothing happening when she'd felt a sharp yearning, a nostalgia for it, her few months of being pregnant, when she would find herself in the pregnancy section of bookshops looking up what a four-and-a-half-month – fifteen-week – foetus looked like, putting a finger to the illustration and thinking, *my baby*. That was my baby.

Tim had always been there. Helping her keep going, keep trying. Five years of IVF, when her body went on not working, and with every hospital visit, every injection she felt further away from herself. From the self she had liked, loved, taken dancing, given new clothes. When she wanted to scream when he touched her, *Stop. Let's stop.* Poor Tim.

He was back in the room, sliding back the doors of the big wardrobe, and Georgie still hadn't moved. How long had it taken them to get that wardrobe right? Tim had wanted cherrywood, with maple for the doors, and drawers for his shirts: she'd walking into the living room one time when she heard him calling the interior designer a cunt because she'd specified the wrong finish, and had stepped back out of the door so quickly she'd stumbled.

Now he swung out the rail with his ties on, fingering them, preoccupied.

She felt it slippery between her legs and shifted, uncomfortable. A tiny movement but Tim looked across quickly. Smiling, level. He turned, approaching and Georgie pretended to yawn, because her own smile went a bit wrong, she could feel it; his head went down and for a moment she thought he was going to climb back on the bed but he leaned under it and pulled out the overnight bag. The little case she'd used last Friday: she heard Tabs turn on her light next door and in one quick movement she swung upright and out of the bed and took it from him.

'Let me give you a hand,' said Georgie when he looked at her nonplussed and Georgie laid the bag on the bed, shielding it from him. Just in case.

'I wonder what the weather's going to do,' he said to her back. She opened the case swiftly. She didn't know what she had expected to see – wanted to see, even. A trace of the night, a clue. It was quite empty. She turned around then to glance at the wardrobe, to make sure the golden dress was out of sight – even at the thought of it she felt a sharp pang of longing, that night and her shining in the dark and the man's smile, appreciative – but Tim was at the wardrobe again, blocking her view. He was getting out his navy blue summer wool, handmade like everything. Even Tim's shoes were handmade: he'd said something about his father always insisting on it, when she'd asked. Tim's father had been a major in the army. The suit had cost more than a thousand pounds.

Georgie sat back down on the bed. She wanted to shower, she felt the stickiness between her legs. She felt it start up, the hum of secrets. *Go away.*

Five or six big private clients, that was all it took, or so he said. Tim managed their money, set up offshore accounts where necessary, trusts and tax-free investments, all that. Within the law. 'They like it,' he always said. 'That I look like a small-town operator.' Smiling down at the suit, brushing off imaginary crumbs. 'On paper, anyway.'

She'd told Cat, business was good, in that hour they'd been alone in the hotel room on Friday night, pulling on her dress as Cat lay on the bed putting on stockings. Cat had been curious, she didn't know why, except apparently when they were fixing the evening up Holly'd mentioned something to Cat that she'd heard, about Tim being a star. Admiring.

'He always was a smart one,' Cat had said, lying back on the pillow in the grubby hotel room. 'Knew how to make friends. Work the system.' And turned on her side, sighing. 'I suppose, well—'

'What?' Georgie had said.

'Nothing,' said Cat quickly, sitting down quickly, one stocking on, the flush of booze on her but Georgie pushed it. 'Harry's a scruffy bugger,' she'd said.

Harry's new job, the reason they'd moved back to be closer to London, was running an office supplies company: it wasn't exactly a step up from his previous job in a brewery but they managed. Just about. Cat hadn't asked her to the house yet: she'd told her, looking round Georgie's big empty kitchen, it was tiny. Two of the boys sharing a room but that was all right, they were still young.

'And he hasn't got Tim's drive. They're just different, I suppose. It doesn't have to be to do with—'

'With what?'

And Cat had rolled over, her voice muffled in the pillow. 'The baby thing.'

'Baby thing.'

'You know.'

'I don't think so,' Georgie had said quickly. 'He's not – it's not that.' Cat hadn't said anything else.

Tim had been unbothered by it, or so he'd said: 'Whatever it takes,' shrugging. His own sperm were low motility, which didn't mean no chance, it just meant almost no chance. His work face on, in that moment in the consultant's office, smooth smiling Tim and the consultant nodding, man to man.

'Think I'll have a shower,' she said, standing up abruptly, needing the cool water, needing to be clean and Tim stepped beside her and put his hand on her, gently, between her legs. She could smell his aftershave and then his hand was gone: carefully he laid the suit on the bed, smiling still, to himself this time, a smile of satisfaction.

The door opened and there was Tabs.

'Go on,' said Sue, holding out the biscuit tin, a frown beginning to appear.

It was halfway through the morning and normally Georgie would have had one, wanted three. But looking down into the tin, again she felt no appetite at all. Sue shook it impatiently, and Georgie dipped in at random.

'I thought I'd take Tabs up to town Saturday,' she said. 'The zoo, maybe.' It sounded quite different to what it had this morning, when she'd said it to Tim. He'd been standing at the counter in the kitchen waiting for his coffee to cool, impatient to go. Then – and she'd hoped he hadn't been able to hear it like she could – she'd sounded nervous.

But he had hardly seemed to hear, looking down at his mobile, just grunted at first. Then looked up.

'Sure,' he said, equably. Encouraging, even. Setting down the phone and lifting the cup to his lips in that slightly fastidious way he had: if he ever spilled anything on himself on the way to work there was hell to pay. 'Why not? Take her to see your father.'

Georgie had relaxed then, just the thought of her father was enough on its own, his old coat and his collection of tote bags full of treats for Tabs.

But it made sense, too, of Tim being fine with it, because he was always happier for them to see Dad in town, or at his sheltered housing, a cup of tea somewhere, than the fuss of him hauling out here, needing collecting from the station, looking round the place anxiously so that Tim would tut despite himself and go off to tennis, or his study.

And then the cup was in the sink and Tim had been reaching for his velvet-collared coat. 'And I won't be back till Sunday night, will I? You'll need something to keep her entertained.'

Now Sue made a non-committal noise and Georgie felt stupid, to have worried. It was half an hour on the train, and people did it all the time.

Not her, though. She'd just been waiting for Tim to look at her sharply and say, 'What? London on a lovely sunny day? What do you want to do that for?'

97

She had had a response to that lined up, as a matter of fact. Autumn colours in Regent's Park, and the zoo. But he hadn't asked: he hadn't said, *Plenty of autumn colour on our doorstep*, which would have been true.

Imagine. Walking down a street and there he is. Mark. Georgie put the thought out of her mind. Almost.

What on earth did you get up to? Tim hadn't asked that either. And it was almost a week ago, it was over and done, it was forgotten. Except it wasn't. Except there were those little traces: a phone number. A lost earring. A bruise or two and a soft voice in her ear. *Hey.*

All the way to school Tabs had been cheerful: she'd got wind of the plan somehow and kept glancing up excitedly, not daring say anything: trains, Granddad and the zoo being all her wildest dreams together. Usually they walked, but they were late today and they drove, round the edge of the village, skirting the trees. The colour was mazy, still green but darkening, bronze here and there: it was in the corner of Georgie's eye as she drove, behind her Tabs kicking her legs gently against the back of her seat.

He might not even live in London, and if he did Georgie certainly wasn't likely to bump into him in the street and if she did she would probably hide – but all the same. The thought wouldn't go away. It felt as though her life had been travelling along a flat, flat road and there was a bump, suddenly, there was a tree or a car crash or a hare hurtling across a field and how couldn't you stop and look at it? He'd been a gentleman, Cat had said.

All morning she felt as though Sue was watching her, Sue who had a teenage daughter and would therefore immediately recognise the stupid thoughts racing around her head, thoughts that had nothing to do with being a grown woman and a mother. Sue might even have heard her, whispering to him by the photocopier. Fantasies, blossoming out of the time she couldn't remember, between the brandy bottle and the next morning. He'd come back to the room with them and then just – left. She'd seen him out, they'd both told her that, Holly and Cat. Had he kissed her goodbye? He'd phoned to make sure she was all right. The panic of the next morning, the hot shame of the journey home had settled into a different perspective: overreaction, silly, hysterical.

At lunch Georgie got out a card she'd brought, to send to Cat. She sat at her desk for five minutes with the pen in her hand and the envelope addressed, but not even knowing how to start. *Let's have lunch. When does the chemo start? Shall I have the boys? Shall I come and hold your hand?* Then she looked at it and saw only her own futile neediness and with a sound of exasperation that did have Sue looking over at her, she tore it up and clutching her mobile phone hurried out into the playground where she ordered a hamper of ridiculous food from a fancy grocery in London that cost several hundred pounds instead, on the joint credit card.

The afternoon crept on, the knowledge of what Tim would say when the bill arrived, of just his expression, snagging on Georgie at regular intervals. She realised only now that he'd never had much time for Cat, she was too raucous or up-front or something and Tim liked a quiet life. He was also funny about illness, always had been, superstitious and judgemental, as if you brought these things on yourself, or they were a sign of weakness or something. He'd been funny about it this morning, when she'd plucked up courage to tell him.

His own parents still alive and living in Surrey, just the other side of London, though they never wanted to see Georgie and Tim and Tabs. Georgie knew there had been telephone conversations, about the IVF, that she hadn't been told about, or that were closed down if she walked in but she didn't let herself wonder, if they never wanted to see Tabs because she wasn't their flesh and blood.

Well, she drinks, doesn't she? As she filled the kettle to make tea for her and Sue – two-fifteen regular as clockwork, with an hour and ten minutes to go of the school day – she could hear Tim saying it. As he examined his row of ties, frowning, pleased with his conclusions. 'There's research linking breast cancer to alcohol consumption, I read somewhere.'

'A friend of mine's got breast cancer,' she said now, handing Sue her cup. Sue stood up immediately, set the cup down, put her arms around Georgie all in one movement, taking her aback, setting her off. How had she known? Sensible Sue. She laid her head just a quick second on Sue's shoulder, inhaling her reassuring scent, freesias and wool-wash.

Stuffy in the office, still hot in the playground. The weather would change tonight they said and not soon enough.

Then Georgie stepped back, rubbing at her eyes, feeling a fool and a fraud. 'Don't know what I'm crying for,' she said, crossly. 'It's her got to do the chemo. And tell the boys. They're only small—' and she stopped because that would set her off again

Sue patted her. 'I know,' she said, 'I—' but then something changed, she was looking past Georgie and frowning and whatever she had been going to say was forgotten. Turning to look Georgie stared, something faintly surreal about it, the conversation about illness, and hospital, but the flowers had been sent here, was all Georgie could think.

A big gaudy bunch, big enough to obscure the man carrying it and for a moment all Georgie could see was a dark green sleeve, the badge of a delivery service and beyond him through the door in reception Janette, peering round her classroom door for a look.

'Miss Baxter, is it?' The flowers went down on the floor and the deliveryman looked from Georgie to Sue and back.

'Mrs,' said Georgie. Immediately Georgie knew they were from Tim, his way of apologising for springing this weekend on her. The man held out a digital pad for her to sign.

From across the desk Sue folded her arms, eyeing the bouquet. It was so big it came in its own box. The flowers were bright, big nodding orange gerberas, pink lilies and fat red rosebuds all trussed up in cellophane and ribbon. They sat there in the middle of the office floor, out of place, demanding attention.

'Sorry, sorry,' said Georgie when the man had gone, hurrying forward to claim the box. Awkwardly she shuffled it round the side of her desk, out of sight. Not quite: the cellophane and a stiff rosebud were still visible: she could see that it had been dipped in a kind of glitter. Sue rolled her eyes.

'Sorry why?' she said. 'Nice of someone.' A theatrical sigh. 'My Al wasn't ever the romantic gesture type, was he?' Sue's husband Al had died young of cancer, or youngish, when Sue would have been mid-thirties. 'I mean he had his ways, but—'

'Tim's sprung this weekend away on me,' Georgie said quickly, glancing down at the flowers beside her. She could see the corner of the tiny envelope had come dislodged from its clip and slipped down inside the cellophane: she didn't want to read it, she realised. She knew what it would be: something he'd asked the florist to make up, something from a list. *Best wishes*: Once he'd sent her flowers with that on it, long ago, and they'd laughed about it. Or at least they had after a moment or two, Tim looking affronted. 'That'll be it. He only told me yesterday.'

When the bell went for the end of day it seemed everyone had seen the flowers arrive, because half the school, including Janette and Mrs Floate who cleaned and the reception classroom assistant who was only there two afternoons a week crowded into the office to coo over them, and Georgie trying to get them out to the car like a murder suspect under a blanket. She couldn't have even said what she was embarrassed about, except they all knew Tim – by sight, anyway, they knew his offices in town and his big silver car – and they'd all be gossiping about why he'd sent them, they'd know it wasn't her birthday or anything. She could have wished, she found herself thinking ungratefully, for a smaller bunch, or a less conspic-uous one at least.

It wasn't like Tim to go for bright colours, anyway, she thought, squeezing the bunch into the back of the car while Tabs hopped up and down behind her, *Mummy, Mummy*. Pale blue in the spare bathroom was as far as he'd allowed her, her pale blue tiles.

Tabs clambered in beside the flowers and Georgie buckled her into her special seat. She noticed that it was quite worn down where her small hands rested: soon she'd have outgrown it completely, and with the thought she kissed her quickly, smelling bubblegum and yoghurt.

But Tabs was already straining away, curious to look inside the bouquet. 'There's a card, Mummy,' she said, fishing for it. 'You've got to read the card, it's polite.'

'It's only from Daddy,' said Georgie quickly, and reached to take it. Tabs smiled at her, naughty, holding it back a second and Georgie just waited, her hand held out until Tabs gave in. She put it down quickly on the front passenger seat and Tabs kicked the back of her seat for a moment or two then lost interest. *Read the card before you open the present*: it was Tim had taught Tabs that, and quite right too. In theory.

Stopped with the engine idling at a red light by the church, though, the church with its leaning mossy gravestones and the forest beyond it, the tiny white envelope was still obstinately there in the corner of her eye and she did reach for it, casually, not wanting to rekindle Tabs' interest, and her scrutiny. No eyes as sharp as Tabs', and no pestering as determined, and – and. And what? It was only from Tim.

With half an eye on the traffic lights, Georgie opened it in her lap and looked down. The florist's name on the front in a wreath of roses, she knew the place, a little family shop. Not far away. Not far enough: they'd know her, even if the deliveryman hadn't.

She opened the little card, frowning down at the words. *What—*

Behind her someone tooted and she started, looking up, the lights had changed. Carefully, as if Tim was watching, she engaged first gear, she didn't want to stall, and all the time in her chest her heart was pattering. *What?*

I can't stop thinking about you.

Chapter Eleven

Tim had always been the pragmatic type. A bit of courting, taking her out for dinner and kissing her and telling her he loved her, everything measured and careful and safe.

I can't stop thinking about you.

That was all it said. For a second, two, three, she had run through the meaning of it in her head. The idea of Tim writing – saying – those words. The florist reading them back to him.

Was this the new start? They'd – made love, this morning. The card lay on the passenger seat beside her.

Since this morning. Since he had climbed off her and started looking through his ties for the weekend, Tim hadn't been able to stop thinking about her? Sitting in his office, at his desk, getting up to close the door while he whispered his message into the receiver. With the tiny card in her hand, the neat careful florist's handwriting, another hand to engage gear as the lights changed she had flushed, she had been able to feel it hot behind her ears, because it was a joke, it was stupid—

It was all wrong.

The flowers were in the living room, arranged carefully in a big glass goldfish bowl vase, almost glowing brilliant in the low evening light. Tabs had run upstairs while she filled the vase.

If only, Georgie thought, standing in the kitchen, *they'd come tomorrow*. With Tim away, she'd have had time to think, what to say. Her mind raced. She'd have had till Sunday night, and Tabs would have forgotten about them. She could have thrown them away, surreptitiously.

'Fish fingers all right?' she called up to Tabs and something muffled came back, that didn't sound like no. She got the packet out of the freezer and hesitated, her hand on the fridge door. There was an open bottle of white wine in the door, Tim had drunk some last night. She glanced at the clock: five forty-five, but inside her something hummed, needing to be appeased, needing to be calmed. She took the bottle out of the fridge, poured herself a small glass. Put the bottle back before lifting the glass to her lips, taking a sip, then another. The hum was warm inside her, now.

Close to home, seeing the time on the dashboard, Tabs quiet with the iPad behind her, Georgie'd turned the car around.

Tabs hadn't looked up, until they pulled up on the florist's forecourt. Floribunda, it was called. One in a small row of shops, between a catering supplies place, a nailbar.

'I just—' said Georgie. 'Just a minute, Tabs. I'll be quick.' It was almost four, and a gaunt woman in an apron was

106

hauling a tall galvanised bucket towards a grating in the ground. Georgie hurried up the forecourt, standing there awkwardly while the woman ignored her, doggedly pulling on the tall bucket's handles, lank hair falling either side of her face. She didn't look like she loved her job. Georgie started forward, thinking perhaps she could offer to help and then the woman stopped, straightened, wiping her hands on her apron.

'We're closed,' she said, regarding her. Georgie had never to her knowledge used Floribunda although she knew it had been in the village three or four years now. She didn't know if Tim had ever been.

'I just – I received a bouquet,' she'd begun, 'you made it up.' Even as she was saying Georgie knew she shouldn't, she knew people would talk: the glance the woman gave her was impatient, turning to curious. Pushing the hair from her face to get a better look. 'I don't know who it's from,' said Georgie, lamely. 'I wondered if you—'

'A phone order, was it?' There was a touch of colour in the woman's face now, as she pretended not to know what Georgie meant. Adjusting her apron. What had she thought? That the woman would read out the credit card to her? 'I can go and look through my orders,' she said then, sly. 'What was the name?' When Georgie hesitated. 'Your name?'

It had been this woman's handwriting on the card, then. Her taking down the message. *I can't stop thinking about you.*

She knew all right. Who Georgie was, her address, what this was all about. Everything. And Georgie had stepped back, hasty, turned to look at the car, Tabs' face turned towards her in the backseat window, pale and curious.

Of course it hadn't been Tim who sent them. Of course not.

'Oh – you know, it doesn't matter,' Georgie said, an effort not to just turn and run, 'I think I – thank you, though.' But then she *was* running. And as she swung the car back out into the road, she had seen the woman looking after her, triumphant.

Don't be silly.

In the kitchen Georgie refilled her glass, halfway: she turned the fish fingers over and set off round the house, doing the things she always did, mechanically, drawing the curtains, turning on lights. *Don't be silly. Of course it's not him.* On the side in the kitchen was a rack of lamb, potatoes peeled. Tim hated the smell of fish, and the lamb would cover it. She got out her phone, curling her fingers round it.

But 'him' wasn't Tim, any more. 'Him' was *him,* she knew his name but she didn't want to use it, it felt dangerous. *Mark.*

Of course it wasn't – him. Because how would he know where to send them? Restless, Georgie went into the living room, straightened cushions: she bent to turn on a sidelight and on the table the flowers receded, dimming.

A man who'd chatted her up on a night out, yes, he'd called to make sure she was OK but he hadn't – he hadn't – he'd just been being polite. A gentleman. He wasn't going to make inquiries – who from? – or spend fifty quid on a bunch of flowers. But who else could it be? Some dad from the playground, some lunatic with a crush on her – the idea was stupid.

It was Tim, after all. Tim.

She needed to know, though. Because he'd see the flowers. Or Tabs would say something about them. Or both.

And then, quite suddenly, perched on the edge of the sofa, Georgie felt herself go still, head up. She remembered. He *had* asked her about herself. *Mark*. The name came easier, this time, as the memory popped out of nowhere, complete and distinct, like he was *her* Mark. At the bar, raising the drink to her lips – perhaps she had still been sober then, capable of processing that kind of thing – he'd somehow come around Holly, or was it that Georgie'd been dancing, and then had come back to the bar and found herself next to him? She remembered his forearm resting on the bar, his hand when she looked down only a centimetre or so from hers.

Tipsy but not drunk. She *had* told him.

I'm nobody, I work in the office of a primary school, you wouldn't know it, small village on the edge of Epping Forest – yes. She had said that. Had she said the name of the village? Maybe. Probably. And school would be the only place he would have been able to find her, anyway, wouldn't it? Not her home. A stalker playground dad would know where she lived.

A kind of thrill went through her: if *he* knew where she lived. The danger of it.

The mobile was in her palm. Holly would know. Holly would understand. She was that kind, Georgie thought of her voice, husky and conspiratorial, her smudged make-up, legs with sharp ankles.

She just wanted to tell someone, *He said he can't stop*

thinking about me and who else? Not Sue in the school office. Not Cat, poor Cat. She walked out of the bright kitchen with the phone in her hand, into the living room, into a corner of the living room by the window, half hidden in the curtain and looking at the flowers on the table. She dialled Holly's number.

Tim could be home any moment – or he could be late. She pressed her back into the curtain, feeling her heart pump, feeling herself breathless before she'd even opened her mouth to speak. This was adrenaline, wasn't it? Because this was dangerous. The phone went to voicemail again. She heard something that might be Tim's footsteps, might be his key in the door, if it was he would be prompt, he would be early – but still, she didn't hang up. This time she left a message, jumbled, breathless, *I'd love to see you, give me a call, may be in London Saturday.*

'Something burning?' The front door closing.

Tim was standing in the hall, raincoat on, briefcase in hand: Georgie ran past him, letting him blur, and snatched the frying pan off the stove. Turned the extractor fan to full, her eyes filling abruptly from the smoke – and she didn't know if it was from the smoke or panic, because it was too late to eliminate the smell of fish or come up with an explanation, for the flowers. *Shit shit shit.*

Tim was through the kitchen door now and he just leaned down and kissed her. Then pulled back, the slightest wrinkle between his eyebrows. 'You've started early, haven't you? Not even six.'

'I—' Georgie put a hand to her mouth, eyes darting to the side but she'd put the bottle back in the fridge,

110

there was only the glass. 'I just felt like it,' she said. 'It's been one of those days.'

Tim nodded. 'Never mind,' he said lightly, running a hand from her waist to her hip and letting it rest there.

'I'll—' Georgie wanted to twist away, just to collect her thoughts, just not to be looked at – but she didn't. She smiled up at him instead. Rehearsing it silently, *Oh, those? We thought you'd sent them, but they're from – from.*

'I'll make her scrambled eggs,' she said. Leaning back a little and calling, towards the door. 'Tabs?' Tim held his gaze for just a minute, examining her, then he sighed, and let her go.

Note, yes, there was a note. Not sure where I put it, now. It was in her pocket.

It felt unreal, how could she take it seriously? This man didn't know her – not like Tim, sighing, ironical; Tim following her round the kitchen, tidying, peering in the dishwasher.

I can't stop thinking about you. Whatever she thought rationally the words were powerful. They took effect, like smoke.

Tim had stopped, he was looking around now, expectant.

'Would you like a glass too?' she said, not understanding.

He looked at her as if he didn't recognise her for a second and then he shrugged, 'Sure,' he said. 'Why not?'

What was he expecting to see, then? And then it came to her, of course. He was looking for the bouquet, or some trace of it. The wrapping was already in recycling. It *had* been him, after all, the flowers, the note might have been mixed up with another or he maybe – and the thought stopped her – maybe the sex this morning, maybe

111

he had read something about rekindling your wife's— Had them sent to the school just to get them all talking, she could hear him explaining that to her. *Give those old biddies something to gossip about.*

Pouring the wine for him it tumbled softly down around her and she felt foolish with disappointment. Why would she think… She knew in there was a stir of resentment, even, and she didn't say, not straight away, *Thank you for the lovely flowers.*

Taking the glass, his face amused, Tim walked past her, into the living room: she followed and she was there when he stopped. There they stood gaudy and resplendent, glowing in the low light. Gaudier than the room and she waited for him to grumble – they hadn't got it right, he'd been cheated on the bouquet.

But walked on, set down his briefcase, as if he hadn't seen them.

He set down his briefcase. 'So,' he said, lowering himself into the armchair he always worked in, in the evenings. It had been designed specially for his back. 'What's for dinner?' Humorous. 'Not fish fingers, anyway.'

And then Tabs was in the room, in school skirt and vest, hurtling at him, flying and he put one hand out to slow her down, the other to shield his glass on the low table beside him.

'Tabitha,' he said, 'how was school?' She burrowed her small head into his chest and didn't answer. He pushed her back a little and held her at arm's length.

'Boring,' she said defiantly, sitting back on his knee and folding her arms: they locked eyes, Tim and she, a stand-off.

Tabs was doing very well at school, the words her fond

112

teacher used were *sparky, bright. Challenging*, on occasion. Tim, perched in the reception classroom on a ridiculously tiny chair and grilling the teacher like she was applying for a job, was proud of her. It was what he said.

Now Tabs laid her cheek back down on his chest and looked sideways up at Georgie. They were both dark, but Tabs darker, thick hair, thick brows. She didn't look too unlike him: sometimes people remarked on their resemblance, not knowing. You could choose the physical attributes of the donor. Georgie didn't think about it, not too often, or not consciously, anyway. Tabs was herself, that's all. She'd rehearsed that one enough times, in case anyone said.

Not many people knew. Cat knew. No one's business.

Then Tim made a movement to Georgie with his head and she knew what he meant. 'Come on,' she said gently, leaning down to tug at Tabs. 'Let's make your tea.'

He didn't say anything till later, till Tabs was in bed and the table laid and Georgie was at the stove, flushed with steam from the vegetables and checking the lamb, everything five minutes from being done. And then suddenly he was behind her, very close, his mouth was on her neck. She could smell the wine on him: she'd stopped drinking as he'd started, the desire for it ebbing.

'Nice flowers,' he said, into her hair. He had positioned himself directly behind her, one hand on each of her hips, his body close.

'Aren't they?' Georgie said and as she shifted, sideways, reaching for the vegetables, she heard him make a sound of amusement. If this was a game – she drained them, carrots and peas mixed together, and the steam enveloped her. 'Cat sent them.'

Cat's name came to her out of the air, the only one she could trust, and looking sideways at him through the steam she could see that it took him aback. If it had been him sent them after all – but it hadn't been.

At dinner Georgie was jumpy, she couldn't help it. Getting up from the table too many times – to get the salt, change a napkin. She realised she'd left her phone out on the side and if Holly called back, *if she called* – so she got up again on the pretence of refilling the water jug and swiftly took it into the kitchen. Tim didn't seem to notice any of it, eating stolidly, pausing to look up once and ask her, mild and solicitous, about her day.

'I – I sent something to Cat. You know, to help out – a hamper.' He nodded, raising the fork to his mouth. Implying, without saying it, that Cat had sent the flowers in some way in connection with her own illness, in gratitude for the support, or something. If he said, 'Really?' – and it didn't make much sense, after all – she didn't know what she would say. But he didn't.

She didn't tell him how much the hamper had cost. She'd cross that bridge when she had to.

It wasn't till later still, in bed, that she understood, he hadn't believed her.

'We should have them over,' he said, in the dark. 'Cat and her husband. What's his name?'

'Harry.' Her mouth dry.

And he stroked her hair in the dark for the longest time while she lay there, stiff and silent before finally he settled back on the pillow and went to sleep.

Chapter Twelve

Friday

Friday morning was boxing, until summer came around again.

The boxing gym was old school, which suited Frank, torn posters and sweat in the air and a concrete floor. There was even a glass booth where you paid your dues to ancient Jules with his shaking hands; Parkinson's, he said, sitting under a dog-eared ten-year-old topless calendar.

It had to be done. Frank liked his food and he needed to keep in shape. He liked a beer. He tended his niche among the older men jealously but limited himself to the punchbags. He was too canny to offer himself up to anyone with a grudge, because however laidback you were, however easy you took it and however many people you tried to please, someone could come out of the woodwork.

The door opened and Frank saw Matteo come through it, looking round for him, raising a hand.

'Eh.' The Cinq's bouncer was a man of few words. He was already in his kit, it didn't bother him to plod through the streets in tights and shorts. Like Frank he mostly restricted himself to the punchbags, but for different reasons. He was built like a truck and it was hard to find anyone to fight him. Steadily they swung and dodged, getting a kind of rhythm up although Matteo moved much less, rooted like a big tree. With every glimpse of the bouncer's square shaven skull, his bulky shoulder, from around the big swinging bag, Frank found himself thinking of Matteo's life on the pavement. Quiet, invisible, unless he needed to take a step towards you. It occurred to Frank that he saw things.

Afterwards they sat side by side on the bench, drinking pint glasses of water they refilled from the wall tap in meditative silence.

'Teo,' said Frank abruptly. 'You remember a tall guy, Friday night? Tall skinny guy?'

Matteo turned his big head and looked at Frank reflectively. He frowned, taking his time. Eddie had a fondness for Matteo, and Frank found himself wondering if maybe he came in handy beyond his duties on the Cinq's doorstep before dismissing the idea. Eddie was a landlord, he wasn't a gangster.

Matteo was a bit slow, maybe he *had* taken a few punches before he got this big, Frank did wonder. He did know how to treat customers and you couldn't do that, if you didn't pay attention to who was who – coming in, going out – and what they might be up to. And if the guy had stuck in Frank's mind, chances were—

'Maybe with a couple of women? Leaving with them?' he persisted.

Matteo reached for his sweat-towel, mopping his forehead delicately.

It took him a while: Frank had shifted forward on the bench ready to give up and go when finally Matteo nodded.

'I see him, sure. No two women, three. 'E leave with them.' Cockney Italian, Frank's favourite accent in the world, the voice of the melting pot.

'You know any of the women?'

Matteo jerked his head back, *maybe*. Then nodded, took a long pull at his energy drink – how he made the muscles, Frank wouldn't touch the stuff – and dabbed at his mouth. Fastidious for a big bloke but Italians were like that.

'Yeah,' he said. 'That Holly, I seen her around, since I been here.' Matteo had arrived in London as a skinny kid from Palermo almost ten years before, working in shops and restaurants till he settled on building muscle. Holding the can loosely between his hands, on the bulk of his thighs. 'She chat to me, now and then, back when I work at the Capri.' The Capri was like the Cinq but a bit rougher, down at the Leicester Square end of Soho.

'Oh, yeah,' said Frank, nudging him. It was like nudging a truck.

Matteo studied his forearms meditatively. 'Some lady, they like always to have a man to talk to. You know what I mean? So if she don't like the look of anyone in the club and her man hasn't turn up again – she talk to me.'

'Is he her man?' Frank asked, curious. 'The tall guy?'

Matteo shrugged. 'I never see her guy. She talk about him all the time, he goin' do this, he goin' take her there, they goin' get married but he never turn up, not when I am on the door. So could be. Not my business.'

'Huh.' Frank turned it over in his head. 'Always the same guy?'

117

'She don't come so much to the Cinq, and Eddie don't want me talking to clients, so I don' know no more – but that was what it sounded. Same guy on and off, for years.' The dent of a frown appeared briefly in his big impassive face, at the thought of some crazy women, maybe.

'But the guy last Friday night left the club with them.' Waiting for more. 'The skinny guy.'

Matteo looked up, mild again. Thought a long moment and finally said, 'Yes.' Set down his can, folded his sweat towel with care. 'He get in a minicab with them.'

That was an idea: Frank turned it over in his head: he felt something squeeze inside him as the picture materialised. Two of them had had wedding rings on, not that Holly, mind, and what did he think he was going to get up to with three women? Unless he was Holly's man and she'd talked them into something pervy. He shifted on the bench at the thought of them crowded into a minicab: at the thought of her. Georgie. Pressed up against the skinny guy, uncomfortable, the martinis making her soft and dreamy, unprepared.

The bar had been packed by the end of the evening, and she'd been dancing. Getting into the dancing, with her girls. And when she settled for a breather she hadn't come back to the bar so Frank lost track. There'd been the usual clamour, girls pounding on the bar for Cosmopolitans, endless pints for the lads. By the end of the evening anything a foot back from the bar always turned into a blur. Not his fault.

And besides, he'd seen Holly since, so there was nothing to feel bad about. But he did. He felt bad.

Because he *had* glimpsed her, late in the evening. At the far end of the bar, the door end, her hand had lifted, fluttered and he hadn't seen her again. If she'd been saying goodbye, he hadn't registered it.

And if he'd known. The tall skinny guy had a look about him, like he knew what he was about, one leg down off the barstool, biding his time. Ready to make his move.

He leaned back against the brickwork, feeling the sweat patch the back of his T-shirt. Still hot out.

'So you didn't know the guy?' he asked, just casually, and Matteo leaned his big head back against the peeling paintwork of the brick wall, where a hundred heads had rested. Gazing off into nowhere, he had long lashes for a big bloke, just a touch of the feminine. And then Matteo shrugged, and leaned forwards, elbows on his knees.

'Just a suit, they all look the same, don't they? English men, all look the same to me.'

Frank nodded, saying nothing. *Not to me*, he thought. Frank would know the guy, if he saw him again. Beside him Matteo raised his head, still sweating. A big man took a while to cool. 'Is a problem with him?'

Frank pondered a moment, as to whether to confide, and decided against it. Confide what? He clapped a hand on Matteo's big shoulder and got up to go. 'Nah, forget it,' he said. 'See you later, mate.'

Out on the street there was a wind, cold in gusts, colder suddenly than it had been even before he went into the gym. Leaves were coming off in Soho Square. Frank stopped to check his phone, looking up into the

119

sky as he listened to his answerphone. Eddie didn't do text messages. There was a lot of cloud scudding across bright blue, behind the forests of scaffolding, the hoardings on half-demolished buildings.

Come up here will you Frankie? To the house. I got a job for you. Quick as you can mate.

All very easy, all very laidback, that was Eddie. Except when he said quick, he meant, *now*.

When Georgie woke, Tim had already gone. She knew straight away, it wasn't just the quiet, she always knew, it was as if the whole house relaxed, all his systems turned to default silence, the hi-fi speakers in the kitchen, the hum of the heating. She sat up in a hurry, as if she'd done something wrong.

Whispering at the photocopier. Lying about the flowers. She *had* done something wrong.

All right, she told herself. *You don't have to go.* Because she realised part of the feeling was to do with London and the trip with Tabs, tomorrow. The memory of it, of the fever of sudden, inexplicable excitement in which she'd planned it, the way she'd proposed it to Tim not quite telling the truth, all made Georgie feel slightly sick.

'Tabs?' Silence. Georgie sat back against the headboard.

Don't go. Stay away. But the reason she should stay away was the same reason she wanted to go. London. Where it happened. Where he was, drinking his coffee in a bar in Soho, maybe. Thinking about her.

She'd already told Tabs they were going. She made herself think. Around her the quiet house began to reassure her. She didn't have to decide now. Tabs might forget.

And on cue she heard the door to Tabs' room creak, the feet soft on carpet on the landing, a little intake of breath, a little humming. A surreptitious click and she knew that Tabs was at the control panel for the speaker system, she loved playing with it, making the radio come on in the bathroom, filling the house with noise. It drove Tim mad: Georgie tried to excuse it, when he shouted up the stairs to Tabs, raging, *Stop messing about with it, you'll break it.* But she couldn't tell him what she knew to be behind the obsession, which was that Tabs was lonely. 'It's my sister,' she'd said solemnly once to Georgie, when singing came from the bathroom.

The crackle of voices came from downstairs, and even knowing he wasn't there, the sound made Georgie uneasy.

'Tabs?' This time Georgie was out of bed and on the landing in time to see her dressing gown flying round the corner at the bottom of the stairs and into the kitchen. She stopped at the control panel to turn the radio off. You could do it from your phone – or Tim could, anyway. It occurred to her that one of the things he didn't like was that at five, Tabs understood the technology better than he did.

Perched on a stool in the kitchen, Tabs had already poured herself some cereal, another thing she wasn't allowed to do when Tim was here. She must have known as instantly as Georgie had that they were alone in the house. There was a slop of milk on the counter. Georgie came up behind her, hugging, breathing in her hair, and saw a little stack of cans on the floor beside the store cupboard. Beans and peaches and tomatoes: and then she remembered that today was harvest festival.

121

'Tabs,' she murmured into her soft fragrant hair. 'Clever girl.'

The school was already full of it when they got there, the commotion that went along with every occasion, the harvest art display moved to prominence, year fives dressing up as sheaves of corn, a big cardboard box in reception filling up, and Sue's dry expression. She'd already seen twenty harvest festivals.

At eleven they all filed out, in coats: it was colder again today, and half the children were in gloves. The little church at the far end of the village was where they held all the religious observances, and as a C of E school there were a few of them. Candlemas and Easter and carol services: it was an old church, or some of it was, five hundred years old, built when this was a long way from London, when it was proper countryside and silent.

Carrying a cardboard box each holding the offerings that would go to the old people's home in the town – the town where the station was, where Tim's office was, that in truth was joined to the village by a thread of bungalows – Sue and Georgie brought up the rear of the procession. They wound through the village past the handful of original buildings – a thatched cottage, the manor house, a row of Victorian cottages – glimpsing the rest, the little housing developments, closes and lanes, houses all separate from each other, swathed in hedges, screened by garages. And then the church was there and up ahead Georgie could see Tabs at the front of the line, being asked to open the gate. They waited.

The graveyard was full of old stones, tilting and mossy, and beyond it the forest: you could see just what it would have been like, a hundred, two hundred years ago, only the sound was different. Only the soft roar of traffic. And of course once you were round the woodland the whole other forest of glittering glass and tower blocks would come into view – but today, in the new bright cold, with the crocodile of children obediently filing through the gate, holding hands however reluctantly in their grey and red uniforms, it might have been Victorian times.

It was why they had moved here, out of London, she and Tim, the old-fashioned values, the blazered uniforms, the neat verges. It had seemed so safe here when they got here, ten years ago. So quiet. They trooped inside and heads turned: the church was already full of parents, and it was stuffy though outside it was cooler, at last. They said it was going to get cold tonight.

There was a stir, suppressed excitement among the children as they saw their parents, the parents waving, covertly taking photographs. Tim should be here. Last year he had been, standing up in his pew to photograph Tabs, getting pissed off when they told him he couldn't. Proud dad. Five minutes of shuffling and at last they were all seated and Georgie risked a quick look round.

The rows of faces: of course by now she knew most of them by sight, if not by name. She knew those two, Maya Jason's mum and Kyle Roberts' mum, inseparable in the playground, yummy mummies if you believed in that kind of thing. Georgie fervently didn't want to believe it. They were both wearing the uniform, tight jeans and soft pale sweaters with discreet gold jewellery and expensive padded jackets – and as her glance snagged on them, exactly at that moment Maya's mum turned and whispered to Kyle's, her eyes on Georgie. Georgie's hands went instinctively down to tug at the comfortable old dress she'd put on, to herself, the tummy she'd never got rid of since having Tabs. She turned quickly, so she didn't have to see them, but it was as if she could hear someone whispering even from here, a buzz in her ears.

Sometimes she thought it was about the IVF, sometimes she imagined everyone knew. Not just imagination, either: Maya, year three, had once asked her. *Miss. Miss. Did your baby grow in a test tube, Miss?* Asked quite innocently, it hadn't been in class, to make everyone laugh, it had been at lunch, when Georgie had been helping serve and only the school mum helping that day – Georgie had endeavoured to forget her name since – had heard, moving her head quickly so Georgie couldn't see her face.

Georgie was fairly sure they thought of her as less than them: Maya's mum, Kyle's mum. Was that why? They all liked Tim. He was good-looking in his suit, his hair cut short, he was charming. Last year, he was Father Christmas. They clustered round him at fundraisers, though he hadn't been to many lately. Georgie wanted to turn round again, quick, to catch them, but she resisted. She was proud of Tim. It was just that – they didn't know. There was more to him.

They looked at her as if they would like to be in charge of her kitchen, *they*'d be able to keep the crumbs from collecting under the toaster.

The service dragged, even more than usual, an endless procession of children each with their cake tin or bag of pasta collected from the cardboard box to be taken to the altar and deposited in a big cloth-lined hamper, for show.

It would all go back in the boxes for transportation to the old people's home. Two hymns. Three. Covertly Georgie looked down into the bag to see if there was anything. Messages, on her mobile.

She should go and see Cat, not just phone her.

No messages, from anyone. Surreptitiously pushing the phone back down she saw the little leather box and flipped it open cautiously with one finger. The remaining earring sparkled up at her from the white satin lining, the London jeweller's name in gold on the satin: she could go in there, maybe and ask, if they could make her another? Hatton Garden. She had a bit of money in her own account: Tim gave her cash and she put some by some months. The earring was bigger than she remembered and the thought of cleaning out her savings made her sigh. Beside her Sue gave her a glance and hurriedly she squirrelled the box back down into the depths of her untidy handbag.

Head up. Eyes front. Another thought came to her: a long shot but. She could go back to the club and ask. That nice barman, ask him. Frank. Had that been his name or had she just made it up, because of Frank Sinatra? The idea settled her, it was almost a warm feeling, the thought of going in there and he'd smile, he'd remember her, the girl from Brockley Rise. He'd probably shake his head straight after, *sorry darling*, but somehow that didn't matter. He'd be nice.

And then there was the commotion of everyone getting up and they were leaving at last, eyes front.

At lunchtime with her lunchbox in front of her – ham and mustard, her favourite and because Tim was gone she'd put butter on too, but they tasted of sawdust

125

– Georgie was sitting on one of the playground benches bundled up against the new chill in her scarf when the phone rang. It was quiet because the children were inside eating, but soon they'd be out, shrieking and wheeling around her. The screen told her it was Tim. She snatched it up.

'Sweetheart,' he said. In that moment the word sounded odd on Tim's lips, it sounded soft and romantic and then things shifted and it was just one of those words he used for her.

'I'm on the motorway,' he said and Georgie heard the hollow sound that meant the phone was on speaker. Tim was always careful when he was driving. 'Sorry not to say goodbye,' he said, 'you were spark out.' Merrily. 'Snoring away.'

Georgie pushed her lunchbox aside. 'I wasn't,' she said, stupidly upset by the idea. She could imagine him, in the cream leather of his car's interior in his suit, laughing about her. Kindly – of course. Kindly. And then he *was* being kind. 'No, sweetheart, of course you weren't.' There was a silence, she said nothing to fill it, knowing she should laugh too. Then Tim said, 'I've been thinking.' When she still said nothing, *Sulking? Acting like a child*, but he didn't say that, 'Georgie?'

'Yes?' she said.

'You've been looking tired. I do notice, you know.'

'Have I?' She could hear herself, her voice faint, frightened.

'Well, not – still my beautiful wife of course, just – I thought I'd like to treat you. A weekend at a spa, something like that?' When she said nothing he kept going.

126

'I'd have Tabs or – or she could stay over with a friend again. One of those places with saunas and exercise machines, lovely healthy food, all that.'

Georgie's hand reached out for the lunchbox and she looked down into it, the yellow butter on her sandwich. 'Yes,' she said obediently. 'That'd be lovely. Thank you.' Automatically. She repeated it in her head, *so thoughtful, so considerate*, but she felt almost on the edge of tears at the thought.

The double doors to the hall burst open and they streamed out, a pack of boys breaking off with a football. She'd dreamed of Italian cities or Indian temples or blue seas, waking up in a sunlit bedroom with Tim, Tabs playing in the sand. She supposed it might be nice, a spa. Towelling dressing gowns and massage and diets. Maybe she would feel better after it. Maybe she'd come home glowing, and ready for the new start.

Tim's voice broke in. He was still talking, kind, solic-itous, but the subject had changed. 'Did something happen?' he said. 'When I was leaving I saw a dent on your car.'

'What? No – is there?' Georgie tried in panic to remember, where had she been in the car? Bumped against anything? Her mind was a blank.

'You didn't have a prang, did you? I mean, you're all right? You didn't say anything about it last night.' Concealing impatience, not too well.

'I – I didn't see a scratch,' she said. 'I don't – I didn't hit anything. Where? I mean where's the damage?'

Tim didn't seem to be listening. 'It probably won't need the whole panel replacing, a couple of hundred maybe, there's that place near the station—' She waited until he'd

127

finished. Tim wouldn't let her take the car in for repair, he always said they could see her coming. Listening and not listening, Georgie felt the approach of something she couldn't control, a sense of despair. How could she have dented the car? She hadn't.

Georgie looked at the children, the girls huddled together with bare legs and white socks, feeling a shiver just at the sight of them she pulled her coat around her.

The sky was almost clear. They said there might be a frost tonight.

Georgie searched the suddenly crowded playground for Tabs and for a second couldn't see her then there she was, running, the hood of her coat bouncing up and down. 'Darling?' said Tim, his voice suddenly sharp. 'Did you hear what I said?'

'Yes,' she said, 'yes.' And repeated back to him everything he'd said, until he was satisfied. She thought but didn't say, stubborn, *But I didn't dent the car. I'd know.*

There was a pause, then as if he knew what she'd been thinking, tentatively Tim said, 'I thought maybe it might have happened,' he hesitated, 'Saturday morning? I mean, coming home from London you were fairly . . . out of it? They do say the morning after a big night, you can still be . . .' he trailed off.

Georgie felt her mouth open, she hadn't driven Saturday morning, she'd got a taxi back – but she said nothing. 'Anyway,' said Tim, brightly, 'have a good day, sweetheart. I'll call again. See you Sunday evening.'

The text message came as Georgie was ushering them back inside: she was on the threshold, chilled to the bone after sitting so still and she felt it hum in her pocket. She knew it would be Tim, sending her the body-shop's number so she could fix a date for him to take the car in. She didn't remember scraping it against anything. It alarmed her. The thought that she might have been distracted, the thought that some malign neighbour, some teenager, might have wantonly damaged her car, the thought that Tim had it before she did. But then everything alarmed her, at the moment: she could almost hear Tim sigh. Worrying for her.

At her desk, Georgie got the phone out to look, only wondering at the last minute if it might actually not be from Tim – he was driving after all, he would never write a text at the wheel. Cat?

No. Not Tim, not Cat.

Sue had her back to her, feeding something into the photocopier. Georgie stood up, feeling herself flush hot, knowing any minute Sue would turn around again and look at her, and she had to turn and walk out of the office carefully, into the reception area, where the school library was, staring at the spines of the books then – then, she *dared* to look back at the message.

Something happened. Something *did* happen. How could Cat not have seen it, or Holly? *She* knew it, in her insides turning to water.

Did you like your flowers? Her heart turned over. The number wasn't recognised by her phone but she knew whose it was, already. Another message. We'll do it again, soon. M.

She remembered something, it was suddenly sharply in focus and in that moment she felt as if anyone could see, through the walls, Sue's head turning, just visible through

129

the reinforced glass panel in the school office door. M for Mark. She remembered him close up against her, in the hotel room, in the dark, or almost dark, holding her phone. He had her phone in his hand. That was how he had her number.

And then she knew. He had dialled his number from her phone, then handed it back to her. Clever. How clever. The phone clasped between her hands, held against her front, between her breasts, she stood very still. On the shelves of the little library the words on the books' titles jumped and blurred. *How Things Work.*

We'll do it again soon. That wasn't just being a gentleman. That wasn't just being polite, checking you got home safe. That was something new. Something not safe.

None of it had been safe, had it? From the minute she reached across Holly, holding her glass out to him. Asking for it.

'Georgie?'

Tomorrow she'd be in London.

It was Sue, standing in the school doorway looking at her, holding up one of the photocopied sheets. 'George?'

'Yes,' she managed. Dropping her hands as casually as she could, smiling mechanically. Phone in pocket.

'The return date on the school trip – has it been changed?'

Sue was looking at her oddly. Georgie knew she must be flushed, her whole body felt hot. Something told her she should sense danger and she did, she did. But it was as if she had been inoculated against it by something else, her system flooded with pleasure at this mad thought. And most of it down to their secret, the words on the

130

screen translated into his voice full of intimacy, *We'll do it again soon.*

Stop it. *Stop it.* School trip.

'Yes,' she said, calm and level. 'The centre wanted to add in an extra activity, canoeing, and they said they wouldn't charge for the last night so the price would remain the same.'

'Oh, right,' said Sue, but her body language, the sheet of paper held high between both hands, almost up to her mouth, her eyes over it still inquiring, said she knew something was off, something was happening.

Do what again?

Following Sue back into the office, suddenly small and crowded, Georgie sat. She had to fill out a form for uniform orders online: she looked from paper to screen, her fingers tapped. *White polo shirts, medium, times twelve. Sweatshirts with embroidered logo.* But the danger was still there, it wouldn't go away: it felt too good. She remembered details of him, his collar, the shape of his head, the feel of his suit. His hands – she remembered his hands, long-fingered. The sound of his deep voice, talking low just to her and the brush of his lips. Her fingers hovered over the keyboard, and she trembled.

Do what again?

Chapter Thirteen

Frank headed up east on the tube, a long way, then a walk from the tube, trees, hedges, big houses, birds singing and as foreign as Zanzibar to Frank. As he plodded he could see it in glimpses, down at the end of a street or beyond a stretch of dual carriageway, the big forest. Epping, a place of murders and satanic ritual, to believe his old mum, a wilderness to her. He found himself turning to search for it, disappointed when it wasn't there, when all there was was another neat terrace, stretching off, bay fronts as far as the eye could see. Epping Forest had trees older than the city, he had read somewhere, places to hide the bodies, swamp and all.

Eddie's house was big, ugly red brick at the top of a drive with a massive stained glass window, hideous to Frank's inner London eye but what did he know? It cost a fortune anyway but Eddie was smart, he'd have claimed it against the business somehow. Frank had been here a couple of times before, but never inside, just to pick Eddie up. He rang the doorbell, hearing the chimes, and saw a bulky shape behind the stained glass. Eddie stood there in slippers and a suit next to a stack of big removal boxes, looking him up and down. 'You take the scenic route?' It had been forty minutes, since he picked up the message – to get right out of London – but Frank knew better than to defend himself.

As he stepped across the threshold Frank could hear a shower going and caught Eddie's eye, unwillingly. Eddie winked. *Oh shit*, thought Frank. *Is this about Lucy?*

He kept a straight face. He stood there like a plank in the hallway, stiff with nerves. 'You never seen the place before, have you,' said Eddie, though it wasn't really a question. 'I'll give you the guided tour then, shall I? While her ladyship performs her toilette.' Eddie had a voice that was soft, like velvet. He went straight for the wide staircase and Frank had no choice but to follow.

The master bedroom was all pinks, the feminine touch like the eyelashes on Matteo, fooling no one. Over the bed was a big portrait in oils of Lucy, naked and of course Frank couldn't look anywhere else. Sitting up on the bed, elbow on one knee, looking straight at you. He gave the painter his due, it was Lucy, head-on stare and all. They'd been married five years: she must have been twenty-four or something. Frank stood there like stone, listening to the shower still going and Eddie just looking at him, laughing his head off inside: Frank could smell her perfume, the stuff she washed with.

He thought of Brockley Rise and getting the train to go fishing near Bromley with the old fellers and their rods. Hurtling around the school playground like a kid and the girls staring. He didn't want to be here.

'So what's the kitchen like?' he found himself saying, just to get out of there, and then Eddie *did* laugh.

What the kitchen was like was massive, and masculine where the bedroom was feminine: island in the middle, all granite and steel. There was nothing on the surfaces except an expensive coffee machine.

'What's the job, exactly?' Frank said, hands flat on the speckled granite surface as if it was the bar at the Cinq, brusque out of desperation. He could see Eddie's face go still and watchful but Frank felt it again, the sudden itch to get out of there. On cue, upstairs the drumming of the shower stopped. They looked at each other, him and Eddie, then Eddie said, 'Come on, then.'

It was the boxes, the ones he'd seen stacked in the hall. Eddie wanted them driving up to town and stored at the club. 'Some old papers,' he said though Frank had not asked. Of course he hadn't. Another wink. 'And just for the meantime, all right? Just temporary.'

Eddie fished in his pocket and handed the Jag's keys to Frank. 'Get going, then.'

He stood there in his slippers watching as Frank sweated, four boxes, and heavy. He could have had his driver take them up, Frank knew that. When he dropped the boot shut and turned Eddie wasn't in the doorway any more. He came inside shutting the door behind him quietly. Wary. He could see Eddie's slippered foot wagging in the living room, and could hear him, on the phone.

'Coffee, Frank?' Lucy's head came around the kitchen door, her voice bossy like a teacher's and Frank watched

134

her move, getting coffee out of a cupboard, filling the machine, knowing where everything was. He let out a breath warily, wondering what this was all about. He didn't usually get waited on by Lucy.

Eddie's voice murmured away, across the big hall. Both doors between them were standing open: if Frank took two steps, maybe three, across the kitchen's underheated stone floor, Eddie's nodding slippered foot would come into view. 'Milk?' Lucy twisted to look at him over her shoulder and her robe fell back, he could see her thigh. He shook his head. Swallowed.

As the machine rattled, grinding its beans and the smell – of morning, of breakfast and Soho, far away – filled up the big room, Frank didn't move. It was a test and he was going to pass it. How could Eddie still be talking? On and on. The coffee machine's noise stopped and suddenly Frank could hear Eddie's voice more clearly. 'No, no, mate,' he was saying, soft and persuasive, and despite himself Frank took a step towards the door. He'd never been curious about Eddie before: something had always told him, it wasn't a good idea. But he couldn't help himself now.

'Be patient, these things take time.' A business associate, but not quite business they were talking. Eddie didn't distinguish between friends and business acquaintances. Frank heard a low chuckle. Then, 'When he's done it we'll get together,' insinuating something. 'Get the girls together.'

At the coffee machine Lucy looked back at him over her shoulder and rolled her eyes.

Was it about sex? Eddie's conversation. That was what it sounded like. Sex was business too, for Eddie, he'd got other properties in Soho than the Cinq. They might be in someone else's name, Lucy's maybe, and at least one of them, Frank was fairly sure, was being used for immoral purposes, or whatever they called it.

Frank had always thought it wasn't his business and safest to go on thinking that way but something about sitting here in Eddie's kitchen was making him ponder it. How Eddie made his money. Why he'd brought Frank here: it felt like he was being shown something, or told something, or warned off something. Off Lucy? No need for that.

And there on cue was Lucy, coming round him, setting down the coffee he didn't want. And she sat herself, ladylike, opposite Frank, one leg up on the stool he sat on and then her robe fell open and she leaned toward him to put her hand on him, and ladylike was a thing of the past.

In a hurry Frank got off the stool and took two steps, three, away from her. She leaned back against the breakfast bar, amused. Crossing her legs and taking her time adjusting the robe.

Frank didn't know what her game was. Jealousy? Not Lucy. But then why had she mentioned to Eddie that he'd been chatting up a customer? For a second he wondered if Matteo might have mentioned his questions already, about the women, to Eddie or to Lucy – though why would he? – that everything had felt different since he'd taken an interest in what happened to those women, Friday night.

Eddie murmured on, his voice fainter now because Frank, putting a safe distance between him and Lucy, was at the window, looking out into their back garden. A marble statue of a naked girl holding her boobs. With an effort, Frank made himself focus.

'What's Eddie talking about?' Asking out of desperation, to change the subject, work out what you've got yourself into. Something to do with feeling trapped here. The more information, the better, when you were under threat, even if you couldn't work out where the threat was.

'I don't know who it is,' said Lucy, not moving from the breakfast bar, cupping her chin between her hands. 'Someone he's doing a favour for.' When Frank stayed where he was she straightened, shrugging. 'You know Eddie, always doing a favour here and there.'

And then the door opened behind her and there was Eddie, looking preoccupied.

'Good coffee?' he said, looking from Lucy at the bar to Frank in the window, a faint smile appearing. He knew all right.

'Better get that lot shifted, then,' Frank said, and he was out the door.

He could feel Eddie's eyes on him as he turned out of the drive into the avenue, spinning the wheels on the gravel, just wanting to get out of there.

At the end of the road, waiting to turn, he came face to face with the tangle of woodland, a stream of cars passing. Frank had to be patient, gazing at the old trees, not knowing their names. And then his thoughts shifted, with the memory of Eddie's voice, dry and sceptical, to the phone call. *Get the girls together.*

There was a gap in the traffic and Frank pulled out, smooth as he could manage, trying to keep it all under control, just like he'd been trying and failing to do all day, and as he straightened the long car, took his foot off the gas, it dawned on him. He had cameras in that house, Eddie did, security or whatever. Spy cameras, for security – or so he knew what Lucy was up to. It would explain the smile. Set up.

Frank heard himself make an impatient sound and reached to click on the radio: some classical station, that was Eddie, showing his class. Clicked it off again. Alongside him the woodland ran on, dusty, mysterious and empty and then to his relief a junction came into view, a blue sign for the motorway and he told himself, *Get a grip*. Why would he care, anyway? He joined the traffic, eight lanes of it.

Should have waved, after, a cheery wave to Eddie and Lucy? He hadn't touched her. She'd touched him. But all the same, he felt like he'd been set up.

Do what you're told: if he wants you to put the boxes in the club or if he wants you to chuck them in the Thames then just do it. All women are the same, none of them is worth it and stop asking questions.

Message received.

Georgie was lying on the sofa in her oldest jeans with a drink, bare feet up, radio on. A glass of nice cold white wine balancing on her belly. She still wasn't hungry. Which was strange because all her life she couldn't remember ever not being hungry. Once when she'd been nine or ten she'd spent her money on a loaf of bread hot out of the baker's and thought she could eat it all. Now leaning back on the sofa, stretching her toes, she tried to remember the cravings. Toast with butter, always taking one more bit. Tim wasn't interested in food: he ate cereal with skimmed milk, every morning, mechanically, then the bowl straight into the dishwasher.

The morning after Tabs had been born Georgie had been ravenous. Dad had brought a bunch of roses and iced buns in a paper bag to the hospital and she could remember licking the sugar from her fingers while she fed Tabs. Tim had brought magazines, slick and shiny, that had kept falling on to the floor from the bed until the man who brought round the tea took them away and put them in the visitors' room.

Coming in with Tabs after school and knowing he wasn't there, seeing her drop her things carelessly on the floor, Georgie had just stood there not picking them up and for a moment it was like watching grass grow long. The house shifting around them. A garden without a gardener.

There was a cottage on the corner near the church, on the edge of the forest, where until a couple of years back an old lady had lived: spry, solid, cheerful, with a little dog and a very neatly tended front garden. The dog had been old, greying round his muzzle, and then he'd died. One day, pushing Tabs past in the buggy Georgie had seen the old lady just standing there, looking lost without the dog. May or Mary she'd been called, something like that. And a month later she'd died herself, and within weeks, days, even the garden had changed, the small lawn not velvet any more but ever so slightly shaggy, the browning heads of roses unclipped, dandelions springing up in the gravel path.

Someone had bought the house and tarmacked the garden and now there was a huge car parked in front of the cottage, obscuring the downstairs windows. Lying on the sofa Georgie tried to think why she had thought of that cottage. Things change, was that it? People move on, move out, move in: this might not be her house for ever. Their house. All she could think now was, the view from the old lady's front room would be of the owner's car.

She'd picked up Tabs' school bag and gone upstairs to get the discarded uniform, put on the wash. But everything had been done more slowly, leisurely. It didn't matter if the grass grew a bit longer, did it? If a dropped sock lay in the hall half an hour before she noticed it. Georgie lay her head back on the arm of the sofa and set the glass down carefully on the carpet. On the wall the clock said 6.59 and if Tim was here he'd be reaching for the remote to turn on the news.

She'd read Tabs her goodnight story: she might be back down, there might be the patter of feet but she had seemed sleepy, a wide luxurious smile after Georgie's kiss good-night, at the thought of the weekend just the two of them. In the kitchen the radio played some seventies tune.

The clock's hand moved and on cue somewhere underneath Georgie on the sofa her phone buzzed. Someone was calling her, but the wine had taken the edge off, she sighed, sat up, groped for it. Tim.

'Hey,' she said, a little light-headed.

'Sweetheart!' Tim sounded buzzy, like he was having fun. 'Just checking in.' In a bar: she could hear glasses chinking.

'You got there safely, then?' she said, pointlessly.

'You still planning on going up to town tomorrow?' he said, as if he hadn't heard. 'I've been thinking, you really ought to. You don't need to just – just sit around waiting for me to get back. Have some fun at the zoo.' Georgie lay back again, let her hand fall so it touched the glass on the floor.

'Yes,' she said. 'Yes. I think I – I think we will.'

Running the bath for Tabs an hour earlier she had been sure they wouldn't. Tentatively she'd started to say, with Tabs standing there in her vest, hopping from foot to foot. 'I thought tomorrow maybe—' But she didn't get a chance to finish.

'The zoo, Mummy, yes, yes. I told Lydia we were going.' She'd obviously picked up on it from yesterday and played it cleverly, biding her time. Thinking about it all day.

Georgie had leaned down, testing the water, straightening back up before proceeding, cautiously. 'Maybe we could go and see Granddad too,' and now Tabs was jumping, jumping for joy. 'Yesyesyes, Granddad!' she said, pulling off her vest and clambering into the bath, singing at the top of her voice.

Beside the tub Georgie had sat back on her heels. Suddenly it felt easier, it felt safer. See Dad, a cup of tea and a bun in some old café somewhere. She'd call him in the morning.

'Tabs can't wait,' she said now. But Tim had moved on; Georgie half listened as he talked about the conference programme for tomorrow, a lot of detail she didn't need and perhaps it was the wine but she found herself wondering, *Why does he think I'd be interested?* Because she should be. Because he was her husband.

141

'And you called the garage?' That registered. Georgie sat up quickly and the wine slopped in the glass. 'I – yes – no—' she said. Improvising, because she had forgotten. 'That is, they said call back on Monday.'

Tim clicked his tongue, the sound of dissatisfaction. The wine had gone on her hand, she could smell it. 'I see,' he said. 'Friday night, get off early.'

'Well,' said Georgie, and she leaned down and licked the wine from the pad of her thumb. Not thinking. 'It's Friday night for all of us, isn't it?' And then a silence. She heard a slow intake of breath and waited for him to say it. *It's not a bloody holiday, you know.* But he didn't. Sighed, instead.

'Well, you just have fun, darling,' he said, and his voice was soft, now. Behind him she could hear the hum of voices, glasses chinking. Someone laughed, a woman's voice. 'Better go,' said Tim. A pause. 'Sleep well.'

Putting the phone aside Georgie got up from the sofa on stiff legs. Looking down, to her surprise she saw that her glass was empty, and in the kitchen the music was still playing. She wandered in there, barefoot, poured herself some more and set it on the side carefully. Swaying – she liked this song – she could see herself reflected in the glass door, darkness beyond it. She moved her hips and lifted her arms, nodding.

What would Tim do if he could see her? She turned, arms up, feet knowing where to go, from memory. Put his hands on her hips and move with her? He'd never done that: Tim didn't like dancing, it made him uncomfortable, but most men were like that. Except the ones who practised, the man in the hat twirling her in the dark. The barman silhouetted against his rows of bottles watching. And *him*. He hadn't danced with her, but he had liked looking.

She turned again, looking for her reflection and in silhouette she looked almost graceful even in her old jeans, almost — what was the thing she most wanted to be? — willowy. And then something else moved beyond her reflection, further off, a flicker of white, and Georgie stopped. The song sounded tinny suddenly, and all the grace seemed to drain out of her, she felt cold and stiff. Stepping up to the window she looked, hands flat against the glass. A cat in the garden or a pale branch moving — or just her imagination.

Imagining being looked at: that was what she'd been doing, after all. There *was* a bit of wind: she peered closer. She could see the big philadelphus moving at the back, her ear to the glass she could hear it, even. There was no curtain she could close, but she switched off the light, instead, and the radio sang on, in the half dark. Leaving her drink on the side, she slipped through the door and ran on quick feet upstairs, to the bedroom. Left the light off.

The wardrobe door was open, Tim's suits hanging there in the dark, a smell of dry cleaning from them. It was open because she'd been looking at her little section, wondering what to wear tomorrow. Her soft-coloured cashmere jumpers — Tim got her one every Christmas — raspberry and apricot and rose, hadn't seemed quite right, then Tabs had called her to get her out of the bath and she'd forgotten to close the doors again.

Now Georgie went noiselessly past the suits to the

143

window and stood, just off to one side, looking down into the back garden.

Once her eyes adjusted to the light it looked as usual: neat and empty. The heavy wooden table and chairs, the big terracotta pots, the cropped grass. Tim would be better at looking: he could see a cigarette butt in the lawn from thirty feet away, when the nice Hungarian man who laid the patio had left one in a plant pot Tim had got them to take thirty quid off the bill. The big shrubs along the back of the garden didn't look any different, no branches broken, their carefully trimmed shapes intact. Behind them was the six-foot fence: Georgie could go and inspect in the morning, but she knew it was just her imagination. She wouldn't even mention it to Tim – well, of course she wouldn't.

The list of things she wouldn't mention to Tim seemed to be getting longer and longer: the thought simultaneously frightened Georgie and made her want to laugh. And made her remember something: the garage. She could call in the morning, they were there Saturday mornings, she knew that even if Tim didn't. And then she found she wanted to see this dent, this famous dent, that Tim had noticed and she hadn't.

Outside on the front path in bare feet and jeans, she shivered: maybe it was the wine but the long warm autumn wasn't warm any more. The car sat there on the drive, the perky sensible little car Tim had chosen – well, they'd chosen it together, really. For the fuel consumption, or whatever. It was white – so he could see her coming, he said, the safest colour for a car to be according to the surveys although secretly she'd have liked something chic and dark, like navy blue.

Georgie came alongside it, running her hand over the bodywork – where had he said it was? She should have brought a torch, maybe, she couldn't see much but the light at the street corner had come on and there was the tiniest bit of light left in the sky even though it was getting late. Long shadows, from the neighbour's hedge, the neighbour she still hardly knew to talk to after five years, shadows from the two round bushes at the end of the drive. She held her wristwatch up to catch what light there was and saw that it was almost nine: she wondered at how much time seemed to have passed since Tim phoned, it unnerved her. Left alone, without Tim inside watching the news and reloading the dishwasher, time seemed to have turned more fluid. Flexible.

Maybe that was it, the thought came to her as she felt the smooth cold metal of the car's wing under her hand, that night out with the girls, it had just been the unfamiliarity of being without Tim, then staying up most of the night. Maybe that was what had turned things uncertain, in her memory. She let the thought move on and out the other side, not worth dwelling on. Maybe she would finish that glass of wine when she got back in.

And then she stopped because she felt it before she saw it. Much more than a scratch: she had imagined someone knocking against the car while it was parked, or at most keying it, although this wasn't the kind of car vandals picked on. She stepped back to get a better look then remembered her phone, in her jeans pocket and held the glowing screen up to the place. Rear door, passenger side, a proper dent and scrape about six inches long, requiring force, a flake of red paint against the silver: it

145

wasn't a question of someone keying it. Georgie felt herself sway, unsteady with disbelief.

She didn't remember doing that. Not at all. She swallowed, feeling tonight's booze in her system.

Stepping back from the car Georgie looked at the dent, where it was, halfway down the body work, just beyond the passenger door. Odd. Something odd about where it was. A low bollard? Bollards weren't painted red.

She tried to think when she'd last used the car. Driving to the florist's, yesterday? She couldn't remember that for sure, either. She'd been in a state, it was true but this – this. It would have been loud. She'd have heard it. Tabs had been in the car too, and she'd have heard it. Slowly Georgie put the phone back into her pocket: the dark shadows of the drive seemed longer suddenly. And then she turned and ran, light on bare feet, back in, back inside her house because if she hadn't noticed that scrape then what else? What else? Someone might have slipped inside, behind her.

Once back in she downed the wine without thinking and put the glass in the dishwasher, set it going though it was only half full. She checked the back door, the wide glass sliding doors of the sitting room, then paced the house quickly, quietly, from room to room, under the little lights of Tim's systems, the thermostats and security monitors and sensors that should reassure her but didn't, not quite. Her heart bumping.

Of course there was no one there. Of course. Georgie came to a stop at Tabs' room, pushing gently at the door and standing in the doorway. And there she lay in bed, curled like a dormouse in a swirl of duvet and cushions, mouth half open in sleep, precious and golden in the glow of her nightlight. All around them the house was quiet.

Georgie took a pill. She hadn't done that in three years. She thought about taking two, and decided against it. Even opening the little medicine box and seeing the packet churned her: an episode, not long, when Tabs had been one or so and Mum had finally died after all those years getting less and less recognisable, six months or so when everything had panicked her. Everything had frightened her. She'd been good about it, though. She'd done her research, she'd stopped taking the pills when they advised it even though Tim had reassured her, another month or so wouldn't do any harm and look how much better they made everything. He'd been kind.

It didn't take long before she felt things soften, as if the house was growing warmer around her. Georgie opened her drawer in the wall of drawers and compartments and hanging space to look for something to wear in bed and took out the pretty slip, silk and lace, that she'd worn in London and pulled it over her head. In the soft dark of the room, alone, it slipped down and settled on her and it felt just the right thing, not too warm, not too bare. She closed the doors carefully on the shelves and drawers and the row of dark expensive suits and slipped into the cool bed, luxuriously alone.

Drifting, only half listening now to the sounds that reached her, the rustle of cats in the undergrowth, a hum of far-off traffic, the clicks and ticks of the house talking to itself, closing down, it was the feel of the suits that came back to her, and Tim, on their wedding day.

Clean-shaven and bright-eyed in a pearl-grey morning

suit with tails, a top hat, although they'd been twenty-four and twenty-six respectively. Dad as smart as he could manage, aghast at the sight of the limo and the flowers and Tim, specially Tim, with Dad in his best suit that was shiny at the elbows and a frayed tie. Mum in the care home and long past any of it, they couldn't even get her out of the bed most days so he'd been on his own.

Ten, twelve years ago, they'd been so young: but Tim had pressed ahead, eager. He had been infatuated with her, it occurred to her now, dreamy on the pillow in her silk slip. Behind her eyelids the memories flickered, the feeling came back to her, excited and awed and anxious, of how it had been to be on the receiving end. It didn't seem so hard to believe in that warm encouraging quiet, lying there with her eyes closed. He'd been obsessed with what she wore, the make-up she put on: he had wanted sex every night, twice a night, he had wanted to be married. And he'd wanted them to try again. For a baby. In the bed Georgie shifted, feeling heat, unease.

Nowadays she heard Tim tut over couples who went into marriage without pre-nups, when he saw the after-math in his clients' accounts – but he'd never asked for one when they got married. Tim Mr Organised, Mr Professional, Mr Practical. In the dark Georgie turned over on her side, wondering. If they got married now, would he ask for one? Life was long. Marriage had to last a long time.

Georgie slept.

In the Cinq they were crowded up against the bar four deep, and even Dom was moving at something like normal

148

speed, on the edge of flustered as he leaned across from pouring four Old Fashioneds to flick on to the late night playlist on his laptop. Friday night and no time to think.

Sometimes Frank wondered where they got their money from. Eleven quid a cocktail, a hundred quid minimum just on drinks, and they weren't trust fund babies, they were anyone and everyone. Kids from the suburbs, from further out, Southend. Kids living in dodgy rentals on main roads. They weren't buying houses, they were living instead and when the living ran out – well. No one knew what happened then.

Shut up and pour. Ours is not to reason why. Frank's shoulder ached from reaching up to the optics and he could feel the sweat dampening his shirt, under the suit. He'd taken off his tie: that much was allowed. Even Sinatra had taken off his tie when things got hot. Frank Sinatra, cool as a cucumber, his vest visible through his shirt like any Italian old-timer.

He'd stashed the boxes down the corridor, under the velvet curtain where they concealed the spirits. They'd weighed a ton: *files*, Eddie had said.

Lucy hadn't said a word to him, but he'd been working hard avoiding her: he didn't know what her game was, or their game, hers and Eddie's – but it was trouble. Frank found himself scanning newcomers, turning every time the curtain at the door was pulled back, in case they returned.

It was only Georgie from Brockley Rise he wanted to see again, only her that tugged at him. The memory of the afternoon in Eddie's kitchen, taken for a mug – it felt to him like only she could wipe that out. Maybe it was all about just wanting to be a kid again, in those streets, ducking when the girl you liked turned the corner. Starting over.

They didn't come back in, of course.

The call came just after midnight: if she'd taken two pills, it occurred to Georgie groggily, surfacing, she'd never have heard it. As it was she had to grope for her jeans on the floor, where the phone was buzzing angrily in the pocket.

It was Holly. Disorientated, Georgie registered a lot of background noise, as if Holly was in a bar somewhere, or a party. A high pitch of noise, too, excitable people. 'Hey babe,' Holly shouted into the phone, too loud, too loose, then immediately broke off to answer someone calling across the room.

Flopping back on the pillow, Georgie waited, woozy still, and a memory came back to her – with the sound of Holly's bright, excitable voice – of long, long ago, when they'd worked together. Holly coming down after the weekends and someone rolling their eyes, ostentatiously rubbing at their nose as she snapped and dozed at her desk. Coke – well, Georgie supposed everyone took it these days, except her that is, except her and Tim. Maybe even little Lydia the personal assistant took it, perky little Lydia with her yellow car. Cocaine. Why had she thought of Lydia? Everything jumbled in her brain, she must have been deep asleep.

'Holly?' she said, and Holly was back again.

'It's you phoned me, remember, sweetheart,' she said, loud. 'No need for that tone, I don't think.'

'I didn't – what tone?' said Georgie, feeling things

150

sharpen, anxiety nibbling at the edges. Holly so spiky, her world was another world. This was a mistake. She'd been dreaming, she couldn't remember what, then she could. A warm soft dream of sex. 'I called you yesterday.'

'Yeah, sorry about that – it's just – hold on a minute.' A muffling of the receiver and then, 'That better?' The background noise had gone, as if Holly had left the party. Out on a balcony or something, at a back door with the smokers.

'Sorry, darling,' Holly said, defiant, then sighed. 'So—' sighing, 'it sounded important.' A silence. 'What's been going on?'

'Oh, just, nothing, just—' Georgie felt stupid suddenly.

'It was fun, wasn't it?' said Holly, lowering her voice as if it was a secret. Dark and sexy and mysterious, their secret. 'Our girls' night out. We should do that again.'

'That's what he said,' said Georgie, before she could think. Holly pounced.

'Oh he did, did he? What was his name again? Martin? Something like that, right?' She hadn't needed to ask who. 'Well, you did get along, didn't you?'

Holly hadn't mentioned Tim – neither of them had. An alternative universe presented itself, in which Georgie was a free spirit. This was just a game, a fantasy. Nothing was going to happen. A man sending her flowers.

'Mark,' and she had given in. She was playing the game. Even more, maybe, because it had an edge of danger. 'He – he's called Mark.'

Holly let out a breath, a tiny sound, but distinct, of satisfaction.

'He sent me flowers,' Georgie said.

151

'Oh, did he, now?' Was it her imagination, or did Holly sound almost envious? 'An admirer. You dark horse, you, Georgie.' Then a sigh. 'No one sends me flowers.'

Georgie sat upright on the pillow. 'I bet they do,' she said, and was rewarded with a throaty laugh.

'Well,' said Holly, pensive, 'I have my moments. But come on, tell me.' Lowering her voice. 'Was there a message with them?'

Georgie felt herself blush. 'Nothing – nothing much. Just – saying he couldn't stop thinking about me.' Was that what he'd said? She had a moment of panic, wondering what she'd done with the note before she remembered. Safe in her coat pocket. She shouldn't be saying this. Talking about it made it real.

'Oh, well, that's not nothing,' said Holly. 'That's nice. Isn't it? I mean, of course you're gorgeous—' hesitating, as if she knew that wasn't the right word for Georgie, 'but I'd be flattered.'

'Oh, yes, well—' said Georgie. That wasn't quite it, though, was it? More than flattered. She could feel it even now, the warmth uncurling in her, the flutter of excitement. 'I – it's just that—' and now she had her opportunity, she wasn't sure if she wanted to ask. 'It's just that I can't really remember a thing about him.' Lamely. And it wasn't true, either. She could remember things. Too many. How his hand had felt. The flutter beat strong inside her.

'Come on,' said Holly, 'he was talking to you all evening. Don't remember that? He seemed really into you. You were cool as a cucumber.'

'Really?' Georgie could hear herself, sounding ridiculously

eager, ridiculously pleased. She was just relieved she hadn't behaved like an idiot, that was all.

'Well, until you let him into the cab,' said Holly.

'It *was* me, then,' said Georgie, stupidly, not cool as a cucumber after all and that feeling ebbing, that warm feeling.

'Well, I suppose it was all of us,' said Holly airily, 'but you were the last one in and he just climbed in after you.' She paused. 'We laughed, didn't we?'

Deflated, Georgie did remember that. Remembered shifting up to make room for him. Did that make it her fault? She remembered the laughing, as if they had all been in on it, it was all of them together, it wasn't just Georgie. Laughing at his cheek, his insouciance. Cat sinking back on the seat, flapping a hand, tired.

'So—' Holly moved on, swift, 'flowers, though, that sounds like fun.' Expectant.

Georgie hesitated. 'He called me. A couple of days ago, just to say—' she faltered. It didn't sound innocent now. 'To ask if I was OK.'

'Sweet,' said Holly. 'So you gave him your number, then.' She laughed. 'Georgie, you really are a dark horse.'

'No – I—' but Georgie hesitated. Explaining it, how he had got her number, his *trick*, was the only word for it, made her look such a fool. An innocent. And she was almost enjoying Holly's disbelief; her admiration. It was all a game.

And Holly was impatient, anyway. 'So did you answer?'

'Of course not,' said Georgie.

Holly laughed that big laugh again, as if she knew exactly what Georgie was thinking. That she'd wanted to.

153

'No? Oh, well, please yourself but it's still fun, isn't it? Life's too bloody short.'

It was what Cat had said. For a second Cat filled Georgie's head, Cat making a weekend of it, letting her hair down, before she had to face weeks, months, of appointments, of being frightened. *Life's too short.* Georgie wondered if she'd told Holly about the cancer, but she said nothing. She didn't want to talk about it behind Cat's back, to make it gossip. But Holly had moved on again, Georgie had a sudden vivid impression of Holly in motion, always with a suitcase in her hand on some doorstep or other.

'So,' she was saying. 'You're in London tomorrow, right? Shall we have a coffee or something, I'd like to meet your – your kid. Daughter?'

'Um, yes,' said Georgie warily wondering about Tabs meeting Holly. 'Sure, shall I call you in the morning?' Remembering she needed to call Dad, first. 'Or we could just fix a time now? A place?'

Holly named a café, north of Oxford Street. 'Let's say I'll be there at five,' airily again. 'It's sometimes hard to get me on the phone.' There was a hesitation. 'Just—' Holly began, then seemed to change her mind. 'Look, I'd better go. See you tomorrow.' And had hung up.

It took a while for Georgie to get back to sleep, although it was quiet outside now, she couldn't even hear the distant hum of traffic that in the day was a constant. She thought of the wide dark forest between her and the big motorway circling the city, strung with lights. The grey suburbs, the arterial roads swooping between terraces, heading for the centre, traffic lights obediently turning green, amber, red, in deserted streets. High rises giving way to grand white

154

stucco parades, the animals in the zoo pacing at night. Closer in and there were those crowded narrow streets, the signs still in windows, *Model, third floor*, men sitting outside coffee bars, baggy-eyed with sleeplessness, the streets still busy even at two in the morning. She'd seen all that, that night, from the taxi, driving back to the hotel and never knew she remembered it till now. She thought of him.

Where had he come from? Mark. Where did he live? Restless on the pillow Georgie had no idea. He knew where *she* was, or where she worked, at least. He could look at the village on the internet from a satellite image, he could see the gleaming slate of the church roof, he could note where the woodland gave way to neat developments; he could zoom in, he could walk the lanes with two fingers on a screen.

London was different. A big place, London. A tangle of rooftops, heading off at all angles, alleys and basements and places to hide, crowds to disappear in. And out of the blue, thinking of the busy streets, Georgie felt a throb of pure happiness: London was where she'd been born, on the long swooping terrace of red brick and cherry trees with Crystal Palace radio mast at the top of it where Dad had still lived till two years ago. And suddenly ten years out here in the sticks seemed like nothing at all. Georgie could see Tabs on their way to the zoo, holding her hand looking up at terraced windows, at buses, her head turning this way and that way, looking at the dogs cocking their legs, old men muttering to themselves, the upturned boxes of Turkish bread and plantain and Chinese cabbage spilling out on to the grubby pavements.

155

The feeling wasn't a sleepy one, it was excitement, it was longing. Closing her eyes Georgie tried to back pedal, to find her life again, her comfortable quiet life with designer bathroom and cupboards for everything and a patio and a barbecue and *all that wonderful green*. Garden and churchyard and woods beyond. It was what Tim's mother had said, approving, when they packed up to leave London and their married life. *So good for the child*. She always called Tabs that. Dad had been encouraging too but with a different expression, anxious, and Tim had said, heartily, nudging him with his shoulder, 'We're not talking the Amazon jungle, Jack.' Dad had looked down at his feet, wanting to be happy for her.

My home, thought Georgie in the dark inside her head, settling on the kitchen because if any of it was hers *that* was but it was no good, the surfaces remained smooth and empty, where the kitchen she grew up in had been cluttered to every corner. The house felt alien, her and Tabs adrift in an alien suburb.

That was the image that sent her to sleep in the end, the two of them holding hands in a boat bobbing on a wide sea, a silver horizon, the white crests of waves. But somewhere in the night Tabs was gone, the boat was gone and Georgie was alone in the dark outside. She was running her hand over a scratch on the side of her car as if it was Braille and she was blind. Red flakes of paint on her hand. She tried and tried, because it was there somewhere, but she couldn't read the message.

Chapter Fourteen

Saturday

Frank was woken by sirens. There were always some, Friday night, Saturday night, any night at all but that particular twenty-four, forty-eight hours in Soho was busy with crime, most of it petty. Drunk and disorderly, a bit of light thieving. The room was cold but light dazzled through the blinds and Frank raised a lazy hand to cover his eyes. Wearily he turned, fumbling for his phone to see the time.

Too late – or too early – for this many sirens. There was usually a squad car or two parked up just waiting for the trouble even though most of the real violence in Frank's experience took place further out, on the periphery of the city, stabbings and that, gang stuff. Tottenham or Walthamstow or Streatham, off those long arterial roads. Dangerous places. Soho was busy, it was safe.

But this morning the sound was close by, slowing to a *whup, whup*, and it wasn't going away. Eight, was it? Frank squinted down at the phone. He hadn't got to bed till three. They were very close: he could hear the crackle of walkie talkies. The other siren that meant an ambulance. He set the phone back face down, fumbled for the earplugs he kept on the bedside table and turned over, burying his face in the pillow. Back to sleep.

The day looked different: it sparkled with frost. The windows were all double-glazed so the house felt the same, warm, but there was light everywhere, bleaching the hall white, flooding the kitchen as Georgie stood, there, remembering it. Last night. The grass of the back lawn glittered in the early light, the birdfeeder was dusted white.

Tabs had woken her at seven, clambering into the bed, her sweet-sour morning breath on Georgie's cheek. Tim had a rule about Tabs and their big bed: Christmas and birthday mornings only, and then grudgingly. Then he would be out and gathering wrapping paper within minutes, leaving it to the two of them.

'Mummy!' Tabs had said this morning, gleeful, when Georgie threw back the covers and Georgie hadn't known what she meant, until she looked down. Nothing dramatic, a dusting of dirt on the sheets – and a trace of mud between Georgie's toes. She'd been out barefoot, though, she hadn't washed her feet afterwards. She'd drunk two – three? – glasses of wine. None of this was normal, and Tabs knew it.

She found herself thinking back: Tim's birthday this year he'd been away, a golfing weekend. He had asked Georgie too and she'd pretended to give it some thought but she had known what he wanted was peace and quiet, man space – and one mention of the networking possibilities had been enough to get her shaking her head, blushing at the offer. It had been May, it had rained all

158

weekend but he had returned with his spirits undented and Georgie had been happy. It was hard to please him on his birthday: she'd lost count of the cufflinks and ties she'd had to return.

'I know!' she'd said to Tabs, pulling her to her side, warm and compact, all coiled excitement ready to go. 'I forgot I'd been out in my bare feet. Better get this changed before Daddy gets home. You go and choose what to wear.' She began to pull off the sheets, weary. Stupid: the last thing she needed. But she should have thought.

When it was done and the old sheets turning in the washing machine, she'd gone into Tabs' room. She'd been suspiciously quiet.

The bed had been heaped with crop tops and shorts, Tabs equating a single day out with the whole summer holidays. 'Tabs,' she said, 'it's freezing out there. Haven't you looked out of your window?' Tabs made a face, refusing to come. They compromised on shorts over woollen tights, a madly clashing jumper half a size too small for her, a bomber jacket Dad had bought her: all the things Tim would have put his foot down over.

She waited to phone Dad. He didn't get up till nine: his treat, he always said, but sadly. When Mum had been alive – well, when she'd been herself, still Mum and not forgetting where the kettle was or who it was in the bed next to her – she'd be up at seven every morning to make a pot of tea whether Dad was awake or not.

'George!' He fussed, lost for words, delighted. It sounded so quiet, where he was: they'd been there a few times, her and Tabs, before he moved in and then after and it was nice. A little world that suited it. A two-room

159

bungalow in a tiny church close. It wasn't home – but then that was probably just as well. He had lost interest in everything after Mum had gone and home had been dusty, bags piling up, windows unwashed. He shied away from touching any of it. 'Really? Really? Well, I can get to the zoo in – let me see—'

They fixed on an early lunch, and the zoo. Ten years older than Mum, he'd always thought he'd outlive her. He'd be tired after, Georgie knew: they'd pay for a taxi home for him. She tried not to think about five o'clock, and tea with Holly but Holly was there, intrusive, bright as a parakeet, nosy and knowing.

When she'd put the phone down Georgie turned to see Tabs all ready, backpack on, hugging herself at the thought of seeing her granddad. *We should be able to do this every week*, thought Georgie. *Why don't we?*

They'd drive to the station, then take the train, it was decided. Georgie had decided. With Tabs strapped in, her backpack on her knee, coming back around the wing of the car, where the scrape was, Georgie hesitated. Bending she couldn't see the red flake of paint any more and didn't know if she'd dreamed it, or it had been dislodged in the night.

She'd had a car accident once only in her life, almost ten years before and it hadn't been serious, but she still remembered it. Coming round the rear of a bus in pouring rain, barely moving, the bus had somehow shifted and forced the wing mirror back into the quarter light: there'd been an explosion of glass into the car and she'd stopped, stunned. The noise of it.

Cat had been with her in the car, in London, they'd

been on their way somewhere. Shopping? She couldn't remember. But she could remember the noise. The startling loudness, the shock. In the pouring rain Cat had looked after her, told her what to do. *Indicate, stop here.* She'd driven back home so slowly she got hooted at at every junction but she had paid no attention and when they got there Cat had explained to Tim what had happened, that it hadn't been her fault, while he stood there white-lipped. 'Never mind,' he'd said, but she knew if Cat hadn't been there it would have been something different.

Putting out her hand to the scratch, Georgie knew she hadn't done it. Had someone driven into the car, while it was parked on their drive, then driven off? She couldn't imagine it – but it was possible. The nearest house was twenty feet away, the hedges between the houses were well grown, because Tim liked his privacy. An accident, then. Under her hand the car moved, Tabs wriggling and bouncing for her attention, craning her neck. Georgie could see her mouthing something through the rear window and the other possibility materialised: the one that said, it might *not* have been an accident. She looked down and in the same second pulled her hand back, as if the car was hot.

As if she *had* had an accident, Georgie drove as slowly as she had all that time ago, carefully, the big modern houses sliding past them, the thatched cottage, hedges, the woodland. Past the church. *All that wonderful green.* It had turned overnight, with the cold, it blazed with red and orange. Could someone out here have it in for her? For them? For *Tim*? She settled on that thought, it seemed easiest. Because he was a man? And she was a woman

161

who worked in the school office and tried very hard not to upset anyone, ever. Who could have it in for her? Those women who whispered about her in the harvest festival?

The sign for the station came into view and the turning took them away from the forest, but oddly, somehow she could feel it behind her. She imagined the leaves crunching underfoot in the cold, the smell of the leaf mould and dirt, the knotted roots and cobwebs in the air. *Mirror, signal, manoeuvre.* The station car park was half empty because it was Saturday. She could see a couple of figures on the platform through the picket fence. Turned to unbuckle Tabs and told her to wait, while she got the parking ticket. At the machine she was still going through the motions, *whole day parking*, inserted her credit card, PIN code.

But she was thinking about something else. Could someone have it in for them, really? She made herself consider Tim's work. The neat two-storey house in the town with its forecourt and its receptionist, nothing to scare the horses, the reception area with water cooler and copies of *Country Life*. Could a tax accountant make enemies? She turned and walked back to the car, and for a second her heart jumped and raced, because there was someone in the car, someone she didn't know – and then she stopped, subsiding because it was Tabs. Of course it was, just Tabs gurning, pressing her face against the glass, little hands like starfish either side of it.

A couple of years back there'd been legislation, obliging accountants, like lawyers, to report wrongdoing to the authorities. Georgie remembered Tim scornful of it, *as if*. Accountants did know plenty; they knew about the money.

Idly she thought, *I wonder.* Tim's office, the filing cabinet

162

he kept locked. If he was in trouble, she could help him. He hadn't sounded like he was in trouble, on the phone last night.

'Come on,' she said to Tabs, helping her out of the car. Holding her hand to cross the car park, she looked back. The little white car looked so modest, so anonymous, not flash at all.

They hurried on. Why not dent Tim's car? Key it in the car park of the office? If it was just a warning, or vindictive? At the ticket window she gripped Tabs' hand. She was an easier target, maybe. It felt like it, out here: she couldn't wait till they were on the train.

There was no one she knew in their compartment: although they'd been the only ones to get on at their stop – Georgie looked up and down to make sure, then settled them at a little table. It was half empty. Five minutes into the journey, her mobile rang: Tabs barely looked up from her colouring book, earbuds in and listening to her music.

'Cat!' For some reason Georgie felt false, guilty. The natural thing to do would be to tell Cat what they were doing. She should tell them they were meeting Holly. But she didn't.

'You shouldn't have, George,' Cat said, weary and when Georgie hesitated, 'the hamper?'

'Oh.' Georgie had quite forgotten she'd even done it: the memory set up a panic. It had cost three hundred pounds. Tim would understand. 'Sorry – I didn't know what to do. I wanted – is it the wrong thing?'

'No, love,' and Cat's tone changed, she was wry. 'Foie gras and stilton and chocolate biscuits. The boys are over the moon.' She sighed. 'And they do say I need to eat.

For – reconstruction, you need a bit of belly fat, so—'

'So I'd be all right, then,' said Georgie automatically, and Cat laughed, then sighed.

'You want to stop all that, George,' she said. 'I've had enough of that. Life's too short. You were always the best-looking of us, still are.'

Georgie swallowed, a lump in her throat. 'Shut up,' she said. 'Then, well, anyway. Say if there's anything actually useful I can do.'

'The hamper's great,' said Cat, 'honest. Set the neighbours talking anyway, big handsome delivery man, they have their own vans, did you know? And it's better than some old casserole.'

'How are things?' said Georgie. 'I mean, home, the boys, people. All that.' She felt like she had lost half her vocabulary.

Cat sighed. 'You know what people are like,' she said. 'The mums – well, they seem almost pleased. They come around, talk in those special caring voices—' Another sigh. 'Offer to have the boys, give me food I can't eat.' And she was weary again. 'That's not very nice of me, I know. It's hard. I just want – I just want my life back. Hospitals, well – it's like another world, isn't it? The world of sick people.'

'You'll get it back,' said Georgie. 'We'll be out celebrating before you know it. Dancing.' She tried to sound calm and cheerful, and failed. Briskly Cat changed the subject. 'What are you up to?' Georgie told her. Granddad and zoo, what could be more normal? – but Cat wasn't fooled.

'London twice in a week?' she said, sounding curious, wary.

'Tim's away for the weekend,' said Georgie. 'Conference.'

164

'Ah,' said Cat, as if that explained everything. 'He's doing something right, then. Too important for us these days.'

'He – he's not – actually he did say, the other day, let's get Cat and Harry over. Now they've moved up the road.' He hadn't meant it, though. Georgie wasn't surprised Cat had picked up on that.

She sighed. 'I'm – I'm a bit worried, actually,' she said, hesitatingly. And found herself confiding in Cat about the damage to the car. Lowering her voice so Tabs wouldn't hear. When she finished there was a thoughtful silence.

'You couldn't have done it and forgotten?' Warily.

'No!' said Georgie straight away – but then wondered. Had there been something in Cat's voice? Why was she even asking? 'No,' she said again, hesitating. Glancing up and down the carriage: it was almost empty. She sighed. 'I – this might be just me, but I wondered if – if it could have been done on purpose. If Tim might be in some kind of trouble.'

'Well,' said Cat, 'you know your husband better than I do.' A silence, in which Georgie found herself wondering, if that was true. He didn't encourage it. 'I mean, don't you?'

'I – he's so discreet about work, though,' Georgie said, hesitant. Feeling stupid.

'Well,' said Cat briskly, 'not everyone's so discreet.' The change of subject had cheered her up, at least. 'Your trouble is, you don't gossip. I did hear – well. When I was phoning round, seeing who I could get together for our girls' night, quite a few of them asked about Tim. He's got quite a name. Quite a customer base.'

165

'Yes,' said Georgie, on safer ground. 'I know he looks after plenty of people round here.' Not from Tim, though; from the other mothers in the playground, talking warmly about him to her. 'There's a builder, in the town, and a man runs a team of plumbers—'

'No, I'm talking bigger fish than that,' said Cat easily. 'Doesn't he deal with what's his name, that man—' she named the owner of a chain of gyms, 'the one who went bust? That was very handy, declaring bankruptcy when he did.'

'Oh,' said Georgie, startled. 'I didn't—' Cat knew more than her. People she'd worked with fifteen years ago seemed to know more than her, for God's sake.

'You didn't say any of this on our night out,' she said, troubled.

'Well, why would I?' said Cat. 'That wasn't about husbands, was it? And it's not like I think— you're straight as a die, Georgie, everyone knows that.'

Georgie sat back against the seat, her gaze turning to Tabs' head, bent over the page. She could just about hear the tinny sound of the music she was listening to, Shakira, on the headphones, another thing Tim wouldn't have allowed. She didn't understand. 'What *do* you think, Cat?' she said.

'Oh, I'm not saying he's a crook,' said Cat but she didn't sound sure. 'He just – it's just that – he certainly gives them value for money, is what I'm saying.' A pause, in which the phrase turned meaningless. 'Gamekeeper turned poacher, the best kind of man to have looking after you. You know. Because he'd worked for the Revenue, you can bet he brought a lot of insider knowledge to the game.'

'That's legal, though,' said Georgie. 'Right?' She felt stupid, ignorant. She thought of all those IVF appointments, the injections of drugs that made her feel deranged, and then Tabs. She'd been too – too stupefied, too lazy, too something – to ask Tim about his work, too bound up in IVF and Tabs.

'Oh, you can bet it's legal,' said Cat. 'On paper, anyway. It's a while since I've seen Tim but he's not stupid, is he? He knows what he's doing.' She sounded invigorated. *At least*, thought Georgie with one part of her brain, *I've distracted her.*

'No,' she said. 'He's not stupid.' Was it why she'd fallen for him? Tall, lean clean-shaven Tim, in his crisp white shirt, his tie, standing frowning down over his papers in the sunshine of their home. So fierce in concentration, so intent, so focused. He'd applied the same focus to everything, hadn't he? To her, to getting her pregnant, to making a home for them. 'Are you saying he's working for the kind of person who might damage our car?' At the window Tabs was pulling at her headphones and she lowered her voice. 'My car.'

Cat sighed. 'Well, it could be a creditor, couldn't it? If I know Tim handled the guy's bankruptcy, anyone might. But then again,' she hesitated, 'we've probably all done something, sometime, somewhere, that has made someone angry enough to key our car, if they got the opportunity.'

Georgie was about to protest, *not me*. But she stayed silent, uneasy. And then Tabs had the headphones right off and was tugging at her sleeve. 'Mummy, I need the—' too loud, still at the pitch of the music in her head. And

167

looking round uncertain, not even sure if there would be one, 'I need the toilet, Mummy.'

'Look – I've got to go, Cat,' she said, not wanting her to think she was changing the subject. Wanting to *know*.

But Cat only sighed. 'Look, George, there's probably nothing—' relenting. 'I'm sure there's nothing to worry about.'

'I'll call you back,' said Georgie. 'All right?'

'Sure,' said Cat, but she sounded abruptly deflated, worn out. 'Maybe – just not today.'

Making her way down the carriage to the train's toilet with Tabs' hand in hers, Georgie couldn't stop wishing she could see Cat, face to face. She could ask her – well, whatever. She could trust Cat. But it was Holly she was going to see, Holly who thought it was all just a laugh. Cat said what she thought. But Cat had more urgent things to do than listen to her whining.

'Here?' The toilet was certainly cleaner than it would have been during the week but still enough to have Tabs wrinkling her nose in disbelief, looking up at her.

'Sorry, Tabs,' she said. Kept her outside while she wiped down the toilet seat with paper then lifted her on to it, holding her safe. She stood bending down, between Tabs and the locked door. Her small face looking up into Georgie's was uncertain, as if she couldn't quite believe that her mother authorised this situation.

She thought again about Cat, asking her if she might have damaged the car herself and not noticed. Tim asking the same question. What did they think of her? Soft old Georgie, head in the clouds, trotting up to Tim's office to say goodbye on her way to London, off she'd gone.

Head up her own backside. Georgie waking up in a hotel room, her mind a blank.

Tabs tilted her head, anxious.

So much, thought Georgie, making herself smile back. *There's so much I don't know.*

Chapter Fifteen

'Is everything all right, Georgie?' Dad leaned across the plate of fried eggs towards her. He looked worried. His old cap was on the table beside him, but he had his best checked shirt on buttoned to the neck, and a corduroy jacket she knew he'd bought in a charity shop. Georgie tried to buy him things – the shirt had been from her – but he liked to be independent. It had been a sign of him getting his spirits back, his afternoons browsing for cast-offs.

He'd chosen a greasy spoon off Baker Street for their lunch. 'Brunch,' he said to Tabs, excited as if it was something that had just been invented – because he knew he could afford it and whatever Georgie said, he was going to pay. Tabs' eyes had lit up, to Georgie's relief.

'And sausage?' she'd said, goggle-eyed at the choice on the stained menu. '*And* beans?'

Covertly Georgie examined him for signs of change,

of age and deterioration, as she always did. But aside from the pouchy, anxious look to his face at these fleeting moments, when Tabs relaxed her attention and his gaze rested on Georgie and saw something in her, she didn't know what, Dad looked the same. His hair was being cut regularly, his nails were clean, his clothes were getting washed – and he was even, she guessed from their un-ironed look, managing it on his own.

'Yes,' said Georgie now. 'Everything's all right, Dad.'

He shook his head, not believing her, then looking from her to Tabs, and sighing. 'You're looking tired,' he said, uncertainly.

'It's just me getting older, Dad.' She did feel as if her body was running twice as fast, lately. Ever since – ever since.

'Never,' said Dad, gallantly, 'not my little George.' And then a boy was at their table, plates up his arm brimming with beans and eggs and piled with toast. But when he'd gone Dad still looked bothered. 'Is everything OK at home?'

Tabs' head shot up. 'There's a scratch on the car and Daddy's angry.' They both stared at her.

'Well,' said Georgie, with a stiff quick shake of her head to tell Dad, *Don't, don't ask,* 'There's that. Come on, Tabs, eat up now.'

Dad said nothing, she knew he wouldn't, just a brief quick pressure of his arms around her shoulder in the doorway as they left. He walked ahead of her holding Tabs' hand as she bounced beside him along the pavement, walking down Baker Street with its funny assortment of shops, a nail bar with a fish tank in the window and from behind Georgie watched them. She knew the stories he was telling Tabs, a lifetime's worth, the ones he'd told Georgie and for a moment she yearned so fiercely not to have to go back on the train but to stay here – in the crowded streets roaring with traffic and people, with all the familiar sights of her childhood, the Planetarium and the flaming trees in the park – that she stopped, just for a second, half a second, and heard herself make a sound. Go back and start again, just the three of them, her and Dad and Tabs, start again.

In that half second she blinked: she didn't know what she was thinking. Tim angry about the car, the house that must be kept tidy, those things were nothing next to a happy marriage, a steady life. Did she think – she could leave him? Was she imagining she could set up home with someone else, just because he'd touched her hand in the dark? She moved again, hurrying to catch them up: they hadn't noticed.

There was a long queue for the zoo and Georgie found herself hesitating before joining it. Suddenly Dad was moving more slowly, suddenly he *did* look tired, and old. She thought of the tube journey he'd made to get to them, just the steps down to the ticket hall would be too much for him now. 'Dad,' she said, and he nodded.

'Let's look at the giraffes through the fence then I'll be on my way,' he said. They crossed from the entrance to the giraffe enclosure, and stood at the fence where there was a good view: they weren't the only ones. Another family was a little further down doing the same. Tabs' eyes were round and her mouth was open at the sight, her small hands high up on the railings as if she wanted to climb inside with them. They all fell silent watching them, the towering beautiful creatures undulating, unearthly, like something from a dream.

Georgie had stood here as a child herself, holding her father's hand. What had she wanted? Dreamed of? She couldn't remember. A pair of shiny lace-up knee-high boots. She glanced sideways, down at Tabs, who hadn't moved.

'I met someone,' she said without thinking she was going to say it. 'I met someone from Brockley the other week.'

And it came back to her, the club, in the dark, leaning over the bar to him. Frank. How far was the club from where they were now? Not far. On the way, in fact to the bar Holly had mentioned.

'He recognised my accent,' she said, wondering. 'Can you believe that?'

Dad laughed, disbelieving. 'Oh dear,' he said, joking. 'And all that money on elocution lessons.' He frowned. 'You never miss it, though, do you? Not out there in paradise?'

And suddenly, stupidly, she felt tears well, burning. 'No,' she said choked. 'Oh, Dad.'

'You'd tell me,' he said, quietly. He'd positioned himself on the other side of her from Tabs. Georgie looked at the brown-patched giraffes swaying in among high branches, gliding, gazed at their soft knobbed heads, their eyelashes, not at him. 'You'd tell me if you weren't happy? If he—' he hesitated and cleared his throat. 'If he was – doing anything? To make you unhappy.' Georgie felt hot, her eyes felt hot, her fingers as tight on the wire of the fence

173

as Tabs'. What could she say? Nothing. She made herself turn and look at him.

'Tim hasn't done anything,' she said. 'I would tell you.'

She didn't know why he'd even said it. Except he had always prided himself on knowing things before she did.

She hugged him as they said goodbye. A taxi waited at the kerb as Dad kissed Tabs and found a little net bag of chocolates for her as if by accident in his pocket, while Georgie slipped the driver a twenty, hoping it would be enough. Georgie knew Dad must have made a special expedition to find the chocolates, the right ones. Pretending not to see what she was up to with the driver, Dad straightened and hugged Georgie again. 'I wouldn't blame you,' he said, so quietly she didn't even know if she'd heard him properly, then he'd turned and was climbing into the taxi, pulling the door shut. What had he meant? His old white face at the window looking back at them.

When they finally got inside the zoo was crowded, and suddenly, mercifully, Georgie was entirely distracted by the need to keep up with Tabs. It was busy, an autumn weekend, trees turning bright in the park, a long queue of parents for everything, plenty of dads, taking on the kids for the weekend. One of them had tried talking to her in the queue, a man with two small boys, twins they looked like, which always made Georgie wonder if they were IVF too. So she had smiled back when he smiled. About her age, nice-looking, signet ring: 'Custody weekend,' he was saying.

It took her a couple of minutes to realise, Tabs pressed against her hip eyeing the little boys suspiciously, that he was chatting her up. That he thought a woman on her own with a child at the zoo at the weekend might be divorced too or maybe he didn't even think that, was just taking his chances, and then Georgie had to stop herself literally stepping back, away from him, into the cordon keeping them in line. She wondered why she was so stupid. She felt jittery, as if she was coming down with something, and she knew it was to do with him. Not the divorced dad, but *him*. Out there beyond the park somewhere, out there in the city. To do with him and to do with Tim, in the weirdest way they were entwining. Away from her, Tim had morphed into something else. Not familiar any more, a dark outline, forbidding. What *had* Dad meant?

He'd never loved Tim. As they walked between the cages, she settled on that, uneasy: his crumpled face when they got married. It wasn't unusual, was it? For fathers to be wary of their sons-in-law. It was cold but the sky was brilliant blue against the trees all golden and orange, there were the smells of the elephants and monkeys and the screeching of the birds, netted black overhead in the aviary.

In their enclosures the animals paced up and down: the tiger matched them step for step, invisible in the striped shadows, making Tabs shriek and grab her when she realised it was there.

The biggest distraction was Tabs, she skipped and ran, her face pale and wild with excitement, not disappointed by the empty penguin pool with its curves and steps, not disappointed by anything. The paths were littered with rusty fallen leaves, splashed with startling yellow: some had even found their way into the white bottom of the pool. Georgie had to jog to keep up with her, it would have been too easy to lose her. Holding her hand tight once she'd finally got hold of it, slowing her down. They queued for an ice cream.

'Are you sure?' Georgie had said, because it was so cold. But the little hand was hot in hers, burning through energy from who knew where, and Tabs had nodded, certain. *She's going to be exhausted*, Georgie thought automatically, *we can go straight to the station, she can sleep all the way home on the train* – and then she remembered. Looked at her watch: it was only three o'clock.

They sat on a bench in front of a row of smaller caged bird enclosures while Tabs ate her ice cream with concentration, feet swinging. Georgie got out her phone and dialled Holly's number. It rang. The sun was warm now and the birds hopped, from one branch to another and back again. A big toucan sat so still and bright it might not be real, except for the beady black eyes, keeping track of every movement beyond the wire.

Maybe.

Listening to the phone ring, rehearsing what she was going to say, to put all this behind her: *look, Holly, we're running late, I think maybe*— with another part of her brain Georgie wondered how they chose which birds were put in the big netted aviary and which down here, under the gaze of passing humans. The ones that flocked, they got more space, they could wheel a bit up there. These looked like the jungle species, used to the hot damp dark.

The phone was still ringing: where was the answering machine? And then, abruptly, it clicked off, dead. Georgie frowned down at it, all her excuses and evasions on the tip of her tongue unsaid. Beside her, the ice cream eaten down to the tip of the cone, Tabs hopped off the bench and at the movement one of the cages suddenly filled with colour as a dozen small pastel-green and pink birds took flight, whirring and twittering. Georgie recognised them from somewhere: the phone still in her hand she bent to look over Tabs' shoulder.

'Lovebirds,' she said, into Tabs' upturned questioning face, leaving out the rest, *monogamous pair bonding*. 'Aren't they a pretty colour?'

It went round and round in her head, what the placard said about the birds. Monogamous pair bonding. The heavy phrase had set her heart pounding, ridiculously, it frightened her. She made herself smile down at Tabs and with relief she saw tiredness, Tabs had run out of energy at last. 'Time to go,' she said firmly and saw Tabs decide not to protest.

It was a quarter past four when they got on the bus, Tabs insisting on upstairs but almost having to be carried up there and leaning quiet against her now while Georgie's heart pitter-patted. Seeing Dad had shaken her up, not calmed her down. Why did he think— But Tim *did* say that. Tim sighed, when she talked about having Dad over, having him to stay, complained about him getting Tabs overexcited.

The traffic was choked and the bus didn't move. Georgie looked down on to the wide pavements, a group of European tourists in quilted jackets emerging from the Planetarium, a woman with a buggy, a couple hand in hand bundled up in coats, leaning in to each other. What did she even think she would say to Holly, with Tabs there? But when she looked down Tabs was asleep against

177

her. The bus moved a few hundred yards, then stopped again.

And then Georgie had her phone in her hand, and his number on it. *I can't stop thinking about you.*

The journey was so slow. The phone was back in her pocket.

They got off a stop early. She had to shake Tabs gently awake, pressing her face against her warm cheek to soften the blow then pulling back to look down. The small face pale and blank as she emerged from sleep, from somewhere strange where tigers padded up and down.

Funny how the geography had come back to Georgie last week, even in the dark, even after the time away, even with all the changes, the cranes and new building. They walked between hoardings, Tabs dragging her feet. Fifteen minutes in hand: Georgie suddenly felt an access of dread, at the thought of seeing Holly. Seeing her with Tabs in tow, too: what if she said something? What if she even hinted?

Holly had no idea about kids. Of course she didn't: she wouldn't understand how quick they were, to pick up suggestions, to ask awkward questions, to worry.

Georgie stopped on the pavement, because here they were, it was on the way after all, here they were outside the club and as she was telling herself, *No, there'll be no one here anyway*, instructed herself to walk on past the black-painted door when it opened and there he was. Frank the barman, a bulky kitchen machine in his arms, with a plug dangling, something like an ice maker. He stopped stock still in front of her, looking properly astonished.

Carefully he set the machine down on the step. He looked pale by daylight, stocky, dark eyebrows. He was wearing a white shirt rolled neatly to the elbow and a tie pin.

'Well,' he said. 'It's you. It's Georgina from Brockley Rise.' And laughed uncertainly, registering Tabs at Georgie's side, rubbing her eyes with a fist. 'Been a long day, has it?' he said. Standing there.

She felt herself go red. 'Only my mother-in-law calls me Georgina,' she said stupidly and blushed harder, not having wanted to mention her mother-in-law. 'This is Tabs,' she said, 'we've been to the zoo and now we're off to meet – a friend.'

'Just passing, then,' he said, still uncertain.

'Actually I came this way on purpose,' she said, hurriedly, 'Because I – because—' and her hand crept to her earlobe, the flush intensifying. She bit her lip. 'I'm sure you haven't found anything. Seen anything. But I lost a diamond stud.' He was nodding. 'They were a present and I'm in a bit of trouble.'

Georgie fumbled in her bag, fishing in all the crap, still hot, still anxious, before she found the box, holding it up, opening it.

'I believed you,' he said, smiling, then shrugged. 'Sorry,' he said. 'There's been nothing found,' he said. 'I'll ask—' he hesitated, turning his head toward the club. 'I'll ask around. Do you want – if you want to leave a number. Or just call the club and ask for me. I'm Frank.'

'Yes,' said Georgie, 'I remember.' And he smiled, and she smiled and it seemed all right. In that moment, it all seemed – manageable. Replacing the earring, meeting

Holly, getting home, putting all this behind her. Last Friday night, gone and forgotten.

His hand hovered above Tabs' head as if he wanted to rest it there a second but she looked up at him in that moment, eyeing the hand haughtily, and he laughed instead. 'Looks like you,' he said, then looked embarrassed.

'I'll give you my number,' said Georgie. Frank got out his phone and punched it in carefully, big fingers and Georgie was suddenly uneasy.

'Thanks, I think – I'd better go,' she said, apologetically, 'I'm meeting someone, at Fanelli's, that's not far, is it? I mean, I'm sure you won't – I'm sure— Thank you. Anyway.' And she was off, tugging Tabs behind her. When they got to the corner and turned she saw that he was still standing there, the ice maker on the pavement beside him.

Georgie had looked up Fanelli's. Tim had always praised her thoroughness, her scrupulous attention to detail, when they worked together and it occurred to her now as she shepherded Tabs ahead of her that partly she had been that person obediently for him. And then he hadn't wanted her to work for him.

It wasn't far from here, she knew that much. Down the side street they followed the light was going: overhead the sky was bright but pale. Georgie looked at her watch: five past. Damn: they must have stood talking longer than she thought. He'd been nice, though. She'd have liked just to stop there a bit longer. At her side Tabs stopped. 'Who was that man, Mummy?' she said distinctly. 'And where are we going now?' Tugging her hand downwards like a bell pull. A stubborn look on her face, a dark look

180

to her brows. She looked foreign, sometimes, though the donor, they said, had been British. He'd said Tabs looked like her.

Making herself be patient – she could see the illuminated sign to the café, if Holly gave up waiting and came out they'd see her – Georgie lifted Tabs, small and heavy as a couple of sandbags. Smelling sweet, of ice cream, she stuck out her lower lip. 'We're going to have a cup of tea with an old friend of mine,' Georgie said. 'She wants to meet you.' Tabs' shoulders dropped, but she nodded.

Seven minutes past, and the café was crowded. There was no sign of Holly: Georgie scanned the heads once, twice. There was a long bar with stools, all taken: she saw a woman's crossed legs, stockings, a slim ankle swinging – but it wasn't Holly. More a bar than a tea room, not quite right for Tabs: Georgie felt a strange mixture of panic and relief and disappointment.

'Can I have hot chocolate?' Tabs was craning her neck, impatient. She'd perked up, pink in her cheeks.

Resigned now, relief uppermost, Georgie began her backtracking 'Sorry, baby, we must have – there's nowhere to—' But then a couple were getting up and Tabs was already heading for their space, weaving at table-top height through the crowded room.

Following her, apologising right and left in the cramped space, Georgie realised she was gripping her phone tightly in her pocket: she stopped and with an odd sense of dread stole a look. Missed call. She thrust it back in her pocket: Tabs hated her looking at her phone when they were together. Always asking who it was.

181

What would happen, if she knew? Knew another man was interested in her mother.

A man she'd met once. Georgie's belly dissolved, with the danger.

Maybe Tabs would just look up, bright, intent, and nod and that would be it. Children were adaptable. People – people's lives changed sometimes. Everyone adjusted, didn't they? For a second Georgie glimpsed something far off, like sunlight, a different house in a different street. But that wasn't going to happen.

A hassled waitress brought hot chocolate for both of them, but when she lifted it to her lips Georgie found the smell turned her stomach, and set it down. It was like being pregnant, this constant queasiness, this fluttering: the thought made her almost laugh out loud, or cry, she couldn't have said which. With Tabs absorbed in her big cup she looked at the phone again. The missed call was from Holly's number. Of course it was.

With one hand covering her ear in the sudden noise of the room, Georgie called back, averting her eyes from the full cup of chocolate on the table. The line was engaged. Across the table Tabs had pushed her cup aside half full and looked up at her, flagging again. Her shoulders drooped. Georgie put the phone away and signalled to the waitress.

Standing to leave, Georgie was suddenly worn out, too, disappointed and relieved all at the same time. There had been something wrong about being here with Tabs, concealing things from her, bringing her to this place, to crowded dangerous London, where men turned to look at them. And it was too noisy, too hot. Getting out her stuffed purse Georgie paid and added a tip and thought she heard the waitress make a sound of disparagement. She got up hastily, the chair scraped loud and for a second people turned, everyone was looking.

Tabs came obediently round the table and Georgie steered her ahead of her. There was something – something odd, her peripheral vision seemed fuzzy suddenly, as if she'd stood up too suddenly, and she kept her hand on Tabs, steering herself now through the crowded room. She didn't remember it being so dark when they came in and she focused on the doorway out of the café, the rectangle of greying light, the railings of the buildings opposite, still stupidly far away, more tables still to nego-tiate as if they were multiplying. A man standing on the far side of the street. Was this the place, was this where it happened?

Where what happened? She didn't know what, and that was the truth. Holly could have told her, but Holly wasn't here. Where a strange man kissed her goodnight. She knew if she looked down there was still the bruise on her shin she'd woken up with, the morning after, the other that had appeared inside her thigh, as if a thumb had pressed there. Both yellow now. And if she chose to remember it, the feeling of dread she'd woken up with, when her body had ached in strange places, her neck, her jaw, and she couldn't remember how she'd got to bed.

And then suddenly Tabs wasn't under her hand any more, and Georgie didn't know if she'd tripped or lost her balance but she stumbled, she was over, half in, half out of the café doors and Tabs nowhere to be seen.

And out of nowhere a hand was under her arm, it was rescuing her. There was a man looming over her, blocking what was left of the light, the darkening sky electric with the evening. A man with his hand under her elbow: he held her up, raised her up. She knew him.

Chapter Sixteen

Saturdays got started slowly and Frank was restocking the bar. Reaching up to fix a bottle of Aperol into its optic – Frank didn't like the stuff, which he found sticky and orange as Lucozade – he couldn't stop thinking about her. Georgie.

Walking out with the ice maker, looking for Joe who was supposed to be collecting it for repair, Frank couldn't believe it when he saw her. Right there standing on the pavement outside the Cinq, wearing jeans, no make-up and a little girl in tow and looking – tired and a bit scared, if he was honest. Looking lovely. She'd showed him her diamond stud in the little box. He remembered seeing them in her ears, then, but they hadn't looked that big. Her husband must be loaded.

Ruth was the Cinq's cleaner, a Brixton girl with a gold tooth and she was fairly straight. She'd turned things in before that she'd found: a chain one time with a little letter hanging off it. The girl had come back for that – but mostly people didn't come back.

Wiping the counter, Frank wondered if she was scared of her husband. 'I'm in trouble,' Georgie had said, her mouth twisted up as if she actually meant it, it wasn't a joke. Maybe she was trailing all over looking for the stud, hotel or wherever she'd stayed. They'd stayed.

Frank had stood in the street watching her and the little girl go off to Fanelli's, just thinking of what Matteo had said. About the skinny guy going off with them, getting in their cab: Matteo had known there was something funny about it, ever the wise old monkey himself. For a stupid second he'd thought, *he took it*, he took her diamond. The tall skinny guy: he saw she had money from those sparklers in her ears and he went after her. But when you thought about it, that didn't make any sense at all, why take just one? How would you even do it?

Something was wrong, though. With him, with the man. Frank was quite sure, from the minute he'd seen him set his foot down off the barstool. He'd have taken the earrings if he'd had the chance, he'd have taken something. The women might have thought, there was three of them, they could handle him. But he'd been after something, Frank was sure of that. And Frank had been right.

He should have gone after her then and there, and he would have, just to make sure she was – just to stop her looking frightened like that. To say, *It's just an earring, love, I'm sure he'll let you off.* Except at that moment Joe had turned up in his white van and there was the ice maker

186

to sort. And then Joe wouldn't stop talking, about the murder.

There had been a police van up on the pavement just around the corner when he'd gone out for breakfast: outside an old brick building he knew nothing about, shutters at the windows, a lightwell, six bell pushes. Frank had stopped to pick up coffee on the corner and asked if anyone knew what it was and the Filipina lady who ran the greasy spoon he favoured got all flustered, hands up in the air, he gave up. It wasn't till later he'd found out, bumping into Matteo on the corner around midday.

Joe, whose face looked like a walnut, had run his electrical store in the next street since the sixties, and he was up in arms about it. He blamed Crossrail and everything getting dug up and sold off. He blamed the old landlords for being greedy, and Airbnb and the internet. He blamed foreign pimps. 'It'll be one of them Romanians,' he said. A woman had been raped and strangled, in a top-floor flat. Joe was certain she'd been a working girl – prostitute – working out of an Airbnb. Matteo had said the same. The cleaner had come in and found her.

It had shaken Frank, when Matteo had told him, the two of them standing there in the busy familiar street between delivery vans and motorbike couriers. When he'd lived in Streatham a few years back there'd been for ever a street taped off for muggings, stabbings, gang fighting. But not Soho.

He should have gone after her sooner. But at least he *had* gone, once he'd shut Joe up, getting more and more uneasy the longer he'd gone on about it.

Now in the dim evening as the day turned itself over

187

and over inside him, the club was empty and Frank came round the bar to stand in the doorway. In the week there were after-work drinkers but Saturdays always started later, ten, eleven o'clock.

Dead in some poky flat, one of the thousands behind dirty windows, raped and strangled. Not normal for round here. Too many people around.

There were plenty of girls, too, though. Girls who didn't look where they were going, or who was watching them.

Down the street a long vertical green and red neon sign blinked. Soho wasn't a place where you got murdered. Too busy, too full of life. But maybe the place hadn't been secure, these Airbnbs could be like that, ramshackle conversions, old doors easily forced. And it was a dangerous business, selling sex, everyone knew that. Frank shifted in the doorway: he had never been to a prostitute, wouldn't dream of it, it felt dangerous to both sides, to him. Frank liked it easy, he liked it friendly.

Catch people in their soft spot, say the wrong thing and they lose it.

It was dark outside now, but not the warm autumn dark he'd got used to.

Frank poured himself a mineral water, ice and lime, taking care, setting it on its little round mat. Lucy wasn't in yet, Dom was still out the back and he must know something Frank didn't know, namely that there was no chance of Eddie coming in as the smoke was spicy with dope, you could smell it from where Frank stood, wafting in the still air. Not a soul in. Frank sipped, leisurely. Time to think.

He'd got there just in time: he wasn't sure if she'd

tripped or fainted or a combination of the two but her face had been quite white. Picking her up off the pavement in the doorway of Fanelli's, there'd been a moment when he thought he'd scared her himself, coming after her like that. The little girl beside her standing back wide-eyed and shocked, the first time you see your parent poorly, or not in charge, it *was* a shock, wasn't it? Frank remembered that feeling.

He had brought her back inside Fanelli's and asked for a glass of water for her. Frank couldn't remember when he'd last been in there but the dark guy behind the espresso machine seemed to recognise him and the water came straight away, someone got up and gave her a seat by the door. The air outside was cold, and someone closed the door and looking out through the glass, Frank saw him. Standing in the doorway opposite, leaning against the stone surround, half in shadow, looking down the street.

'Holly never came,' she said beside him then and he bent to hear her better.

'Holly?' he said.

He couldn't work it out. Coincidence? He doubted that. The guy was watching her. Them. The tall skinny guy in the cheap suit who'd got in the cab with Georgie and her friends, the guy she shouldn't have gone near – he could have told her that – was watching her.

Had she seen him? Coming out of Fanelli's with her little girl holding her hand? No wonder she'd looked the way she did, white as a sheet. And very frightened. His arm was half round her now, hovering, not presuming to touch her and she looked up at him. A bit of colour coming back into her cheeks.

'My friend Holly,' she said, 'last week, she was the one—'

'I know who Holly is,' he said and after a second's surprise she went on.

'We were supposed to be meeting her here.' Her voice almost a whisper.

The little girl had been staring at him and he'd tried to give her the right kind of smile, reassuring her. Dark eyes almost like she might have had some foreign in her, a cloud of hair. But her mother's mouth and then she smiled back at him and awkward: suddenly he'd patted her shoulder and had bounced up, away from them. 'Well, she does look like she's always on the run somewhere,' he said, 'Holly does.'

When they came out through the door the entrance was empty: Frank looked quickly up and down the street but he was nowhere to be seen. He hadn't wanted to take any chances, though. 'I'm getting you a cab,' he said. She'd begun to protest but his hand was already up and a black cab sliding in to the kerb. 'You don't want to keel over on the tube, do you?' he said and the little girl was already peering through the glass at the leather and the flip down seats. 'Your husband wouldn't want that either, I'm sure.' Frank wished he hadn't said it because then she'd gone white, all over again.

The cab had hardly moved off when Frank spotted him again. He must have just moved up the street to a new doorway and he stepped out of it as the cab came past him, towards it, as if he wanted to be seen. And when the cab turned off he moved fast, away from Frank. Raincoat, hands in the pockets, collar turned up to hide his face but it was him.

Frank had followed him all the same, just to see. Not sure what, just to see. Waited till they were in a lane off Tottenham Court Road – and who said London wasn't a village any more? There were lanes, still, there were alleys and Frank knew most of them. The man went past, sauntering, hands in his pockets, Frank pressed back against a doorway that stank of piss. Frank called after him, *hey*, and he stopped.

Relaxed, his face quite open. Just standing there with his hands in his pockets, curious, not moving. Who did he look like? Joseph Cotten, only taller. High forehead.

'Do I know you?' the man said and he sounded like he found it funny now.

'You know me all right,' said Frank, and he had stepped out of the doorway, the smell of urine in his nostrils propelling him. 'What were you doing there? What are you after?' He didn't know where it came from but he was on full alert, all of a sudden. The man's stillness, like an animal waiting to run. 'It's against the law you know,' he said. 'You were following her. You were watching her. Stalking, it's against the law.'

He'd gone too far with it, he thought then: the man just looked amused. Too far to go back, though. 'She's married,' said Frank, and took another step so he was square on to the man. At the end of the alley behind him people were passing down Oxford Street, Saturday shoppers in the last of the light. He was watching Frank steadily, not afraid but calculating. Joseph Cotten. Or someone else? 'Didn't you see the kid?' said Frank, moving so his face was in the guy's. 'The wedding ring?'

He was disturbed by how much this stirred him up.

191

He could see Eddie's face, Matteo's, Lucy's — see them shrugging, *Why do you even give a shit?* Because she was Georgie, from Brockley Rise. Because she was frightened. Because she'd said, *I'm in trouble.* And because — he just didn't like this fucker.

And then at last the man had moved, only shifting his weight from one foot to the other but light fell on him from overhead somewhere. 'I don't know what you're on about,' he said easily. In the yellow light Frank knew him from somewhere closer to home, it wasn't just old movies. Maybe from a while back? The guy was uneasy now, shifting again and the light was gone — but the face was still there, imprinted, the cheekbones, deep set eyes. The sense that Frank had seen him somewhere, *grinning*, didn't go away.

He took a step back and Frank took a step forwards. The next thing the man could do was run, but he wasn't at that point yet. 'You went off with them, the three birds,' said Frank. 'Last Friday night.' And the certainty gripped him that there was something off, here. Something wrong. Women got picked up, men too, people did things they shouldn't on a Friday night in Soho, even married women with kids, it had been known, but something was wrong.

'What are you up to?' said Frank and it was his turn to sound curious. The man shook his head then and began to turn away: galvanised by the movement, Frank grabbed his arm. Stopped him. 'You knew she was going to be there,' he said, working it out, at last, or some of it. 'How did you know she was going to be there?'

The man had looked down at Frank's hand on his arm,

then back into his face, weighing something up. Frank persisted. 'How did you know?'

Behind the bar now, Frank heard himself sigh. There was something wrong with all this. Something very wrong. And it had happened here, in his club.

What was it with Frank? He wanted to protect them. If anyone asked him he wouldn't know why. It was stupid, in this day and age, wasn't it? Except if someone needs help maybe it isn't stupid.

The man standing in a doorway opposite Fanelli's, watching the woman called Georgie and her kid. Joseph Cotten only taller, grinning down, a lecherous look in his deep set eyes.

How had he known she was going to be there? Georgie. Well, he'd had his explanation.

In the alley off Oxford Street the bloke had just looked him up and down like he was nothing: Frank had felt the bicep under his hand but he reckoned he could take him. If he had to.

'How did I know?' And he'd leaned forward to Frank. Sour breath. 'She told me herself,' he'd said softly. 'That's how.'

Now behind the bar Dom had decided to come in from the yard, sidling up to him before he'd even taken his coat off, and he was talking about the dead woman straight out of the blocks, in that wondering way he had, sing-song, like he was talking about something not real, some movie or three-part series or bloody *Teletubbies*.

'They're saying she was on the game.' Adjusting his bow tie, looking in the mirror behind the bottles. 'Strangled then raped.' Incurious, with no sense of the word meaning something.

193

'You ever seen anyone dead, Francis?' Turning back to Frank to smile because Francis was his joke and spoken so cheerfully Frank had had to resist the urge to punch him.

'Shut up, Dom,' he said instead, keeping his voice steady but Dom's eyes widened.

He had. Heroin overdose in the toilets, four years back, the guy sprawled half under the door. Frank had tried mouth to mouth, all that, the body sluggish as a sandbag under him but he'd known it had been no use. It had taken a long time for the club to recover from that. Eddie pacing around, shouting. And Frank, come to that. When his granddad had died his mum wouldn't let him see the body.

He thought about where the dead woman was found: Airbnb. A house on a dark corner, let yourself in and out again. Close circuit easy to dodge in Soho, if you know what you're doing. Go in one door, come out another. The old loading yards and alleys.

'Keep your hair on,' said Dom, as uncomfortable suddenly as Frank had ever seen him, affronted even. Frank just turned away, unaccountably depressed, he should be used to the bloke's idiocy by now. He heard Dom move off, hang up his coat, start again on a subject with a customer. Adjusting his tone to serious and high-minded, with an effort.

More than depressed: it came to Frank that what he was feeling was disgusted; had been feeling since this afternoon, and the feel of the lanky bastard's bicep under his hand. The customer having moved off Dom had opened his laptop now. Frank didn't move, a hand still on the counter of the cloakroom.

The man had shaken him off, a quick easy movement, shit on his shoe, and gone. That woman, Georgie from out of town (where? Out east if she was going for Liverpool Street). Georgie with her kid and her soft anxious little face. Would she have? Would she have? Women, though. You thought you knew them.

Lucy came in at nine on Eddie's arm and they walked past the bar without a word. Frank heard murmuring down the corridor but when he turned his head the curtain was pulled sharply, a rattle and a shush of velvet, and the voices disappeared.

'Raped her *after*.' Joe the electrician had said the same thing.

They hadn't said yet who she was.

Chapter Seventeen

Sunday

The sound was the sound of emergencies and it would rouse her out of any sleep. Even this one, a soup of alleys and dark brickwork and pale faces, hurrying down crowded streets where someone had a knife. Holly. Had Holly got the knife?

Georgie started upright: she hadn't drawn the curtains and the room was flooded with light. The sun was high in the sky, bright clear crystalline blue. The house was quiet except for the ringing telephone. The landline, used now by almost none of their friends, only the elderly, or the authorities.

Something had happened to Tim.

Her heart thundering. Something had happened to someone, Georgie knew that with absolute certainty and Tabs – where? Georgie rolled across the bed to Tim's side where the phone sat and grabbed up the receiver. As she spoke into it, breathless, there was Tabs in the doorway in her pyjamas, a tuft of hair sticking up.

'Hello? Hello?'

They'd both slept in. That was all. That was all.

Not all, something had happened, last night—

'Georgina.' Georgie felt things unravel, *should never have taken her to London, should never have—* The voice was querulous, she recognised it straight away. 'Have I woken you up, Georgina?'

The voice was her mother-in-law's. 'Jennifer,' she said, trying to inject enthusiasm into her own voice.

Hesitating, Tabs crossed the threshold, began to wander the room. Pulling open drawers. Helpless, Georgie followed her with her eyes then thought, *Sod it.* Tim wasn't here. Let her. It's *her* house. *Her* parents' bedroom.

Tim's parents lived on the other side of London. Surrey, in a big house with many ornaments and an immaculate drive: an old-school version of the house Tim had built. They'd stayed once, early on in the relationship, and Georgie had felt Jennifer's disapproving eye on her wherever she sat, whatever she said. They'd been given separate bedrooms.

'How nice to hear from you, Jennifer,' she said politely. 'How are you?'

Tim was their only child. His room with model aeroplanes displayed on shelves was as he'd left it. A filing cabinet: he had a filing cabinet in his room. Jennifer had told her with pride that he'd asked for it for his twelfth birthday.

'How *am* I?' Jennifer sounded impatient, almost affronted. She played tennis, went to health farms. Of course she was all right. 'Look, Georgina, I'd like to speak with Timothy, please. If that's not too much trouble.'

'He's not here,' said Georgie, feeling a surge of rebellious satisfaction. 'I'm sorry, Jennifer. He's away at a conference.' She knew Jennifer never called him on the mobile because she thought it was expensive: Tim hadn't disabused her. She wasn't sure if even he liked his mother, or his father, either, but he wouldn't hear a word against them.

They didn't call often, anyway, they were great believers in children standing on their own two feet – unlike her own father, who anxiously believed she would always need him. Tim's parents had a lot of money from his father's time as an oil executive, but they didn't like spending it. When Tabs had been born Jennifer had sent a Marks and Spencer's voucher for fifteen pounds.

'Oh! Oh, *really*.' Irritably, as if it was Georgie's fault. 'I thought – he – oh. I received an email from him last week.' Hesitating. Evasive. 'Well, perhaps I shall – when does he return?' Jennifer's telephone mode was personal assistant, with a rod up her backside. If Tim had been here, Georgie wouldn't even have dared have that thought. He'd have seen it in her face.

'Tonight,' said Georgie, trying to sound bright. Feeling anything but, suddenly: there was so much to do. Dinner, cleaning. Maybe the flowers – maybe she should – then she saw Tabs was at the bedside table, Tim's side, pulling out the drawer. Georgie half stood to attract her attention, shaking her head, and Tabs skipped away, to the dressing table where Tim kept cufflinks and collar studs.

A disgruntled silence. Not even the sound of a radio on behind her. Georgie wondered where Tim's father was, on a bright cold Sunday morning. He was called Jonathan. Playing golf perhaps, or maybe he had a girlfriend some-where. He had goosed Georgie once, while drunk, at a long-ago Christmas drinks and she'd shoved him off, glaring. She'd never said anything to Tim.

'How's – how's the child?' Jennifer couldn't bring herself to call her anything but that.

'Tabs?' Georgie's head cleared, abruptly. 'She's absolutely lovely.' Defiant. Tabs' head flipping up from the dressing table, beaming, and then she was on the chair beside Georgie, nudging into her, reaching for the phone to talk to whoever it was had expressed an interest. 'Doing so well at school, she—'

'Very good,' said Jennifer, interrupting her. 'Timothy does keep me up to date with all that, she may not be – he'd do anything for – for her, you are aware of that?'

'Yes,' said Georgie, uncertain. Anxious, suddenly, at the thought of the conversations Tim had been having with his mother about them. About Tabs. But Jennifer wasn't listening. 'Anyway. Tell Timothy I'll telephone – well. Perhaps it would be better if I called him at the office. Tell him I'll call him in the morning, if you would.'

One thing Tim *would* have told his mother about, she realised with a small shock, was her night out in London. She would have disapproved: there'd certainly been plenty unspoken in their exchange. Tim would have told her in order to incite her disapproval, somehow. He'd probably told her about the earring, too. Jennifer's idea of Georgie amplified: a slattern and a slut. Both.

Really? She told herself to stop it.

'Yes,' said Georgie, but she spoke into thin air. Jennifer had hung up. The air around her swirled in the silence. Tabs had gone, she didn't know where, but Georgie didn't get up to call her, she sat very still.

199

This happened. This happened.

Holly. Last night.

Georgie put a hand to her forehead and felt a sudden sweat. They'd got home, gone straight to bed, asleep by nine. But then there'd been a phone call. Not a dream after all, not a nightmare: a phone call. That call. Groping for the mobile plugged in and charging on the bedside table, squinting at the time. Eleven fifteen.

Her stomach turned to water.

Why was it that things that happened in the night had a different shape? The room had been quite dark, the nearest street light a long way off, the only light the phone pressed to her ear. She remembered listening to the words without understanding, her heart thumping in her throat.

Now she walked back to the bed and picked up the phone: call history, and there it was. She hadn't dreamed it. A call from Cat that had lasted ten minutes. Before it, her call to Holly that had gone unanswered, at five fifteen. At the head of the stairs, listening for Tabs downstairs, Georgie called Cat's number: she answered on the first ring.

She still sounded frightened, breathless. From the kitchen came the sound of Tabs pulling a chair across the floor so she could stand on it to reach the cereal.

'It's true, isn't it?' said Georgie. 'I thought – last night, it was so late – I thought—'

Holly's face. Her morning-after face, tired and human in the bathroom of that dodgy hotel, her hand lifting Georgie's hair out of the way as she raised her head from the toilet bowl.

'It's true,' said Cat, dully. A shaky sigh. 'It's true. They found her yesterday morning. Some rented place.'

Holly's dead.

'Look—' Cat began.

'I'm coming over,' said Georgie.

Cat hadn't been in much of a state to give directions, but that was what mobiles were for. Tabs in the back, headphones on. For a moment or two as she opened the door for Tabs Georgie had registered the dent, again, but vaguely, because it couldn't matter, any more. Lost earrings, a dent in the car, a face in a doorway – but she shied from that thought. None of it. None of it. Next to Holly being dead.

She had to make herself drive slowly. All of it churning in her head: she had thought, the first time she drove over to Cat's it would be for fun, it would be her best mate finally just around the corner and all the chat and the gin and tonics and kids playing in the garden. But this. Not this.

The house was in a terrace, small as Cat had said but nice, homely. A few roses in a crowded front garden.

Pale in the doorway, Cat stepped back to let her in. 'The boys are out with Harry,' she said. 'Football.' She stood motionless as Georgie hugged her, finally patting her on the back. The tiny back garden had a rusting climbing frame in it and Tabs went straight for it.

They drank instant coffee in the kitchen: Georgie made it while Cat paced. The hamper sat on the counter, ridiculously big, an embarrassment. It looked like it had already been raided, at least: a packet of expensive chocolate biscuits half empty on the top. Pushing aside a stack of school folders on the table they sat, Cat staring down into her mug.

'Her mum called me,' she said. 'Holly's mum, I haven't spoken to her in years but she must have found my number somewhere. I never thought I'd have counted as one of Holly's best friends.' She sighed. 'It sounds like they found her yesterday morning, in some Airbnb in Soho. They're not saying anything. I called the police again this morning but they won't say.'

Georgie felt like her head was made of wood. Why wouldn't it sink in? 'Was it – did she – it wasn't an overdose or anything? She didn't—'

'Someone killed her,' said Cat bluntly. 'She was murdered, probably by someone she had let in. No question. Her mother said – I don't think she could even think about what she was saying. I don't know when Holly last saw her, but I'd say they hadn't been close. She—' She stopped.

'What did she say?' Georgie almost whispered.

'Her mother said she was raped and strangled.' Cat's voice shook.

'What?' said Georgie, stupidly, her head turning automatically, in terror, to Tabs in the back garden, perched on the old climbing frame, then back to Cat's face. Thinking of Holly's sharp ankles, her long legs, her face rough in early morning light. Thinking of Holly having a mother. '*What?* No. No.'

'I know,' said Cat, and Georgie saw a shiver pass through her, from her shoulders to her hand around the mug, unsteady with the horror. 'I know. She didn't actually *have* a home, it turns out. The last boyfriend kicked her out – they're talking to him, but he isn't even in the country, so it wasn't him.'

202

'She was supposed to be meeting me yesterday,' said Georgie, numbly. 'And she didn't turn up.' Cat's mouth opened, then closed again. Holly had a mum. Holly had been living out of an Airbnb and no bloke looking after her, after all. Rather the opposite. Holly and her wheelie suitcase.

She remembered the last thing Holly said, or tried to say. *Just be*— and then nothing. Just be careful.

There was a silence. 'They can't find her phone,' said Cat, and she was mumbling, in an odd voice. Perhaps it was shock. 'I left my number with the police.' She hesitated. 'In case they want to ask, about, you know. About Friday night.'

Dazed with the horror of it, Georgie felt that thud into her, remotely. 'Friday night,' she repeated. 'Yes, of course. Of course.'

'I'm going to call again later. Shall I—' her gaze, on Georgie, flickered. 'Shall I give them yours?'

'Yes,' said Georgie, immediately 'Of course I should talk to them too.' Cat nodded, still looking down.

Because it was all in her head, because nothing had happened. She'd done nothing wrong. Why wouldn't she talk to the police? Tim would be all right with it, he would probably even encourage it. Probably.

'And shouldn't you be—' Georgie changed tack because if there was anything Cat hated, it was being told what she should or shouldn't do. 'Isn't your treatment—'

Cat looked up then from the coffee mug but her face, her bright tough face that was always so alive, set and blank. 'My first appointment's tomorrow,' she said.

'Oh, shit,' said Georgie, the word escaping her. 'Oh, it's

such shit, Cat.' Then, 'This must be the worst bit. Waiting for it to start. Is there anything—'

Cat just shook her head. 'Harry's taken a month off,' she said. 'The company say it's OK.' She shrugged. 'If it goes on – well—' and Georgie's hand shot out despite her knowing Cat hated this pity crap, and Cat's came out to meet it.

Chipped nails, her knuckles dry from washing up but always elegant, that was Cat, in her careless way. Georgie took it, squeezing, tight and tighter.

'I'm glad you came, George,' said Cat. 'I'm scared, you know? It's scary. All of it. Cancer, Holly, all of it.' Looking into Georgie's face. 'Where did it come from?' she said. 'I don't understand.'

Then into the silence there was a commotion at the front door and the tiny house was full, crammed with boys kicking off their shoes and shoving. And Harry was in the kitchen door, his face anxious at the sight of Cat's face – both their faces. And it was time to go.

In the back on the way home Tabs kept up her babble, she was hungry and what was for lunch and this was what she wanted and Georgie delivered answers randomly, trying to get them home in one piece. Trying to find a way out, of all this.

Where *had* it come from?

She had heard it. Seen it. That small hesitation of Cat's.

Cat had thought she'd be reluctant to go to the police. Cat was skirting round something, even Cat with so much on her plate, had seen something, remembered something, detected something.

There could be any number of reasons for it. Who

wanted the police round? Cat knew Tim well enough: she might never have been to their house, with its hedges and security systems, in its exclusive close, but she knew he wouldn't want a police car outside it. And she'd been puzzled, at Georgie's trip back to London, more puzzled now at the thought she and Holly had arranged to meet.

Cat wasn't stupid.

Georgie had sat on the bus in traffic, Tabs asleep against her and the mobile in her hands. Her heart in her mouth, her fingers trembling so much she had to type and retype the few words. *I'm in London.*

He hadn't answered.

She'd deleted it straight away. He didn't see it. Perhaps that was it. She told herself that. Her heart thumping so fast she thought Tabs would feel it, she thought she might have a stroke, there on the top deck of a bus in London.

He didn't even see it. It was a good thing. A good thing. The only good thing. *Thank God*: a small rush of relief.

They got home, in one piece, in the sunshine, back inside the house, the cool empty clean house. Tabs opened the fridge straight away, something she wasn't allowed to do when Tim was there. Tim would have taken her hand off the door and held it up, high in his own hand while he closed the door, keeping Tabs there, half dangling, while he explained. No eating between meals.

She took out a yoghurt and Georgie got a spoon for her and she ran outside with it, a splash already on her skirt. Georgie turned on the tap, reached for a cloth, intending – but she lost track of what she had been intending.

205

How could she have even thought of messaging him? How could she have let him have her number? Not objected, to the text, to the flowers. Georgie held the phone tight between her hands now, in the kitchen, in the sunshine. She would like to throw it into the garden, into the trees, flush it down the toilet. She could tell Tim she'd lost it. She knew she wouldn't do it. She was already talking herself down.

If she'd seen him.

And she trembled. There had been a moment, on the threshold of the café, when she'd imagined – but it hadn't been him. When she'd looked up there'd been no one there. If she had even bumped into him in the street, if she'd allowed him to talk to her, smiling down at her. So dangerous. So dangerous. She'd be – like Holly. If Tim, if Tim—

In a dangerous place, cut loose, living hand to mouth. What had she been thinking? Just because he'd kissed her. And anyone could say, *I can't stop thinking about you*, couldn't they? Just words. And then it stirred, again: the unease. *We'll do it again, soon.* He'd kissed her, and then he wasn't there any more and she had woken up in a strange bed, and only Holly had known what happened in between.

And now Holly was dead. Under her hand the water was running cold and Georgie stared down at it without understanding for a second, before hastily turning it off.

Tabs would need a clean skirt. She walked upstairs, standing on the landing. One way, Tabs' bedroom, the other way theirs. Hers and Tim's.

I hardly knew her. But. Her sharp knees, on that other bathroom floor with Georgie the morning after. Whispering. Cat asleep on the bed, snoring. The only person who could tell her what happened that night, who could make sense of it, because Georgie couldn't remember. Just couldn't remember.

And she was dead.

In the bedroom Georgie's clothes were everywhere. If Tim had been here he'd have had a go. Her keys on the floor.

She went into their room, bending to pick things up, keys in her handbag, knickers in the linen basket. Setting things back to rights. Bending, she felt her belly, smaller and found herself thinking of Tim, suggesting she should get away, go to a spa. He'd be pleased, when he got home. She could get back on track, she could love her house, her work. She shouldn't have upset the apple cart by going off on a night out, she'd just wanted to see Cat, that was all.

Not Holly: she'd hardly remembered who Holly was, to begin with, had she. But Holly had been – vital, in her way. What would they have done if Holly hadn't come, if it had been just the two of them? They'd have stuck together. No man would have got between them. Got pissed, danced, taxi home holding each other's hand tight.

Holly had been a kind of conduit, hadn't she, opened the evening up, with her little suitcase and her carelessness, her languid, intimate way with the barman. With the hat-check girl.

Opening up another world of secret communications

with men you hardly knew. Because deep underground, Georgie still felt the reverberations of shame, the misery, of him not replying to her message. The message she didn't even know if she'd sent. What had she thought would happen? They would have a drink together? How would she have explained him to Tabs? Reckless. Stupid.

Holly had been reckless. She gave it off: she'd open the door to a stranger, she'd have a one-night stand. But she shouldn't be dead. She should be sleeping it off, she should be picking herself up and starting again. She'd opened the door to a stranger, and he'd raped and strangled her.

Blindly she went on, tidying, tidying, till the room was clean and neat, the bed smoothed, all drawers closed, the suits neat in the wardrobe. She was shutting the doors on them, trying to still the voices in her head, when the phone blipped. She didn't go to it straight away. She made herself wait. It was from Tim.

Home by five, six at the latest. Met some good people. Can't wait to see you, what's for dinner? Of course, he had no idea, it wasn't his fault. Had he even remembered Holly? Had Georgie even mentioned her? Holly the loose cannon, Tim's idea of hell.

Downstairs the flowers were there in their big glass bowl, the water stained dark.

It's all right, Georgie told herself, over and over, *it's all right. You've done nothing. It's not too late.*

Too late for Holly, though.

Sunday morning and Frank was running. Up through cluttered Soho, rubbish on the pavements, empties, grey stone, sparkling sky. Winding through Mayfair, Harley

Street, clean red and white façades, all those doctors and private hospitals, up to the roar of the big road, beyond it the park.

Passing the private hospitals he thought of Holly, taken down some narrow stairs and out in a body bag.

Matteo had told him. Holly.

Two in the morning and the Soho night still young but Frank had stepped out through the curtain, hands stuck down in his pocket, wishing he hadn't given up smoking. Two minutes, he'd said to Dom, because he'd had a sudden feeling of suffocation, or panic, or something, like a premonition, and there'd been a lull. The door quiet: he'd brushed Matteo's shoulder as he emerged and Matteo had turned, cleared his throat.

Frank had seen straight away how pale he was. He looked – Frank couldn't quite make sense of it because he'd never seen Matteo anything but stolid, calm – he looked frightened. 'Holly,' he said. 'That girl—' he pronounced it *gew*, like a real cockney, 'the one they find dead? Is Holly.' Then Frank saw the police car parked up the street, saw its light come on as it pulled away.

'But she—'

'Is none of our business, Frank,' Matteo said, stopping him, looking both ways, but Frank persisted.

'She wasn't a hooker, though,' he said, bewildered, stunned. A woman he'd seen, whose perfume he'd smelled. Matteo's hands on his shoulders, stubborn, 'They said the girl was—'

'I don' know what she was,' said Matteo, with as much urgency as Frank had ever heard in his voice. Jerking his head to send Frank back inside. 'Is not our business.'

209

He'd just been shocked. So shocked — although he had opened his mouth it didn't make sense so he didn't say it. He didn't say, *But her friend Georgie was on her way to meet her, yesterday afternoon.* She never turned up: the random guy had been waiting there instead. Not so random after all.

Inside Dom had been bouncing from foot to foot behind the bar, pointing into the air, punters waiting. Lucy's pale oval of a face framed by her velvet curtain, watchful.

Frank was too heavy to run, really. Hard on the knees. Once through the iron railings he set out across a diagonal path, watching the other figures doing the same as him on other paths, all of them moving like some board game, like air traffic control. He passed one, a whippet but grim-faced. It was a pretty morning but that just made him think of her dead, too.

Holly with her big smile and her wheelie suitcase. Holly with her eyes on the prize, but what prize? Dead in a body bag. He thought she wanted a man, but what did he know? Standing on the pavement under his window and gazing up at some guy like he was Marlon Brando.

That guy. Jogging, Frank squeezed his eyes shut a moment, trying to remember him. Anything about him. Dark blue suited shoulder, her fingernails scarlet against the fabric, curled round his upper arm.

Matteo talking to her on the doorstep of the Capri about her mystery man, her prince bloody charming. And now what? *Is none of our business.*

The park looked beautiful. The sky bright blue. Frank had been coming here since he was a kid, the little boats on the lake, the playground where he broke his wrist on the roundabout and Mum coming in her overalls, furious, to haul him off to the hospital. He remembered the little toilets just for kids, tiny porcelain behind the doors and a ferocious Jamaican auntie in charge. Railings and autumn colour just beginning and a freshness to the air. The roar of the big road was steady and comforting to Frank's ears, Ally Pally a distant spire in the misted sky.

He had looked scared, though. Matteo.

Maybe he knew more about Holly than Frank did: certainly he did. But he wasn't going to talk about it.

He bumped into Lucy in the corridor, getting her coat on, at two: the car came for her at two, Eddie's car. She looked like she wanted to run, her pale pointed face, she began to push past him and without really thinking, he stopped her. Took hold of her by the arms like Matteo had him. A sacking offence, if Eddie knew. Touching the boss's wife — but there was no one to see.

'What were you and Eddie talking about, earlier?' he said. 'You knew her, didn't you? Holly. Who was killed. I saw you talking to her, that night. Friday before last.'

She pulled away. 'I don't know what you're on about. She was a punter, is all.' She tried to push past him but he blocked her and for a second he saw a flash of something, fear. Panic. 'Look, Frank, I don't know what you think you're—' Blustering.

'It's not one of Eddie's buildings, is it? Where she was found?'

'I don't know what you're talking about,' she was holding her ground, haughty, coming the boss's wife over him.

He was patient. 'They're saying she was a prostitute,' he said. 'Did you know that?'

211

She made an impatient sound, pushed his arm off her. Frank stepped back. 'I don't know the woman,' she said. 'But Eddie's not a pimp.' Something in her voice, a wobble, and then she cleared her throat. *Was* Eddie a pimp? The thought hadn't occurred to Frank. But Lucy's voice was firmer now, defiant.

'From what I heard the coppers saw thousands of pounds of fancy underwear and her camping out in an Airbnb in Soho and drew their own conclusions.' Pulled her coat shut, triumphant. 'Now if you don't mind. Eddie doesn't like me being late.' A threat in the words.

Would she tell? Tell what? *Frank's asking bloody questions again.*

Frank was coming past the children's playground now. The playground was empty, new slide, roundabout gone – he remembered throwing up on that roundabout when he was a kid – but the little toilet block was still there, white-painted brick.

He wondered how she knew, about the underwear. The cleaner? Some dodgy copper? It would be Eddie: Eddie knew everyone. Including policemen.

Frank tried to think of the last time he'd talked to the police, and it was a while. They parked up for their coffee early mornings and knew who he was all right, they exchanged nods, but Frank kept his distance. It seemed only wise. He didn't know how their minds worked.

Frank thought he might make a loop round the northern canal and seeing another runner in the corner of his eye found himself wondering about that guy. The one he'd seen watching Fanelli's yesterday afternoon: wondered if he'd see him again. Get a chance to work out where he knew him from. For no reason except he was the same build, roughly, tall and skinny.

Had it been him, on Holly's arm? Then Frank saw some tattooed guys swinging their legs above the water and knew he was too near Camden and he turned back, wondering if he could ever live anywhere but London.

Turning for home, the last stretch, straight down between the wide avenue of mature trees that bisected the park, Frank was tiring now. He narrowed his vision not to include the morning dogwalkers, the old blokes on benches, the other runners, but focused on his stride, lengthening it. Trying to imagine himself one of those animals that was solid but still graceful as he headed for the big road, roaring already with the morning's load of commuter traffic. He wasn't graceful, he was heavy, but he slogged on.

He wondered about those boxes, the ones Eddie had him stash in the club.

He wondered about Lucy putting her hand on him in the kitchen, calculated, and Lucy and Eddie in the cloakroom, murmuring. Taking him for a mug.

He didn't like it. The loneliness had receded but Frank felt lost in all this. At sea: him and Georgie, too. Frank had Georgie's number now: he could give her a call, ask her if she was all right, but he knew he wouldn't. In another world, she'd have his number and would phone *him*. Ask for his help. In another world they'd have circled each other in the school playground until he'd plucked up courage to ask her out. But they hadn't and he hadn't and Georgie was a married lady, home with her little girl and her husband, safe. He hoped so, anyway.

213

Reaching the gate in the long railing fence he stopped, gasping, and feeling every year of his age, every pound on his gut, Frank bent over. He gave in.

Chapter Eighteen

The mobile rang again when they were almost at the checkout.

Tabs loved the supermarket. Always had, since she was a tiny baby, newborn, gazing up from her car seat wedged into the trolley at all the lights. Georgie babbling nonsense to her as they moved through the aisles, in heaven back then, in a daze of wonder.

These days of course Tabs was grabbing everything in sight and talking back, asking for stuff non-stop. All the same Georgie still felt a certain kind of safe in the supermarket, happy even. Couldn't admit that to anyone, probably, barely to herself, it was almost outrageous. This one was a big place, wide aisles, bright with natural light. Upmarket: once, a year or so ago, she'd gone to one of the cheap ones, she'd heard from some mum in the school about how they were good for this that and the other, German biscuits or ham or prosecco and then Tim had frowned at the stuff in the fridge.

'Mummy?' said Tabs, pausing in front of a fridge full of desserts, tarts and pies and cheesecakes. 'Can we?' She knew they weren't supposed to have pudding every day, but she also knew Georgie liked them as much as she did, the two of them conspiratorial at the fridge. Holding out a box of eclairs. A way along the big refrigerated section a slim woman in running gear gave them a side-long glance.

Better class of person at this one, Tim said. Georgie hid from them, the better class of person. School governors, women in officewear, ladies who lunched. And today, perhaps because it was Sunday, men cruising the aisles following the click of heels: Georgie wondered why she'd never noticed that before. She recognised a woman who took her kids out of the school to go private.

Tim was always talking about doing that: 'It's just your insecurity,' he said, last time they had the conversation. 'You think they'll look down on you, the other mothers. Isn't it?' Spoken kindly, but it had hurt her. Did she? Tabs was so bright, so shining: she just wanted Tabs to have what she had. A scruffy little school you walk to every day.

Why would they look down on her?

Georgie imagined her dad's face if she gave in. Bewildered: she remembered him doing homework with her every evening, him beaming when she collected her A level certificates, the praise he heaped on the system that had got her there. It's why she had gone to work in the school office, when Tim said no to her working for him. And her working there was why he let Georgie keep Tabs in the school – for now.

He talked about funding issues, class sizes, music classes: he would have his way once she was eleven, he'd send her to the convent in Brentwood, or even boarding school. Georgie felt a knot inside her. Till death us do part: and she stopped short in the supermarket as she found herself thinking, *It doesn't have to be like that.*

Divorce. It happened. Tentatively she prodded at the thought, it bloomed. What had brought this on? Something. The turbulence of the last week, since. Just her and Tabs. Tabs in any school Georgie wanted. Was that how it worked? She suspected it wasn't.

They came around the bakery aisle, a row of wicker baskets, the morning smell of fresh bread and there was a young woman in tight jeans, late twenties maybe, something familiar and unfamiliar at the same time. Ponytail, wire basket slung over her arm. Then she was gone.

But you love Tim. The after image of the young woman mocked her. Springy and lithe and fast, no one holding her down, no cumbersome trolley for her. She could see Dad's face again, bewilderment becoming alarm. Cat's: he'd done so well. Steady old Tim, who'd built all this up, who'd stuck it out with her, bringing up another man's child. How could she do it to him? Of course she couldn't. What was she thinking? And besides.

And then it rang. Her heart jumped in panic, in anticipation, knowing it was going to be Tim and she got the phone out of her pocket looking around to locate Tabs.

But DO you love him? The thought nagged, because she couldn't make sense of it. What did that mean, love? Looking after someone?

And besides. He'd never allow it.

There she was. Tabs, looking at the packaged buns, tentatively reaching out a hand to squeeze one. Her mother, always after something sweet and comforting.

'Hello?' In dread.

Why was she thinking about Tim this way? It was all messed up. Like the ground was shifting.

'Hello there.'

She knew the voice again straight away: it did something to her insides. Deep and soft. She hurried with her trolley past Tabs, looking for shelter. Into mineral water and squash. No one there. Kept pushing, between the ranked bottles, Tabs hurrying to catch up.

How few words had she heard him say? She could repeat all of them. She was terrified.

She gabbled, 'You can't, I can't —' She heard him laugh, softly.

'Calm down,' he said, sounding amused. She stopped, obedient. Like a dog, like a puppy ill-trained. 'It's OK, Georgie.'

She swallowed: she didn't know he knew her name somehow and yet of course he did. He sent the flowers. His voice was very soft, it was kind. She didn't dare say anything, in the silence she could feel herself straining towards his kindness, his approval.

'I shouldn't have sent that message,' she blurted. 'You shouldn't be contacting me.' *Mark*. She didn't know if she said his name, whispered it. She should just say, leave me alone or − but she still strained, for his kindness.

Why was she like this? She'd always been like this. Mum exasperated, at the stove, I'm *busy*. Needy little Georgie.

218

There was a sigh, not impatient. 'OK,' he said. Reasonable. 'I understand. Really, I do. I just thought —' and now he sounded — what? Bewildered, regretful, sad, even. 'I got the wrong idea.' Stiff now. 'I apologise.'

And like the dog again, Pavlov, she began to apologise herself.

'No,' she said desperately, 'No, I'm sorry, it was—' because of course, it was her fault, too and she didn't want him to feel bad, that was the last thing she wanted, and then she was laughing, and he was laughing.

She was laughing because she was afraid. Because she didn't know what the way out was.

Someone walked past the end of the aisle, a blur against the light coming in through the big windows. Walked back. Georgie looked for Tabs and there she was, standing still for once, holding on to the trolley, alert. Georgie took a step away, just one step. Her hand shielding the phone.

'I'd like to see you again,' he said gently. 'Is that wrong?'

'Well, why didn't you—' she blurted, wrongfooted. *Why didn't you answer the message?* No, she couldn't say that. It had been a mistake to send it, she had been glad he didn't answer. It didn't sound wrong, but it was. A silence, that she filled with apologies, in her head.

And then he said, 'Yesterday? My phone died.' Sorrowful. 'I didn't see the message till it was late.'

'I'm sorry,' she said, holding her voice firm, 'but can't you see it's impossible?'

It was as if he hadn't heard. 'I thought I'd just rather talk to you,' he said, still gentle. 'I mean all this, messages and all that. So much easier, face to face.' A rueful laugh. 'Well, you know what I mean.' She hesitated but it was

219

too late. 'Where are you?' he said, his voice lower, confiding, intimate. 'Are you at home?' She turned, looking around, she has temporarily forgotten. Where? The rows of plastic bottles, the striplighting.

'In the supermarket,' she said, faintly. Looked up and there was the woman in jeans, stock still at the end of the aisle, a couple of feet away. The woman with her ponytail and her basket, a salad box, a Diet Coke. Looking at her, head on one side as if wondering.

Georgie didn't know what it was she was feeling, something rushing, rushing in her veins.

Terror: it was terror. Of something she couldn't see. And then she turned to see her trolley and no Tabs. Where was she? Where? 'I've got to go,' she said into the phone, her breath evaporating, and hung up, began to run and almost tripped over her. Tabs. Tabs had been there all along, squatting at the foot of the little bottles of squash she always wanted for lunchboxes. Why hadn't she seen her?

Georgie leaned down and gathered her up under the arms, feeling her heart pound, letting the warm weight of Tabs soothe her until she wriggled free, 'Come on, darling,' she said, her voice strained as she pushed towards the checkout in a kind of desperation to be out and done, as if he hadn't been on the phone but was in there. And only then, arriving at the row of tills, realised she still hadn't bought anything for Tim's supper when she's about to unload. Losing it.

Go back. Walking past the sushi, the tuna steaks, she got a chicken, potatoes, garlic, parsley, lemons. She made herself walk slowly, Tabs trotting beside her. Green beans and carrots: she wanted comforting things. Things from her childhood in South London and Mum at the stove.

The supermarket was too bright, suddenly. It wasn't a safe place, after all, was it? They were all watching her. The girl with the ponytail was watching her.

Swiftly she steered the trolley to the checkouts, looking straight ahead now, Tabs sensing something, running to sit obediently to wait in the window beyond the row of tills. The light behind her made her look small: it bleached out the figures, the rows of parked cars beyond the window, like an old photograph.

Unloading the contents of the trolley, Georgie worked fast, piling everything up hastily, not speaking, not making eye contact. The checkout girl wasn't a girl but an older woman in the company overalls, thick grey hair, many rings on her fingers, and within seconds was gauging Georgie. Quick glances, as she passed the stuff over the scanner. Silence attracted attention. Sitting there all day what is there to do but judge people? By their shopping, their chat, their silence. Neurotic, standoffish, bad mother, alcoholic. But she didn't dare say anything, not even, *Nice day*.

At the other side of the checkout Georgie piled things into the bags they'd brought, careless.

He'd go away, wouldn't he? His voice was still there, persistent. But his tone had been innocent, reasonable, what had he done? What had he actually done? He'd sent her flowers. Her heart told a different story, racing, on and on, in time with Tabs' fast swinging legs.

There was something else. It wasn't just flowers and a soft voice, her body knew something different. The soft black space between climbing out of the taxi and waking

221

up the next morning in the hotel bed. The family room, the main road roaring outside.

She didn't pause for Tabs, just pushed on past and she hopped off the seat and ran to keep up. Obedient still, knowing something was up and it was as if the little movement jolted something in Georgie's head, and she knew. Where she'd seen the girl with the ponytail before.

Lydia's best friend, Tim's secretary's best friend, and she had been watching Georgie as she whispered into the phone. She had been listening. *You can't.*

She wouldn't even have needed to hear the words, would she? Just to see Georgie's face, her whole body, curled around the phone. Guilty.

You can't. I can't.

Guilty.

The phone rang again as they skirted the forest in the car, on the way home. The church came into view, grey against the trees all suddenly bright with autumn colour.

The phone was lying face up on the passenger seat beside her and Georgie dared a glance at it. Cat. Georgie pulled in to the layby beside the church and stopped.

Cat launched straight into it. She was fired up.

'They're saying she was working as a prostitute,' she said, her voice ragged. 'I won't have that. I won't have it.'

'A – a what?' Georgie didn't dare repeat the word, Tabs was quiet in the back, the engine ticking down. Georgie sat very still, staring into the haze of green under the trees. Light falling down through it as she thought of what Cat had said. Holly, sitting on the bathroom floor with her knees up, knowing what Georgie was feeling.

Someone was walking, far off. Sunday afternoon she supposed dully, it's what people did. Though she never saw anyone walking here.

'Just because she was living on her own in Soho?' she asked. Incredulous.

Cat exhaled angrily. 'Apparently it's because she let the killer in. They're saying he was a *client*. She had plenty of nice knickers and a vibrator and that's all it takes.' A furious edge to her voice. 'I'm going to talk to the police again. I *know* what had been going on in her life, and they're just guessing.'

There was noise in the background, someone shouting. A man: it would be Harry. 'You can't,' said Georgie quietly. 'You're not well enough, Cat. You can't – let me talk to Harry.' Looking quickly round to monitor Tabs, but she was asleep, head tilted back, mouth a little open.

'I—' Cat began to protest but then suddenly the fight went out of her. 'All right.' Flat and low. 'All right, I'll get him.'

Her hand must have gone over the receiver because everything was muffled. Georgie rested her head against the cool glass of the window. The figure in the woods was walking, steady, calm. The lights fell down between the trees, the hummocky mossy ground. It felt like the weirdest time and place to be talking about this stuff.

'Georgie?' Harry sounded like he was at the end of his tether. Pain translated as anger: he'd always been that way: Tim was so different, so quiet, so reasonable in every situation Georgie had used to wonder how Cat managed it, but she did. 'She can't go to London and talk to the police,' he said, savage. 'Her chemo starts tomorrow. The kids are desperate as it is.'

How would Tim be, if she was ill? With a dull sensation of dread, Georgie knew how he would be.

'OK,' she said quickly. With no clue of how she could do it. 'I'll persuade her.' Silence, just Harry's uneven breathing. 'OK?'

'OK,' he said. 'OK.'

Then Cat was back, snatching the phone from Harry. 'Look—'

'I'll go,' Georgie said, before she could start. 'I'll tell them what I know – how she was with us, what she said in our last conversation, everything I can remember. And I'll pass on what you know too, until they can confirm it with you. OK?'

Haltingly Cat told her. Began by cataloguing the boyfriends but gave up, there had been too many, she lost track, sounding weary. 'She always ended up getting dumped.'

'It was never she dumped them?' Georgie was taken aback.

'She was a softie underneath it,' said Cat and Georgie thought of Holly in the bathroom, the morning after. Over breakfast in the hotel's stuffy dining room, when she had thought she wasn't being watched. Her face going from animated to lifeless. Older, sadder. 'She was a romantic even,' said Cat quietly, thinking of something else. 'Believed in happy ever after, love, all that. It's what kept her going.'

'The most recent one – what happened to him? I mean – could it be—'

Cat sighed. 'He's gone. It hadn't been a big deal, then he just got a job in New York and left. Two weeks ago he just left, and she was out on the street. *That* was why she was in an Airbnb. It was that or move in with her mum.'

'So when she came along with her suitcase – she'd just split up?'

'Yes—' said Cat, then stopped.

'But—' Georgie hesitated. 'She didn't seem down.'

Cat went on, slowly. 'She called me Friday. I can't stop thinking about that. I only spoke to her Friday. She was – happy.'

'Me too,' said Georgie. 'That's when I spoke to her. She *did* sound happy. I can tell them that. What did she say to you? Did she tell you why? Was there someone new?'

'I'm not sure,' said Cat and suddenly her voice was odd, as if something had just occurred to her. 'I actually – I can't think straight at the moment.'

'You're shattered,' said Georgie. 'You get on with the chemo, I'll go to London.' With no clue of how she was going to work that, but – but. 'I'll find out what they're saying at the police station. Whatever it takes. But if there's anything. Anything you remember.'

'Maybe she'd just been drinking, maybe – I don't know,' said Cat but her voice was still distant. There was a pause and then Cat said, 'Are *you* going to be all right?'

'Me?' Georgie was taken aback.

'Tim's away, didn't you say that? And there was that thing with the car. The dent.'

'I'm fine,' said Georgie, thinking, *that dent*. 'Tim's back tonight but—'

But then there was a racket somewhere behind Cat, a door banging and raised voices arguing. 'Got to get on,' said Cat quickly. 'Sunday dinner.' A breath. 'You take care.' And she was gone.

Parked up beside the road Georgie looked out over the tombstones in the afternoon light. He'd stopped, whoever he was, silhouetted against the hazy downlight through the trees. Quite relaxed. He'd got a small backpack on and his thumbs were hooked through the straps. They looked at each other, although neither's face could be distinguishable, he was too far, she would be just an oval through a car window.

The sound of Cat's voice, distant, echoed in her head. The sound of her not saying something. *You take care.* It was what Holly had said, more or less. Holly's last words to her.

Georgie started the car, indicating carefully, and pulled out into the traffic. As she reached the green bend she looked back, in her rearview mirror and whether she had been looking for him or not, she saw him. Emerging from the trees to stand beside the road, a tall man, lean, a little stooped he was so tall. He watched her disappear.

Chapter Nineteen

Frank was on his knees in the curtained corridor that led from the cloaks to the back yard. He was searching for the boxes he'd lugged in here Friday evening.

Searching wasn't quite the right word. They weren't there.

It had got cold. Eddie must have had the boxes. He couldn't have lifted them on his own, though. Frank had had enough of a job of it.

He was on his own in the club, for the moment. Sunday evenings they barely opened anyway, just a couple of hours, for the ravers to wind down, the alcoholics to pretend they were social drinkers, mellowing out. No one had said who'd be on the cloaks, no one had said anything. Eerily silent, was how it was today. He stood up, brushed at his knees.

He'd thought Eddie had asked him to shift the boxes as an excuse, to get him out there. They could have had bricks in them, for all Frank knew, although he had thought from the weight of them and the way their contents shifted as he carried them, that they were full of papers. None of his business anyway.

But then Frank's mother had called that morning. Which she did, most Sundays, and he'd sat on the edge of the bed and let her mild grumbles about the weather wash over him, with her little dog yapping away in the background and the ex-policeman who'd been her boyfriend for years moaning at the television. It had never been anyone but him and Mum growing up, in Brockley, Frank had no real idea who his dad had been or where he'd gone. But this morning the grumbles were different: she had a bee in her bonnet. She'd gone on and on about Holly until he'd let it slip, he knew her, well sort of.

'A customer, Mum, that's all.'

But it had been too late and she'd been on about Soho not being safe and what kind of a club was it again, he worked for? She knew well enough: he'd even brought her in for a drink early on. He'd introduced her to Eddie.

And now she was suggesting he worked for gangsters. 'Mum,' he'd tried. 'It's a bar. People come here after work for a bit of a dance. Girls on a night out.'

When she appeared to have got the hump very suddenly and hung up, with just a *whatever*.

It was normal enough, for Mum. She saw something in the news and drew conclusions. But it had unsettled Frank: he saw himself. Never curious, never poking his nose in where it wasn't wanted, never asking questions. Until now. Partly Mum, partly Lucy telling him to stay out of it, telling him it was none of his business.

So he'd let himself back in, careful to lock the door behind him, and gone to look for the boxes.

Frank hadn't turned any lights on: why hadn't he done that? Two hours till opening, he could have been in and out.

And then he heard the door go and darting forward on instinct closed the door between the bar and the corridor and in the next movement, quietly stepped back, behind the curtain that lined the corridor, and everything shifted round; this wasn't his turf, suddenly. This was unfamiliar territory. Frank was hiding in the dark for a reason, he just wasn't sure yet, what that was.

It was Eddie, and he wasn't alone.

They were talking in low voices, standing in the bar, the other side of the curtain that closed off the corridor. Frank held his breath: he wouldn't come out the back. Would he? Eddie never came out the back. He couldn't hear all of what they were saying: he caught phrases from Eddie, more at ease maybe on his home turf. He didn't know the other voice, talking in an undertone.

Eddie was telling him not to worry about something.

'. . . all sorted. Easy. No worries. I can handle her.'

Handle her? Lucy? Lucy had stuck to her story, Lucy had run for the waiting car, so yes, Eddie could handle Lucy. If that's who they were talking about.

One of them must have stepped against the door at the end of the corridor because it opened a crack and light spilled into the corridor where Frank stood. Behind the curtain he stepped back, silent, and pressed himself against the wall where the boxes had been. Carefully he turned only his head, to look, left and right. They were gone, all right, you could see in the dust where they'd been. A single sheet of paper curled up against the wall and invisible unless you stood where he was standing.

The boxes had contained papers, then, he'd been right. Eddie had wanted them gone while he worked something out? Eddie had a shredder, Frank knew that too. He knelt, very carefully, picked up the single sheet, folded it and put it in his pocket.

He waited for them to leave.

Tabs was drawing in the sitting room, papers all around her on the floor, when the car pulled up on the drive. The solid chunk of the door closing sent Georgie in her apron hurrying from the kitchen. Too hasty, she tripped, catching herself on the low table.

'Daddy's back,' she said, her hand on her shin to stop it hurting and at the same time trying to smile. Straight away Tabs understood, making a pile of her papers, sitting up straight, and Georgie went into reverse, careful, brushing herself down, trying not to limp.

Tim called from the threshold, loud and cheerful, which was already not like him, and when he saw her dropped his bag, holding out his arms. Georgie stepped into them, reaching up for the kiss and then his hand was on her backside. She smelled aftershave, the air freshener he used for the car, dry cleaning. He held her against him, tight: squeezed, she looked up into his face, it was the only movement possible. He smiled down at her. Those eyes, somewhere between green and brown, smiling, deep set. *You've known him since you were twenty-three.*

Her eyes darted through the kitchen to the door into

the garage: she hoped she'd closed it behind her. *Poking about.* That's what Tim would call it, poking about. His tools hanging at the wrong angles.

'I've missed you,' he said and his voice was throaty.

'Me too,' Georgie said, brightly and couldn't stop herself, she pulled back. 'I — there's something on the—' and moved back, awkwardly, turning for the kitchen as quick as she could so he couldn't see her face. She saw it herself, a glimpse in the sharp-edged mirror as she passed: pale, drawn. She saw panic and guilt. She saw fear.

There was a light haze of smoke from somewhere in the kitchen, for a moment she couldn't remember what she was even cooking, she was only listening for his footsteps. He didn't come straight after her, but he didn't go upstairs, either. She could hear him, waiting. A soft sound as he took a step, a sigh with a hint of impatience in it.

The garage was Tim's domain, always had been, as much as his study. His study was locked so she'd gone into the garage when they'd got home from the supermarket on the same blind impulse, to understand him. Her husband. To make it better.

All that equipment: the tools he hardly used although he always showed them off, to every builder and roofer and paver that came to the house. The tent furled in its nylon bag, the new long wooden box holding whatever, some new drill. Two big red gas cylinders, for camping: she had knelt beside them because she couldn't remember one, let alone two. Rolled them gently to see if they were full or empty: both full, heavy. She had stood them back up again, carefully. Brushing the flake of red the movement had dislodged out of sight.

231

She was kneeling at the stove – it was chicken, the oven was too hot, that was all – and he came up behind her. His hands were light on her waist, he leaned past her to close the oven door, raising her up. Still behind her: she froze. His lips were on her neck, he was sliding one hand up her skirt.

'Tabs – Tabs is—' her voice was high, she didn't want to turn round.

'She's fine,' he said. 'I saw her in there, making a mess. She's fine.'

She's not, thought Georgie wildly, thinking only of the haste with which she'd tidied. Not making a mess, or not fine? Tim's hands were heavier on her now and still she didn't turn round. He lifted her skirt and she heard him gasp: he was rough. It hurt her.

He mumbled something into her neck, like *I've missed you*, again. Something about it having been a long time.

Georgie held on to the kitchen counter, trying to stay silent. The counter digging against her soft thighs, the pain still throbbing in her shin. She didn't turn around, she wouldn't stop him. It felt like a kind of game, or a test, or something, she couldn't protest. Their game, they both knew this wasn't normal, this wasn't *them*, it wasn't just because he'd been away. He wanted her to turn around, and she wouldn't. He wanted a reaction, that was why he was pushing her. Her mind spun, out of control, her breathing ragged, what was it he wanted to know?

What she'd done.

She could hear his breathing ragged in her ear, she could smell booze somewhere, not on his breath but in his skin, and she had a vision of his weekend, smoke-filled

232

rooms, staying up drinking with other men, conference speeches before an audience of the hungover, the unshaven. Holding her breath till it drummed in her temples.

And then suddenly he was finished. His breathing eased, and when she turned round he was buttoning himself back up. Peering down at a speck on his shirt. A blotch of colour of his neck, already fading.

He wasn't looking at Georgie but she looked down at herself. Her knickers halfway down her thighs, her skirt ridden up. She could feel the slime between her legs. She tugged at the skirt, she could feel the knickers rolled and twisted underneath it, she could feel the heat in her face. Haltingly she began to lay the table. Mats, plates, knives, forks. She found herself staring at the setting, unable for a moment to remember which way round the cutlery went. Tim walked out of the room and in a second she could hear his voice, murmuring to Tabs.

Tim didn't usually carve but in the bright hot kitchen he insisted on it, humming something under his breath. There were beans and carrots and broccoli, three vegetables, all done to four minutes as Tim liked them, plus roast potatoes. She saw the food pile up on his plate, saw him look around for gravy, saw Tabs looking from one of them to the other then back down to her plate. He ate greedily but the hunger seemed to be to do with her, in the way he looked at her across the table not caring if Tabs intercepted the look.

In the sitting room after the meal he flicked between channels restlessly, still looking across at Georgie. The news came on, something in North Korea. Georgie hesitated: did she really need to tell him? He'd hardly known Holly.

233

'You remember – when we went out?' she began. 'In London? The three of us, me and Cat and Holly?' He grunted, watching the fat Korean president in his blue suit, raising his hands to a huge crowd. 'It's – well, Cat phoned and she told me Holly's – something's happened to her. She was found – she's died.'

He looked across at her, frowning, as if he didn't believe her. Then abruptly leaned forward, his elbows on his knees. '*Died?*' he said, incredulous. 'What, like, heart attack? Drugs or something? Wasn't she the one who used to—' Then he sat back again.

'Not drugs, they don't think. They think someone killed her.' Georgie could feel herself growing agitated, Holly's violent death had no place in the quiet sitting room, the evening news. Tim's frown said as much. He raised the remote as if to change the channel, turn down the sound, but did nothing. Then he blew out his cheeks.

'Bloody hell,' he said, sober. Darted a glance at her. 'Well, I'm sorry to hear it. Christ. Good job we left London when we did. All these stabbings, every night another one.'

She didn't say, *She was strangled*. Raped and strangled and left there in a bedsit. Tim seemed almost irritated, as if she was spoiling his fun, letting him know she hadn't been in the mood, back there in the kitchen.

It flashed up in her as she sat there that the truth was she couldn't imagine that mood any more, she couldn't imagine leaning over to him in bed and putting her hand on him. There was a second in which neither of them moved or spoke, then Tim sighed explosively, and leaned to set the remote back down on the coffee table.

234

'And the car, then?' he said, such a change of subject that she had no idea what he meant for a moment. 'The prang?'

Georgie stared. Any idea she'd had of saying, she was going up to town to talk to the police about Holly evaporated. 'I don't know,' she said, 'I honestly can't remember. I couldn't have done it without noticing, it's a big dent.' Feeling panic close her throat, in response to the way he was looking at her patiently, sceptically. And as if on cue Tabs flitted to the door behind her, clutching her papers, a little ghost and Georgie got up, gratefully, to put her to bed.

In Tabs' bedroom she sat a long time reading aloud in the bed beside her: she could feel the small head hot under her hand as she stroked Tabs' hair, she could sense the small heart pattering, pattering, in time with hers. So long she heard the television go off downstairs and through the door saw the lights disappear, one by one, kitchen, hall. And still she stayed, Tabs asleep now, slipped down beside her on the pillow, until there was silence.

Padding across the landing she was as quiet as she could be, holding her breath in the dark room, watching for movement and seeing none – but there was something in the air, like electricity. There were marriages where there were separate bedrooms, where that was quite normal. She didn't want to touch the bed, let alone to get under the quilt, but she did it.

His hand went out to her.

She'd known him fifteen years: she repeated that in her head. *This is your husband, you've known him fifteen years, your husband, father of your*— not quite, though. Was he? And now everything was wrong.

He was on top of her.

Lying awake afterwards she made her plan. On her back staring in the dark at the ceiling, making patterns, sorting, shaping.

There would be no need to tell him about Holly, all that, about going up to London to try and talk to the police. She would let him go off to work and she would take Tabs in as usual. She would tell them she was feeling sick — and she was — because they could manage without her. She would call one of the other mums and ask them to have Tabs after school for a couple of hours in case she was delayed. She would call the police and talk to them.

Fifteen years: but when she scanned the years somehow Georgie couldn't see Tim, she could only see herself, scurrying, scurrying. Lying on her back in a white room while her ovaries were plundered for eggs, she could feel the lump in her throat, of fear. She could see the walls going up around her, glass and concrete, sharp edges, higher and higher.

It rose in her throat, her sinuses throbbing with it, the saliva rushing into her mouth, and she scrambled out of bed. She got to the toilet in time and vomited, strings of chicken, carrot. She tried to be quiet but couldn't, she went on retching until yellow bile came out. And then sat back against the wall, her face wet with tears squeezed from her eyes. She could hear Tim snore.

He knew something. How could he know what she didn't know herself? And Holly the only witness, gone.

Gone, gone, gone. Raped and strangled, beside her little suitcase, her nice underwear, policemen looking between her legs for evidence.

But not the only witness, *Cat might have been dead to the world but you were there, Georgie.* You were there stumbling on the stairs, up in the family room, saying goodbye on the doorstep. You were there. And so was he.

Georgie squeezed her eyes shut until sparks flew behind the lids like fireflies and there in the dark was the shape of a man, coming out of the forest. A tall man, he stood and watched her. He was patient.

Chapter Twenty

Monday

Frank woke at ten out of dreams of women in need, a flickering black and white movie of train tracks and dark water and his hand went straight to his mobile, on the side table. It was ringing.

Bright sun again: he had to shade his eyes, squinting: Mum. Again. On a Monday? She launched straight into it.

She wanted him to go, to leave Soho. She didn't like him working for Eddie.

'It's Benjy,' she said, cryptic. 'He said I had to say something.'

Benjy, her ex-policeman boyfriend. Sitting on the bed in his boxers Frank tried to make her understand.

'Three strip clubs, a massage parlour, this block of apartments and the Cinq,' he said, patiently.

'And the rest,' said Mum, sharp. 'There's one house in Soho, where that girl was found, B and B if you say so but most of the guests seem to be single women and no doubt booked in someone else's name, so that's one brothel in my book. And seven more out of town.'

238

'What?' Frank sat there half stunned, scratching his head. 'Mum—'

'That's what Benjy says.'

Frank had always thought Benjy was only interested in fishing and crossword puzzles.

'Eltham, Bromley, Wanstead, Harrow.' She reeled off the names. 'Benjy says, they've been trying to get a case together against Eddie for fifteen years. And now this girl. Murder.'

'Eddie isn't a killer,' he said, automatically. But he didn't know if it was true.

It wasn't like he hadn't been thinking about leaving. Since Vince gave him that Sunday evening look in the dim club and mentioned Savoy-style. But this was crazy.

Holly was in everything now, since they found her body. Even Vince had mentioned her name, lowered voice, but his eyes sliding away when Frank said, 'You knew her?' Mumbling, changing the subject. And Frank had begun to wonder about the man he'd seen her with on the street, the man she'd gazed up at, searching his memory. Could have been anyone. Anyone not fat, anyone who owned a dark suit. The details were sparse, the sharpest of them her knuckles, her hand on his arm.

Mum was still talking. 'You never would listen to me,' she said, exasperated and he was back in Bromley and her smacking him across the back of his bare legs for coming in late. 'All right, Mum,' he said, feeling alarm start up in him and just wanting to think. Time to think. 'All right. I get it. I just – it's a lot to – let me—'

'Benjy's retired, love,' she said, on the edge of defeat. 'It's not like he wants to get you involved, get you asking

239

questions, he just thinks you want to be out of the picture. Soon as.'

'Yes, Mum,' he said, obediently. 'I will. I'll – get out, soon as.'

The thought of it, though, the picture of him and Eddie having a little chat, gave him a nasty feeling. Something told him he'd have to be very careful what he said.

Frank got the impression Mum could have gone on another half hour but he must have convinced her, or the dog needed taking out, because suddenly she gave in and hung up and he was left there with the phone in his hands.

Oh, shit, he thought. Because he'd forgotten he sent it, until now. Never text after midnight, he'd heard a couple of girls confiding that one at the bar more than once. Never text when you're pissed or after midnight. He hadn't been pissed, but there'd been a cold beer in his hand and he'd been winding down up here, one o'clock in the morning and looking down to the street when he'd texted Matteo.

After Matteo had already told him, stop asking questions. *Who was he, Teo? The guy I saw Holly with the night before she died?*

Now he opened the messaging app and peered at the little screen: the message had been delivered, had been read, two little blue ticks, but no answer from Matteo. And then as he was looking something happened. Something changed. Matteo's profile picture disappeared. The little line of information on when he was last seen, gone. It gave him the weirdest feeling, like Frank had watched someone take him.

It dawned on him: Matteo had blocked him. Or someone else had.

The buzzer went and he jumped, nerves jangling, but by the time he got to the window the pavement was empty, someone else had let them in. He stood a long time in the hallway waiting for whoever it was with his heart beating too fast, but the lift went on up and he knew it was just someone had forgotten their keys. But the danger was still there.

Mum was right. He had to go.

Tim left early, whistling.

Georgie hovered on the landing, distracting him with brushing imaginary dust from his shoulder, his hand resting on her backside, and he'd left the study open. Holding her breath as she listened to the car reverse, turn, rev loudly, recede – she went inside.

She only wanted to be helpful. To be a supportive wife. That wasn't quite the story in her own head, but it would be her excuse if he caught her. *If he came back, if he parked on the corner, if he let himself in, quietly.* She reprimanded herself: why would he? Why would he do that?

The desk was clear, the filing cabinet was locked. There wasn't even a laptop, but Tim didn't do all his work on a laptop.

Once, when they'd been watching the news, a piece had come on about a businessman who'd been convicted of fraud because the police had found evidence he thought he'd deleted, on his computer. Tim had laughed and said – and with hindsight he had been talking more or less to himself, he had even forgotten she was in the room with him – 'Keep it on paper, mate. Paper you know how to destroy.'

Lightly, still holding her breath or so it felt, Georgie ran her hand over the desk top, picked up the framed photograph: her and Tim with Tabs between them. His hand on Tabs' shoulder. Tabs bright, bubbling with excitement. Georgie peered closer, at her own face: a blank. A blank of fear, call it apprehension, call it anxiety or nerves or— but it looked like fear. She remembered the photograph being taken, Tabs' first term at school and Tim initially dismissive, irritable at the thought of being dragged into school then somehow taking it over. He had been rude to the photographer and she had been quietly resistant to his rudeness and that was where the fear came from.

She wasn't sure what she was looking for, and in a way the empty desk and the locked filing cabinets were an answer to the question she hadn't known she was asking. What did her husband do, that he didn't want her to see? He had never wanted her to work with him, he kept his study locked. He didn't trust her. And then quite abruptly it flipped around in her head: *You don't trust him.* That's what this is about. You *can't trust* him. She put out a hand to the filing cabinet, took a deep breath and tugged, and as she felt the resistance there was a sound from downstairs. A sudden, slithering rush of a sound and then a sharp rap, in that instant so shocking that she backed away, out through the door, almost tripping on the landing.

The post. The post had come. She saw it on the mat, she heard the sound of the postman's feet. Groping, Georgie picked up the wastepaper bin automatically and took it downstairs, picked up a bunch of catalogues from the mat. Gardening tools, cooking equipment, bedlinen. Tim liked nice linens, a neat kitchen. She dropped them all into the bin.

Sue had offered straight away to have Tabs after school. Take her to the swings, give her her tea, whatever. Tara would love to take care of Tabs, always wanted a little sister. Cue an inquiring look. Georgie knew Sue only had one kid because her husband hadn't wanted any more. 'You're an angel,' she said, meaning it. Perhaps with too much warmth because Sue gave her a bit of a sharp look, then. The truth was she felt like she could vomit again at will, only there wasn't anything left.

Sue got up from behind the desk, taking off her glasses, peering. 'Are you sure everything's all right, hon?' Georgie abruptly robbed of the power of speech, tears just asking to come. 'At home, I mean?'

'I—' she blinked, feeling a sweat on her forehead. 'Yes, oh, it's just—' Sue didn't move, just frowned at her, uneasily kind. She wouldn't be sympathetic if she knew – or would she? The messages on her phone. Dragging her daughter up to town, dragging her dad out and in the back of her mind was the possibility she might glimpse a man she knew nothing about. 'I don't know why you'd think—' She started again, trying for a wan smile. 'It's just something I ate.'

Maybe she'd heard something. The girl in the supermarket yesterday could have guessed – what? Something. Enough to start whispers. And the flowers, the florist gossiping about her flying out of the car to interrogate her on where they'd come from.

243

The school was noisy with Monday morning, filing into the assembly hall. Soon they'd begin to sing. 'You know what this place is like,' said Sue, smiling a little but still watchful. Georgie didn't know, not really. She thought of a rumour, a cluster of rumours going round the village, like wildfire. Until they got to Tim.

After last night, the thought petrified her. The smile she forced out for Sue felt like a grimace. 'Just need a bit of a lie down,' she said. And went, turned for the door, one foot behind the other. Behind her she could tell Sue hadn't sat down again. Wondering.

Walking away through the cold bright playground Georgie tried to calm the panic. A latecoming mother with flying hair and a child on each hand gave her a quick glance she didn't dare return.

Someone had sent her flowers. So what? Nothing had happened yesterday in the supermarket, just her talking animatedly on the phone. What had she actually said? *You can't phone me. I can't talk to you. Nothing happened.* She had said that.

He had made a sound at that, hadn't he? A kind of laugh. Conspiratorial. As if – *That can be your story, if it makes you feel better.*

In traffic alongside a row of fast-food joints near the station – chicken, kebabs, ribs, her stomach churning – Georgie remembered something. She'd forgotten to take the lasagne out of the freezer for supper: *All right. All right.* She indicated, turned. Back against the morning traffic that was ebbing now, lights, a stretch of green that was the forest, insinuating itself between the arterial roads, the church.

No one was walking under the trees this morning, Monday morning. The woodland canopy was motionless, quiet, motes of something in the slanting light. Afterwards the forest would always be there, the backdrop to the picture she was about to be shown, and everything holding its breath.

She turned into the close.

A little bright car was parked outside the neighbouring house: as she let herself in it snagged on her thoughts. She knew that car.

There was someone there. There was someone inside the house.

Chapter Twenty-One

She heard the sound from upstairs as she pushed the door open, that soft sound, and knew what it was in the same moment. And knowing what it was, everything around her shifted, it felt as though things really moved sideways, the kitchen door frame, as she stood in the hallway in the sparkling light, seeing herself in the metal-framed mirror as if she was someone else, her mouth half open, her keys in her hand.

Georgie had been in an earthquake once, in Italy, only a little one, but that was what it was like. The corner of the room shifting.

Uuuhhhh. His voice, low.

Georgie stopped, there on the mat in the hall. She opened her mouth, but what was she going to say? *Who's there?* She knew who was there, because she'd seen her car at the kerb, seen it but it hadn't sunk in, no more than the vaguest, mildest question. *That looks like Lydia's car.*

Lydia oh Lydia, now, have you met Lydia?, where did that come from? She was standing there in her own hall and listening to her husband fucking his secretary upstairs and *that* was going round in her head. She could hear the name on Tim's lips, too often, it seemed to her now, too casual. An old-fashioned name for a twenty-five-year-old. Lydia was shiny and polished for a girl her age, though, heels and stockings and everything. *Girl. Girl.*

Outside her car waited on the kerb. Tabs at school, she should be on the train to London. She should be at work. *That's what they thought, Tim and Lydia, how often—*

They were still at it. She could hear him now, groaning, a sound she recognised as if from a long way off and the hair on her head stood on end, literally. She hadn't known that really happened but then Georgie had led a fairly sheltered life. Lucky Georgie.

What was she going to do now? The lasagne had to be taken out of the freezer or there'd be no dinner and Tim — for a mad second she thought, *I could text Tim from the train and tell him to do it. While he's here.*

Tabs was always starving when she got home from school and the microwave was on the blink — *they were still going.* She squeaked, Lydia did, who knew.

Inside Georgie something churned, like a tornado, a rope twisting tight. She walked the four, five steps into the kitchen, opened the freezer, took out the lasagne and put it on the side.

The car park was very full. The taxi behind her peeled off to drop its passenger at the front of the station and she slowed, moving up and down the rows of cars. A little yellow one appeared and for a fraction of a second Georgie's impulse was to smash into it, but she drove on, her head turning to look at it as she passed.

At the ticket machine in the station car park, although she'd done this before a hundred times, the instructions refused to make sense and she had to stoop, peering at them. A man in a suit gave her a funny look as he walked past and Georgie realised she was crying.

The machine clicked and the paper ticket was extruded behind its little Perspex shield. Other women, Georgie supposed, would have gone up there, would have taken the stairs two at a time to catch them at it, would have stood in the doorway and screamed. In her head, she was screaming at him. In her head it all unravelled from that moment, dismantle the house down to the foundations, brick by brick, pick up Tabs' ragged teddy from the rubble, her nightlight, Mum's mirror. Leave all the rest, the clothes, the gadgets, the limestone floors, the kitchen. Leave it behind, pick Tabs up and run.

Leave the flowers in the vase. Turning at the edges this morning, their water brown in the sunshine.

But that would never work. He wouldn't let that happen. Tim wouldn't let her leave. And Tabs: she saw in that instant, his property, like the car she drove and the food she bought, he'd never let her have Tabs.

The station was busy, a blur of people: she had to queue for her ticket. The train wasn't due for ten minutes but Georgie saw a seat on the platform.

Sitting forward, elbows on her knees, her face between her hands, she felt sick to her fingernails, to the roots of her hair, every cell of her body. She needed a plan.

Or not. She needed overwhelmingly to think of something else or she might throw up right there, in the cold sunlight on the platform, on the shoes of a man in a suit, on the concrete next to a woman with a baby in a sling. A metallic announcement came over the loudspeakers: she registered that it concerned her train. Nine minutes delay. Georgie sat back, got out her phone. She was here for a reason, she would get the train, go to London, see the police.

Then come home again. The lasagne would still be sitting on the kitchen counter, waiting for her to put it in the oven. With clumsy fingers she dialled. Cat.

Too late, she remembered it was Cat's chemo today. She could hear hushed voices in the background, a mechanical hum. 'It's all right,' said Cat, dry and weary. One of the voices identified itself as Harry's, low and grumbling. 'It's done. I'm at the sitting around phase, waiting to be allowed to go. And you don't – apparently the effects don't kick in straight away, not for thirty-six hours. I could have gone to the police station myself.'

'No,' said Georgie and with the word, things around her shifted, the poison in her ebbed. 'I'm on my way.'

'Just tell them,' and then the voice broke off, muffled, she was talking to someone, and when she spoke to Georgie again it was obvious she'd moved away from the voices. 'All right. They let me go out into the corridor, Harry's talking to the nurse, I don't want him to – he worries.'

'What do I tell them?' said Georgie.

'That she was a romantic. She wasn't a prostitute, or an escort or whatever they want to call it. She had a proper job. Tell them she always fell for the wrong people but she was holding out for love.'

249

They wouldn't be interested in that, not second-hand, not from Georgie. They'd want hard facts. Something about the sound, still ringing in her ears, of Tim and Lydia in the bedroom had clarified something, in Georgie's head. Romance: what was that? It was nothing. It was worthless. But she let Cat go on.

'What wrong people?' she said. They'd want names.

'She never said his name,' Cat faltered, clinging to the romance. 'She just told me – it was all going to come good. She said a man she'd been in love with a long, long time was going to look after her. Marriage, children, everything.' Cat, who never cried, sounded like she would cry.

Georgie tried to imagine Holly with a baby and the thought tightened her throat, too, because it would never happen. She could believe she'd wanted it, suddenly. Holly resting her chin on her knees in the bathroom, watching Georgie with her cat's eyes.

'You think that was true. Not just – like her putting on a front?'

'Well,' said Cat, and her sigh was long and weary. 'It wasn't true, was it? Whoever he was, he didn't look after her.'

There was a silence. 'Look,' said Cat, her voice low and tired. 'Just send them to me. Tell them to talk to me.'

'No,' said Georgie again. 'I'll tell them as much as I can.' Then Harry was there, talking insistently, and Cat had to go.

There was movement on the platform: the train was limping in, slow, a blur of faces. Georgie stood, thinking of Holly, of the man who had been going to make it all

250

all right for her. Where was that man now? What was he thinking?

There were men all around her on the platform, in suits, in jeans, in velvet-collared coats, carrying computer bags, backpacks, briefcases. She'd spent a long time thinking men were like Dad, gentle, uncomplicated, loving. Wanting to fix and repair, to protect and build. She'd thought Tim was like that. She stood back, waiting for them to climb on.

Tabs didn't have a dad like that. Tabs had a dad who was shagging his secretary.

The sounds still hummed in her head. Tim grunting. A moan, the squeaking. The whispering, as she stood stock still in the hallway: conspiratorial. She was suddenly sure they had been talking about her. *Stupid Georgie, dopey Georgie.*

Georgie who had secrets of her own, though.

She stepped forward to climb in, not even bothering to look for a seat, she'd stand. Someone was behind her. A couple of guys.

A woman with a toddler in reins and a buggy was blocking the entrance, bending to fold it while a bald man looked down at her with irritation. Patiently Georgie held back: whoever was behind her was patient too.

Maybe the friend had told her, the ponytailed girl in the supermarket. And Lydia hadn't been shocked, Lydia had been delighted. Maybe Lydia had run straight to Tim. Behind her was a small sound, a breath, not impatient, not yet. Had that sparked something between them, Lydia consoling him, perhaps Lydia had had her eye on him for a while – but no. This had been going on a long time.

251

The toddler looked up at Georgie, candid, blue-eyed, while her mother struggled. 'Can—' Georgie leaned forward but the woman just shook her head and wouldn't make eye contact, jaw set.

This weekend conference – Georgie was fairly sure there had been no conference. He'd been with Lydia.

Then she remembered last night, Tim in the kitchen pressing her against the counter. Tim leaning over to take hold of her in bed – and at the memory a sweat broke, nausea flooded her mouth. Something was going on. Something weird was going on.

And then the woman straightened and the buggy was out of the way and she was looking for a seat, the toddler's reins wound tight round her hand. Georgie moved forward and the men who'd been behind her did too, they came around beside her, matching her step on to the train, separating. Seeing their feet move in unison she lifted her head and saw the one to her left – a teenager in a base-ball cap, a line of spots along his chin – move into the carriage a little way. She turned to lean against the div-ision of the compartment and she was looking into the other man's face.

There was a high-pitched beep as the doors closed but she hardly heard it, standing with her handbag clutched against her as if he was a thief. It was him. It was Mark.

He didn't seem to notice: he put a hand up and touched her cheek and she knew they were all looking, the bald man leaning against the opposite door peering over an iPad, the woman with the toddler clutched on her knee staring down the aisle in derision.

252

She knew then that it had been him she saw, standing in the hazy green light on the edge of the forest with a backpack on. Watching her. Following her.

'Hello there,' he said softly.

A brewery truck outside on the pavement was unloading noisily. Soon Frank was going to have to go down to the club and start all over again. Another evening.

Eddie's not a pimp. Eddie'd pimped his own wife, hadn't he, unless it had been her idea to show him her tits in their kitchen. Had she said, *I can handle Frank. Stop Frank asking questions about customers*?

What did three women on a night out have to do with Eddie's business? Frank still had no clue.

Seven brothels in the suburbs. Frank wasn't stupid: he knew what those places were like because now and again one was raided and you saw it on the news. Eddie would have them in someone else's name. He'd have his people keeping it separate.

He leaned down and picked the piece of paper from the floor, where it had ended up: for a second he'd forgotten where it came from then he remembered, in the dust at the back of the club, all that was left of Eddie's boxes. It told him almost nothing, at first glance. It was the headed notepaper of an accountant. Eddie's accountant. He stared at the name and address.

The police might well have it in for Eddie, they might often get it wrong, but Frank figured they also probably got it right now and again. Mum might be old but she'd never been stupid. Frank turned the piece of paper over, then back again. It was about the sale of a house in

253

Wanstead Flats to a property company. All above board, no doubt.

He held the paper in his hands and thought of Matteo's profile picture disappearing, of Eddie holed up out there in Epping, where the big houses sat hidden behind hedges and security lights, a shiny car on the front drive. He held very still, thinking.

Brothels were one thing. If Mum was right – if Benjy was right about the building Holly had died in belonging to Eddie, that was a bit different. Lucy's outrage on the subject hadn't been convincing. And strip clubs were one thing, brothels worse, but a woman strangled *then* raped? After she was dead.

That would mean, one way or another, Eddie was involved with some horrible people. He thought of Matteo, pale and urgent. *Is not your business, Frank.* Of Lucy desperate to get past him in the corridor and back to Eddie.

And Frank was involved, too, after that trip out to Eddie's, shifting boxes while Eddie talked business and all of it no doubt on the security cameras. Not moving fast enough when Lucy stepped close, placing her hand on him, and it occurred to him that there were probably security cameras in there too. That made him part of the family: Frank moved his head from side to side, trying to work it out.

Outside the crash and clink of shifting bottles stopped, there was the loud rattle of a metal shutter and then a sudden silence. Frank remembered being hip high to his mother, her standing at the sink while he pulled on the strings of her overalls. She had worked as a cleaner for forty years: she'd seen it all.

And she was right: he needed to get out. Out of the club, out of Soho, and start by getting out of this flat. It wasn't his, never had been, Eddie could have come in and out with his own keys a dozen times and Frank wouldn't have known about it. Frank pulled on a clean shirt, tie in his pocket for later, passed a cloth over his shoes. At the door he hesitated.

Lucy had known Holly, Georgie had known Holly. Matteo had said he didn't know the lanky guy who left with the three women, that night; said he'd never seen Holly's mystery man. Lucy kept saying, *I don't know what you're talking about.* The man who had reminded Frank of Joseph Cotten, old-time lanky movie star only with a bit of sleaze layered over the top.

See no evil, hear no evil, speak no evil. Suddenly no one knows anyone, no one saw anything.

Frank was fairly sure he'd seen the lanky guy somewhere before, eyes sliding away from him, standing in a doorway. Working the door at a strip club? Something like that. If he'd seen him, Lucy would have.

Pulling the mobile out of his pocket he scrolled through the numbers till he got to hers. Somehow he thought he'd already warned her, because he'd said it in his head enough times, but he hadn't. He dialled.

It went straight to answerphone and he heard her say, *This is Georgie Baxter* but he didn't get a chance to leave a message because the door opened in front of him, his own front door opened inwards.

And there was Eddie.

Chapter Twenty-Two

Her legs felt like jelly, out at the big station with its soaring girder roof, the noise all around her, echoing. Georgie knew he was walking behind her.

His head tilted, his face looking into hers, smiling in the crowded carriage. And everyone watching: her stomach turned to water. 'Excuse me,' she said and began to move through the carriage. The toilet was two carriages along, and mercifully unoccupied. It stank, but she sat there, staring at the smeared mirror, dirty water trapped in the little steel sink, the sticky floor, as long as she could stand. Longer: she only left it because someone rattled the door.

Hurrying along the platform, weaving between the other passengers, she saw a baseball cap, bobbing among the heads, not far back and when she swayed, looking for him, something hard caught painfully against her ankle. Georgie stared down at a wheeled suitcase; reaching a hand to rub at the spot, looked up at its owner whisking it irritably out of the way. Not Holly, of course not Holly: a man.

She couldn't see him but she knew he was there. She dipped down towards the tube, hurrying, faster, faster. Knowing it was useless.

A train had just left: the tube platform was empty except for a cleaner in a fluorescent tabard. The illuminated display said the next train would be in one minute, and Georgie stood, paralysed, waiting, exposed. She could hear a far-off rattle, it receded, then returned, the rails began to click and whisper, the warm wind that always came before a train blew, soft, in her face, pushing back her hair.

Jump, she thought, out of nowhere, *just jump*, but instead she stepped back, with a jerk, back from the platform, just as the train rattled out of the tunnel. There were suddenly more people on the platform, a small group of Italian tourists had drifted from somewhere chattering, cushioning her and as the doors opened she thought, *It's all right*. Stepped on to the carriage, only registering it was half empty, Georgie moved blindly to a seat. The Italians had got on in the next compartment, looking along she could see their black leather jackets through the greasy window. At her ear the beep of closing doors, an announcement, and she sat back.

Someone blocked the doors and they juddered, then slid open again to admit two, three more bodies. Georgie didn't look, because she knew whoever it was, he would be among them.

'Don't—' she said, as he swung into the seat beside her, stretching out his legs. Long legs, to chase you with.

'Calm down,' Mark said easily but softly, looking around,

257

restless. Down the tube carriage. Whoever had got on with him was standing in front of the doors, strap-hanging with his back to them, though there were plenty of seats. She could see earplugs, his head nodding.

Turning to her, he smiled. Mark. He started talking, as if taking up a conversation, as if they knew each other. Like they were friends.

I don't know you, Georgie thought, looking at him, frozen. Unable to do anything but look. His hands with bitten nails, his restless long legs, his jawline, his hair. Darker than Tim's. Thicker. Tim's nervous movement, his hand always moving to his head, tentative, smoothing his hair.

She felt herself nod, stupid, hardly daring to look around. Not wanting to draw attention to them. He was talking about the woodland, *could have been cleaner but then what can you do so close to the city*, his little hiking weekend, a nice B and B. Her mind jumped and started at the thought of him, in someone's house not far from hers, hanging up his clothes at night, going out to walk the streets.

The whole weekend. He'd known where to find her. Since the flowers arrived at the school, before. Since that night, when she'd babbled, about her job.

Now he was saying something about people looking for mushrooms out there, about nature. Georgie couldn't take it in, she just sat very still in the neon-lit train with his voice talking softly, staring at the ads overhead without seeing them, alert for the sound of the wheels slowing. She was running ahead in her mind now and fixing on the police station. He wouldn't follow her there, would he? She tried to think about what she had to say to the police but her thoughts scattered.

Leaning her head back a little Georgie looked up at the tube map – how many stops? and he was in her face, quick. 'Am I boring you?' Smiling, easy, but with an edge to it. She looked away, up and down the carriage, but there was only the strap-hanging boy and an old man leaning forward, looking down at his shoes.

'No,' she said, 'no, I—' Three more stops. Just be polite. Tried to smile. 'What were you doing out there, did you say?'

'Oh, I always do a bit of walking, weekends,' Mark said, leaning back, elbows on the armrest, hands steepled together. Pleased with himself. 'Gym gets a bit boring, doesn't it?' She said nothing and he leaned towards her. 'I'm not saying you living out there had nothing to do with it.' Smiling, his eyes crinkling, conspiratorial and she felt it, the panic. What if, if he – if Tim – But Tim had been away, hadn't he?

'Nice pub, too. Friendly.' He took hold of her hand then, in a quick easy movement, without asking, and as he did so the boy standing beside them turned, with his earbuds and she saw the baseball cap stuffed in his top pocket. Him. The lad from the train. His head still bobbing to the sound in his ears, holding his phone up and peering down at it.

'No,' Georgie said, feeling sick suddenly. Pulling her hand away. 'Mark,' she said, trying out his name, her mouth dry. 'Look, this is – I don't know what you think, but nothing's going to happen. I'm married.'

The train was slowing, they were approaching a station, the sooty tunnel walls giving way to advertisements but even as she felt the surge of relief, other people, other passengers, the world coming in through the window he leaned down across her, he was on her. He was kissing her, his mouth hard then soft, pressing down on her, she pulled her head back, struggling, overwhelmed by his different smell, different taste. Horrified. He was holding on to her too tight, the train slowing, slowing and then just as it came to a halt he took hold of her hand and thrust it down between his legs. She could feel it. His erection.

Over his shoulder she saw the young man, his face turned their way.

'You can't,' she said, frantic now, pulling back. And as she broke free she saw the young man, grinning. He had his mobile in his hand, the mobile that was also a camera, these days.

'Married?' he said, standing up and the tube had stopped now, the doors were opening and Georgie sat there as if pinned back in her seat, a hand on either armrest. 'You didn't seem very married last week, darling,' he said, malicious, and as he said it the doors slid open and he turned and stepped out through them, not looking back.

The youth stepped out of the way with a little movement, the beginnings of a bow and then followed him, sauntering, reaching to pull the cap out of his top pocket and slapping it back on his head. Tugging down on the visor and sliding a glance back her way as he stepped through the doors, and then other passengers were getting on, someone sat beside her with a sigh.

When the train moved off it caught up with them, standing in the entrance to the white-tiled tunnel leading off the platform. They didn't care what she saw, they didn't bother to look at the departing train, and as she watched, hypnotised, she saw him, saw Mark clapping the boy on the shoulder with one hand, the other passing him something, folded money. And then the train was in the tunnel and she could only see her own white-faced reflection.

Trembling, Georgie sat back in her seat. *Why, why.* She didn't know what had just happened – and then she did. Didn't know why, still, but to the roots of her hair she understood, she'd been shamed, publicly, she'd been exposed. She'd been set up.

One night, a taxi ride, a polite goodnight on the doorstep, flowers. That hadn't been enough for him.

She knew what this looked like. She knew. He was her lover, meeting her a week later, kissing her, holding her in his arms in a public place, shameless, heedless. She rubbed her lips, rubbed and rubbed until they looked at her. She reached her stop and got up, tasting blood in her mouth.

All the way up the escalator, the dirty stairs, Georgie had to fight panic. Around her everything felt squalid from the gritty tile underfoot to the posters to the other passengers, old men scratching their crotches with dirty fingernails, a girl in front of her whose skirt was so short her knickers were visible, a long ladder in her tights. She came up out of the exit as if she had been diving, gasping for oxygen and Soho was bright around her, dazzling. The sunlit curve of old dark brick fronts shone away from her into Chinatown and she turned along them, into the sweet smell of dried glazed meat, hanging burnished red in the windows.

In her head Georgie knew where she was going, she

had mapped her route out in advance and now followed it like a blind person. Right, then right, across the choked traffic of Shaftesbury Avenue, threading between buses straight on then left. A motorbike roared behind her, so close she felt the wind from it move her hair but she barely flinched.

The police station was in a building from the nineteen-thirties, Georgie could even visualise it as she walked, head down, a building she must have passed dozens of times in the old days, the days when she was a Londoner. The blue lamp over the doorway and the plain handsome lettering of the period, a sober building. You never thought a police station applied to you, it was something glimpsed on a television screen, it was a backdrop. She had never thought, consciously, that she would ever climb the steps, walk inside. Georgie had never spoken to a police officer.

He could still be following her. How had he known Georgie would be on the train, how had he known she wouldn't be at work? It seemed almost supernatural: every nerve in her body jittered, uneasy.

Hurrying now, outside an old-fashioned restaurant with dusty red lampshades Georgie sidestepped a big man in a camel hair coat who seemed to have planted himself in her way. She stopped, risking a second, had to look up because otherwise she would have bumped into him.

Smooth looking, old, swept back grey hair. He stared, then made a sound and was out of her way.

'A word,' Eddie said.

The first thing Frank saw as he stepped aside to let Eddie in was the piece of paper on the table, from Eddie's accountant. He stopped, looking down: he had his phone in his hand and he set it down on the table slowly. Face down.

The letter was official side up. He focused on the letterhead again, the name. The address. He frowned, and then there was Eddie, beside him and without a pause Eddie leaned past him across the table and took the piece of paper, folding it, tucking it into the pocket of the camel coat. He sauntered over to the window and stood in front of it, his overcoated bulk blocking the sun, and smiled.

'What do you want?' said Frank, just letting it happen. The first time he had ever spoken to Eddie that way.

'Frank, Frank,' said Eddie in that easy way he had. And sighed. 'You're involving yourself in something that is not your business. You see? You're just a barman. Just a fucking barman.'

'I'm leaving,' said Frank immediately, before he knew he was going to say it but he could see straight away that wasn't enough.

He couldn't just walk out, get on a bus to Brockley and Mum and forget all about it. Lucy had made her own bed, but Matteo? Musclebound Matteo running scared. Maybe he could leave Matteo, too, he was a big kid for all he was still a kid. It was Georgie – the thought of Georgie, standing there looking scared with her little girl on the pavement outside the bar, that made his chest tighten.

Even if Eddie let him walk away, it was too late.

Stepping back from the window so that the sun flooded back in Eddie said, 'It's too late.'

And in that still bright instant Frank felt his own head move back, a small involuntary recoil, as he worked something out. Or saw something, more like: he saw the man's face, looking down at a woman. The skinny guy waiting in the doorway opposite Fanelli's: Frank knew where he'd seen him before. The realisation came with a tingle of shame, because where he'd seen him before was in a porn movie. Not even a movie, a clip on the computer, how long ago? A couple of years. Between girlfriends, after the Spanish bird who'd gone home and before the roller-skating waitress.

An appearance in a porn clip didn't make you an actor. It made you someone who'd do a range of things for money. Frank couldn't remember the woman, but he could remember the man: that was the thought that made him swallow, uneasy. He remembered the man, and the settee they'd been having sex on but the woman's face had gone.

Eddie was turning towards him. Of course he could be involved with porn, of course he could. It was bigger business than ever. Frank's head hurt from trying to make this all connect, like holding wires up in a Bond movie, except that would be to defuse the bomb, wouldn't it? Not set it off.

'I need you here, Frankie,' said Eddie easily. 'I don't think I'm going to let you go.'

'What?' said Frank, feeling stupid, on the tip of his tongue to say, *you can't stop me*, but once anyone went head to head with Eddie, they were going to lose. He had to keep it quiet.

'You knew that girl, didn't you? The one that died,' said Eddie smoothly and Frank went cold.

'Holly,' said Frank, feeling his scalp prickle, 'No, I didn't know her.' Speaking slowly. Lucy did, he wanted to say but managed not to. Lucy did, Matteo did.

'You sure?' Eddie's pouchy eyes, hard as stones. 'You sure you didn't have a quick one with her, round her place? You were seen over there, I'm sure someone said that.' Scratching his chin ruminatively, stubble coming through white, Frank noted, mesmerised. 'And she was easy, you know. She was anyone's.'

Trying to goad him. In the certain knowledge that he was being fitted up Frank said slowly, 'What are you on about?'

Eddie slotted his hands in the slanted pockets of his camel coat and tilted his head to one side. 'You want to be careful,' he said gently.

'It's to do with that night,' Frank said before he could stop himself, because it slid into place, the wires joined. 'The night when those girls came in, Holly and the other two. And that guy was hitting on them.' And then he realised he needed to keep very quiet indeed.

The night Lucy had been so keen to distract him. 'Never mind,' he said, feeling himself begin to stutter.

It was you, Frank thought looking at Eddie, but he still didn't know how or what or why and Eddie was smiling at him as if to say *Not my style, mate, you should know that by now. I don't get my hands dirty.*

The guy picks up a married woman, climbs into a taxi with her and her mates.

The married woman happened to live out there not far from Eddie, out there in the suburbs, in all the green, in the woods. Frank knew that because she told him the station she was travelling back to when he helped her into a cab outside Fanelli's.

And Georgie's voice, on her answering machine.

This is Georgie Baxter. Please leave a message.

She was married to the accountant. The name on the headed paper of Eddie's accountant had been 'Baxter'. T. C. Baxter whose wife was called Georgie, whose daughter was called Tabitha, looking anxiously at Frank while he got a glass of water for her mum.

It had been a set-up. It came to Frank there and then. Some kind of sting, blackmail, a version of getting Frank on tape with Lucy's hand down his trousers. He could see, if there were seven brothels in false names, that Eddie might need leverage over his accountant. And Holly must have been part of the set-up, and now she was dead.

Eddie was circling on the spot, taking the room in, as if assessing it for the bailiffs. Looking up at the damp patch in the corner, the handful of books on the shelves, the curtains. The bed. He was looking at the bed now.

Face down on the table Frank's mobile pinged, as a text came in. Eddie stopped, eyeing it as if it was part of the deal, his to buy or sell.

'That'll be—' Frank groped for someone innocuous, 'That'll be Mum,' he said, pocketing it. Eddie's eyes stony, like a lizard's.

And Eddie's hand was heavy on his shoulder. *Careful*, thought Frank, *no fast movements* but there wasn't much chance of that. His brain felt like it had been put in the deep freeze, or hibernation.

Eddie sighed.

'I'm off home,' he said, lazily. His hand was still on

Frank's shoulder. 'Got to look after the wife, if you know what I mean.' His big fingers working at Frank's trapezoid, gauging how much muscle there was there. 'But how about a quick one, first. Just you and me.' Smiling, but joyless. Grim. 'Set the record straight, how about that, then?'

Frank tried to work out if he had a choice. He didn't think he had.

Chapter Twenty-Three

The police station was as she remembered it from that other life, on a corner, anonymous as an office block except for the blue lamp. Behind the bland façade it was dingy and busy, a murmuring underworld in a neon-lit reception area contained by swing doors and two rows of grey plastic seats. Four or five of them were occupied by motionless figures.

Tentatively Georgie approached the reception desk, which sat behind a wire-reinforced security screen like you'd find in an all-night off-licence. There was a sign about the penalties for abusing the staff and an officer who looked like he worked out sitting behind it, blunt fingernails curled around his biro. He looked up at her with a brief smile. Georgie hesitated, and a man who could have been any age in rags started up from the seating beside her, scratching his groin savagely and beginning to pace. Gripping the counter Georgie held her ground, and he walked the other way, off towards the door.

'I need to talk to someone about the death of Holly Walker,' she said in a whisper, on tiptoe to get closer to the wire screen.

The desk sergeant had to ask her to say it again.

The officer who eventually came to get Georgie – DS Andrea Mills – was a woman of roughly her own age: solid but not fat, square-hipped in the uniform trousers, thick ponytail. Following her through the swing doors Georgie reminded herself it wasn't likely they had allocated a woman out of consideration for her feelings, more like they got better results, women maybe would say more to another woman. Which was what she wanted, they wanted, everyone wanted, wasn't it? To solve this, but that didn't explain her sick feeling, her panic. The sense of guilt that threatened to flood her in the grey corridor, to make her blurt and flush. They headed down some stairs.

She focused on the policewoman's back, instead. A bulge under the fabric of her shirt where her bra was too tight; Georgie sympathised, on safe ground. From behind Georgie could see she was wearing an incongruously bright scrunchie in her hair, too, like it might have been borrowed from an eight-year-old's bedside table at the last minute, late for work.

'Here,' said the woman, opening a door, not into the kind of grey featureless cell Georgie had expected but a big bright room with two long tables in it, a man at the end of one who barely raised his eyes from his computer. No window: they were underground, but no privacy, less formality than she'd expected. When Georgie didn't move with an audible sigh the policewoman – DS Andrea Mills, *What had made her choose the police force?* thought Georgie, frozen – pulled out a chair at the free desk. Georgie sat.

'So,' said DS Andrea Mills, planting herself in another chair across the corner of the desk, 'I'm not quite clear,' the trace of a frown, down at the paper form she had in her hand, 'what it is you're here to say, Mrs Baxter. Georgina, is it?'

'Georgie's what – people call me,' said Georgie, wanting suddenly to change the subject, to talk about anything but this, *How old's your daughter, mine's five?* 'I knew Holly Walker a bit, we went out a week or so ago. My friend – Catriona, Cat, she came too, she knows Holly better than me but she's—'

'Yes, I got that. Catriona Marston. She's already called the station, talked to a colleague of mine. I believe Mrs Marston is undergoing treatment—' Shuffling papers, peering down. 'For—'

'For breast cancer, yes.' Feeling the lead weight that was the thought of Cat hooked up to a machine, Cat lying in the dark. But Holly. She made herself focus on Holly. 'Holly was – Cat said she was in love with someone. Had been for years and years, Cat said not to judge a book by its cover, she looked like a party girl, you know, but—' A frown notched itself above the bridge of Mills' nose.

'Look,' she said, leaning back, 'Ms Marston did also seem to think we were acting on the assumption Holly, Ms Walker was a – an escort, sex worker.' A glance down the room at the man, who seemed oblivious, her voice lowered a little anyway. 'But we aren't. We can't afford to

270

make any assumptions at this stage. But she let someone in, or went there with him.'

'A man,' said Georgie but then she remembered, *strangled then raped*, wondering who, what kind of man could – just as the woman's eyes flicked up at her, warning her. 'Yes,' said DS Mills. 'A man.' Curt but not unkind.

'She wasn't a – an escort,' said Georgie, hearing her voice rise. 'She had a job – I mean a real – a different job. She worked in . . . in advertising. Cat said, she had relationships – she—' None of those things ruled it out, a secret life. For a second her own kitchen rose into view, Tim doling out housekeeping. Don't judge a book.

'All right,' said DS Mills, holding her hand up. 'Sure. But—' a hesitation, 'I'd like to know what *you* think. Not your friend Cat, we'll get back to her eventually—' So there'd been no need for her to come? No need to lie to Tim, to take the train. She could leave. But then she remembered, with a scalding rush – how could she have forgotten – that it hadn't been just her, lying, her with a secret life and it looked so flimsy, so squalid, an evening of flirting with a man, getting too drunk to know— Not just her. All the time Tim had—

With the policewoman's eyes on her she remembered standing in the hall, unable to move, hearing the sounds from upstairs. Tim with Lydia, on top of— the lasagne on the kitchen counter. She sat very still, obedient. None of this had anything to do with Holly's death. Did it?

'Don't you have an opinion?' said Mills, gently.

Holly was dead. Nothing else mattered. This was what she had to do. 'I didn't keep up with her,' said Georgie, haltingly. 'It was years ago we worked together, me and my husband and Cat and Holly, but I left not long after she arrived. Before she died, before Cat told me – I only thought she was, you know, not after a steady relationship.'

'So you're telling me the impression *you* had of her was the direct opposite of Mrs Marston's.' Chewing the side of her mouth, perplexed.

Helpless, Georgie shrugged. 'I didn't really know her,' she said. 'Maybe she thought I was too – too boring, too married, I wouldn't understand. Cat's more – she's more—' More angry. And happier.

Not relevant: the state of her marriage against Cat's was not relevant either. Georgie felt herself flush.

DS Mills nodded, thoughtful. 'All right,' hand up, 'that's fine, sure. But you went out together. After not having seen her in, what, years?' Georgie nodded. 'Whose idea was that?'

'Well—' Georgie hesitated. 'Cat's. I thought there'd be more of us, I didn't – I didn't really know who would turn up, I was mostly interested in seeing Cat.'

'Is it the kind of thing you do often? Going up to London for the evening?' Georgie shook her head. In the policewoman's faintly perplexed questions it all sounded – odd.

'You know, these girls' nights out,' she said. 'They can be – a bit random. Whoever's free.' It didn't sound convincing, but DS Mills nodded.

'And how was she? How was Holly, that night? Up, down, wired, anything odd?'

Georgie made herself think: if she just focused on the question, she'd be safe. 'She was cheerful,' she said finally. 'She was really upbeat.'

272

Mills nodded, thoughtful. 'Did she meet anyone she knew, when you were out?'

'I think she knew the hat-check girl. You know, the cloakroom girl.'

Mills wrote something down. 'And her mood?' she asked, without looking up.

Georgie thought, shrugged. Frowning. 'She did seem happy. I mean, she had — a relationship had just ended, a man had ended it, she even had her things still with her, her suitcase, she looked like, well, maybe a bit rough round the edges the next morning but she didn't seem — depressed, the opposite.'

'The opposite.' Mills paused, pen in hand, and looked up, questioning as if she didn't know what the opposite of depressed would be.

'Excited?' said Georgie. 'Cheerful anyway.' The police-woman reclined in the chair, leaned back, removed the scrunchie and put it back in, sweeping back her hair, watching Georgie.

'There are three missed calls from your number on her phone,' she said. 'So you hardly knew her but you were in touch three times? Keen to talk to her?'

'So you do have her phone,' said Georgie, too quickly.

'We've got *a* phone, yes,' said Mills, regarding her warily. 'It took us a while to track it down. It had been left in the postbox attached to the apartment.'

'*A* phone? You're not sure its hers?'

'It's hers all right. What I meant by that was plenty of people have more than one,' Mills explained, patiently. 'People with — people who want to keep parts of their life separate. There's a certain amount of evidence that Holly had another phone.'

'Such as?'

Mills hesitated a second as if considering the wisdom of giving any information to Georgie: Georgie held her gaze: it came to her in that moment that whatever it was that was making her feel guilty, she wasn't. She wasn't guilty. Had Tim had a second phone? In case she picked his up from the kitchen table or the bedside, while he was in the shower, or mowing the lawn? 'Such as a receipt from a pay-as-you-go top-up, in her purse.' She leaned forward, elbows on the table. 'So why did you call her? Three times. Once late that night, the Friday night?'

'We were supposed to meet again,' said Georgie, faltering. 'Just me and her. I phoned to organise that. She – well, it was the Saturday afternoon. She never – never turned up.' She didn't know what Mills was getting at. 'Have you got any other leads from her phone?' she asked. 'The one you found?'

Mills just shook her head briefly without looking up, not saying if she meant, no, or that she wasn't going to say. Making more notes. Then she lifted her head. 'So when she didn't turn up you tried to call her?'

'No,' said Georgie, heat rising under her collar with embarrassment, 'I just left. I – my daughter was tired.' It sounded lame: it sounded implausible. 'I'd been regretting – coming to London, it was too much for Tabs, she's only five—' her voice pleading for sympathy but DS Mills just looked at her incuriously. Maybe she had no child after all, no daughter waiting at home. 'I wanted to get home,' she said. 'I thought Holly – I thought she maybe—'

'You thought she was flaky?' Mills laid down her pen: Georgie felt tears coming into her eyes.

274

'No,' she said, cleared her throat. More firmly. 'No. I thought she'd been delayed somehow and I just didn't want to wait. I was being the flaky one. Just running off home. London's – it – I'm not used to London any more. The tube—'

And quite suddenly she was thinking of him. Mark. That was what a secret life was, when you didn't want anyone to see inside your head, when you didn't want to give names to people and make them real. Mark. She thought of Mark, on the tube, of Mark putting her hand on his groin, and that kid, that boy smirking down at them.

You didn't seem very married last week, darling. And Holly the only one who knew what he meant. Only Holly knew what happened that night.

And him.

'So you went home without attempting to contact her again.'

'There was a missed call from her,' she said, numb, because she had forgotten that. 'I tried to call her back but there was no answer.'

'Ah,' said Mills, looking down. 'Yes. Yes, that's right.' Tapping her teeth with her pen. Georgie could see the policewoman hadn't washed her hair, it was thick hair with a dusting of scurf at the centre parting.

And then something about the room, the strangeness of it, of being in a police station, entering another world where bad things happened and must be dealt with and Georgie's mind crept back again. She was confined here under the flicker of the striplighting, the smell of disinfectant over grease, fast food carton in the bin and it crept back — *she* crept back. Back to that night. She had told herself she had no clue what had happened — but that wasn't quite true. There were clues. There were signs, at those crossroads in her brain, those neural pathways. If she sat very still, there was something, if she worked backwards: if she forced herself.

What she had needed to know was that Mark was not a good man. He was not a gentleman. Putting her hand on him in front of people: she had wanted to cry. She had looked around, horrified, and people had turned away.

She remembered the cab. Flashes of street lighting as they passed under the lamps. The memory of a sensation, a bruise on her shin, the railings along an area.

An old railing. Georgie saw her hand on the old railing outside the cheap hotel, but she was walking down, not up to the room, down into the dark. Down into the old building's lightwell.

A gentleman. Had Cat said that, or Holly? Not Holly, with her sleepy look, her side-sliding eyes, her amusement. Georgie had seen him out of the hotel. She had gone down the stairs with him, Holly had told her that much. Georgie's hand crept up to her throat as it came back, it invaded her: she couldn't stop it, whether the policewoman chose that moment to look up, to examine her or not. Not a conscious memory, nothing her brain had processed but something more indelible. His hands on her shoulders, fingers digging into the soft space above her collar bones, pushing her down.

Down below the pavement, stone steps and a sharp smell of piss. *Where are we going?*

She must have been completely out of it, drunk or — or

something. The whisky, his back to her and then he turned and gave her the glass. Out of it, and yet Holly had let her go with him. When she got back upstairs Holly had been witness, to whatever had happened, to whatever state she had been in. At best, too out of it to take off her own clothes.

And Holly was dead. Witness Holly. Maybe more than a witness: it had been Holly had reached into her bag for the brandy.

She thought of him, when she'd last seen him, cheerfully handing money to a kid in a baseball cap on the tube platform, his eyes flat and uninterested, his hand on hers, thrusting it between his legs. A man who would do anything. He'd known Holly, all along. Pretending not to know each other had been part of the game.

'There was something,' she began, making the mistake of beginning to say it before she knew what would come out. DS Mills raised her head: had that been a trick, too? Looking away to lull her into a false sense of security? 'Something happened—' and then she stopped.

What was he going to do next? Mark.

Georgie had never really understood before, about those women who didn't go to the police when something bad had happened to them, because they don't think they'll be believed.

The policewoman was looking at her, curiosity hardening into something else.

'Something?'

Georgie froze, gave a stiff little shrug, forced herself to sigh, reluctant. 'Oh – nothing. Just the next morning, she was very kind, I was hungover.'

DS Mills was very still. 'Right,' she said, and it was clear to Georgie that she had not been believed. True and yet not true at all. The next morning Holly *had* been kind. She had told Georgie nothing had happened, but her eyes had said something different.

They both waited, and finally Mills sat back.

'Well, you've been very helpful, Mrs Baxter,' she said, clapping her notebook shut and Georgie felt a kind of desperation, as if with the sound of the book closing her chance had gone. But she was frozen, her throat choked with something. 'Really very helpful. Would it be all right—' a hesitation, a tiny sideways look, 'would it be all right for me to contact you at home, about this? If I think of anything else?'

'Yes,' Georgie managed through dry lips, thinking of the home phone, her lifting the receiver and Tim watching her. Cleared her throat. 'Sure. Of course.'

The man didn't look up as they left but she heard the sound of his chair as the door closed. As DS Andrea Mills escorted her back out – letting Georgie go ahead of her through the door, on the stairs – she didn't say anything more. But Georgie felt her watching.

Past the reception desk and the plastic chairs, past the ragged man still pacing and scratching and the big glass doors opened, letting her out, into the cold polluted air. Halfway down the steps she turned and the doors had closed but there was the policewoman, still watching.

Tim had always been scornful of the police: bottom-feeders, he called them; chavs, kids who left school without qualifications, the boneheaded and the violent and the stupid. Georgie, who had never knowingly spoken to one before, didn't think Andrea Mills was stupid. Turning back into the blinding sunlight she nearly walked into a passing car and stopped, feeling her heart pound.

The possibilities jumped, sprang. If it was him. Him. She didn't know him at all, this Mark, after all, she didn't know one thing about him. You made it all up, didn't you, when you were infatuated, in love, maybe Holly had been the same, maybe she had trusted someone. This secret life built itself in your head and you thought there was no harm in it, but you built it around another human being and there was your unknown quantity. You never knew, did you, what was going on in another human being's head? You never knew.

And then in her pocket her phone came back to life, it pinged, once, twice, three times.

Two missed calls from Tim. And a message, but this one wasn't from Tim. Georgie raised a hand to her forehead to shade her eyes, so she knew what she was looking at. Although her mobile refused to recognise his number, she already knew it by heart.

And he had sent her a picture.

No more than mid-afternoon, but the traffic was heavy, *how the fuck, how the fuck* was going round and round in Frank's head as he drove, his hands sweating on the Jag's leather steering wheel. He shouldn't be here.

Slow and stupid in everything he did. He stood there behind the bar fancying himself as Frank Sinatra or the head barman at the Savoy but he was a trained gorilla in a sharp suit, he was thick as pigshit.

They were in north London, Tottenham, edging uphill

between terraces with dirty windows, their paintwork dingy with the fumes.

The traffic had ground to a halt again.

Holly, on the floor of a rented bedsit, call it an Airbnb but they were all bedsits. With damp under the window sills showing through a hasty coat of magnolia, with scale in the toilet, with curtains too thin to keep out the light. Holly raped and strangled. Strangled then raped. Did it matter which way round that happened? It mattered. It mattered to Frank.

'I thought we'd just head back to my place,' Eddie had said, watching him as if he knew what he was looking down at, while he waited at the flat's door. 'If that's all right with you?'

Before he'd put the phone away he'd seen that the text was to tell him he'd missed a call, from Matteo.

Why would you block someone? To stop messages coming in. If Matteo had been with Eddie, Eddie reaching for his phone like it was his own property? Funny, that Frank was more worried about Teo than Lucy. The big bloke just wanted a quiet life.

And in that second Frank had unclenched, he'd seen his chance, right or wrong. He'd nodded. 'You're the boss,' he said. And even as he said it, a suspicion crept up on him. *What if?* Matteo was from Sicily, he was strong enough to strangle a woman one-handed. He might have been given no choice. The idea was ridiculous. Outlandish. Not strangle and rape. Not Teo.

The satnav said another twenty-five minutes, a red line of traffic. Behind him Frank could hear Eddie laboriously typing in a message to someone. He'd never got the hang of using thumbs, Frank had seen him, jabbing at the screen with a forefinger. He could hear Eddie's breath, heavy and fast.

It was possible that Eddie was in the shit, and needed Frank's help. It might start with a dead girl in a building that could be traced back to him. And that was what this was about? The boxes moved out of his house, then disappearing from the Cinq. About money and dodging taxes – was that how Holly had ended up dead or was that just an unforeseen consequence? It occurred to Frank that he should go to the police. The thought was so impossible he almost laughed.

And then abruptly as the traffic eased the houses thinned out, old brick semis fronted with shrubs and cherry trees and tidy hedges. Then the roundabout so big it looked like a park, and beyond it the wide roads disappearing into the woodland. Here they were again.

As Frank took the roundabout from behind him Eddie's phone rang: he left it two, three, four rings, then answered. Frank tried not to move his head, not to show he was straining to hear. Whoever it was, was worked up: Frank couldn't hear the words but the voice was animated, insistent. It wasn't Lucy. A man's voice.

Turning his head slightly Frank could see beads of sweat at Eddie's glossy hairline, under the silver curls. Eddie wasn't so laidback, after all.

'No,' Eddie kept saying, keeping his voice low but Frank could hear the warning edge to it. 'No, no, that wasn't the idea, no. Don't go off on one, no. I told you. I didn't know, did I? How was I supposed to know she'd come down here? No, don't do that. I wouldn't do that, mate.'

She. Who? Georgie had come to London on Saturday, holding her little girl's hand.

All in a level voice, at one point even catching Frank's eye in the rear-view mirror before he could look away, smiling, shrugging, as if to say, what can you do? Then with finality, 'Look mate, I've done my part. I've done what you asked me to do. Maybe best if we don't talk for a bit, right? Radio silence. I think that's best.'

Almost inaudible to the human ear, but Frank was tuned in: the sound of Eddie close to losing it. The jab of a finger, his breathing heavy then the soft hydraulic whine of the Jag's rear window and Frank couldn't stop himself looking, turning to look at the phone flying out, a tiny flash and gone. A small cheap thing. Then abruptly, Eddie said: 'Turn off here.'

They were beyond the houses, beyond the suburbs: they had just driven past a little church and there was a turning, a narrow road but tarmacked at least.

Automatically Frank did what he was told: of course he did, it was what he was used to. He felt it creep against him: despair. The sign was low down, Private Road, low down, seen too late, like the tarmac, unmaintained, crumbling at the verge.

The road surface was poor almost immediately, the low-slung Jag bumped and crunched. All around him the hazy green of trees, one after the other like reflections in double mirrors, nothing to see but trees. The church behind him, the road, civilisation: they were all out of sight. He peered across the steering wheel, searching for something that would indicate there was an end to it, to the dusty woodland, the silent trees.

282

'Here,' said Eddie and there was a turning, a track that Frank hadn't seen coming.

There was someone there. Was it Matteo? Big Matteo sorrowful, who'd tried to warn him.

And his foot went down on the brake, sharp.

'Hey,' said Eddie into his neck, thrown forward by the abrupt stop, nettled at last.

But it wasn't Matteo, stepping out from behind a tree into a space that – from the untidy trampled aspect to it, a dirty bottle, baby wipes, the glint of silver from a blister pack – had been used before.

It wasn't Matteo but it was a man Frank had seen before. A black backpack rested at the foot of the tree.

He could turn here, he could drive away. He wrenched the car into reverse, turning to look over his shoulder, for trees, for the space to do it, always too cautious and then Eddie was there, and Frank could smell the sweat on him now, never mind see it. Eddie's big body, taking him by surprise, barrelling between the seats with a grunt and reaching past him, past the steering wheel before Frank knew what was going on.

Too slow, Frank, too slow.

Eddie plucked the keys from the ignition. And as Frank, galvanised at last, reached to grab them back off him, the door beside him opened.

Chapter Twenty-Four

Tim sounded completely reasonable, completely calm. But he was asking where she was.

She was home.

Standing there on the pavement, with the police station at her back, Georgie hadn't opened the picture message. She had stuffed the phone down into her pocket, deep down and she had walked stiff-legged to the tube station. Down, down, down, into the bowels. The escalator rattled, faces turned to look at her but Georgie stared straight down at her feet. As she descended, into the warm breath of the underground, between the tiled walls, she felt as though she might not come back up again. Standing on the platform, climbing into the carriage: it all felt like something from a horror movie, people peering at her, every face shadowed unpleasantly.

When Georgie did emerge with the flow of the crowd, out into the vaulted din of the mainline station, the mobile was dead. Of course it was: she hadn't charged it up before leaving. For a brief breathless moment, though, it felt as though something had intervened, to stop all this. If she dropped the phone into a bin, flushed down the train toilet, threw it on to the tracks, would it all go away?

She didn't throw the phone away, though. It sat in her pocket all the way home, but she hadn't dared even put her hand in, to touch it. She didn't know what he would be sending her a picture of. Him. Mark.

In the part of her brain that opened and closed her mouth and communicated with police officers, the part that got on to trains and off them again and found her car in the station car park – Georgie didn't know what picture Mark would be sending to her. But there was another part of her brain, where memory blinked and pulsed.

The car had been where she left it. Georgie stood there, at the rear left side, looking at the dent. More of the white paint had flaked off, and it looked ugly.

She put both her hands in her pockets as she looked and there was the phone. It felt warm, from being against her body. She hadn't pranged the car, therefore someone else had done it. That realisation ticked down in her conscious mind, her rational sensible mind, as she found the key, started the car. Drove home, plugged in her phone to charge.

Had *he*, Mark, had he been here, had he been watching her? He wanted her to know he'd been there.

She put on the kettle. It was after five o'clock, and getting dark but she didn't turn on the lights, she stood there quite still, in the kitchen. She thought she should call Sue and get Tabs back but something told her, leave her where she is. Just for a bit longer. Waiting for the phone to charge.

Using the landline would have meant whoever she phoned would know where she was.

But they seemed to know, anyway. Mark did. How could he have known? This morning Georgie hadn't known herself where she was going to go.

How long had he been here, in his Airbnb? How long had he been here, following her? Up to town and back again. Had he been watching when she got the flowers, when she raced to the florist's? In the supermarket with Tabs' hand in hers?

Georgie walked softly into the sitting room: it was darker inside than out, as the light faded beyond the wide wall of glass, so she didn't close the curtains. She paced the house out, metre by metre, going up the stairs carefully, on bare feet, standing beside each of the windows, theirs, Tabs', the bathroom window that looked out to the side, the fence that protected the back garden. She couldn't see anyone.

Only then did she come back down, pick up the mobile and call Tim.

'Where are you?' he said, without any preamble.

'Tim—' she couldn't help it, she heard the voice she used to placate him. But she didn't want to tell him. She hesitated.

'When you didn't answer the phone, I called the school,' he said, just a hint of puzzlement in his voice. 'Sue told me you'd gone home sick.'

'I know,' said Georgie.

'But you didn't go home?' The puzzlement more pronounced, not quite disguising something else. He wanted to know what she knew. She let the silence lengthen.

'No,' she said, 'I lied.' She was in that moment completely calm. Her knowledge of what Tim had done – was doing, with Lydia – sat there in her head but she said nothing about it.

'You what?' There was something new in his voice.

Or not quite new, it had always been there. Georgie knew him so well, she realised in that moment. Obviously not well enough to see he'd been fucking his secretary but come to think of it, she'd probably even known that, deep down. She'd always known he kept his life secret from her, she wasn't allowed to see inside his office, that was why he didn't want her working there. When he opened his computer he would always turn it so she couldn't see the screen; when he looked down at his phone he tilted it away from her.

She knew his every intonation, she knew when he was lying, when he was angry, when he was hiding something. He never admitted he was wrong.

And now she calculated, the old calculating Georgie, so sharp at school and at work. She knew that Tim had come downstairs and seen the lasagne out on the side in the kitchen and he had wondered if it had been there before. When he let them in, himself and Lydia.

And she wondered, too, had she left it there on purpose? So he would know she knew. And it was then that sharp calculating Georgie faltered, uncertain. Her subconscious was evading her. She didn't know herself what she was capable of any more. She took a step back against the kitchen counter, pressing herself against it so she couldn't be seen through the kitchen door.

The picture he'd sent her was still there, unopened, on the phone that was pressed against her ear as she waited for what Tim would say next – what she would answer.

How do you say it, anyway? *I heard you fucking Lydia upstairs.* You don't say it. Instead you make no effort to be quiet, instead you take the lasagne out of the freezer and leave it there.

'Why did you call, anyway?' she said; she heard her own voice, careless. He wouldn't like that, her sounding casual and unworried when he must have been bricking it. A phrase he would have winced at if she'd said it out loud, unladylike, betraying her South London origins.

But when Tim had called the school and they told him she'd gone home, he must have been. Bricking it.

'My mother phoned,' he said. 'She called me at the office. Why didn't you tell me she'd phoned the house?' Still reasonable.

'You phoned to ask me *that*?' Georgie realised she didn't care that she'd forgotten to tell him: she remembered Jennifer's tone with her. She felt as if she'd been cut loose, and she knew what the next step would be. She'd never had a row with Tim. Ever. Not one where she answered back.

'She said she'd call you at the office, anyway,' she said, not even defensive. 'Obviously it was something she didn't want me listening in to.'

'Don't be childish,' Tim said harshly. He didn't *sound* scared. 'Where were you?'

Georgie didn't know what Tim scared would sound like, though, because he didn't do that. He went straight to angry. A near miss in the car one time on a slip road, Tim cut up by some bloke and Tim's lips white with fury.

'I went to London.' He was waiting, so she went on. 'I went to see the police.'

And then there was a silence, and she heard it bubbling up, eloquent. The anger: it could be there for all sorts of reasons. Because she had found him out, because she had got away from him, that she had done something unexpected. 'The *police*?'

'About Holly. You remember Holly?' How had that note of sarcasm crept into her voice?

'Holly.' He spoke without comprehension, as if he really had forgotten who she was, and that she was dead.

'Cat asked me—' Georgie began trying to soften it, and then she thought, leave Cat out of it. 'I just wanted to tell the police about how Holly was, when we were with her. That she was happy, she had things to look forward to.'

She wished in that moment that Tim could understand: she knew he wouldn't. He'd never had any time for it, what he called being sentimental. When she found herself talking about anything like that, about Cat being ill, or Tabs at school, or her dad, hearing her voice wobble, his jaw would set, he would look away, impatient.

'Well, I'm sure they were very grateful.' She heard him being careful not to meet her sarcasm with some of his own: he only sounded condescending, but that wasn't what he was feeling. Georgie could hear that too, with her new sharpened senses. He was enraged, that she had gone to London to talk to the police, that she had involved them in this – mess. It would just look like a mess to him, that he wanted nothing to do with.

And then for some reason Georgie found herself thinking of the man in the camel-hair coat on the Soho pavement, blocking her path. He had stared at her as if she didn't belong, as if she shouldn't be there. As if he knew who she was.

'Tim—' she began uncertain, but he interrupted her.

'Where's Tabs?' and his voice was mild, still giving nothing away, but Georgie's hair stood on end at the sound of it, of danger. Of menace, that was the word. Softly she disconnected the mobile from its charger, and backed out of the kitchen into the hall.

It had got quite dark in the hall, with the only light from the misted pane in the front door but Georgie could see herself, a motionless outline in the metal-framed mirror. This was what it was all about, this new world, where she could see and hear everything so clearly, it was about making her space smaller and smaller. For all this time she had worked on the assumption that Tim was on her side, but he wasn't. Never had been. They were his possessions, her and Tabs, in this house he built, for his own purposes. His garage, full of his things, his locked boxes, his clothes in the wardrobe.

'Tabs?' he repeated, patiently.

'She's—' she didn't want to tell him.

So many years since she lost that baby, lying in the overheated hospital ward, lying very still, her head hurting under the bright lights, and Tim had been there, whenever she opened her eyes he'd been there. Tim had been all around her, telling her it would be all right, they could try again and she had thought, *I don't want to. I want that baby back.*

'She's — she's over at one of her friends',' she said, looking around herself, trying to formulate a plan. Where to go. 'Playdate.' A lie: she suspected he would hear it was a lie.

'Right,' he said, soft. 'Well, I've got one or two things to wrap up here and—' his voice trailed off. Lydia, was she one of the things he needed to wrap up?

Georgie had thought, the first, maybe second time in bed with Tim, that something wasn't right. That it wouldn't last. She remembered only now, as though it had been hidden from her. She remembered clear as day sitting up in bed the second time, the morning after and watching him brush his teeth and she hadn't liked the way he did it: so weird to have forgotten that. She had suddenly wanted to leave and had made an excuse, she had to get in early to work. He had asked her to come back to bed, wheedling, and she'd given in.

And now here she was staring at herself in a mirror in the dark and suddenly Georgie knew what to do next. Upstairs, suitcase. Moving up the stairs sideways, with her back against the wall, careful steady steps. Tim still didn't know where she was, did he? Not for sure.

'Right,' she said. 'Well, I'll go and get her in a bit.'

It occurred to her that there were couples, many of them, old married couples who went over and over the details of their meeting, their falling in love, the first time they did this or that. Two days after that morning when she'd faltered he'd asked her out again and she'd thought, *How can it matter?* The way someone brushes his teeth.

291

She'd slept with him again. Then she had got pregnant, and he had been so loving, so happy. And Georgie hadn't been able to face having an abortion and she thought, *that was that.*

'You do that,' said Tim, silky-voiced.

'Yes, I'm—' Georgie was in the bedroom now. Outside the lawn had turned grey and velvety in the twilight, the shadows of the big shrubs lengthening. It was getting harder to see if there was any movement there. 'I'm just going now,' trying to sound casual. 'OK?'

'How was London?' said Tim, 'I mean – nice day? Get anything else done while you were there? See anyone?' Wrongfooted – hadn't she told him, she'd been there to see the police. Did he think she'd have wanted to fit some shopping in after? – Georgie sat down abruptly on the bed. He was the one who knew people in London, not her.

That man she half recognised in Soho, on her way to the police station, the man in the camel coat who'd looked at her. She remembered him, from somewhere, sometime. He had a connection with Tim, she was fairly sure. A client, an associate, someone from when they were in the big tax office together? He had turned to look after Georgie as she hurried past.

Say nothing. Don't let him know you guess, you wonder, you think at all.

'I didn't do anything else, after the police station, I—' Flustered, she changed tack. 'I – I came straight home.'

Hang up, then go upstairs and break into his filing cabinets and find out.

A soft sound, like a sigh, barely audible. 'So you're home. You're there now.'

'Yes,' she said. He already knew, though. She could hear that in his voice.

'I won't be long,' said Tim, and he was gone.

And there on the stairs in the half light falling from the landing above her and her heart pounding Georgie looked down at the phone. Slowly she went to the message, and opened it. She made herself wait for the photograph to download.

It was a picture taken from above, taken with a flash, and the first thing she saw was a hand, bleached white, spread like a starfish, against old railings. She could see her wedding ring, white gold, because that had been what Tim wanted. Her right hand was elsewhere, she couldn't see her right—

Seen from above. The flaking black paint on railings, the hand grasping for them. The fair crown of her hair, the swirl of it, the dull gold sparkle at her shoulder where the dress had begun to slip from her shoulder and his hand on the back of her head, pushing her towards him. Dark hairs on his knuckles. Holding her against him and that was where her right hand was, on him.

The hand went to her mouth now, on the stairs in the failing light, saying something like, *no I no I didn't I*

In the picture she was clearly recognisable, you could see her. She was trying to look up, one hand out to the side, flailing, her eyebrows, her eyes. Her eyes were glazed, she was a fish frozen under ice, she was terrified. She had his cock in her mouth.

And suddenly now she was scrambling, half falling to get upstairs. Georgie staggered. On her hands and knees she kept climbing on the hard wood because she had to get to the bathroom, before – *before she*

293

And feeling the stairs bark her shins she remembered that too, those other stairs. Remembered the bruise the morning after from falling upstairs drunk – more than drunk. The half bottle Holly got from her bag. Holly. Georgie had been insensible. He'd shoved her back up the stairs, his hand hard on her backside.

And then Georgie was in the toilet and vomiting. All around her Tim's house, Tim's stuff. She sat back up and there was someone outside. A car pulling up.

Frank had never been good at school. There were things that wouldn't go in, and the more the teacher yelled at him, the tighter his brain closed. There were times when he just froze.

'What are we doing here?' he said. 'What's he doing here?' Eddie was sitting in the passenger seat beside him, and the doors were locked. Outside the tall guy had retreated to lean against the tree, smoking: he had the car keys in his pocket.

Matteo must have been trying to warn him.

In the seat beside him, Eddie adjusted his bulk in the seat. 'You just keep asking bloody questions, Frank. Keeping bits of paper.' He looked down at his hands in his camel-hair lap. Fat fingers, gold signet ring on the left pinky. 'How do I know I can trust you? And when I found out your mum was shacked up with that old copper—' He shrugged, looking sideways at Frank. 'You been saying things to your mum, have you?'

Frank felt his scalp prickle. He could only think long-ingly of that night, when he was in charge, behind his bar, everything in its right place. When the tall bloke now standing against the tree waiting had been just a punter, trying his luck with some women on the raz. 'I wouldn't—' he began.

'Shh, shh,' said Eddie equably, like he was Frank's dad. Eddie had no kids. Didn't want them, according to Lucy, never had.

The address on the accountant's headed paper was out here somewhere, too. Satnav had shown him that much, driving out. Five miles, maybe six, from where Eddie lived, separated only by the forest.

T. C. Baxter CCAB.

The accountant whose wife had been set up so Eddie would have something on him, just like he had something on everyone.

'That girl,' he said. 'Georgie Baxter. She was nice. She'd never have gone with him.' Nodding towards the bloke leaning against the tree. 'You set her up.'

Eddie didn't answer, he was just smiling, those hooded eyes, the grey lips. Had they always been grey? 'Not me,' he said, shaking his head. 'Put people in touch, that's all.'

'Was it pictures, blackmail, what was it?' Frank was incredulous.

Eddie just shrugged. 'Like I said. Not me.' But he looked off, somehow, a sheen of sweat.

The lanky man had pushed himself off from the tree and began to saunter slowly towards them. Frank rested his head back against the seat and the future unspooled, how far was this going? If he was lucky he'd just get the shit kicked out of him. He could take the tall skinny bloke, maybe but there was Eddie too. And he didn't feel lucky. He sat forward.

'Was it not part of the deal, her getting strangled?' Eddie closed his eyes. See no evil. 'Was it him did that?' Frank said, turning to look at the man beyond the window because it seemed too late to pretend. Holly hanging on to some bloke like he was Marlon Brando. 'Her loverboy?' He wasn't going to mention Matteo. Keep Matteo out of it.

The man, Mark, took another step towards them, a hairy-knuckled hand going up on the roof of the car and he leaned down, grinning. Frank had been sure he was the guy with Holly, now he wasn't so sure. Something was wrong about it. About the right build, he thought.

Mark, the man with wood – *raped and strangled* – went back to the hotel or wherever with the three of them, but he was after Georgie, not Holly. Would Holly have let him do that, if he'd been the one she loved, gazing up at him that way? A threesome, foursome in a hotel room. Maybe. People did all sorts in the name of love.

'Did he do Holly? Rape and strangle her, did he do that for you?'

But Eddie's face was grey now, not just the lips. 'You want to know, now, do you?' he said and there was a smell in the car that hadn't been there a moment before, sharp and rank, of sweat. Eddie was leaning against the door with his shoulder, shoving to get it open, sweating.

'No, I—' But Frank couldn't form the words. Once he knew, he was a dead man.

But then something else was happening. Eddie wasn't waiting to hear. Eddie was climbing out, his broad back briefly blocking the door, then he was standing, heavy against the car. Frank wondered, in that moment as the

296

outside air came in, about the big world. About the seasons, the sky, the trees, all of the world beyond Soho and beyond this soft green land, this ancient burial ground, all the world he was never going to see.

'You stupid cunt,' but Eddie wasn't talking to him. He was talking to Mark. A wheeze as he drew breath. 'You were supposed to show *her* the pictures, not him too. No bloke wants to see that, does he? His wife – like that?'

For a second Frank was bewildered, a prickle at the back of his neck, remembering Lucy's hand on him in the kitchen. No man wants to see that, not even Eddie, who'd probably asked for it.

Eddie's bulk was in the car doorway, Frank could see his gut, the camel coat swinging open. 'You don't know him,' he was saying. 'Accountants – mild mannered? I don't think so. And now what? Now what? All this mess. Just so he gets the kid, not even his flesh and blood.'

The kid. Little girl on the pavement. Think about her later.

Now.

Frank got the door open and began to run.

They got him down in under five seconds, he hadn't even got to the trees, but then Eddie was gone, somehow. Out of the corner of his eye Frank saw him stagger, off to the side and then he had the guy down, and underneath him.

And saw it. It wasn't him. The bloke he'd seen Holly with from above didn't have this much hair. And with the realisation he loosened his grip for an instant and between his knees Mark twisted and was out from under him,

297

reaching for the tyre iron that Frank hadn't thrown far enough.

Caught off balance, Frank fell. He didn't even have the time to turn and see where it was coming from.

Chapter Twenty-Five

'I just drove by to see if the car was back yet and – Georgie?'

Sue was standing on the doorstep, Tabs' hand in hers. She was looking worried. 'Georgie. Is everything okay?' Peering at her from the porch Sue was wearing jeans, something she never did at school and for a stupid instant Georgie longed to just have a silly conversation, about clothes or the kids or awful bullying parents. Other people's lives.

'Yes, yes – I—' Georgie plucked at her shirt, it was sticking to her where she was sweating.

Take her away, keep her, just a few hours more.

All this time and she hadn't seen it. No wonder Sue always looked sideways at Tim, or frowned when she and Georgie had that conversation about pushy dads, the ones who would stand in the doorway not moving until you had to deal with them, the ones you bet pushed their wives around behind closed doors, and worse.

Tabs ran past her before Georgie could say it. *Keep her safe.*

'Georgie?'

'It's – he's—' She wanted to come out with it, *it's Tim,* but she didn't know where to begin.

'It's all right,' said Sue. 'I – well, perhaps I can guess—' Advancing on her, pity in her eyes and Georgie stepped back.

'Can you?' she said, faintly, because in that moment all she could think was that Sue had seen the picture she'd just seen. That she knew about him, Mark, that he'd sent the picture to all of them, got their numbers from somewhere, hijacked her phone.

Maybe that was it. The phone. It was in her hand: she should have thrown it from the train, after all. 'You know about—'

Sue stopped, not quite across the threshold. She sighed, lowering her head. 'It's the girl, isn't it? The secretary. Tara saw them in the pub one lunchtime, heads together, she was hinting she thought there was something—' Her shoulders dropped. 'I told her not to gossip.' She couldn't meet Georgie's eye.

'It's all right,' said Georgie mechanically. So it hadn't been just a one-off. A fling. She should care but she didn't, her mind was racing, round and round like a rat. What mattered was what she'd seen on the phone.

The nasty squalid mess of it: her and Tim, both the same. Is that what Tara would say, and Sue would have to agree with her daughter? Caught at it. Except she hadn't, except she wouldn't, she would never have.

He gave me one of those drugs. Him and Holly, Cat snoring

300

on the bed. Had they given Cat something too, so she didn't see anything?

Sue didn't know the half of it, looking at her that way, with sheepish sympathy. *I wouldn't have done that*, she whispered to herself, in her head but the words sounded stupid, lying. Behind her she heard Tabs coming back down then felt a soft bump against the back of her legs, the small arms around her thighs from behind.

But she still didn't understand: there was a piece missing. Why would they do it? Mark and Holly? Was it just money? Or they'd tell Tim, was it blackmail?

Maybe that was why Holly was dead. Her share of the money? There was no money. Where would Georgie get money from? Why hadn't they asked for it already?

She twisted to look down and saw Tabs' upturned face at her hip, plaits coming undone, the little vest grubby at the neck and she knew, finally. She's why.

Sue's hand was on the door jamb, she was going to come inside.

'Look,' said Georgie, because she knew quite suddenly, that she didn't have time for conversation. They had to leave. They had to get out of there.

'We – I've got to – we've got to – I'm sorry, Sue, thanks for worrying about me but we've got – we've got to get going.'

Sue stepped back, startled and Georgie began to close the door immediately. Sue put up a hand to stop her and for a second they were pushing against each other. Georgie put her face to the crack. 'Tim's coming home,' she said. 'Do you understand?' She could see the questioning look in Sue's eyes, the reluctance hardening and then Georgie simply had to close the door, setting her back against it.

'Mummy?' Tabs in her vest and pants, looking up at her. Georgie put a finger to her lips.

From outside silence, and then the sound of Sue's footsteps receding, the car door slamming.

Georgie could have told her everything. Asked her to stay and help. Two against one, or three with Tabs, or would he bring Lydia? She wasn't going to wait to find out.

Telling her everything would have been the problem, too: with Tabs there, bewildered and Georgie trying to interpret Sue's expression, not knowing if she was disgusted, or fascinated, or angry. And someone dead, Holly dead: that would have frightened even Sue. And there wasn't *time*. It was too late.

'Upstairs and get your jeans on,' she said to Tabs. 'Quick now.'

Tabs just stood there.

'*Quick.*' Her eyes were wide. 'We've got to go and see Granddad,' Georgie said, into her wide eyes, not quite improvising because it had occurred to her, once or twice in ten years, more often if she admitted it, that that would be the excuse she'd use. 'He's not well. And you're coming with me.' And she turned Tabs in front of her and hurried her upstairs.

With Tabs distracted, pulling open her drawers Georgie quickly took the teddy from her bed, old Stanley, worn at the paw Tabs hauled him around with. Nothing else. Just be quick.

'And socks and jumper and trainers and put your pyjamas in your backpack.' She hurried out before Tabs.

There was a big suitcase in the landing cupboard and Georgie hauled it into the bedroom. Open on the bed it looked too big, suddenly she didn't want to take anything, nothing from here, nothing of his, she didn't want to wait one minute more. But there'd be no money, not for a while, she'd have to have clothes. She'd need another job, Dad's pension wouldn't— and she paused, feeling the weight of it, the breadth of it, a whole wide unknown horizon. Georgie wavered, the ragged Stanley in her hands. She couldn't do it. How could she?

Then she thought of Tim: his voice on the phone. His whispering, up here, in this bed, to Lydia. His fucking her, last night, in the kitchen and again in the bedroom, when she hadn't wanted it and yet she hadn't been able to say no. How many times had that happened?

Hundreds.

And when he found out, when he knew, when they told him: she didn't have money to pay blackmailers, if that was what this was. Holly and Mark. Maybe he already knew. Maybe they'd gone straight to *him* for money, and maybe that was what she'd heard in his voice. He'd already seen that picture.

And the fear blossomed inside her, rich and dark as blood.

She had to do it. She dropped Stanley into the suitcase. A handful of underwear, at random, jeans, trainers. She tugged open the wardrobe and there they hung, Tim's suits, orderly, mothproofed, dry-cleaned after four wears, every time. She shoved them aside. Dresses – what would she need them for? Offices, interviews, Christ knew – she felt herself on the brink, looked round for the time, the bedside clock said six, and beyond the window it was dark. All the lights blazing, advertising their presence – and soon he'd be home. He was on his way. She grabbed a dark thing off a hanger at random and then saw it, gleaming, the gold dress.

Take that too because if you don't, he'll use it. Evidence: your evidence not his. She almost stopped with that thought. It was outrageous, it was mad, it was extreme, to be thinking in terms of evidence. But that was where they were. Today she'd been in a police station. Just from one telephone conversation with Tim – *I lied*, she'd said, defying him – and the playing field was laid out.

He'd known this was where they were going. Had he even wanted her to find him with Lydia? She stopped, dead, as something suggested itself. Where had she put it? The phone.

She scrabbled on the bed and there it was, hidden in a fold of the bedcover and as she saw it she saw a greyish smudge of dust from the suitcase, too, for a mad second she thought she was going to have to change the sheets, so Tim wouldn't be angry. Too late for that.

And she knew Tim. He started things and sometimes they didn't finish the way he liked. For some mad reason, sorting the clothes frantically in the suitcase, thinking: shoes, *where?*, listening for Tabs, at the same time she was remembering when they'd had the drive laid and the border finished too far from the kerb and he lost it. Screaming at the Hungarian blokes until they just got in the van and drove away, back door banging. If things got away from him, he got angry – because control was all important, when you were doing accounts, wasn't it? If she'd had a fiver for every time he'd said that.

She'd read something. In a newspaper? Tim said newspapers were a waste of money but one of the supermarkets gave them away free and she would sit in the car, in the supermarket car park and read, luxuriously, disposing of it in the car park's waste bin before going home.

It had been about surveillance. Husbands watching wives? She remembered that piece, of course she did, remembered thinking Tim would like to do that, as she read that there had been husbands – controlling, possessive or simply divorcing husbands – who installed an app on their wife's phone called, *find my phone*, or something. She stared at the apps, half of them she never looked at, no more than wallpaper. Frowned. Saw nothing.

'Tabs?' Tabs came to the door of her room, jeans on, trainers on, backpack on, sweatshirt on inside out. Little Tabs, obedient, hurried, sensitive to every tone of voice, anxious. All the signs you could look for, if you thought to do it, and she'd been trained to, before she went to work in the school, the signs of a child uncertain in her own home, a child from a place of danger not safety. Was that what Georgie had been doing while she ran around after Tim all this time, trying to keep him happy? Keeping them in a place of danger.

'Make sure you've got everything,' she said, in a whisper, and obediently Tabs went back in, without a question or a murmur. Georgie hurried back into Tabs' room and scooped up the pile of clean washing that sat on her chair, folded and ironed, *that would do*. Dropped it into the suitcase.

305

Slammed it shut.

Lugging it on the stairs, too big, too awkward, Georgie stopped, panting, the suitcase painful against her ankle. Her back to the wall and Tabs upstairs, waiting to be told what was next. She'd known what he was like, known she didn't love him, worse. Had known he frightened her for years, ten years and more, the look that came into his face when things didn't go his way.

And still now, the house was holding her back, the dishwasher to unload, Tabs' school uniform to fold. Tabs: Tabs was holding her. Tim had paid for Tabs, he had got Georgie pregnant with another man's sperm. He had wanted the wife and kid.

And the thought sprang, alive, into Georgie's head as she stood there on the stairs: that if she said one word, one word against him, it would only end one way.

With that thought Georgie felt herself begin to shake and in that moment the mobile rang, in her hand. And she dropped it: she didn't know why or how. Still ringing it skittered down the stairs ahead of her and tipped by the sudden movement and the weight of the suitcase she could feel herself teeter, losing her balance.

She went down.

The pain in Frank's leg was astounding: it throbbed, up his side, but there was no blood. He held it stiff in front of him, in his two hands: he couldn't have spoken if he wanted to. If he opened his mouth in that moment he thought he would vomit.

Standing over him Mark crossed his arms, the tyre iron dangling from a hand, looking towards Eddie for instruction.

Covertly Frank moved his arms back, straight down, hands palm down on the ground to either side of him. Mark was frowning across at Eddie still, impatient now. Frank raised his knees, slow.

In the twilight Eddie's face was white: he was old, wasn't he? Years out of the gym. He wasn't up to physical force any more. And with the calculation, before he even knew he was going to do it himself Frank pushed, all the strength he had going into it, his body had never felt so heavy but he was off the ground and up. He heard a grunt come out of him that turned Mark's head, too quickly. He caught the tall man off balance, and with the advantage lunged, elbow up, and jabbed him sharply in the throat.

The tyre iron fell and Frank went after it. The leg stood up under him, but the pain was still there, like fire. He straightened, with the bar in his hands. Mark was swaying: he had both hands at his own throat, and his mouth moved but nothing came out.

'It wasn't you, then,' Frank said. 'Holly? You didn't kill Holly.' Raped and strangled: he'd been so sure. What kind of man could do it? Fuck a dying woman. A man who'd do anything for money, who'd fucked on screen for money, that's what Frank had thought. What did *he* know? You wouldn't do that unless you hated the woman.

Mark was shaking his head now but it wasn't clear what he meant by it. He was looking at the bar in Frank's hand. He was probably wondering if Frank had the balls to use it: Frank was wondering that himself. He didn't want to. Why were they making him?

'He'll let you go down for it, though,' he said. 'You know that?'

Mark looked at Eddie and Eddie was murmuring, saying something, but he seemed to be having trouble forming words.

'Don't—' said Eddie, faltering, taking a stumbling step towards him and still Frank didn't understand.

'Was that the favour you were doing for your mate on the phone?' Jerking his chin up, talking to Eddie like he was Matteo, or some guy Matteo had just put out on the street.

Eddie was pale, blue round the mouth. 'It was a bit of fun,' he repeated, but the words sounded mumbled. 'I don't know that Holly from Adam, she was the one—'

'She was the one what?'

'It was her idea,' said Eddie.

Out of the corner of his eye Frank saw Mark shift, one foot to another, looking for his way out of this. 'I never knew anything,' he said, his voice rising, pleading to Eddie for confirmation. 'It was just an evening out.' Eddie didn't look back at him, his hand was under his coat again, rubbing at something.

Eddie was looking at Frank, and Frank looked back at him, ignoring Mark.

'*Her* idea? Did she know him, then? Did Holly know this mate of yours, the one you were doing the favour for?'

He should go. But he kept talking: slow old Frank, always the last one to the party. He needed to understand. 'The husband is your accountant, right?' No answer, which was confirmation. 'That was him on the phone, the one you chucked out the window.' Still no answer.

'So – you owe him one, I bet. All these years moving

your money around. Your property. I read somewhere these days accountants are like lawyers, they have to tell the police if anything illegal is going on. That right?'

'It's just,' Eddie began, 'it's just maximising resources.' But it was as if he ran out of breath, he sounded old, feeble.

'And the rest,' said Frank. 'So you were doing him a favour, setting his wife up? And where did Holly come into it?'

Mark was saying something, he'd stepped forward again, his long face pale in the darkness, 'She was his—' but Eddie shook his head, sharply, the old Eddie at last, and with the movement took a step towards Frank, then another.

'That didn't sound like leverage, on the phone, when you chucked it out the window, it didn't sound like black-mail. It sounded like something had gone wrong,' he said, and then Eddie was right there, leaning heavily against the Jag's bonnet, the driver door between them. And Eddie began to shake his head, eyes watery. 'Not—' and then he seemed to topple, clutching at one side.

There was a moment when everything seemed to hang suspended, and Frank was out from behind the door, round it and grabbing at Eddie as he went down.

'You,' he said sharply across Eddie's body, heavy against his legs, to Mark who was backing away again. Stopping him, rabbit in the headlights. He was never a killer, Eddie had picked the wrong guy. 'Get over here.'

It was a split-second thing. Do you run or do you stay? Frank would never know, would he? Just do it.

Between them they hauled Eddie into the back. Frank straightened, reached for the keys, reluctantly, and handed

them to the guy. The ex-porn actor, lanky streak of terrified nothing, but Mark took them. You never knew. You
just had to try.

'You're driving,' Frank said, and then he was in the
back, leaning over Eddie, ear to his mouth, listening for
a breath. 'Just find a fucking hospital.'

Chapter Twenty-Six

It all went through Georgie's head as she tumbled, the suitcase catching her sharply above the ear. Tabs behind her bedroom door, Holly dead, Cat on the machine that was pumping shit into her veins. The hard lump of cancer in her.

Tim on the way home, his face above the steering wheel in the dark. Calling to make sure she was still there, in his house, with his child.

And then abruptly it stopped, Georgie stopped falling, wedged at the bottom of the staircase with the suitcase below her and the phone under it, still ringing.

'Mummy?' Tabs' voice from upstairs, from behind the bedroom door.

'It's OK,' she managed, grappling for the phone.

She struggled upright, shoved the case out of the way and grabbed it. It wasn't Tim, it was Cat.

'Georgie?' She sounded terrible, her voice low and

311

dead. Georgie heard her try clearing her throat, a painful sound. 'Sorry, it's the chemo,' she said, 'I'm not supposed to be feeling bad yet, would you believe it—' trying to joke, failing. Starting again. 'George? I just – I just – there's something I need to tell you, George.' A sound in the background, another voice pleading with her that was silenced. A door closing.

'I can't talk,' said Georgie, desperate suddenly. Tabs in car, Tim on his way home, suitcase packed. 'Can you – look, I'll call later, in an hour—' Was that all it would take? They'd have to drive for more than an hour before she felt safe.

But Cat had interrupted her, her voice a low painful rustle she barely heard, words she could hardly make out. There was something in the sound of her voice that made Georgie stop. 'Where are you?' she said.

'I'm at home,' a hint of the old impatience, mixed with pleading. 'Look. Georgie. You have to understand. You have to believe me. I had no idea. Not that it was still going on. I'd have never—'

Leaning back against the wall, Georgie drew her knees up under her. 'What do you mean?' she said stupidly, but Cat was still talking.

'I thought it was over long ago,' she said, dully. 'Him and Holly, I thought – I'd never have—'

Around her the house was quiet, breathing, waiting. 'I don't know what you're talking about,' Georgie said, though she did, she could feel it rising, lifting her hair at the roots, something dull and awful, something dangerous and twisted, rising like a storm. 'Him? Him? Who's him?'

'*Tim,*' said Cat, blurting it, anguished. 'It was Tim, he

was the one Holly was in love with all this time. Since way back. Since we all worked together they've been an item. I swear I never knew – well—'

Here it comes, thought Georgie. She said nothing.

'Well – I knew there'd been something, but that was fifteen years ago.' Cat faltered then. 'That was before you—'

'Before I got pregnant.' Georgie spoke dully. She felt as though she had been in a car that had crashed, her ears were ringing. Then something roused her. 'No – no. Wait. He's – he wasn't – he's been fucking his secretary this past year.' It came out too blunt, too brutal. 'He—' She stopped.

'Well, he might have been fucking someone else—' and Cat made a sound of distress, almost a moan, but Georgie had not space to feel sorry for her, not in that moment. 'I'm so sorry, Georgie. I didn't know. I thought Tim was a good guy. He was so keen for you to have the evening out, he contacted me, he transferred me a hundred quid to pay for drinks.'

He hadn't said anything about that. Georgie tried to get her head around it. 'A hundred pounds,' she said slowly. 'Yes – well he would have been keen, I suppose. To get me out of the house. To get me—' she stopped, trying to fit it all together. The money, Lydia and Tim waving them off – and not just so they could have a night together. But—

Cat didn't seem to have noticed she'd even spoken. 'I had no idea,' she said again, slowly 'All I know is, Holly was in love with him, all right.'

'How do you know? How can you know?' Georgie felt sweat on her forehead, found herself thinking stupidly

313

Was the heating on full blast? Tim would be angry – he would—

Cat cleared her throat. 'I got a card from her, from Holly, in the post this morning, I only opened it when I got home, an hour ago, I was feeling shit, I didn't even recognise her writing—' she broke off, and when she spoke again she sounded desolate. 'She said by the time I got the card it would all be done, they'd have gone together, gone away. Her and Tim.'

A silence, into which everything she had learned about Tim over fifteen years, learned and never admitted, settled and took shape.

'He was just using her,' said Georgie, and she heard herself, cool and distant, clear-headed, the old Georgie, the prehistoric, pre-Tim Georgie. 'It's obvious, isn't it? He'd have been stringing her along – had been all these years. A bit of a shag when he didn't have anyone else. Promising her all sorts.' She thought of Holly, that next morning, in the bathroom with her. Her bony knees, looking a bit rough, excited underneath it. Making sure it had gone off all right, their plan. Georgie and Mark. A kids' rhyme from the playground was in Georgie's head then, *Mark and Georgie, sitting in a tree, K-I-S-S-I-N-G.*

Did I really, she thought of the image on her phone, *did I really do that—*

And the side of her hand was at her mouth now, rubbing hard against her lips, like she was wiping something off. *I didn't. I didn't.* And then the sickness, the creep of shame hardened into something else. Rage.

'They set me up,' Georgie said, her voice hoarse. 'Holly and Tim between them, and that man – that man. His

314

name's Mark, I don't know where they found him.' She thought of the other man in the camel coat, sidestepping her in Soho, the look on his face. The client.

Cat seemed stunned into silence, and Georgie went on, still cool, adding it all up.

'They set us both up,' she said. 'You were dead to the world, weren't you? Out for the count. That wasn't like you, when I knew about the cancer I thought it was just that, you'd gone for it. But he spiked both our drinks, between them they did and Holly got you into bed and sent me back out, with him. To kiss goodnight.' She paused. 'He could have done it in there, in the room, with you passed out but maybe he thought you'd wake up, make a noise, maybe Holly didn't want to see it—'

Dead Holly.

'All I remember is bits. The staircase. The railings. There were bruises—'

'Bruises?'

'I saw them next morning.' She was brusque, dismissing them: it wasn't the bruises she cared about. 'I don't remember – it. But he's got evidence. On his phone.'

'*Evidence?*' Cat sounded like she was going to pass out again.

'I've got it too,' said Georgie, 'he sent it to my phone. He's been following me. I think he scratched my car.' It sounded completely nuts. Tim and Mark, monitoring her every move. Gathering more evidence.

And maybe – maybe—

Maybe Tim hadn't been on a conference last weekend – she'd thought of that already, except she'd assumed, since this morning, that he'd been with Lydia. But maybe he

315

hadn't been with Lydia, either. Maybe he'd been in London last Friday night, at least, he might have gone to Bournemouth after that, of course. A weekend with Lydia and then he had come back to his wife. Wanting his tea on the table, wanting to fuck her. Feeling like a man.

Georgie didn't know where this language had come from that was in her head. This rage. She felt as though she had been turned into something else, not even some*one*. What was she worth? Would Dad even take her in, if he knew, her and Tabs scuttling away in the dark? She took a breath: speak it out loud, speak it plainly. 'They set me up. He used her for that.'

She could hear Cat hesitate, before she spoke. 'In the card,' she said. 'The card she sent me, Holly said Tim wanted a divorce, he wanted your— he wanted Tabs, she was helping him get all that.'

'Yes,' said Georgie. 'Yes.'

Put Tabs in the car. He won't get her. I get her.

'Georgie,' said Cat, pleading, 'Georgie, say something.'

'I've got to go,' said Georgie. 'Listen, Cat. You do something for me. I know you're feeling bad – you'll feel worse tomorrow. You need to call the police. You call the police and tell them it was Tim.'

'Tell them *what* was Tim?' Cat sounded panicked now.

'Tell them. About him and Holly. Because I might not be able to. Because he's on his way home right now. Tell them I think he used her – then he killed her.'

She hung up. Staring down at the phone blindly, thinking of the two of them, Mark and Tim, always knowing where she was, mapping her movements. It had to be.

Then she saw an icon that said, *extras*. She opened it.

It won't be there it won't be. It was there. Find my phone. *Find me.*

Georgie stood, stepped over the suitcase and walked through the house to the back. She opened the kitchen door, walked to the end of the garden and flung the phone, as far out as she could. There was a rustle in the dark as it landed, far beyond the fence.

Now. She ran, back into the house. And as she reached the hall, the suitcase there waiting for her, she heard it. She heard the car.

Upstairs, she heard Tabs' footsteps, the creak of her door. *Daddy's home.*

Chapter Twenty-Seven

They'd come into a town, they'd passed the sign and it had rung a bell but Frank didn't have the time. Street lights, ye olde pub. Very nice, very safe. Commutersville.

Frank had called Lucy. He just said, no time to be kind, 'Eddie's having a heart attack. We're on the way to the hospital. Epping.'

Frank had gone from thinking Eddie was going to kill him and bury him under the trees and Lucy was in on it, to knowing it was just a fuck-up. Eddie wanted to frighten him because he was shitting himself at the thought of that girl dead in one of his places.

Mark was following his phone's satnav. He was a bad driver, unsteady, jerky – or maybe it was the circumstances. He kept looking back over his shoulder.

Half lying across the back seat and Frank crouched over him, Eddie was breathing, but his colour was bad. Despite himself, Frank held his hand. He'd known the bloke near on his whole life.

'The police are going to want to know,' said Frank. He was talking to Mark, leaning forward so Eddie wouldn't hear. 'I mean – you say you didn't kill her but . . .' A pause, for it to sink in, Mark at the wheel, staring grimly ahead. 'You're going to have to come up with some kind of story and if you didn't kill her – raped and strangled, I heard – the truth is probably your best bet. They're not all thick, coppers. So what was it you were up to that night, you and Holly? Eddie put you and him in touch, you and that Georgie's husband? You know she's got a kid, don't you? Little kid.' Mark's eyes slid sideways to him then back to the road. 'Going back to the hotel with 'em, three women. Did you spike the other one's drink too? So you and Holly could sort out just what you wanted between you.'

'She was begging for it,' said Mark, knuckles white on the wheel, but his voice was dull. 'Couldn't get enough of it, you know what they're like, these women, let 'em loose, can't hold their drink.' It was like he was repeating something he'd been told. 'It's not illegal.'

'That's not going to convince anyone,' said Frank, softly. 'Rape and blackmail are illegal, as a matter of fact. Just not as illegal as murder.' He saw Mark's jaw begin to work, but he said nothing, and Frank went on. 'Have you done this before, then? What, for money, or just for fun?'

Mark's head whipped round then, the ghost of a smirk on his pale face.

'They never go to the police,' he said again. 'You use enough stuff they can't remember anyway. No one needs to pay for sex these days. It's out there, you just take it.'

Frank stared back at him, expressionless, wondering if

319

he should stop it now, right now, open the door and leave them to it. But beside him on the back seat Eddie was struggling. He was trying to right himself from his sprawled position and Frank could see his face, slack with pain. He was trying to say something, reaching up with a hand to the window and Frank leaned down, but it wasn't even words.

The street lights strobed as they passed, down into the car's interior, lighting them all the same yellow. It must be almost six, but the shops were still open. There was a sign, the black H that directed them to the hospital. It came to Frank, then, a little bounce of memory, that it rang a bell for a reason, that sign. Twinned with wherever in Germany, the town was where the accountant's offices were. *T. C. Baxter CCAB*. A little high street, all cosy, London beyond the trees.

Frank wondered if it was too late, from what Eddie had said under the trees to Mark, having a go at him. He'd sent proof to her husband, of what they'd got up to.

Continue for one mile, said the mechanical voice.

'He knew Holly,' said Frank. 'What was she to him? His bit on the side?'

They slowed: red lights up ahead, and a handsome old house with all the windows lit up, with a little car park, a professional sign he couldn't read. Mark rested back in his seat and gave Frank a look. 'She thought she was,' he said, sullen. 'Silly bitch. Pathetic. She fixed everything for him, where the girl was going to be next day, I'd have caught up with her then if you hadn't turned up.'

'You said Baxter's wife told you she was going to be

320

at Fanelli's herself,' said Frank. Baxter's wife, now, not Georgie any more. He'd liked it when he could call her Georgie. 'But it was Holly told you?'

'It was him,' said Mark. 'It was her husband, they were planning it together, him and Holly. To start with they were going to fix for her to meet Holly and Holly could, like, encourage her to see me again. Tell her what a sweetheart I am. Only then he calls me and tells me why don't I go instead. And it's going to look like we've got something going, witnesses and everything. He didn't say the fucking kid was going to be there, though, did he?' Irritable.

'And Holly couldn't go, could she?' said Frank. 'Holly was dead.'

A grin, then Mark was looking through the windscreen again. Either he was too dumb to understand or he didn't give a shit.

'He killed her. He killed Holly.' No one said anything.

They were level with the tall red-brick house now and the last window went dark. The front door opened and the blue-white of a security light came on, illuminating the sign. And there it was, literally in black and white, *T. C. Baxter, Chartered Accountancy Services*. Frank stared, and in that moment Eddie flailed beside him, managing to locate his arm, his hand, tugging with surprising strength.

Frank pulled away, his brain running like a train in another direction. He said, 'Let me out here.' Something in his voice turned Mark's head, eyebrows up in surprise. '*Now.*'

But Eddie hung on, exhausted, white, in the back, panting. And till trying to say something.

'I'm sorry, Eddie,' said Frank, his free arm on the door

321

handle. Up ahead the lights had gone green. 'Lucy's going to be at the hospital. You'll be all right, mate.' But Eddie's head was moving, side to side, *no*.

And then he spoke, with an effort, slurred but his grip on Frank's arm was tight. 'Don't go near him,' he said. 'Baxter. 'S'not safe.'

Mark was revving the engine now, engaging gear. 'How was I to fucking know?' he said, loud and clear at last but not turning his head, talking to the windscreen. 'Bloke's a fucking psycho. I thought he'd like to see the bitch sucking cock.'

'He'll kill her too,' said Eddie distinctly, and he fell back.

Chapter Twenty-Eight

And there was the sound of the garage door opening.

The mechanism was smooth as silk, and quiet, Tim had insisted on it but Georgie had always registered it, almost as a vibration through the house. How many times had she heard the big car purr up on to the drive at six thirty and gone to the front window to look out? To see Tim behind the gleam of the windscreen, just a silhouette, head and shoulders, arm raised to point the remote at the garage door.

The feeling was there now, in the pit of her stomach, it had always been there when she heard that soft sound that meant he was home but now Georgie knew what it had meant. She leaned down and raised the suitcase, setting her back against the wall. In her head she saw the inside of the garage, the tool bench, the row of heavy wrenches and spanners on the wall. She knew what came next. She knew. The detail was what escaped her: that was what she needed to work out.

'Mummy?'

Tabs was out of her bedroom, standing at the top of the stairs, looking down. Her voice was high with anxiety and her eyes were wide, taking it in. Georgie wanted to reassure her but her face wouldn't do it, it was a mask, and behind it she was calculating. Tabs could see the mask, and she was frightened.

Georgie heard the car now on the drive, heard him engage gear, it was pulling into the garage, the door was coming down again. She smiled up at Tabs, holding her gaze, and willing her to understand, *this is me, this is Mummy,* she beckoned. A finger to her lips. And solemn, careful, one hand on the banister and her eyes never leaving Georgie's face, Tabs came down.

Her own car was on the front drive, on the paving, Tim would have glided past it. As Tabs descended Georgie remembered the Hungarian builders again, driving off and Tim shrieking after them.

The soft whine of the garage door, and then silence. It ticked away. No sound.

Where was he? Why hadn't he come in?

She could see him sitting in there, in the car. *Find my iPhone.* How close could he get, on the little map? She could see him behind the wheel in the dark, the little glowing screen.

It occurred to her for a brief leaping second that a certain kind of man might never come out of the garage, if he'd seen what Tim had seen. What she thought he'd seen, the woman he loved with another man. Seal up the windows and doors, run a pipe to the car, run the engine. Not him. No. Not Tim.

324

Tabs reached the bottom of the stairs, and stopped. Georgie – wishing Tabs' daddy dead and slumped behind the wheel – knelt.

Her bag was upstairs. She calculated. No time, the car unlocked, the keys upstairs. *He can find me but he mustn't find her.*

'Sweetheart,' Georgie said, encouragingly, 'I want you to go out and get into the car. Very quietly.'

She tried to make her voice sound calm and reasonable, but she could hear the hoarseness in it. Tabs' face questioning, then frowning, stubborn.

Georgie took her hand. Leading her, two steps, three, to the front door and clicking it open as softly as she could. The cool evening air came inside and with its breath she could hear a sound, from inside the garage. Tabs lagged, pulling away.

In the doorway Georgie leaned down, felt the small warm head against her breast, breathed in soft hair. She whispered, through the hair. 'You wait for Mummy in the car, now. You climb inside and lie down on the back seat and have a little rest. You hide so I can't see you.'

As Tabs looked up Georgie saw it, saw her trying to understand, saw her beginning to grasp it, seized her chance. 'Stay very quiet, all right? I won't be long. Wait for me.' There was no more than a second of hesitation now in Tabs' dark eyes – those eyelashes from elsewhere, the thick black hair – and she nodded and was gone. Out into the dark on soft feet.

Georgie closed the door behind her and her heart squeezed in her chest. The suitcase sat there, too big, stupid, why hadn't they just *run* when they had the chance, why had it taken the sound of that garage door for her to understand and now it was too late, too late—

No. Just move. Move. Georgie ran, swift, to the stairs and up, two at a time.

If he thought she was in the garden, if he looked at the app that told him where her phone was and it said she was hiding out there, that she'd run out into the dark to escape him – then she'd have time. And even if she didn't – just do it. Upstairs, keys, car, drive.

If Tim thought she was in the garden he'd go back outside.

He wouldn't take the door that led from the garage into the house. The door that led to the utility room, then the door at the back of the hall – he wouldn't come inside. She was in the bedroom but she couldn't see her bag, the bed was covered in – and then she saw it, a couple of inches of strap and grabbed.

And heard the door, downstairs. He was going to come inside.

All right, reconfigure. New plan. Her heart was in her mouth but she slowed right down, straightened her back. Keys out of the bag and in her pocket, the bag – purse, driving licence – over her shoulder. Downstairs on quick feet, to the hall.

Then she could hear him, not just the door from the kitchen to the garage opening but a sound she didn't recognise, a horrible dragging, then a clank, that filled her with dread. She shifted, beyond the corridor that would lead him to her, so he wouldn't be able to see where she was standing, wouldn't guess anything.

He was in the house.

The suitcase stood there, though. In the middle of the hall.

'Georgina?' The name his mother used for her, in his voice. Inside her something tightened: the walls seemed to tremble and close. She needed to breathe.

Breathe. Don't pass out. Georgie gauged the distances, the steps, three, maybe four, across the hall in plain view, and she'd be at the door. Leave the suitcase, fuck the suitcase, this had gone too far for plans, for clothes. But she'd walked herself into a corner in the hallway, trying to keep out of his line of sight. She was behind the hard chrome console table he had chosen, she could see a corner of herself in the pale wood mirror – and there he was. Watching her in the mirror. She stepped out from her hiding place.

He was standing in the kitchen doorway, his body half concealed from her. His head and half a shoulder out. She shifted the handbag back over her shoulder. 'You're home,' she said, breathlessly stupid, and he smiled to hear it.

His head disappeared, she heard the soft sound of something being set down that she couldn't see and then before she could move he was out in the corridor, all of him.

'What was that noise?' she said, before she could stop herself. He didn't like being interrogated.

Tim had his phone in his hand: he looked down at it as if he didn't know what it was doing there. It was as if he hadn't heard the question, his old trick. 'Hello, sweetheart,' he said, pulling at his tie to loosen it. Sweating, which wasn't like him, sweating as if he'd been exerting himself.

Usually he would set his briefcase down next but he didn't seem to have brought it home.

Standing frozen in the entrance to the corridor Georgie made a tiny movement with her head, looking over her shoulder back to the front door, a tiny crack ajar. Cautiously took one step backwards. Tim was still talking and if she interrupted him he might—

'Sweetheart,' he was saying, ruminatively, 'that's what we are, aren't we, childhood sweethearts? Were. They do say you never leave them behind, the first one, however many—' but then he stopped.

'Where are you going?' he said, and his voice was hoarse suddenly, she heard the danger. He had taken another step and was looking past her, at the suitcase.

'Oh, I – no – my dad—' She was turning as she spoke, thinking, not about what she was saying or how she was going to end the sentence but how to block him, how to get to the door before he reached her. Little plump Georgie always last in the hundred metres, the sack race, the egg and spoon: the stupidest thing to be thinking of at a time like this, Dad on the sidelines cheering her, a faded long-ago summer.

He caught her before she'd got halfway, and his arm was round her. Pulling her into his side. From the outside would it look like they were lovers? She struggled briefly, feeling the hardness of his grip, pinching, and subsided, feeling her heart pattering, her breath quick. Once the fight began in earnest, she'd lose. Her only hope was to be submissive, eyes down, let him think she'd given up.

All these years. Why hadn't she fought before, why hadn't she run— She felt the tears in her eyes and stopped them. No time.

Tim was steering her into the corridor, arm tight around

her, squeezing her shoulders. She needed to be in a better position. To run. She needed a clear route. She needed him to loosen his grip.

He was taking her back to the kitchen. Before the door he turned her, quick, and she was against the wall, her back against the wall. Tim had one arm up, blocking her path back to the front door. The other hand was under her hair, on her neck.

'Where's Tabs?' he said. Looking around. 'I've got something to show her.'

'She's with Sue,' said Georgie, desperate, and she could hear it. He smiled, except that it wasn't a smile, and shook his head.

'No she's not,' he said and his lips were on her skin, at the temple, at the hairline. Kissing her.

Was he – was he going to— her hands clenched.

Raped and strangled. It felt like he was already strangling her, her throat tight as if it was in a noose and just at the feel of his fingers, under the hair at the back of her neck.

But Tabs. Why would he be asking about Tabs? She had lied. He had caught her in a lie. His fingers tightened on her hair in that moment and he pulled her head back so she had to look up into his face.

'She's not with Sue,' he murmured. 'I went there first – of course I did.'

'What – what did—'

'What did I want to show Tabs?' He tilted his head.

His hand twisted in her hair, tugging it, tighter. The pain was nothing. She hardly felt it: it was as if there was something in her veins that numbed her. 'Hold on a minute,' he said, as if he was going to produce a present, *surprise!*, and then he was holding his mobile in his hand.

'It's this,' Tim said softly, his thumb moving across the screen. Manicured: he had them done, once a month. The phone was in the hand that had blocked her path back down the corridor, but she didn't dare glance that way. His other hand tight in her hair still.

'This—' and a speck of saliva appeared at the corner of his mouth. 'This is what I want her to see.' He held the screen up to her face, too close, it blurred. His face beside the screen and still with the smile on it that was not a smile.

She didn't look. She looked at him. She saw his face go dark and then his fingers dug into her, he had grabbed her ear, twisting it, and she thought wildly of the earring she'd lost. It came to her that he probably had that, too, taken from their bedsheets, hidden away to use against her.

'Look,' he whispered, forcing her head round, and she felt his saliva speckle her cheek. The image was there, her hand splayed white against the railings, her wedding ring. Another man's body thrust into hers, his flesh red in her mouth—

'I've seen it,' she said, finding her voice, out of nowhere. 'I've seen it. You know how – you know—'

He didn't let her finish. 'I know *what*, exactly?' he said. 'That you go up to town on a night out, I give you my blessing, I give you money, I take care of *our child*—' and he paused, so she would know what it had all been for and her insides went to liquid, Tabs in the car. 'And you're shagging a stranger? In the fucking *street*?'

He believed it: she could see in his eyes that he believed everything he was saying and for a second she wondered if she'd got it all wrong. No. Holly. He'd been having an affair with Holly, they were running away together. Holly had been the one had got out the bottle of brandy.

'You're mad,' she said, the words escaping her before she could pull them back, but they were true. 'You did it. You did it. You and Holly. She spiked my drink. I woke up the next morning and I – I—'

She couldn't go on. The knowledge of what had been done to her was there at last, it was in every cell of her body. She felt heavy, like a doll stuffed with sand, she felt as if a tide was rising around her and she would drown.

'Don't tell me you didn't enjoy it,' he said and then she felt it rush like fire through her, the rage, and she hung on to the feeling, she twisted, away from him and ran.

He was on her in a second, a hank of her hair still in his hand, and the back of her head struck the stone of the kitchen floor, hard, she felt her peripheral vision go and for a second – she didn't know how long – she blacked out. When she opened her eyes he was on top of her, ripping at his trousers. She could hear a hiss, and shook her head to clear it, but the sound didn't go away.

And then he stopped. His flies undone, his penis flaccid. Was that what this was all about? She remembered Dad's worried face, when they'd talked about IVF, donor sperm, his eyes darting to Tim next time they saw each other.

'I thought it was what I wanted,' he said. He leaned back and his face was blank and dead as though this, the truth, this brief moment of calm and lucidity was strange and alien to him.

She felt herself hauled round, roughly: he was astride her on the floor looking down; he leaned low over her. A hand on either side of her neck but not around it, not yet. His fingers were in the hair behind her ears, stroking as if for a love scene. She felt her neck go stiff with the effort of looking up into his face, waiting.

'When was the last time you gave *me* a blowjob?' he said, nasty and in the silence that followed she knew what that hissing was, it was coming from the kitchen. The clanking she'd heard as she stood in the hall came back to her: the sound had been familiar and now she realised what it was. A smell, familiar and strange at the same time. She turned her head towards the kitchen and there was the shadow of something, in the corner of her eye something propped inside the kitchen door. Familiar and unfamiliar, in the wrong place, like the sound of a gas bottle being hauled over her kitchen floor, just like the smell of gas, in a kitchen that was all electric.

Flakes of red paint. He'd used the bottle to damage the car, it must have been heavy. He must have hit the car like he wanted to hit her.

Stay in the car, Tabs, stay, she heard in her head, *if I die and he dies at least – there's Dad but then—*

'Your mother's not having her,' she said. 'Not your fucking mother,' and he hit her so hard her head turned sideways on her neck and she saw what it was, standing inside the kitchen door.

The butt of a shotgun, and now she knew what that box had contained, the long locked box in the garage. And now it was out of the box and resting there, waiting for Tim to remember what he wanted to do next.

Before the first scream had left her mouth Georgie realised her mistake. Her terrible mistake. A tapping, a child's insistent tapping, at the door.

A voice: a small voice. '*Mummy, are you all right?*'

And then Tim hit her, again, she could see his face, judicious, considering, glancing sideways at the gun then back at her. He reached for it.

Georgie could see it coming as if in slow motion and she didn't feel the pain for a second, only blood in her mouth and in her eyes.

If she even gets in. If she even sees this.

Tabs.

Chapter Twenty-Nine

The girl on the forecourt – in her high heels with the keys swinging in her hand as behind them the traffic honked and growled – had stared at Frank blocking her path. His shirt was untucked, he could feel a bruise beginning to throb on his cheek and there was a look in her eye he didn't quite understand.

Not as if he was a lunatic, exactly, more as if she had known something really bad was going to happen and she was trying to work out if he was it. When she stood her ground, he had asked her her name.

Lydia. Funny old-fashioned sort of a name. As she said it he could see she had been crying. In the white glare of the security lights the tears looked black. 'Listen,' he began patiently, without much hope of any of this working out, not Eddie getting to the hospital, nor Lucy, nor him stopping what Eddie knew was coming to little Georgie Baxter. 'This might sound funny, but I need to get to your boss.'

And she'd started to cry again. He'd put a hand on her shoulder and she'd looked up and said, 'I'll drive you.'

Crammed into the passenger seat of her little yellow car Frank could see straight off that she was scared of him, her employer. 'You all right?' he asked.

Lydia looked sideways at him and rubbed at her little upturned nose with her knuckle. 'He's—' she hesitated, settled on, 'he's never shouted at me before. I was – he was really—' Then she turned back to face the road, eyes big.

Then they were at the entrance to a small close, three, four houses, sloping drives, hedges, a good distance between all of them. Lydia pointed. 'That's where he lives,' she said, pale.

A small car was on the drive, its door open. Inside the house all the lights seemed to be off but there was a gleam, around the big garage door. There was no sound.

'Did he hurt someone?' Lydia said hesitating but Frank didn't get a chance to answer.

A small child was screaming. '*Daddydaddydaddy.*'

'Call the police,' said Frank. 'Tell them he killed Holly Walker and he's going to kill his wife and child.' And he was out of the car and running.

She thought she would probably die, but she had to speak. Shout. The blood bubbled in her mouth, she could feel it running and she couldn't see out of one eye.

'Back,' she said. It sounded like something else, *bag.*

Georgie knew he'd hit her, not shot her, hit her with the butt of the gun. Then she felt him begin to rise off her and – *not dying yet not dead yet* – from somewhere in the blood and hurting she found her voice.

335

'Back, go back, Tabs, go back back in the car go back.'
A bubbling breath. '*Now.*'

Shrieking.

He was standing over her, swaying, and the smell of gas was in her nostrils with the taste of blood. She knew he would hit her again but she reached up and grabbed him by something, she didn't know what, his trousers, and craned, twisted to see behind her and the front door.

Tabs stood there, upside down in her one eye but it was Tabs. Not coming in. *Good girl.*

And with swift careless violence with his polished leather-soled shoe Tim kicked Georgie in the head.

She heard it before she felt it, a crunch and crack – and far off, too far off, a siren heading somewhere else – and her vision blurring so she couldn't be sure if what she had seen through his legs at the back door framed in the dark glass was Tabs or someone else, Dad come to save her, God or angels, before it was all gone.

Glass and Tim and Tabs, all gone black.

The little girl was standing in the doorway.

If he ran, rugby-tackled, Frank knew he could get her out of the way. The child. The kid. That sound '*daddydaddydaddy*' was an alarm that hurt his head. Frank never had a daddy, never wanted one.

But he stayed back. Since when had he been anything but a bull in a china shop, blundering in? Skirted the house, trying to see. The kid didn't turn her head, she could see something happening inside and as long as she didn't step over the threshold maybe he had time. Time for surprise. She was smart. He had seen that in her sleepy face outside Fanelli's. Be smart. And soundlessly he ran, staying back.

There was some light inside the house after all, falling from inside somewhere and then he understood, the garage must access the house, the light that was on in there. He was at the big garage door: if the little girl turned her head she would see him, but she didn't turn. He pushed tentatively at the top of the metal shuttering, to see if it would give: it didn't. He moved on, round the side of the house and as he did he caught the whiff of something, a smell.

Gas. *Shit*. Quick. Quick now. Too late to go back to the front. A side door, sturdy wood, locked. He scaled it, feeling every pound, every extra ounce he was carrying as the wood dug into his belly and he was down, on a paved path with a loud crunch. *Shit*.

Grass, quiet on the grass and he skirted the house. A wide sitting room window, all dark – then a glazed door. That faint light falling through it on to the glass.

It would be locked, wouldn't it? Of course it would be. *Wrong, Frank, wrong, blundering again*, and he paused, gasping, hands up on the glass in time to see him, the silhouette of a man straddling her on the floor, her head raised and then it fell back. She didn't move.

Her husband. He wore a suit, his hair was thinning, and he was holding something, Frank had never actually seen one before except in the movies, a shotgun. He was bringing it up to his shoulder and beyond him in the doorway, the little girl.

And under Frank's hand – too soon, too late – the door opened and he crashed inside stumbling and the man turning towards him with the gun in his hand.

337

He smelled the gas. A spark would do it, even the light switch would do it as Frank blundered on, hands outstretched.

And then her hand came up from the ground and pulled him off balance, and Frank had him on the ground and the gun, when it went off, was beneath him.

She knelt over him, unbuttoning his shirt, pulling out his tie. She could feel his eyes on her, she could see saliva bubble at the corner of his mouth. She pushed herself back off him and tied the tie around the top of his thigh, twisting it tight and tighter. She could feel him staring up at her but she didn't look back. She turned instead to find Tabs. She could see nothing at first then the soft edge of her head, her hair, the other side of the doorway into the hall. Hiding behind the door.

He'd shot himself in the thigh. 'You,' she said, gesturing to Frank, not capable of more than that but he understood and reached to take the tourniquet. Twisted it to keep up the pressure.

She stood between Tabs and the kitchen and leaned to pull the door shut behind them. Time enough as it swung closed to see his head turn, to see the look in his eyes and then to see it change. Hatred and outrage becoming something vaguer, loosening, leaving.

Tabs' head in Georgie's soft belly, her mouth moving. Georgie held on to her, held on for dear life.

Chapter Thirty

There were police cars first, then there was an ambulance.

Georgie could see them from where she sat, in the car with Tabs' head in her lap.

The police wouldn't go in straight away. They talked to her through the glass, because she wouldn't open the door or the window. She told them there was a gun and gas and they just stood there, in a huddle, until she opened the door and said she would show them.

Then Frank had been in the doorway swinging the gas bottle and all the doors and windows had been open in the house and Georgie had wanted to say, *I don't care. Throw a match. Let it all go up.* But she had just stared, and held on to Tabs.

They had been trying to get her to go to the ambulance but she just sat there, holding on to Tabs until suddenly he was there in the car door. Frank was there, leaning down, his big hand on the top of the door, his strong square face looking at her.

'Come on now,' he said, and she could see he had a bruise on his face. 'Let's take care of you.'

Postscript

Tim didn't get to hospital: he bled to death in the ambulance. Apparently it hadn't been quite painless, or quick, he had had time to call the paramedic a bitch and threaten to sue. But Georgie didn't tell Tabs any of that, of course. She was glad he'd known he was dying. She was glad he'd had time to understand what he'd done.

Georgie thought they'd move back into town permanently. Somewhere near Dad's, that swooping row of South London terraces, where she'd been small herself. There would be time, and brains enough between her and Dad, to formulate an explanation for Tabs, a story, that would make sense to her. She wouldn't have to know everything. Tim had not even, after all, been her biological father.

Frank's mum, Lena, it turned out, lived two streets away from Dad, and when he came to visit – he was working at a Savoy-style bar on the Thames owned by a friend of a friend these days – he called in on them, sitting in the back garden under the overgrown roses drinking a beer with Dad. Georgie loved Frank, and so did Tabs. So did Dad.

Tim's mother had engaged a solicitor to try and gain custody of Tabs, within hours of his death. Citing Georgie as an unfit mother with tales Tim had told her, more than one tale, of Georgie's instability, her promiscuity.

Even without that as an incentive, Georgie would have gone to the police with a complaint of sexual assault against Mark Cutler, erstwhile employee of Eddie Starling of Starling Property, currently under investigation for tax fraud and living off immoral earnings. Showing them the photograph: holding it up, because no shame was involved, only anger. Only rage. Evidence of Tim's attempts to blackmail her, his calling in favours to have her drink spiked on that night out, to have her abused sexually, so that he might have a better chance of gaining custody of Tabs. Not his biological daughter, as Georgie pointed out then and on subsequent occasions, which was perhaps why he felt he needed more weaponry, more leverage.

The police had not yet been able to trace Mark Cutler, but they were confident they would. They asked her repeatedly, if she was sure she would be prepared to go to court, and repeatedly Georgie had said, yes. Yes. Yes, she would.

And as she sat beside Tabs every night, holding her hand as she went to sleep in the bedroom where she herself had slept from infancy, that was the word in Georgie's head, the word for the life that awaited them. *Yes*.

Acknowledgements

I'd like to thank, as always, my incomparable agent, Victoria Hobbs, my indefatigable editor Maddie West, the publicity and marketing team at Sphere, spearheaded by the unstoppable Kirsteen Astor, and Thalia Proctor for her patience and unvarying efficiency.

To Richard Beswick, my thanks and love for a couple of decades of friendship and literary encouragement, and last but not least, my wonderful, clever family for their love and forbearance.